for Josh,
the first one out of the nest

The Angel Knight

"Magnificent . . . richly textured with passion, and a touch of magic."
—Mary Jo Putney

"Ms. King, a visual writer extraordinaire, has blended a mystical and historical tale so precise that the reader will be drawn in and won't ever want to leave."
—*Romantic Times*

"A romance of tremendous beauty and heart. Readers will not be able to put this one down. . . . Her books will stand the test of time."
—*Affaire de Coeur*

The Raven's Wish

"Powerful, magical, and delightful . . . a memorable romance that will keep readers on the edge of their seats."
—*Romantic Times*

"Destined to be a major voice in the genre."
—*Affaire de Coeur*

"A storyteller of wit, charm, and pure magic."
—Jo-Ann Power

The Black Thorne's Rose

Laird of
the Wind

Susan King

A TOPAZ BOOK

TOPAZ
Published by the Penguin Group
Penguin Putnam Inc., 375 Hudson Street,
New York, New York 10014, U.S.A.
Penguin Books Ltd, 27 Wrights Lane,
London W8 5TZ, England
Penguin Books Australia Ltd, Ringwood,
Victoria, Australia
Penguin Books Canada Ltd, 10 Alcorn Avenue,
Toronto, Ontario, Canada M4V 3B2
Penguin Books (N.Z.) Ltd, 182–190 Wairau Road,
Auckland 10, New Zealand

Penguin Books Ltd, Registered Offices:
Harmondsworth, Middlesex, England

First published by Topaz, an imprint of Dutton NAL,
a member of Penguin Putnam Inc.

First Printing, August, 1998
10 9 8 7 6 5 4 3 2 1

 REGISTERED TRADEMARK—MARCA REGISTRADA

Printed in the United States of America

BOOKS ARE AVAILABLE AT QUANTITY DISCOUNTS WHEN USED TO PROMOTE
PRODUCTS OR SERVICES. FOR INFORMATION PLEASE WRITE TO PREMIUM MAR-
KETING DIVISION, PENGUIN PUTNAM INC., 375 HUDSON STREET, NEW YORK, NEW
YORK 10014.

ACKNOWLEDGMENTS

To George Bittroff, for sharing his knowledge of falconry, and for inviting me to watch his beautiful goshawk, Sammy.

To Julie Booth, for support and some late hours, and to Jill Jachowski, for leading me to the hawks.

To Dr. Mary Furgol, Scottish historian, for helping me sort through some historical complexities.

And to my cousin, Jolie Chamberlain, who bravely stayed with three boys so my husband and I could go to Scotland.

"Though that her jesses were my dear heart-strings,
  I'd whistle her off, and let her down the wind
  To prey at fortune."

—Shakespeare, *Othello*
Act III, Scene 3

Prologue

Scotland, the Lowlands
February, 1305

A flash of light, followed by velvety darkness, stilled her utterly as the vision began. Isobel clenched her fingers on the arms of the chair that supported her, and closed her eyes.

She saw a man emerge from the shadows and stride forward. Tall, wide-shouldered, cloaked and hooded like a pilgrim, he moved with the easy grace of a warrior and the carriage of a leader. On his gloved fist, he supported a hawk.

Mist whirled around his silhouette, and he was gone.

Isobel frowned, puzzled. No words, no name, no understanding came with the vision—just the vivid, haunting image of a man, now vanished.

"Isobel?" Her father's deep, commanding voice, which suited his impressive height and breadth, was deliberately hushed. John Seton spoke as if he stood in a church, but he was in his bedchamber watching his only child, the heiress to his property of Aberlady, prophesy once again. "What do you see?" he asked.

She shook her head slightly and kept her eyes closed.

Had she opened them, she would not have seen the shallow bowl of water on the table or the gleaming surface that had sparked the first vision. She would not have seen the stone walls of her father's bedchamber, or the glowing hearth, or the three men who watched her so intently.

She was blind.

The darkness of her prophetic vision always took her

earthly sight, for an hour, or several hours, sometimes for a day or more. Each time it happened, she waited on sheer faith for her sight to return. Each time, she struggled against the fear that one day the blindness would remain.

She drew in a slow breath as images formed behind her eyelids. Myriad and swiftly changing, faces and scenes passed before her, as if seen through a sparkling, faceted crystal. Words formed, urging her to speak.

"Treachery," she said. "Murder."

She heard low murmurings among the men who stood nearby—her father, her priest, her betrothed. She watched the scene unfold, and waited for more knowledge to come.

"What sort of treachery, Isobel?" her father asked.

"Aye, what do you see, Isobel?" Sir Ralph Leslie— her father's choice for her husband, and her father's friend—had a smooth, pleasant voice. She heard him step toward her, a heavy sound, for he was a short, powerfully built man. And she heard the hawk, which Ralph had brought with him, chirr on its perch in the corner of the room.

"Stay back, Ralph," John Seton murmured. "Father Hugh sits near her to write down what she says. Dinna question her. Let us do that. And keep your hawk quiet. That bird has a poor temper."

Isobel heard Sir Ralph grunt assent. She had been betrothed to Leslie at Whitsunday in accordance with the wishes of her father and her priest. This was the first time that Sir Ralph had watched Isobel speak prophecy, and she dimly realized, at the outer perimeter of her thoughts, that he did not know how to behave during the session.

She had not wanted him present—nor had she wanted the betrothal—but her father and the priest had made the decision, just as they had made so many concerning her. Sir Ralph would be permitted to watch, but not to distract her.

Isobel frowned, letting her eyes roll behind her lids as she tried to regain her intense focus on the rapid, bright images that slipped across the dark field of her inner vision. Silence filled the room, but for the hot crackle of the hearthfire.

"I see an eagle flying over Scottish hills," she said. She watched while the images came swiftly, easily, as they always did when she sat down to foretell at her father's bidding.

"Hawks pursue the eagle," she continued. Her visions often unfolded as a blend of real and symbolic. This time, her gift seemed to favor birds of prey as metaphors. She watched the birds, and understanding flooded into her.

"They are men," she said quietly. "A hawk of the tower, a hawk of the forest, and others. Southrons and Scots both, come to take a man, the eagle, in treachery. He is a leader whom they fear and would stop."

John Seton, Ralph Leslie, and the priest remained silent. She heard a hawk call out—*kee, kee, kee-eer*—but the sound did not come from Ralph's hunting bird.

"I see a gray goshawk on a gloved fist," she said as she watched the picture form in her mind. "Its master has led the others here. Hawk of the tower, hawk of the forest, both are there. They trap the eagle—the leader— in the middle of the night. He resists, for he is strong in body as well as heart."

She watched the huge man struggle violently while the others dragged him away. "They mean to accuse him of crimes and kill him. But 'tis sacrifice—'tis murder—for their own ends." She paused, watching as the man was taken away on horseback, amid a shower of white-feathered arrows.

"The hawk of the forest will loose the white feather," she said. "He will flee through heather and greenwood."

"And the eagle?" her father asked.

Isobel sucked in her breath as she saw vivid images of cruelty. "His great heart will be torn from his breast," she said, and paused, clenching her fist in anguish until the disturbing vision changed.

"The English lion will claim the triumph. The hawk who betrayed the eagle—his friend—will vanish into the forest."

"The English lion must be King Edward," Father Hugh murmured. She heard the scratch of his sharpened quill over parchment. "But the eagle, the hawk of the tower, the hawk of the forest—who are they? What more do you know, Isobel?" he asked. His voice was quiet and textured with age.

So many visions flew past, brilliant as paintings on glass, that she could hardly describe them all. Insight flashed through her mind, too quickly to grasp it.

Profound sadness and a devastating sense of betrayal made her want to cry. Suddenly she knew that the strong, brave man—the eagle—would die before autumn.

And she knew, with startling clarity, who he was.

Dear Lord, she thought, *let me warn him. For once, let me help, and not simply foretell what will come.* But she heard no answer to her plea.

Let me remember, she added desperately. *Please let me remember this time.*

Usually her visions vanished from her memory. If she wondered about them later, she asked her father or the priest what she had said and what the visions meant. Otherwise, they rarely discussed them with her and told her not to concern herself. Once spoken, the prophecies were out of her care, they told her, and rightfully given to men who could understand them.

But she wanted to be part of that. She had begun to foretell as a girl, twelve years past. For years, her father had overseen all matters related to her life and her remarkable gift. But she was a woman now, and asked pertinent questions of her father and the priest. Their answers did not always satisfy her.

She knew that the priest spoke of her prophecies throughout his parish, and word spread from there. She was aware that he had sent copies of her predictions to the exiled king of Scotland, John Balliol, and to the men who acted as the Guardians of the Realm, the governing body of Scotland in the King's absence. She knew that the English had heard of her prophecies, too.

Her father told her that she was a blessing to the cause of Scotland. She was glad of that. The awful strain of the visions seemed worth the price if the Scottish people benefitted.

Isobel fluttered her eyelids and rolled her eyes slightly. The images spun on, sparkling, fascinating, devastating.

"Who is the eagle, the man taken?" Father Hugh asked.

"The rebel leader William Wallace." Her voice was low, hoarse with regret. She did not want to utter his fate, and yet the words came. She could not hold back the power of truth.

"The English king will butcher the freedom fighter to appease his own anger," she continued. " 'Twill be called righteous justice. Wallace is the eagle among the hawks. He will be betrayed by a hawk."

She heard her father and Ralph exclaim softly, heard them murmur to each other. "Go on, Isobel," her father urged.

The dark, frightening scene had passed. Now she saw a lovely scene of a goshawk flying gracefully on the flowing wind, above the green treetops of a dense forest.

"The laird of the wind," she said quickly when the words came to her mind. She almost smiled, feeling as if she shared the bird's freedom for a moment. "He is the hawk of the forest."

"Who is he?" her father and the priest asked together.

"He has no home. He lives in the forest and flies free." She watched the hawk's soaring, blissful flight, then frowned at what came next. "Other hawks—other men—hunt him. He flees for his life." She joined her hands and twisted her fingers together. "He betrayed, but not by choice. Now he is betrayed. Oh, such pain, such treachery!" She turned her head back and forth to dispel the anguish that filled her.

"What treachery? Who betrayed him? Who did he betray?" Father Hugh asked. His pen whispered over the page.

"Isobel, tell us what you know," her father said anxiously.

The feelings that flooded her were devastating. She could barely speak, and fought tears. The visions did not often pull her into their vortex like this. She felt bitter grief.

She watched with relief as new images flickered over the dark field of her inner vision. Mists formed.

The man in the cloak, holding a hawk, stepped out of the veil of fog. Her heart gave a small leap.

"I see a pilgrim." She described him, and then understood more about him. "He has a penance of the heart, and longs for peace."

"Who is he?" Ralph asked.

The answer came to her. "He is the laird of the wind."

"Isobel, make sense," Ralph said impatiently.

Isobel hardly heard him. She watched the man in the pilgrim's cloak, fascinated, enthralled. He was tall and strong, and stood alone in the rain on the steps of a church, his hand lifted to support a gray goshawk. Below his wide hood, she saw a handsome, somber face: deep blue eyes, a firm jaw, an almost gentle mouth, brown hair streaked with gold.

His eyes seemed heavy with sadness, with pain. And she sensed more—bitterness and rage, stifled. Somehow she knew him as well as she knew herself. Yet she did not know who he was.

He left the steps and strode through the rain-soaked yard toward a hawthorn tree. Rain pattered softly as the man paused by the tree, released the hawk, and walked past. The goshawk fluttered onto a branch of the hawthorn.

"The goshawk guards the secret of the hawthorn tree," she said impulsively. Somehow there was truth in that.

"What secret?" Ralph demanded. "Who is the man? Where is this tree? John, what is the lass talking about?"

"Ralph, keep quiet," her father growled.

" 'Tis likely symbolic," Father Hugh said calmly. "Hawks, trees, pilgrims—all symbols of a greater meaning. I shall study my notes on her words carefully. Look at the way her eyes move upward—she sees more. Isobel, tell us what comes to you now."

Isobel could not answer. For the first time in twelve years of saying prophecies, she saw her own image in a vision.

A woman glided across the rain-dampened grass: tall and slender, wearing a blue gown, her black hair streaming like midnight down her back. Stunned, Isobel watched as she approached the hawthorn where the goshawk perched. The bird's bronze-colored eyes gazed at her, unblinking.

The man in the pilgrim's cloak turned. Isobel felt his gaze pierce hers. He raised his hand and beckoned to her.

She felt an overwhelming desire to go to him. But something equally strong held her back. As she hesitated, the rainy churchyard faded from sight.

Now she saw high stone walls, bright in sunshine. Isobel recognized the curtain walls of Aberlady Castle, her home.

Arrows whined overhead, arcing over the battlements. She heard men shouting, screaming. She smelled smoke and felt a cold, heavy hunger in her belly.

"Siege," she whispered. "Siege."

She cried out. The vision disappeared even as she tried to hold on to the fading images. Pray God she would remember, she thought.

When she opened her eyes, the darkness remained.

August 3, 1305

He ran silently through the moonlit forest. Breath, step, and pounding heart blended with the sound of the wind. Onward, never slowing, he slipped like a shadow between the trees, his long legs leaping easily through the bracken.

Pray God he was not too late.

He ran through forest and over moorland, until his breaths heaved in his chest and the air burned his throat, until his powerful legs ached. But he would not stop. He could not, because every pounding step brought him closer to his goal. He had to thwart a tragedy.

Finally, a light gleamed far ahead through the trees. As he ran, he saw blazing yellow torchlight, and a house, looming between the trunks. Then he saw horses and armored men, and heard indistinct shouts, angry and determined.

Dear God. They had reached the house before him.

He stopped behind an oak, sucking in long breaths, his heart slamming in his chest, his tunic damp with sweat. Men in chain mail, some on horseback, some on foot, filled the moonlit yard of the house. Twenty—nearly thirty, he decided.

A dead man lay on the ground. Someone kicked the body aside. Others brought forward a horse, its rider securely bound and gagged: a giant of a man, bent forward. The blood streaming from a head wound was black in the moonlight.

A guard struck the man again, and the watcher swore, a low, desperate sound. Silent and stealthy, he pulled out the bow slung behind his back and strung it quickly. He withdrew an arrow from the quiver at his belt, nocked it, and aimed.

That guard, about to deliver another savage blow to the huge man, fell hard from his saddle, an arrow in his chest.

From among the trees, a second arrow was fixed, drawn, and swiftly released. A soldier raised a crossbow and looked around, ready to use it. Then he went down like a felled oak.

The men surrounding the prisoner shouted, wheeled, drew swords, loaded their crossbows. In the moonlight, the white feathering on the arrows was visible to all, obviously sprung from the bow of the forest renegade called the Border Hawk. Someone shouted his name.

Watching from his place behind the tree, the renegade thought he saw the prisoner turn and nod toward the trees, as if grateful to his unseen ally, a man he had always called friend.

The renegade saw the pale shape of a small, flat object flutter to the ground, dropped surreptitiously by the prisoner. He noted it well, and resolved to fetch it as soon as he could.

A quarrel slammed into a tree trunk near the archer. Rather than retreat, he slipped forward, a dark shadow, and loosed another shaft. A scream cut the night.

Three guards less, now; nock, draw, aim, release. Four. Still too many to take alone. But several arrows remained in his quiver. Each one would count for a life before the night was done. Even so, without a horse to follow his quarry, without men at his back, he had no hope of winning back his friend, taken in treachery.

Treachery to which he had contributed. The knowledge sliced through him like a razor's edge. He drew the bowstring and let go.

Five on the ground now, moaning or silent. The rest of the men mounted swiftly, leaving the others behind as they circled their horses and led the prisoner out of the yard. Bolts from their crossbows hammered into the trees and the ground as their horses thundered away.

He lunged forward like a wildcat, running after them, leaping over bracken, his bow gripped in his fist. The horses were English breed, powerful and long-legged. They soon pulled ahead of the runner, who dashed among the trees beside the earthen forest track.

He paused, feet wide spaced, to draw, sight, and loose another arrow, and another, and yet more. He shot so fast that he did not think about his aim. Each arrow was an extension of his will and his rage, and each found its mark.

Ahead, he heard shouts and ran forward through the bracken. The horses were nearly out of range now. He climbed a slope with long, rapid strides to overlook the earthen road.

Eyes narrowed, he saw—with the pristine clarity of vision that had helped to earn him the name of Border Hawk—the glimmer of armor ahead in the moonlight.

He had two arrows left. Though he knew the distance would lessen his accuracy, he aimed, drew, and shot. The bolt found a man's arm, but the wounded knight rode on with the others.

He knew these men intended to escort his friend toward a horrible death. The man they had taken this night was a leader and a rebel, and had driven the English king to mad obsession. Neither justice nor mercy would be shown.

He had one arrow left. He nocked it, drew, sighted.

And lowered the bow.

For one fervent instant, he wanted to take his friend's life with a sure, swift, honorable arrow before the English could do it with torture and humiliation.

He raised the bow again, eyes steady, jaw locked. Though his heart sank within him like a stone, he shot.

The arrow fell short.

Chapter 1

September, 1305

Rain pattered on moss and stone as the pilgrim mounted the low steps to the abbey church. He pulled open the heavy oak door and stepped through the arched entrance. Shafts of light, silvered by rain, pierced the dimness in the high, rounded vaulting of the nave. Plainsong drifted toward him, chanted by monks in the choir space beyond the altar.

Danger shadowed him like a demon, even here. Although he knew that he must not linger, he paused and closed his eyes briefly. Peace enveloped him, tangible and lovely, like the evening mist that veiled the nearby hills. But such serenity, for him, was as fleeting as the fog.

He was glad for the simple blessing of shelter from the rain. The forest had been his home for years. He was unused to the profound stillness of enclosed air or to the feeling of flat, smooth flagstones beneath his feet.

He drew his cloak closer over his wide shoulders and dipped his fingertips in a small piscina basin in the wall, crossing himself with the swift, practiced gesture of a trained monk. With a cautious glance, he moved along the shadowed right aisle behind the massive carved columns of the nave.

English and Scots alike hunted him daily now. The summons of a friend had brought him here to Dunfermline Abbey, but he would return soon to the sanctuary of the forest. If he was discovered here, his capture—or his escape—would disturb the hard-won peace of the abbey.

A year earlier, the English king had stayed at Dunfermline Abbey, summoning Scots nobles to pay him submission and dispensing what he called justice. When he departed, King Edward ordered the holy Scottish site burned, though his own sister lay buried beneath the abbey stones. The blackened ruins of the refectory and dormitory lay but a stone's throw from the church, which had survived.

The pilgrim genuflected at the side of the altar and moved past it. In several years as a fugitive, he had never submitted to King Edward as most of the Scottish nobles had done. He had taken a pledge of freedom—for himself and for Scotland.

Months ago, he had been wounded in battle, captured along with two of his cousins, and sealed in an English dungeon. Even then, although one cousin had died beside him and the other—a woman—had been taken away, he had not signed a pledge of fealty to King Edward.

What he had signed, in the end, had been far worse. He set his mouth grimly and moved along the side aisle.

His tall, strong warrior's build naturally attracted glances wherever he went, but he made an effort to bow his head and appear unremarkable. The scallop shell pinned to the shoulder of his hooded cloak, and the brass saint's badge beside it, identified him as a penitent man.

Dunfermline Abbey was a frequent stop along the pilgrimage route that lay between Saint Andrews to the northeast and Compostela in Spain. Few curious glances would come his way, so long as he wore the cloak and the badges.

He glanced about for the man who had promised to meet him after the vespers service. Several worshipers knelt or sat along narrow benches, absorbed in prayer. The smell of incense lingered in the air, and plainsong filled the church.

He remembered the melody well, a *kyrie* that he had sung countless times himself, long ago, in what seemed another life. Even that soothing sound could not ease the roughened edges of his soul now. He had changed irrevocably.

His deerskin boots were silent over the stone floor as he entered the small chapel of Saint Margaret at the east end of the abbey church. In flickering golden candlelight, he moved toward the massive carved marble tomb of the sainted Scottish queen.

Pounding rain and chanting blended as he knelt beside the plinth. He took up a taper and lit a candle in homage to Saint Margaret, who had been a friend to pilgrims and to those in need. Then he folded his hands in prayer beside her tomb, and waited.

After a while, he heard quiet footsteps. A monk wearing the black robe of the Benedictine order entered the chapel and knelt beside him to murmur a Latin prayer. The monk bowed his head, revealing a clean tonsure above his brown hair and long face.

"Pilgrim, you have traveled far on a poor day," the Benedictine whispered when his prayer was done.

"Far enough, and so I hope to hear good news."

"I wish I had that for you, James Lindsay."

James glanced sharply at his friend. His heart seemed to sink within the cage of his breast. He waited for the monk to speak, and knew exactly what the man would say.

"He's dead, Jamie," the monk whispered. "Wallace is dead."

James nodded slowly, though grief and anger slammed through him with vicious force. He steeled his jaw, his fists, and the core of his will against its effect.

"William Wallace, taken by foul treachery. Christ have mercy on his soul," the Benedictine said, shaking his head. "They captured him but a month past, Jamie."

"I know." The words were wooden. He knew too well when Wallace had been taken. He could not wipe the memories away.

"We had word of his death just days ago. He was brought to trial in London, found guilty of treason, and executed on the twenty-third of August."

"What treason? He never declared fealty to King Edward," James murmured. "They condemned him on false grounds, John."

John Blair nodded. "They accused him of deeds he never committed—some he did, aye, but naught to merit

what they did to him. He was dragged to the gallows
and hanged until he scarcely lived. When they took him
down, he begged to hear the psalms read while they . . .
cut—" Blair stopped. "I canna tell you the rest. Not
here in this holy place."

"Tell me," James growled. "I would know."

Blair lowered his head and murmured in a low, ravaged whisper, detailing cruelty, agony, and superb courage. James listened without expression. But his blood
surged and pounded in a hot tide of sorrow and rage.
He felt a strange prickling in his eyes and drew breath
against it.

One well-placed arrow, he thought, could have
averted such agony. But if he had succeeded in that grim
deed weeks ago, his debt to Wallace would only have
deepened. And now none of it could ever be repaid.

The monk's hands unfolded from prayer and re-
formed into fists as he spoke. James looked down at his
own hands, clenched white-knuckled at his sides. His
spirit seemed to harden within him, as if the last tender
part of his heart turned to stone and became impossibly heavy.

"They have martyred him," he said when he could
speak.

"True. His death will spark the fading fire of the Scottish cause, just when King Edward thought to extinguish
it forever."

"Aye. John, join us again, in the Ettrick Forest."

"The life of an outlaw ill suits me now," John said.
"I left it to return to Dunfermline and write an account
of Wallace's life. The truth of his deeds must be known."

"Write your chronicle in the forest. The *vita contem-
plativa* always suited you ill."

"The contemplative life suited us both ill, Brother
James," John reminded him with a quick glance. "You
left our order years ago to join the cause of Scotland.
You were knighted on a bloody Scottish field, while I
took priestly vows."

"And yet we both ended up forest rogues. John, we
could use your steady hand with a weapon, and your
good sense."

"You have others with you in the greenwood."

"Few, now. Surely you know the rumors."

"I know you're hunted again, with a vengeance this time." John Blair frowned. " 'Tis widely said that Wallace was betrayed by Scotsmen—the lord of Menteith sent his servants to take Will into custody. But the rest are unknown."

"Not all are unknown," James said carefully.

"Do you mean the earl of Carrick? I doubt he took a hand in this treachery. Thought he pays homage to Edward of England, I believe that Robert Bruce favors the Scots in his heart."

"I dinna mean Robert Bruce," James said. "I have seen proof lately that he leans strongly to the Scottish side."

"Thanks be to God," Blair commented in a low tone. "I have prayed that Scotland will find a strong leader. Bruce is the only one who can fill that role, Jamie."

James nodded, and let the silence linger for a few moments. "John," he finally murmured, "there is a rumor that William Wallace was betrayed . . . by Sir James Lindsay of Wildshaw."

"Sweet saints in heaven," John muttered. "I hadna heard. They blame you?"

James nodded grimly. "Scotsmen who once gave the Border Hawk their support now turn their backs on me, or hunt me alongside the English."

"But you didna betray Will. You could never do that."

James stared unseeing at the marble tomb. He wanted to tell John—and thereby confess to a priest—what he had done while in English captivity, and the tragedy that had come about because of it. But he could not bear to say the words. Not yet.

Later, when both he and John Blair were past the shock of Will's death, he would explain it. But he had something to accomplish first. And if he survived that, he would return to Dunfermline to unburden his soul.

"There must be some way to take this blame from your shoulders," the monk said.

" 'Tis my matter. I will deal with it."

"What will you do?"

"I will find the man who arranged Wallace's capture," James said. "The same man who brought the blame to bear on me, and now tries to hold a grip over me through my family."

"Menteith?"

"He is one of the betrayers. But I seek another man, who was with those who captured me months ago. He caused the death of one of my cousins, and has another cousin still in his keeping. Sir Ralph Leslie."

"Then you know where he is."

"Commanding a stout garrisoned castle. I canna get to him—or free his prisoner—with only four men at my back."

"Four?"

"Those who follow me now, when once there were fifty and more. Only four men believe I have any honor left at all."

"I think you do," John said quietly.

But I dinna believe it of myself, James thought. He gave John a flat, rueful smile of thanks and said nothing.

John sighed. "Even if I joined you, Jamie, a handful of forest rogues canna take down a garrison. Where is he?"

"King Edward just made him constable of a castle that was taken years ago from the Scots and is held by the English yet," James said. "Wildshaw Castle."

"Jesu," John said. "You do have matters with this man."

"Aye," James ground out.

"I suggest you await his train in the forest and take him when he leaves his lair. Hold a blade to his throat and see if he is ready to offer an apology and return what is yours."

"Ho, priest," James said, a smile flickering over his lips. John smiled slyly in return. "I could do that. But he has more than the castle that is mine by right. Margaret Crawford is in his custody."

"Margaret! Your cousin?"

"Aye. She was with us when we were ambushed by Southrons."

"I know she sometimes insisted on running with you. She always had a stout hand at the bow. But this—"

"Aye. Her extra hand was welcome, and I wouldna deny her what she wanted to do. But now Leslie holds

her at Wildshaw. He hopes to lure me to him by keeping her."

"But if you attempt to win her back by force, you risk
her life as well as others."

"Aye. I have decided to offer a trade for her. When
Margaret is free on a barter, I will exact my revenge."

John watched him in the flickering light of the votive
candles framing the saint's tomb. "What could you have
of such importance that this man would do what you
want?"

"The prophetess of Aberlady," James said.

"You have her?" John hissed.

"I will," James answered smoothly.

"You mean to make a hostage of Black Isobel of Aberlady?" John asked, his voice hushed to an anxious
whisper.

"If Margaret can be held as a lure for me, then I can
hold the prophetess in return," James growled.

"But Black Isobel! I hear the English king applauds
her prophecies. He will be furious if anything happens
to her."

"He is furious with me already, as a close comrade of
Wallace. I have lately heard that King Edward wants
the prophetess brought to him, so that she can divine
exclusively for the English throne."

"Ah. I see. Her price is quite high."

"Exactly. A valuable hostage—for many reasons."

"Certes," John remarked bitterly. "She predicted the
fall of Stirling, the taking of Wallace, the treachery of
the Border Hawk. King Edward wants such good tidings
to continue."

"That wee bird can sing for the king later," James
said evenly. "She isna my choice for a lark, since she set
a noose round my neck with her pretty tunes. If Leslie
pays the price I ask—Margaret—he can have his prophetess and turn her over to the English king as a show
of his loyalty if he wants."

"But why would Leslie want this prophetess?"

"She is his betrothed." The words fell soft but clear
in the silence.

John Blair watched him with an astonished expression.
Then he shook his head. "This is a risky scheme, and

foolhardy. Your heart and gut are ruling over your head. Be cautious."

"Foolish or wise, heart or gut, 'twill be done. Would you rather I simply walk up to the gates of Wildshaw and request my cousin be returned to her family?"

John Blair shook his head. "You would be dead before the words left your mouth."

"I leave for Aberlady Castle today to request an audience with the prophetess. A pilgrim may seek her wisdom, I think." James curled his lip. "Though I doubt true wisdom is hers."

"It might be possible to see her, if you ask permission of her father and her priest," John Blair said, frowning. "But I recall hearing that her father—Sir John Seton, a rebel knight—was taken into English custody following a skirmish."

"His daughter is cut of different cloth," James said. "Leslie, though a Scot, has gone over to the English side."

"Be careful, Jamie," John said. "There may be a guard around her. Her priest is Father Hugh of Stobo parish. If you seek him out, he may grant permission to a humble pilgrim who asks to see the prophetess."

"I am greatly in need of her counsel," James drawled.

John sighed. "If 'twere anyone but you, I would stop this scheme. 'Tis dishonorable to take a woman hostage."

"Tell that to Leslie, who has Margaret. Black Isobel willna be mistreated in my care. Just kept for a bit."

"If you keep her half so well as the hawks you trained in days past, she will be safe enough."

"I learned much from hawking," James said. "Patience will achieve goals. Margaret will be released unharmed, and I will give the seeress to Leslie and the English to enjoy."

"What then, of Leslie? You mentioned revenge."

"The prophetess will soon need a new husband," James said fiercely. "King Edward will find her a suitable match."

"She is kept isolated," John said. "This may not be as simple as you think." He sighed. " 'Tis dishonorable, this."

"Then Leslie and I have a bond," James growled. "Life loves irony. I must commit dishonor to achieve an honorable deed."

"What do you mean?"

"I could do naught when they took Wallace," James said quietly, bowing his head as if in confession. "I was there that night. Too late, but I was there. I saw them take him away."

"Aye. Rumor says you killed half the host that took him."

"But I didna save him." He clenched his fists, opened them. "I could do naught for my men, some of them my cousins, when they were killed at English hands. I canna restore my ruined name. But I can do one thing." He looked up. "I can save Margaret from the beast who helped to take down Wallace. And if I am damned for the rest, then so be it."

"Honor and revenge, my friend," John said, "are often at cross purposes. Be wary."

"As ever." James stood.

"What of Black Isobel's prophecies?" John stood.

"She condemned me long before Will's death with that nonsense about hawks and eagles. She helped to spoil the name of the Border Hawk. I wonder if she is part of some devious game to poison Scotland with rumors of failure—hence her prophecies, which favor the English."

"Aye, witness the marriage she makes." John frowned. "But what if she is a true seeress?"

"Then she has a great gift, and she can divine whatever I want to know," James said bitterly. "Either way, she has value to me as a hostage. She's a useful piece in the game I wish to play." He stepped back. "I must go."

John nodded and sketched a benediction in the air. James gripped his friend's hand, then left the chapel by a narrow side door. He pulled up his hood against the rain and walked past the refectory ruins, where mist gathered among the mossy, fire-blackened stones.

He looked up. A broken tracery window, silhouetted against the sky, framed the distant blue hills. Wallace had loved those beautiful hills, James remembered. He had been willing to give up his life to protect them.

James sighed heavily. He owed Wallace much, and could not even repay the debt now that his comrade was dead and his own name was ruined. No one would follow the Border Hawk now to rally to the fading cause of Scotland.

Black Isobel's prophecy, and the tangled net that had spun out from there—and from his own actions—had helped to make him a traitor.

He bowed his head and walked past the abbey, thinking about the prophetess who had caused such devastation with that cursed, oft-repeated hawk prediction. When he had her in his keeping, while he waited for Leslie's answer to his ransom demand, he would take the opportunity to learn the truth of those predictions. He did not doubt that she served as an accomplice of some sort, or perhaps a puppet, to Ralph Leslie and others.

He would learn the truth, though it would do him no good to know it. The damage had been done.

He walked through the drizzling rain toward the small cemetery beside the abbey. A single hawthorn tree stood in its center. He stopped, gazing at it.

Wallace's mother lay beneath that tree. He remembered the morning that he and John Blair and Wallace had buried her there, in a private, unmarked grave, so that no one would know where Lady Wallace rested. Will had wanted it that way, fearing either the destruction or veneration of his mother's remains, depending on his own fate. James meant to keep that secret forever.

After all, that was the least he could do for a friend.

He walked past the hawthorn and took a steep footpath that led down to the greenwood that spread out below the abbey.

For an instant he wanted to turn and go back to the serenity inside the abbey church, wanted to soak that peace into his heart, into his soul. But he walked on through the rain without stopping. No matter how he craved it, true peace would elude him. He courted danger far more easily than solace.

Within moments he lengthened his stride and ran toward the outer rim of the forest.

Chapter 2

The sandstone walls of Aberlady Castle glowed rosy in the sunset as Isobel Seton climbed the steps to the battlement. She walked forward steadily and resolutely, her head held high and proud, her gaze trained on the crenellated wall ahead of her.

With one hand, she reached up and pulled off her white silk veil, and tucked it into her sleeve. Then she undid her thick black braid, still walking forward, her fingers steady in their task. But beneath the folds of her gray gown and surcoat, her knees trembled.

Hunger and fatigue weakened her, she told herself firmly. Not fear. Never fear. She could not let anyone see that in her. Each day at set of sun, through the ten weeks of this siege, she had walked this path to show the English that she was still here and unharmed. And still defiant.

The breeze lifted the loosened skein of her hair as Isobel moved along the wall-walk toward the crenellations built over the foregate. She looked down through an embrasure.

Vivid sunset light poured over the only access to Aberlady: a rocky slope pitted with ditches. Along that treacherous incline, a hundred English soldiers gathered near cookfires and tents, or hunkered down behind crude wooden palisades set up for protection. Their weapons would be close at hand, she knew, although the day's fighting had quieted.

Her father's men—hers for now, she reminded herself, for Sir John Seton had been captured months ago and was in English captivity—watched from sheltered positions along the wall-walk. Eleven Scotsmen remained of

Aberlady's garrison, though sixty had manned the battlements ten weeks past.

She glanced behind her briefly. The bailey below, with
its massive stone keep in the center, was deserted. The
low, thatched-roof outbuildings were empty of workers,
supplies, and animals. They had let the horses go with
the priest during the one truce day allowed them, and a
few of the hawks had been released. The rest of the kept
birds had been eaten.

And one corner of the bailey had become a graveyard
for the soldiers and servants who had died over the past
few weeks from injury, illness, or starvation.

Soon, they might all be buried in that bleak corner.

The men of the garrison nodded to her as she passed,
their bows held ready, their faces gaunt and grim. But
she knew that they would not object to their mistress
walking the battlements. They knew, as Isobel did, that
she was safe wherever she stood, so long as she could
be seen by the English camped below. The Southron
enemy would not release their arrows or missiles at
Black Isobel, the prophetess of Aberlady.

Her value, rather than her mystery, protected her.
More than once, the English siege commander had
shouted up to her that King Edward wanted her brought
to him, whole and unharmed.

The English king, he had shouted, approved of Black
Isobel's predictions of the defeat of the Scots at Falkirk,
the recent fall of Stirling Castle to the English, and the
capture and execution of the freedom fighter William
Wallace. King Edward was eager to hear the Scottish
prophetess foretell more triumphs for the English.

The news of Wallace's death—which she had tried to
prevent with a note of warning sent to him—had made
her feel ill. But she had stood on the battlements and
listened without showing her reaction. The siege commander had shouted that Black Isobel would be well
rewarded for her efforts by the English king.

She had wrapped a polite note of refusal around an
arrow shaft, which one of her men had delivered by
shooting it quite accurately into the commander's thigh
while he sat his horse.

The grip of the siege had tightened after that. The

English had brought in engines to batter the outer gate and walls, and their archers had sent flaming arrows over the walls of Aberlady.

A cool breeze stirred past as Isobel stood on the high battlement, lifting the rich length of her unbound hair and spreading it out like a glossy black banner. She had removed her veil for just this purpose, just this effect. She raised her chin, stood still and proud, and let the wind pick up her hair and display it. All the while her heart pounded in terror.

In the encampment below, many of the English soldiers gazed up at her, while others practiced with weapons or packed the ditches leading to the castle gates with rubble and branches. A few men repaired the wooden framework of one of the two siege engines used to batter the thick walls.

The delicious smell of charred meat roasting over English cookfires made Isobel's empty stomach rumble miserably. Chain mail glimmered in the sunset as the English ate and talked and settled for the night.

In the morning they would begin another battle, perhaps the last, she thought. Aberlady's few remaining defenders were weak from hunger and could not withstand another onslaught by the English garrison.

Isobel turned to scan the curtain walls. The castle rested upon a high dark crag, which rose from a flat plain. Surrounded by sheer cliffs on three sides and a steep incline on the fourth, where the English were encamped, the fortress was said to be impenetrable. No enemy had ever breached its walls.

Isobel sighed and touched her fingers to gritty sandstone. Aberlady Castle was impervious to all but starvation, she thought. She had been born here, and she had thought to finally die here. *But not so soon, please God, not so soon.*

"Come away from the wall, Isobel." She glanced up to see Eustace Gibson, the castle bailie, step out of the shadows. As he stretched out his hand toward her, his chain-mail sleeve caught a red glint from the sun.

"Stay back, Eustace," she warned. "They will shoot at you."

A grim smile touched his weathered face. "They've

loosed their pebbles and thorns at me for weeks now, and I'm still here. Come, you should be inside the keep." He guided her toward the steps leading down to the yard. As she went, Isobel heard the familiar whine and thwack of an arrow bolt hitting the outer wall, close to where Eustace had been a moment earlier.

"By the Rood," he muttered, "they didna give you much time to leave the battlement before they fired at me."

Isobel turned, tightening her mouth in determined temper, and climbed the steps back to the wall-walk, despite Eustace's protests. She pulled her white silk veil from inside her sleeve, and leaned deep into the embrasure opening.

With an exaggerated motion, she wiped at the fresh scar on the outer wall, then shook the stone dust from the cloth and stood back. The breeze caught the black length of her hair.

Shouts rose from the English troops, cheers mixed with a few loud jeers. Isobel inclined her head regally and turned to descend the steps. Eustace watched, shaking his head.

"You've changed in these weeks, Isobel," Eustace said. "Once I would have said you were too gentle a lass to show such backbone. John Seton would be proud to see his daughter defend his castle with such wit."

"My father, if he were here, would never surrender. Nor shall I." She walked down the steps calmly, but her heart slammed and her hands trembled following her show of defiance. The wit might be there, but the backbone was false. She had learned to hide her fears and convey courage that did not exist.

Another bolt smacked into the side of the battlement above them, followed by sounds of laughter floating up from the English camp. Eustace lifted a hand to deter the Scotsmen on the battlement from returning the shot. He raised a brow in warning toward Isobel, too, to discourage her from another appearance on the battlements. She only sighed wearily and shook her head.

"Would that this was over," she said. "I dreamed last night that help came to us, and we walked out of here into freedom."

"Is that a prophecy?" Eustace asked.

"Just hope," she answered softly. "Only hope." She looked up at the sky. The red glow of the setting sun faded into indigo. The dream had not been prophetic—after all, she could see that lovely sky. The blinding burden of prophecy had not come to her, nor had it come for a long while.

As she looked up, a small shiver rippled through her and she felt warmth on her shoulder, as if a large, gentle hand touched her. She glanced at Eustace, but he was turned away, surveying the battlements.

Isobel frowned, sensing a keen gaze upon her and a strong presence somewhere. She glanced nervously around the gathering shadows in the deserted bailey yard. Naught but fatigue and fears, she told herself sternly.

"There is soup in the kitchen," Eustace said. "Come eat."

"I will." She would sip a small portion, as she had done for the past three days. The thin soup, which she had prepared herself from well water and barley, had to feed all of them.

When the last of the grain was gone—soon, now— they would face an enemy stronger than any army. She already felt the effects of starvation in her trembling limbs and in the hunger, dizziness, and dull headache that had been with her for days.

"There is scarcely enough barley left for soup tomorrow," Eustace said.

"I know," she replied quietly.

"Isobel." She heard the grim note in his voice. "You are the Maiden of Aberlady, and Sir John's heiress. You must give the final order to surrender. I canna do it myself."

"My father wouldna want us to surrender."

"Lass," he said kindly. "He wouldna want us to die."

She looked at him. Eustace Gibson had been part of Aberlady's garrison since Isobel had been a small girl. His skills, experience, and wisdom had been essential throughout the horrible weeks of besiegement. She had relied on his steadfast nature and had learned much from him.

She sighed, torn between concern for the garrison and loyalty toward Aberlady and her absent father. "I thought we could defeat them with resistance. I thought our supplies would last longer than this."

"Isobel, we must surrender."

"Sir Ralph will come soon to help us. Remember, before the siege began, he said he knew where my father was being held prisoner by the English. He went to find him. When he returns, he will help us. He will have my father with him." She heard the brittle note in her voice, but she would not let on that she had begun to lose hope herself.

"I doubt we will see Sir Ralph," Eustace barked. "We must surrender, lass. Your safety is paramount to me. The English willna harm you because their king wants you brought to him."

"But they will harm *you*," she said. "We will be taken prisoner or killed as soon as we set foot out of the gate. Aberlady will be made into a Southron stronghold. This castle is one of the strengths of Scotland. My father would expect us to keep it safe until he returns."

Eustace sighed. "We will put the torch to Aberlady as we leave. At least then the Southrons canna take the castle."

"Torch Aberlady!" She stared at him.

"Would you rather have it captured?"

"We canna destroy it!" The thought of burning Aberlady—her home, her refuge, and her protection—terrified her. "What if we continue to resist?"

"Then we die of starvation."

"Sir Ralph will come for us. He will hear word of this."

Eustace slid her a long glance. "We canna stay, Isobel."

She looked away, silent, and stared at the fading brilliance of the sky. Beside her, Eustace was silent for a long while.

Then she heard him exclaim softly. "We may have another choice, after all," he said. She heard the sudden tension in his voice. Isobel glanced up and saw his mouth draw down in a scowl. He grabbed the hilt of his sword.

"Eustace, what is it?"

"Look there," he murmured, "in the far corner of the yard, beyond the stable."

Isobel looked, and gasped. A group of men—four, five, she counted hastily—emerged out of the shadows beneath the back wall of the enclosure.

They walked boldly into the bailey and came toward the steps where Isobel and Eustace stood. On the battlement, the men of the garrison lifted their bows and held them ready.

Isobel glanced at Eustace. He raised a hand to the garrison in a calm, silent order to hold their attack. Isobel turned to stare again at the five men. Her heart pounded heavily and she felt dizzy, as if all the strain of the past weeks weighed down upon her at once.

"Dear God," she whispered hoarsely, "who are they?"

Unkempt and wild in appearance, they wore simple tunics, leather hauberks, and worn cloaks, although they carried fine broadswords and well-made bows and staffs, as if they were knights. One man moved forward, dropping back the hood of his long brown cloak, pinned with the scallop of a pilgrim.

He was taller than his companions, his shoulders wide, his legs long and lean. His clothing and leggings were worn and faded, and his tangled golden brown hair and darker beard needed trimming. She noticed that his features were handsomely shaped.

He came toward her with a strong, agile stride. His presence seemed to charge the air like lightning, rendering those who watched him motionless. With an inward gasp, Isobel realized that she had sensed his arrival a short while ago, as if his gaze and indeed his hand had touched her then.

He gripped his unstrung bow like a staff and halted close to the last step. The hilt of a fine broadsword gleamed, slung across his back. Nodding toward Eustace, he settled his direct gaze on Isobel.

"Lady Isobel Seton?" he asked. His voice was quiet, with a deep richness that carried well. "The prophetess of Aberlady?"

She nodded. "Who are you?" she asked, clasping her trembling hands in front of her.

He inclined his head. "We have come to rescue you."

She stared at him, stunned and fascinated. The stranger possessed a wild beauty and a startling aura of power, enhanced by his mysterious arrival. His eyes glittered deep blue, like the indigo twilight, and his hands, gripping the bow, were graceful and strong. He seemed beyond the ordinary realm, a man out of the mist, as if he had stepped from legends of the ancient race and the fair folk.

Isobel could not summon an answer at first. She felt almost bespelled. His steady, brilliant gaze seemed to assess her from the top of her head to the roots of her soul.

In turn, she saw the spark of keen intelligence and deep purpose in his dark blue eyes. She sensed the strong current of danger that surrounded him.

She pulled in a breath and lifted her chin. "You know my name, but I dinna know yours," she said calmly, despite her fear. An odd, raw excitement thundered through her. "How did you get inside our walls?"

"Through the postern gate in the northern wall," he said.

Isobel stared at him. "But that small door is hidden by scrub and rocks, and overlooks a cliff more than a hundred feet high. How did you reach it?"

He shrugged. "That took some time."

"Who are you?" she asked again.

"I am James Lindsay," he said in that low, commanding voice. She heard Eustace exclaim, but the name meant nothing to her. "At times," the man said, "I am called the Border Hawk."

"Jesu," Eustace breathed out. "I thought as much."

Isobel gasped softly. That name she knew. The Border Hawk was a renegade Scotsman who hid from English and Scots alike in the vast lands of the Ettrick Forest. His arrival inside Aberlady could mean salvation—or complete defeat for all of them. His loyalties, of late, were known only to himself.

She had heard rumors that the Border Hawk fled north, west, south, even out to sea; that he was a sorcerer who changed his form at will; that he was alive, that he was dead, that he was even immortal, born of the fair race. And, she recalled further, it was said that he had done some heinous deed against Scotland.

She knew that she had mentioned him in one of her prophecies, but she could not recall the prediction. Father Hugh had told her that it was a small matter, and of no concern to her. Now she wished that she knew the whole of that matter, small or large.

"James Lindsay," Eustace said. "I know the name well, sir. You are welcome here if your purpose is fair-minded. If 'tis not—we still outnumber you by a few men." He indicated the parapet, where men trained half-drawn bows on the newcomers.

"What is your purpose here?" Isobel asked. "Surely you didna climb up here just to rescue us. You dinna know us."

"I came here on a private matter," Lindsay said. "We dinna know about the siege until we approached the castle. We thought to bring some assistance to Aberlady's defenders—and some food." He beckoned, and one of his men stepped forward, pulling three limp rabbits from a sack. "I assume a meal would be to your liking."

"Aye," Eustace said. "Our thanks. A few of our men are in the kitchens now. They can prepare the meat." Lindsay's young comrade nodded and turned to run toward the stone-walled keep that towered over the center of the bailey yard.

"I have heard that the Border Hawk has an army of able men hiding in Ettrick Forest," Isobel said. "Are they outside, ready to attack the English and drive them off?"

"We are but five," Lindsay said.

"There are over a hundred English outside the gates!" Isobel burst out. "And you bring us five men!"

He arrowed his straight brown brows together over dark blue eyes. "We will get you to safety," he said, calm but stern.

She gaped at him, then turned to stare at Eustace.

" 'Tis said that a Scottish knight is never truly tested until he has flown with the Border Hawk," Eustace told her. "These men may be few, but doubtless clever and highly skilled."

" 'Twas once said of me, at least," Lindsay remarked. "We can take you out of here the way we came in."

"By the northface cliff?" Isobel asked, astonished.

He nodded. "After you have eaten, and the darkness is deeper, we will leave."

"But the English will take the castle if we abandon it!" Isobel exclaimed.

"We willna abandon it." Lindsay's quiet voice underscored the strength and confidence that emanated from him. " 'Tis Scottish practice to render castles unavailable for Southron use. Either a castle is held by force of arms or destroyed."

"Destroyed!" Isobel exclaimed.

"Aye." James Lindsay began to climb the steps toward the wall-walk, brushing past her. Eustace shot her a grim look and turned to follow him. Isobel grabbed her skirts and ran up the steps behind them both.

Eustace turned. "Go to the keep, Isobel."

"But he means to ruin Aberlady!" she hissed.

"You know 'tis necessary."

"We dinna know this man! We canna trust him to help us!"

"I know his name and his reputation."

"Then you know what they say about him!"

Eustace sighed. "Isobel, think. James Lindsay brings us the chance to survive. He brings hope, where we had none."

"Aberlady will be destroyed because of that hope!"

"With my last dying strength," Eustace growled, "with my own hand, I would have set fire to these walls to keep the English out. This is our only chance. Accept it."

She stared at him, stunned and silenced by the truth.

Eustace turned and walked away to join Lindsay, who stood behind a merlon stone, scanning the English garrison. Isobel hesitated, then ran along the wall-walk after them, halting by an embrasure in full view of the English soldiers below.

Lindsay lashed out and grabbed her arm, pulling her behind the shelter of the merlon. She shoved at him, but he held her firmly. "Are you a dimwit, to stand there?" he asked.

"The English willna harm me," she said with certainty.

"If you believe that, then you are not much of a prophetess," he snapped as he held her fast.

"Look there," Eustace said to Lindsay, from his position several feet away. "Each day, the English fill those ditches with branches and bracken to smooth the incline for their siege engines. And each time, we set them afire, see."

He called to two of the garrison, who turned to prepare fire arrows with cloth, pine pitch, and a torch, materials kept nearby for that purpose. The men loosed the flaming arrows, which sailed through the increasing darkness and fell into the ditches, setting them ablaze.

Held fast in the iron curve of Lindsay's arm, Isobel craned her neck and watched the fires spark and blossom. She saw Lindsay's men, their bows strung, mount the steps and arrange themselves along the battlements alongside Aberlady's garrison.

"When I let go of you," Lindsay murmured close to her ear, "I want you to crawl along the wall-walk to that corner tower over there."

"When you let go of me," she said between her teeth, "I will go where I please."

"Isobel, do as he says," Eustace pleaded as he loaded a crossbow. He ducked as an arrow whined overhead and slammed into a barrel on the wall-walk, followed by two more arrows that clattered on stone and fell aside.

Lindsay released her. "Go! Keep down."

Isobel rose up boldly to face the embrasure gap. She knew that once the English saw her, they would cease to fight. But as she stood, an arrow slammed into her upper right arm with tremendous force.

She spun helplessly with the blow and cried out. James Lindsay grabbed her, pulling her down. Isobel curled forward in searing pain, and Lindsay crouched over her, supporting her with one arm while he pulled at the torn fabric of her sleeve.

"Isobel!" Eustace called. "Dear God, they wouldna have fired, had they seen the lass. She stood too quick. Isobel!"

" 'Tisna serious." Isobel heard Lindsay's reassuring voice through a dim haze of pain. Deftly, he cracked the long shaft protruding from her arm, leaving the broad-head embedded in the muscle. "Can you bear it for a while, lady?" he asked.

She bit into her lower lip and nodded. Arrows fell around them in cruel rain, smacking against stone and wood. Within seconds, an arrow whooshed through the crenel and glanced past the back of Lindsay's leather hauberk as he bent over Isobel.

Another broadhead bit hard into her left ankle. The shaft fell aside. Isobel flinched and screamed, grabbing her leg. Lindsay swore and pulled her to him roughly, shielding her.

"You will be killed out here," he growled, and grabbed her around the waist. While arrows whined and clattered around them, he half dragged her along the wall-walk toward a small corner tower, kicked the narrow door open, and pulled her inside.

He set her down on the stone floor of the tiny, dark room and hunkered down beside her. He took her slender arm in the circle of his hand and examined the wound in the dusky light that came through the arrow-slit window.

Without asking permission, he lifted the hem of her skirt and tore a wide strip of linen from the hem of her embroidered chemise. He wadded part of the cloth around the seeping, throbbing wound in her right arm. Isobel drew the folded silken cloth from inside her sleeve with a shaking hand and pressed it to the bleeding cut above her ankle.

"Arrow wounds are painful," Lindsay said. "I have had several myself. But these will heal well enough. I canna tend them now, but I will be back shortly to see to them. Stay down below the arrow slit while you are in here." He shook his head. " 'Twas foolish to stand up behind a battlement like that."

"The English willna fire at me," she said. "When I am on the wall, they stop their volleys. But they didna see me in the dusk."

He took the cloth from her hand and wrapped it around her ankle. "I hardly think it simple chivalry," he said. "Do you have some agreement with them?" He glanced at her sharply.

She sucked in a breath at his tone. "They willna harm me because their king wants me brought to him. And that has helped us, again and again, in this siege. I stood up because I hoped to halt a battle."

He said nothing, but rose to his feet and gazed down at her, his eyes gleaming midnight blue in the shadows. She sensed deep anger in him and strong purpose.

"James Lindsay," she said, looking up at him. "Why did you come here? Did someone send you here?"

"I came," he said softly, "to find Black Isobel, the prophetess of Aberlady." Something in his tone sent a shiver along her spine. "We have matters between us, you and I."

"I dinna know you," she said, "though you seem to know me."

He shrugged. "The prophetess of Aberlady is widely known."

She remembered that she had uttered some prediction about him, and wished again that she knew what it had been. Silently, she looked up at him.

"Let me make a prediction, Black Isobel," he said in a low, threatening voice. "You will come to know me well. And you will come to regret what you and yours have done to me and mine."

She gasped at his hard tone. "I—I dinna understand."

"I think you do." He turned toward the door. "I will return as soon as I can to look after your wounds. You will be safe here." He stepped through the doorway into a hail of falling arrows.

Isobel stared after him, her heart pounding wildly, and wondered just how safe she was.

Chapter 3

A flaming arrow shaft traced an arc between the merlons, skimmed the wall-walk, and sank to earth in the bailey yard. James stared after it, and looked at the man who stood beside him on the battlement, behind the shelter of the merlon.

"Those Southrons are overfond of fire arrows," Henry said.

James watched another burning shaft sail overhead. "Aye. But if they fire the castle, we willna have the bother of it ourselves." He nocked an arrow and drew back the string. The broadhead found its mark over a hundred yards away when an English archer clutched his shoulder and fell to the ground.

"That," James announced grimly, "is for an arrow-shot lass."

"This morn you were not so protective of her."

"This morn, I didna know she was besieged, or starving, or quite so young." James drew another arrow from the quiver at his belt and set it to the bow.

"Or quite so comely." Henry grinned.

James frowned and deftly released the arrow. "Comely or ughsome, she needs our help in this, at least."

"True. Hah! Look there! I'll wager that soldier would like to know he was just caught in the leg by the Border Hawk!"

"I am sure he would," James drawled, and shot again.

The full moon rose quickly in the indigo sky, and English fire arrows flew like a host of comets. James shot steadily, one arrow after another, with barely time to think or pause. Beside him, Henry Wood did the same.

Beyond them, James saw a few of Aberlady's garrison and his own men—Quentin Fraser, Patrick Boyd, and young Geordie Shaw—all doing their best to keep a steady volley of arrows raining down on English heads.

He knew there was not much point to such a battle, for it could not be won. But he wanted Aberlady's men to know that the Border Hawk and his men were willing to risk their own lives to defend Scotsmen. Proving that seemed more important than killing a few more Southrons just now.

During a lag in the volley, James saw Henry turn. He looked up to see the bailie approaching along the wall-walk.

"Sir Eustace, is it?" Henry asked.

"Aye, Sir Eustace Gibson," the brawny man replied. "Bailie and captain of Aberlady Castle."

"I am Henry Wood." Henry held out a hand.

Eustace put a hand cautiously on the hilt of the sword at his belt. "That's a Southron name," he growled. "And you use a longbow with Southron skill."

"Aye, I'm English," Henry said. "Would you have me use a short bow like a Scot? Scotsmen are a sorry lot of archers. But for Jamie here, I'd think none of them had any worth with a bow. With a broadsword, now, 'tis a different matter."

Eustace scowled. "If you be Southron by fealty, then leave this castle the way you came into it, or bid the world farewell."

"Peace, man." James held up a hand. "Henry is Southron by birth, and a master of the longbow. But he uses that talent on behalf of the Scottish cause."

Eustace looked surprised. "Is it so?"

"My wife is a Scotswoman," Henry said. "Her people have become my own."

"But you fight against your own king."

"Aye, and I'm an outlaw for it. I've seen King Edward's cruelty toward the Scots, and I'll take no part in that."

Eustace nodded, removed his hand from his sword, and glanced at James. "Your loyalty is questioned of late, James Lindsay."

"So they say." James returned an even stare.

"Shall I doubt your fealty?"

"If you like."

Eustace frowned. "We have to trust you for now. So far you have proved helpful. We appreciate your assistance in this skirmish. But if you think to lead us into Southron hands by treachery—" He touched the handle of his sword again.

"My purpose is to help," James said flatly, and turned away. He knew why the man was wary and suspicious of him. But he would not defend his loyalty to every man he met.

"Judge the Border Hawk by what you know of him yourself, rather than by the rumors you have heard," Henry said.

James remained silent, but he heard Eustace make an affirmative, grudging sound.

An English arrow whistled overhead then, and Henry pulled another shaft from his quiver, preparing to shoot. Eustace laid a hand on his shoulder. " 'Tis pointless to return every shot," he said. "They have more men, more arrows, more food—and far greater strength than we have."

James watched the besiegers. A hundred feet out from the castle gates, under the light of torches, a group of men shoved a massive wooden framework into position close to the castle walls.

"That mangonel will be ready for use come dawn," he said. " 'Tis stout enough to damage these walls with scant trouble. They mean to finish you off within a few days."

"Hunger will do that first. You came at our neediest moment, Border Hawk," Eustace said. "Lady Isobel welcomes your help, too, be assured of that. But she fears that you will destroy her castle."

"I will," James said bluntly. "But I mean to free the garrison—and the lady—first."

"Climbing down that cliff is a dangerous venture. Most of my men are weak with hunger, and the lass is sore wounded."

"That cliff offers less risk than giving up to the enemy," Henry Wood pointed out.

"We will all get out of here, with your help," James said.

"Aye then." Eustace nodded. "But I fear Lady Isobel willna forgive you if you ruin her stronghold."

"Would she preserve it for Southrons?" James asked sharply.

"I've already told her the torching must be done, but she loves the place dearly."

James looked away. Years ago, the English had burned his own castle. He knew the devastation of such a loss, and more. In that terrible blaze, he had lost someone precious to him. He had no desire to fire Aberlady. But he had no choice.

"War brings sacrifice," he said harshly. "Lady Isobel will have to accept it." He glanced at Eustace. "When everyone has eaten, and the hour is late, we can make our escape. Go down to the kitchens with the garrison. My men will guard the walls, and I will fetch the lady and bring her to the keep."

Eustace nodded. "We have heavy ropes in storage, if you need them to scale the cliff. Is there aught else we can do?"

"Aye," James said quietly. "Pray to God, sir."

Moonlight sliced through the narrow window opening as James opened the tower door. He stepped into the dark, bare little room, leaned his bow and his broadsword against the wall, and crossed the tiny space in two strides.

Isobel Seton sat on the floor, her head bowed low, her black hair streaming over her shoulders. Blood darkened the sleeve of her gown. She curled forward, clearly suffering.

He dropped to one knee beside her. "How do you fare?"

"Well enough." The words were soft and husky. She looked at him, her face pale in the moonlight, and he saw the keen burden of pain in her taut features. Sympathy whispered through him, and he touched her left, uninjured arm gently.

"The wounds are painful, I know, but you will recover quickly," he said.

She watched him uncertainly. He noticed that her eyes
were wide, large, and extraordinarily beautiful in moonlight. In sunshine, James thought, they might be pale
blue. Now they seemed opalescent, like captured moon-
beams. When she swept her dark, thick lashes down, a
light seemed to extinguish.

"The noise of the arrow volleys has stopped," she
said.

"Aye, 'tis nearly full dark."

"They often send random shots at our walls through
the night." She drew in a shaky breath. "Were any
men hurt?"

"No men," he said. "Just one woman. Let me look at
your arm." When he touched her right shoulder, she
started and winced. "I am sorry," he murmured.

She frowned, watching him with those great, pale,
jewellike eyes. He slit open the sleeves of her gown and
chemise and bared her arm.

When he brushed the silken mass of her hair away,
its cool luxury spilled over his hand. The skin of her
neck and shoulder was smooth silk beneath his roughened fingertips. A soft, warm scent, womanly and sweet,
tinted with roses, drifted up from her.

James felt his gut spin and his loins contract impulsively with a swift, intense desire. He focused his
thoughts and his gaze on the wound, forcing all else from
his concentration.

The broken shaft thrust viciously out of her upper
arm. He took the base of the arrow between two fingers
and tugged gently. Isobel sucked in a sharp breath and
bit her lip to stifle a cry. James murmured a quiet assurance as he narrowed his eyes to judge the position of
the arrow.

A few probing touches, another tug on the shaft, told
him what he most dreaded: the removal would be difficult, and excruciating for her. He sighed and sat back
on his haunches.

"The broadhead is wide and barbed," he told her. I
canna pull it out without doing grave damage to the
muscle." He paused. "I will have to push it through."

She swallowed hard. Her lustrous, stricken gaze
tugged at him oddly. "Have you ever done this before?"

"Nay. But I have seen it done, and I have had it done to me. A field surgeon once pushed a barbed arrow through my leg." Even with the benefit of a few drams of aqua vitae, the pain had been considerable, he recalled. "We should go down to the kitchen for the task. And we need water and wine—a good deal of the last, if you have any left in your stores."

She shook her head. "The wine is gone, but our well water is still clear, if low. We can cleanse the wound, at least."

"Have you herb simples?" he asked. "Willow or valerian? Is there salt left? A saltwater poultice would be helpful if there is naught else to use."

"After ten weeks of siege, we are fortunate to have water and a few grains of barley left." She touched the back of his hand, her gaze entreating. "Take it out now. Here."

He frowned, puzzled. " 'Twill be easier in the kitchen. I will need to cauterize the wound, since there are no medicines."

"Can you do it here?" She looked down. "I dinna want the others to see. My men think me strong. You will be the only one to see the truth. . . . I dinna have the courage for this."

He turned his hand to take her fingers. "You are stronger than you think, I suspect," he murmured. "But so be it. We will do it here if that is what you want." He peeled down her sleeve.

She glanced at him while he continued to examine the wound. " 'Tis so dark. Can you see?"

"I am called after a hawk," he said lightly, "not a mole."

"Surely you need more light for the task."

"I can see."

"I dinna like darkness much. Can we sit closer to the moonlight?" A tremor in her voice made him glance at her sharply. His fingers, upon her arm, sensed the quiver that ran through her body; he felt a cold, strong stream of fear in her.

"Aye," he said softly, wondering if the daunting prospect of the arrow removal made her so fretful. He helped her to shift more directly beneath the window, where the moon cast a bright, cool light.

He frowned as he returned his attention to the wound. He would have preferred her to be deep in her cups when he took out the arrow tip, for the thing was wickedly made. The broadhead, which he had felt through her thin flesh, was wider than his thumb and barbed like a double thorn. The removal would not be easy no matter how he did it.

He encircled her arm with his hand and felt tension thrum through her like a plucked harp string. He murmured a few words of reassurance and felt her begin to relax under his touch. She glanced at him, a quick look of innocence and pleading, and closed her eyes, leaning back against the wall.

Touching her, watching her, he felt her courage, fragile but definite. She did not know its existence, but he did. And he saw something more, too: she placed her trust in him. He was humbled by that. So few trusted him now.

Ironic, he thought. He had come to Aberlady to use the prophetess to regain the trust he had lost. Yet all he saw in her eyes in this moment was faith. He felt suddenly ashamed of his purpose here.

Isobel gave James a tremulous smile. A feeling flared inside of him, brighter than the moonlight, then faded before he could grasp its enticing warmth.

"Do it," she whispered. "Now, James Lindsay."

He watched her hard, thin collarbones rise and fall with her rapid breaths, and looked at the broken arrow shaft jutting cruelly out of her slender arm. He unlaced the wide leather arrow guard that he wore around his left forearm, and handed it to her.

"You might want to bite on that," he said.

She nodded stiffly and slipped the leather piece between her teeth. He angled her torso in preparation for his task. As he moved her, she whimpered and squeezed her eyes shut.

He knelt beside her and took her right arm above the elbow. With the other hand, he gripped the broken arrow shaft.

"Easy, now, Isobel," he murmured.

Eyes closed, teeth pressed to the folded leather, she

waited with a gentle, shining courage. He admired her bravery and wondered why she did not see it in herself. She glowed with it, like a flame inside a horn lantern.

He drew a breath and sighted the angle carefully, wary of hitting bone. Then he shoved the arrow through, fast and hard.

The bladed iron tip burst through her flesh. Isobel cried out once, a low, guttural sound that ripped through his heart.

Biting his lip, aware that he hurt her dreadfully, James pushed the rest of the broken, bloody shaft through her arm and plucked it free.

She dropped the leather piece from her lips and let her head sag forward, heavily, against his chest. Her head rolled in a drunken sort of agony, and her breathing was ragged and fierce. But she neither screamed nor swooned.

"Soft, you," he whispered. "Soft, now, 'tis done. You did well, lass." He touched her head, smoothing his fingers over the silkiness of her hair, and pressed the folded cloth to the fresh wound. She uttered a raw gasp and then was silent.

No matter what else he thought of her, he could not forget the way she had endured the ordeal. He encircled her back with one arm and held the wadded cloth against the wound.

Isobel leaned against him so heavily that he feared she had passed out. She turned her head, reassuring him. Her small, tremulous sob stirred a rush of compassion through him.

He murmured as he held her, soft phrases that he had used while training his hawks or while loving a woman. He had not uttered such phrases in years, for he had not kept a hawk in a long time—and the last few women he had loved with his body had heard no such tender words from him.

Nearly forgotten, endlessly gentle, the words streamed from his lips. He spoke to Isobel as if he held his beloved, as if she were part of his soul, and not a woman who had conspired against him. The warm embrace felt like a fit of glove to hand, giving James as much comfort as he had intended to give her.

Startled by his own behavior, he paused. Then he released her and helped her to sit up.

"Thank you," she said, her voice faint and hoarse. She leaned against the wall, closing her eyes.

James pressed the cloth to her wound and watched her carefully. Her breathing gradually calmed, and color came back into her lips and cheeks.

Even ravaged by pain and distress, she was elegant and delicate, wrapped in cool light and shadow. Her brows and lashes were black against her pale, creamy skin. The thin moonlight revealed the square shape of her face, wide at cheekbones and jaw, curved at the chin, with a full, gentle mouth. Her face combined strength and fragility in exquisite balance, enhanced by her extraordinary eyes.

Her bare shoulder and throat were thin, revealing bony grace beneath the skin. The long limbs beneath the drape of her gown, and the well-defined frame of her shoulders and hips, told him that she was a tall, strong woman.

She reminded him, suddenly, of a female goshawk he had captured and trained years ago. Strong-willed, powerful, and beautiful, the bird had remained partly wild, and yet had given him her exclusive loyalty. He had mourned her when she was gone. He frowned; he had not thought of her in a long while.

He tore a second strip of cloth from the first and wrapped it around Isobel's arm, tying it in place. "That should do for now," he said as he pulled the neck of her gown higher. "Let me see your ankle."

She sat forward. " 'Tisna so bad," she said. She pulled the skirt of her gown higher to reveal her left foot, bandaged in white silk over her bloodied woolen stocking. Awkwardly, using her left hand, she undid the silk and peeled down the hose, biting her lip to smother a wince.

James took over the task from her and carefully pushed the stocking past her long, slender ankle, shoving down the collar of her low boot. Just above the outer ankle, an ugly slash marked where a passing arrow had sliced through the skin.

"This was done by a crossbow bolt," he said. "I saw the shot. You were fortunate it did not shatter the bone." As he spoke, he pressed the torn linen against the wound. She drew in a sharp, whistling breath.

James tied the cloth in place and pulled up her hose, tucking the top under the braided silk garter above her knee. Her leg and ankle, he noted, were lean and hard as a lad's, the bones elegantly shaped.

He stood and held out his hands in an offer to lift her. "I'll take you down to the keep now. I will cauterize the wounds, and I want you to eat and rest. You are weak from this ordeal, and you have fasted too long."

"I havena fasted by choice," she grumbled, and refused his hands, rising slowly to her feet, one hand on the wall, swaying when she stood upright. She stepped forward, and her cry of pain tore through James. He growled and swept her up into the cradle of his arms, though she protested hoarsely.

He carried her down the tower steps and out into the bailey, and strode across the shadowed yard. A few English-sprung arrows sailed over the wall and whacked into the earth not far from them. James stopped to make sure the way was clear and glanced up at his men, who stood sentry on the moonlit battlement.

Isobel looked up as he did. "The English shoot at us almost every night," she said. "We ignore the attacks as much as we can, since we lack the men to return each shot."

"The siege commander has a relentless sense of duty."

Isobel tipped her head and watched him. "James Lindsay," she said. "Did the English send you here to capture us and bring us out of here into custody?"

He stopped, holding her in his arms, and stared down at her. "I dinna take orders from Southrons," he snapped.

"Did Sir Ralph Leslie send you here, then?"

"No one sent me. I came here of my own accord."

"Now why would the Border Hawk do that?" she asked softly.

"To rescue the prophetess," he said irritably.

Isobel's gaze was wary. "I dinna believe you. There is more on your mind than rescue."

He walked on through the bailey without replying. He knew that her faith in him faded as her suspicions grew. Some part of him regretted the loss, but he could not

blame her. Apart from the rescue, she should not trust
him at all.

When he reached the tower in the center of the bailey
yard, he looked up. Like many castles, the upper level,
where the great hall and living quarters would be located,
had no direct access; the upper door stood bolted, its stout
outer ladder removed. He went toward the back wall of
the keep, where he saw a narrow door hidden in shadows.

The door swung open. Eustace Gibson motioned them
forward. "This way. My lady?" he inquired softly.

"I am fine," she answered.

James followed Eustace through a wide, dark storage
chamber. The room was bare except for empty grain
sacks, upturned wooden crates, and a pile of sturdy rope.
Torchlight illuminated some steps in an alcove.

James crossed the room behind Eustace, aware of the
warm, easy pressure of Isobel's weight in his arms. Her
hand was soft at his neck, her torso close and curving, her
slender legs draped easily over his forearm. When he
shifted her for balance, she laid her head lightly upon his
shoulder.

He sucked in a breath, wishing she were strong
enough to walk. He was too aware of her soft, satiny
textures, her feminine scent, her luxurious warmth. She
rode like an angel in his arms.

He would have preferred a hell-hag. When he had set
out to find the prophetess of Aberlady, he had expected
a shrewish, manipulative woman, a perfect mate for Sir
Ralph Leslie. Instead, he found a gentle, brave girl and
her garrison, all in need of help.

But he could not let this sway his original plan. He must
hold Isobel Seton hostage long enough to free his cousin,
and in the process bring revenge upon Leslie's head.

James claimed to be her champion, but he intended
to be her captor. He felt a keen twinge of guilt. However
briefly, she had given him her full trust. The sensation
had been exquisite, sweet and nourishing, unlike the bitter, raw taste of revenge.

He set his jaw and hardened his gaze, and followed
Eustace up the stairs, holding Isobel in his arms. Guilt
be damned. A long while had passed since he had allowed his sins to bother him. He would not begin now.

Chapter 4

The faint rumble that woke her was not the low growl of thunder, as she thought at first, but the sound of men's voices. Isobel opened her eyes, blinked away a fog of sleep, and looked around.

She was alone in the huge, stone-vaulted kitchen, lying on a pallet in a corner near the warm hearth. Voices floated up the stairwell from the storage chamber, and although she could not distinguish the words, she recognized the tones of a few of Aberlady's men.

An hour or two—perhaps more—had surely passed since Isobel had fallen asleep on the pallet of blankets and straw in the corner of the kitchen. The hearth fire blazed at a low fever, but the iron kettle, suspended inside the arched fireplace, was empty. The men had devoured the soup that they had prepared themselves from the barley broth and the rabbit meat.

James Lindsay and Eustace had insisted that Isobel have some as well. The soup strengthened her, although she had no appetite after James had treated her wounds.

She winced sharply at the vivid memory. He had touched the red-hot tip of his dirk to her wounds to burn out the bad humors and seal the flesh. The agony had caused her to black out for a few moments. She had come to awareness with his arms around her, and his soothing voice in her ear.

"Forgive me," he had said softly. She had done so, silently, for she knew that serious wounds had to be cauterized if no medicines were available.

Now, as she lay awake and alone, his warm embrace seemed like a deeply comforting dream that could not be recaptured.

Moving slowly, she sat up and leaned against the wall, wincing at the ache in her arm and foot. Long strips of linen cloth bound her bent arm securely against her side and waist; her ankle, too, was more firmly bound. James had added the outer bandaging before she had fallen asleep. Now she found that the support lessened the discomfort when she moved.

Looking around, Isobel noticed a yellow flash sail past the window on the other side of the room. Fire arrows, she thought with a heavy sigh. She pushed herself to her knees and stood, her movements stiff and awkward. Biting her lip as her injured foot took the weight of a step, she limped to the window.

As she moved, she felt light-headed. Likely that was caused by hunger and the strain of her situation. She breathed slowly, and when she felt steadier, she leaned forward to look out through the open window.

The bailey yard was a vast, dark field, surrounded by the vague moonlit shapes of the high curtain wall and outbuildings. Isobel narrowed her eyes and looked around. In the far corner of the curtain wall, near the postern door that opened on the edge of the cliff, she saw a few men from Aberlady's garrison with one or two of the renegades. The men seemed intently occupied with several ropes, although she could not tell what they did there.

Two more blazing arrows sailed through the night, trailing flames and smoke, and landed in the bare earth of the bailey, quickly burning out. Isobel glanced toward the battlement, but the angle made it difficult to see if the garrison returned the shots. The bailey seemed empty but for smoking arrows.

"My lady? Excuse me, my lady."

Startled, Isobel turned. A young man entered the kitchen from the stairwell and came toward her with long, loping steps. His russet tunic sagged on his thin, gangly frame, and the firelight made a dark halo of his curling, tangled brown hair.

He stopped, his cheeks flushing. "Jamie Lindsay sent me here to see to your welfare, my lady, and if you are ill, I am to fetch him straightaway," he said in a rush.

"I am fine," she said.

"Then I am to watch you close and wait for his signal." He peered intently at her. "Are you truly Black Isobel the prophetess?"

"Aye. You needna stare so," she said, amused. "I willna disappear in a puff of brimstone fire."

The boy's cheeks, faintly whiskered, blushed more deeply. "I ask your pardon, my lady." He cleared his throat as if in an agony of embarrassment. "I didna mean to offend—"

"No pardon needed," she said kindly. "What is your name?"

"Geordie Shaw. I'm cousin to the hero Wallace," he added proudly.

"You are with the brigands? How old are you?"

"Fifteen summers," he said. "I've been with Jamie for more than a year. My father was with him, too. We ran with him and with Wallace. Da died," he said gruffly, looking down. "Six months ago. 'Twas a braw fight that day. He died well fighting Southrons."

"He must have been a brave man, like his son," she said quietly. "My father was taken in battle last spring. He's in an English prison still."

Geordie seemed intrigued. "Jamie was in an English dungeon for months. He finally escaped. Will you ransom your da?"

She shook her head. "We lack the coin for that, and have naught to offer in trade. I dinna even know where he is held. But a friend has promised to find him," she added. "But for the siege, I would have had word of my father by now."

"You will find him," Geordie said. He drew back his wide, bony shoulders proudly. "We have come to rescue you. And then I will help you find your father if you like, my lady," he added sincerely.

"Thank you, Geordie Shaw. I appreciate that." She frowned. "James Lindsay was in prison?"

"Aye, taken last spring. But he escaped several weeks ago, just before Wallace was taken." He swallowed heavily and looked away. Isobel thought she saw the glaze of tears in his eyes. "You willna have heard about Wallace, I suppose."

"Aye, we heard," she murmured.

"How could you know of it, under siege these weeks?"

"The English took delight in shouting reports to us. Once, they allowed us to declare a truce for a holy day, and let our priest come inside to give us communion. Father Hugh told us much news before he left. That was the day he took our horses out with him," she said, remembering. "And the day we let some of my father's hawks and falcons fly free. So 'tis true, then," she added. "Wallace is dead."

"Aye," Geordie said hoarsely.

"Geordie—we heard that the Border Hawk betrayed Wallace."

He shook his head. "Evil Southron rumors. I willna believe that. Jamie doesna speak of it. We few have stayed with him, but the rest have gone, for he is a hunted man. Jamie came here to seek you out," Geordie said suddenly. "But he didna say why. Will you make a prophecy for him? Can you help him?"

She blinked at his blunt, eager questions. "I—I dinna know." Certes, she thought to herself. That must be why Lindsay had come, to ask a prophecy of her. Perhaps he had questions about whatever she had said of him before. But she did not know what that was, so she could not help him.

"Do you trust him, Lady Isobel?" Geordie asked quietly.

"Trust?" She looked out the window. "I dinna know him," she said carefully. "I canna say. Why?"

"Jamie will save you from this siege," he said confidently. "Then you will place your faith in him as we have. If only folk would trust him again, all would be well for him."

Isobel sensed that the lad adored the forest rogue, his hero, so much that he was willingly blind to his faults. James Lindsay was said to be a traitor to Wallace and Scotland. If that was true, she feared that Geordie Shaw would be deeply hurt.

"I will try to trust him," she said, gazing out the window.

Isobel had placed her faith utterly in James Lindsay when he had pulled the arrow from her arm. She remembered the warm comfort of his arms afterward, and his soft, deep voice as he soothed her. Exquisite shivers rippled through her at the memory, and the warmth she had felt then blossomed again.

Had she known only that compassion of him, instead of ill rumors, she would have trusted James Lindsay completely. She would have laid her life in his hands and felt safe—and loved, she thought oddly, quickly.

That was a foolish yearning, born of loneliness, she told herself sternly. She was betrothed to a man without much compassion in his nature. But then, she reminded herself, Lindsay had only comforted her because of her pain.

She sighed and leaned against the windowsill. "Geordie, those men over there in the corner. What are they doing?"

"Jamie told them to knot the ropes and make ladders and harnesses so that we can go down the cliffside. Jamie says the full moon will give us muckle light to climb down. He says we will leave as soon as—" He stopped, coloring deeply.

"As soon as what?" she asked.

He shrugged. "When he gives the word."

She narrowed her eyes. "As soon as the castle is put to the torch? I know what he means to do, Geordie."

Geordie looked uncomfortable. He leaned forward to peer out the window. "I am to watch for his signal."

"What signal? He isna even down there."

"Aye, he is, see. Straight below us." Geordie indicated the area near the base of the keep. "He is talking with the bailie."

She peered straight down and saw his wide shoulders and the glint of his dark, gold-streaked hair. He walked beside Eustace past the base of the keep. Cool moonlight cascaded over his face and commanding form.

The two men strode into the center of the yard. Lindsay paused, standing with a bold, relaxed power, one hand on his upright bow, the other pointing toward the battlement. Eustace nodded in response to something the outlaw said.

Isobel leaned against the windowsill, watching. Though her legs trembled with fatigue, she stayed there, fascinated, as if the forest rogue who had entered her castle exerted some mysterious power over her. She could not look away.

But, she asked herself as Geordie had, did she trust him? She did not know. Even her perceptive inner senses gave her no hint. She only knew that his appearance here had thrown her into a turmoil of fear and hope, of suspicion and faith. She was not certain whether to accept or refuse what he offered.

Why had he come here? She recalled the bitterness in his voice when she had asked him that question earlier. *We have matters between us, you and I,* he had said. The ominous words still echoed in her mind.

But she could not forget, regardless of what mission brought him here, that Lindsay had brought food when they were starving, had helped her when she was hurt, and now intended to get them out of the castle.

He brought hope, as Eustace had told her. Isobel was grateful for that. But she would do well to be wary of him.

Beside her, Geordie waved, and James Lindsay glanced up toward the window that framed them both. Isobel knew the instant that his gaze alighted on her, and she returned it steadily. James motioned toward Geordie.

"He wants to talk to me," the lad said. "I will come back up for you." He turned and ran, descending the turning stairs with pounding, rapid steps. She looked out the window.

Within moments, Geordie appeared beside James. Another of the outlaws joined them, holding a longbow. As they gestured at the walls, Isobel knew they discussed destroying the castle.

As much as she dreaded it, she could not stop it. She understood that it was necessary to prevent the English from entering and taking it. She did not want Southrons to hold the castle.

But Aberlady was her lifelong home and the refuge that she needed. She sighed and watched the men who gathered in the moonlit bailey. James Lindsay was about to take away the haven that surrounded the prophetess of Aberlady. Her father had made certain that she was well protected because of her gift.

Only a few men—including Eustace, who knew only a hint of the truth—knew about the fits of blindness that assailed her when the visions came. No women remained near her now; her mother had died the same year that the gift showed itself, and her nurse and maidservants were gone now, some lost to illness and death, the other gone to live with families far from Aberlady. The last woman to serve Isobel personally had died early in the siege, a victim of age and frailty.

The cocoon that her father had spun around her had grown snug over the years. He and Father Hugh had decided that Sir Ralph could provide the protection of marriage. None of them had thought that Isobel would ever be forced into a situation like this one.

James Lindsay turned then, distracting her thoughts. He looked up at the window where she watched, and a shiver rippled through her. Even through the darkness, she sensed his steady, penetrating gaze. She drew back behind the window jamb and leaned her head against the stone.

In all the years she had lived at Aberlady, she had thought never to leave here. The prophetic gift, which appeared at her own urging most of the time, sometimes burst upon her without warning, bringing glorious or disturbing visions of the future.

She had learned to depend upon the few who understood her singular world. She had been raised to depend on her father completely. But now he was gone, and she did not know when she would see him again.

She knew that Eustace would want to take her to Father Hugh as soon as they escaped the castle. The priest would give her refuge in his home near the parish church outside of Stobo, and would immediately send word to Sir Ralph, who had gone in search of Sir John Seton.

She longed to know that her father was safe, but she inwardly balked at the idea of marriage to Sir Ralph. Beneath the rough manners common to many men, she sensed real harshness. At times, he frightened her, though he had never overtly offended her. But her father and the priest seemed to trust and admire the Scottish knight, even though Ralph had changed his fealty.

He is a practical man who watches the weather of the war, her father had said. *He loves you well, and he has promised me to keep you safe no matter who wins this struggle.*

Safe. She nearly laughed. She had faced besiegement for weeks, and Sir Ralph had not come to her aid. His search for her father must have taken him deep into England. If he had known, surely he would have come to Aberlady Castle quickly.

She had spent those weeks learning new lessons. Now she could lead where she had only followed, and could defy where she had only obeyed. She was far stronger in will than she had been before.

Still, the thought of leaving Aberlady terrified her. Inside the walls of her home, she had learned independence. Inside her cocoon, she could be brave, but she was not a winged butterfly yet. She was not ready for the real freedom of leaving her home.

She leaned out of the window again and watched a rogue contemplate the best method of setting the torch to her home, and the fastest way to rip her away from its protection.

Aberlady would be sacrificed, but its inhabitants would be safe. Homes could be made anywhere, she knew. She sighed deeply and tried to accept what was inevitable.

Another English fire arrow whistled through the dark like a comet, trailing bright flame. The arrow landed, like the others had done, in the earthen yard, flaming and smoking. James Lindsay strode forward and plucked it out of the ground.

Isobel watched as he raised his bow and nocked the flaming arrow. He drew the string taut and released it. The arrow shot upward, its glowing tail tracing a new arc through the darkness.

The arrow smacked into the thatched roof of the empty stable and burst into flame.

Isobel gasped.

Another English arrow flamed through the darkness. Lindsay tore that one out of the ground, too, and shot it forth. The flaming bolt landed on the roof of a storage hut, which caught fire within seconds.

Isobel put a shaking hand to her mouth, unable to move, unable to tear her gaze from the bailey. Golden sparks flew about in the brisk night wind. One by one, the dry thatch and wood in the outbuildings caught flame like kindling.

James Lindsay stood in the midst of the brilliant, growing light, his bow propped upright, and watched the fire spread. Other men gathered near him, and no one made an effort to stop the fire from spreading.

Now Eustace ran toward the burning stable. He snatched up a long stick and lit it like a taper on the low, flaming roof of the storage building. Then he flung the brand toward another thatched roof, and more flames erupted.

Isobel felt as if her heart shattered within her breast.

" 'Tis to prevent the English from taking Aberlady," Geordie said quietly. He seemed to appear beside her; she had not even heard him return. "The policy of scorched earth is based on an old custom of war in Scotland."

"I know," she whispered, and could not look away, although she did not want to watch her home touched to fire before her eyes.

"You can return later," Geordie said. "Repairs can be made. The stone willna burn, just the thatch and the wood, enough to keep the Southrons from taking the castle."

"I know." Tears glazed her eyes.

Fiery patches blazed on the thatched roofs of the smaller buildings now. An apple tree in the orchard near the small stone chapel began to burn, its branches bedecked with glowing necklaces of flame. When flames burst along the gate to the garden, Isobel caught back a deep sob.

"We have to leave here," Geordie said. He circled an arm around her waist and tugged gently. "Come, Lady Isobel. Jamie told me to bring you down to the bailey. He means for us to escape the castle now."

She allowed Geordie to lead her to the stairs. Searing pain shot through her arm and her ankle, and she put her free arm around his waist as he helped her down the steps.

When they emerged from the keep and stepped into the bailey, Isobel moved away from Geordie's grasp. She felt a sudden need to be alone, surrounded by the awful beauty of the raging fire.

Sparks flew around her like stars. The bailey was full of hot, brilliant light. Isobel moved slowly toward the garden, pausing several feet from the blazing gate.

She felt a hand tug at her arm. "Isobel. Come away."

That quiet voice was already deeply familiar, like the voice of a friend. But he could not be a friend, to do this with such thoroughness, denying her even a chance to gather her things and bid her home farewell.

"Leave me be," she said sharply, shaking off his hand.

James Lindsay stared down at her, his face lean and hard in the warm light. "Come away," he said firmly, reaching out again.

"Nay." She limped forward, despite the pain in her foot, despite the danger. The garden had been the heart of Aberlady; her mother had designed it years ago. Memories and need drew her there.

Without hesitation, Isobel moved toward the gate, which gaped wide, its wooden struts flaming.

Chapter 5

Isobel glided through the blazing gate like an angel crossing the threshold of hell. James stared, then strode after her. "Are you mad?" he called. "Come away from there!"

She ignored him, limping along the path, her head and shoulders held proud. James knew that it must cost her considerable pain to advance like that. He followed her.

Flames lingered on the gate, and a few vines blazed nearby, but so far the fire had touched a small part of the garden. Striding along the path after Isobel, James saw the careful arrangement of paths and plant beds—but he also noticed that the garden was already ravaged, without benefit of fire. Stalks and vines were plucked clean, and whole beds had been dug up and not replanted.

Isobel went toward a side wall, where a wooden trellis sagged against the stone. Bare vines clung to it, empty of flowers but for a few ragged blossoms. James was close enough to overtake her in one or two strides, but he paused, ready to snatch her away from there if need be. Behind them, the gate and some dry vines crackled as they burned, and smoke and sparks drifted overhead. But the fire had not yet reached this corner.

A white rose clung to the highest part of the vine, a swirl of pale petals in the light of the fire and the moon. The girl stretched her hand upward to reach it.

James stepped forward and plucked the rose for her, laying it in her open hand. Despite the heavy odor of burning wood, he caught a drift of the rose's delicate fragrance.

Isobel lifted the bloom to her face to breathe in its

scent. "My mother treasured these roses," she said. Her voice was soft and hoarse, and tears glistened in her eyes. James waited, expecting angry accusations from her. But she seemed calm as she ran a fingertip along the edge of the rose. "The garden was all that we had left of her," she said.

"I am sorry," he murmured. "I didna know."

She gave a hollow, hoarse little laugh, surprising him. "The siege destroyed this garden before you set your fire, Border Hawk." She glanced around. "We stripped everything edible, even the flowers. This rose bloomed but days ago. Eustace wanted me to add it to the soup, but I refused." She gazed at the pale blossom, and her lower lip trembled.

She puzzled him, so gentle and sad when he had expected anger from her. But they did not have time to pluck roses, with a fire raging beyond and a hundred English at the gates.

"Isobel, we must go," he said, quiet but firm.

"You didna give me time to say farewell," she murmured, "before you loosed that fire arrow. Let me have the chance now."

James sighed and shoved his fingers through his hair in a gesture of regret. He had been quick to act on his decision to fire the castle; perhaps too quick, but they had little time to spare. He had not meant to cause her this sort of grief.

He remembered his own mother's garden, a haven of scent and color that had provided hiding places for James and his older brother, and created pleasant memories. But it was gone now, burned, as this garden would be soon.

"When I was small, my father brought back the first of these rosebushes from a Crusade," Isobel said. "He said my mother had sweet magic in her fingers for making roses." She smiled. "The garden was always full of roses—white, pink, and red—from spring until autumn. When she died, he buried her in our chapel, so that she could be near her roses, and near us, always." She pointed beyond the garden wall, where a small chapel roof jutted up, its clay tiles bright in the firelight. "Dear God, if the fire reaches the chapel—" she said.

"I have already told my men to soak the chapel roof with water to protect it," he said. "I dinna burn churches."

She nodded. A tear pooled in her eye and hovered there.

James felt a compelling urge to touch her—a hand to her shoulder, a finger to that shining tear, some gesture of comfort. But he held back, fisting his hand against the craving.

And he waited, silent and still, while a slender, ebony-haired girl cradled a pale rose in the midst of destruction.

In some detached, philosophical part of his mind, long ago trained by scholarly monks to see the symbolism in all things, he realized that heaven and hell existed in perfect duality here in this ravaged garden, in the gentle, lovely girl, in the pure rose, and in the darkness and the inferno that surrounded them.

A blaze that he had caused.

"Isobel," he said. He felt emotion constrict his throat, but went on. "Years ago, I lost my own castle when the English set it afire. Those—those who were inside were killed—my kin, my men, my—" He stopped.

She glanced at him. "You know how I feel," she said softly. "You suffered even worse. And yet you set Aberlady ablaze."

"Aye," he said gruffly.

"I know you had no choice," she whispered.

He nodded silently. He had felt hollow, black inside, when he shot that fire arrow toward the thatch. Devastating memories, six years past, had sparked again with that burst of flame. But he had locked them away once again. He had no time, no strength inside to let them out.

Watching Isobel, he would have preferred her to shout at him, to call him vile names, to echo his anger and tap the darkness that he carried inside himself.

But her poignant sadness tugged at him, challenged him, unsettled him. She stood there holding that sooty, bedraggled white rose, and he suddenly wanted—something, and could not name it. He had not felt this raw, this open, in years.

Then she glanced up at him, and he saw in her translucent eyes that she bore no grudge toward him for setting the torch to Aberlady. He saw, God help him, forgiveness.

He turned away.

For one long, dreadful instant, he felt as if the hard casing around his heart began to crack. With the next breath, and the next, he willed the gap sealed again.

He reminded himself why he had come in search of the prophetess of Aberlady, and why he had found it expedient to fire her castle. Isobel Seton might be distressed, in need, and impossibly lovely. But he reminded himself that she was the only pawn he had, and he must use her as he had already schemed.

"The policy of scorched earth is sanctioned by the Guardians of the Realm of Scotland," he said coldly. " 'Tis a necessary action to prevent the English from taking Scottish properties." He turned back toward her.

She blinked up at him. Those sad, magnificent eyes nearly undid him again. But he could not easily look away.

"I know," she said. "But I—I hoped my castle would be spared."

"Dinna be foolish. The Southrons ready their engines to knock down your gates in the morn. You were willing to defend these walls for weeks to keep them out. I have ensured that they will stay out, for now at least, for the good of Scotland, and for your own welfare." His tone was sharp.

She frowned. He saw her temper blossom then, a hard blue spark in her limpid eyes. "I didna think the Border Hawk cared for the good of Scotland," she snapped.

He felt the jab keenly, startled that her words could wound him so easily. But he felt on more certain ground with anger and conflict than with her sadness, her softness.

Many shared the opinion of him that she had just voiced. After all, his new reputation as a traitor had begun with this girl's own words, months ago. His temper surged.

"Come ahead," he said abruptly, taking her uninjured arm, meaning to pull her toward the gate.

She stood her ground. "Why does my welfare matter to you? 'Tis said the Border Hawk is loyal only to himself. 'Tis said—"

"I know what 'tis said," he barked. He glanced through the burning frame of the gate. The fire in the bailey, which lit up the dark sky, had consumed the outbuildings and now encroached on the tower. In the shadows by the back wall, he saw his men and Aberlady's garrison, waiting.

"Come," he said firmly, taking her right wrist. "We have to get out of here. Now."

She resisted his tug. Fiery light gleamed on her fine-boned cheeks and in her glossy dark hair as she looked up at him. "Why did you come here, James Lindsay?" she asked.

"I came to rescue you, whether or not you believe that," he snapped impatiently.

"I dinna believe it," she said. "There is more. Tell me what 'tis."

He leaned forward. "Are you blind, lass? There is fire all around you! We dinna have time for a wee chat."

She gaped at him, and the hovering tears deepened. He could not think why she would be so upset by his remark.

"For now, I am your champion," he muttered sourly. "Later you may call me something else, if you like."

He bent down and scooped her into his arms. Then he strode through the smoldering, fire-spitting gate and headed across the bailey amid a shower of bright sparks.

She might have done him the courtesy of passing out, James thought, as he climbed hand over hand down a sturdy knotted rope ladder. Then he could have carted her down the cliff as he had wanted to do, slung over his shoulder, head down. Both he and Henry Wood had argued with her that she should let James carry her draped over his shoulder; a little time like that would not harm her, they had said. But Isobel had protested the idea stubbornly, and James had relented. He carried her facing him, strapped to his torso.

He had also given in to her insistence that she needed spare clothing and other items. Their escape had been

further delayed while Isobel and Eustace had gone off
to collect her things in a leather sack, which Eustace
now carried down the cliffside.

Although she had not complained, James saw the
traces of fatigue and starvation on her face. He was
keenly aware of her physical weakness as she rode in
his arms. She was a well-made girl, but hunger and injury
had left her scant strength. And he heard every wince
of pain that she tried to suppress.

He glanced to either side and saw the other men, lowering along lengths of rope nearby, moving silent and
steady over the jagged rock face. All of those who had
come out of Aberlady were weakened with the strain of
the siege. James had reminded his own men, who were
fit and rested, to usher Aberlady's survivors down the
cliffside with care.

He glanced back at Isobel. "How do you fare?" he
asked.

"I dinna envy birds," she said wryly, her pale face
inches from his own. She was face-to-face with him, her
legs circling his hips and her uninjured left arm around
his neck. James had fastened her to him with a rope
harness, like a bear cub to its mother, leaving his arms
and legs free to manage the rope ladder.

"Ah, then, I promise we willna fly," he said with a
half laugh. Isobel grimaced and glanced down, and the
grip of her arm became choking strong. "Dinna look
down," he said quickly. "Be at ease. You are safe." She
loosened her hold around his neck and tucked her face
against his shoulder.

The cliffside was high, raw rock, plunging straight
down in some places. The northern face, where they descended was steep and jagged. Mossy ledges and crevices
provided hand and foot holds, some large enough to
stand upon. Each man proceeded carefully; in the moonlight, a loose bit of turf or rock could be mistaken for a
secure hold. Mist drifted over the cliff face in torn, gauzy
veils, making the descent even more dangerous.

James and his men had climbed upward in fading daylight, using ropes fastened to scaling forks, which they
tossed up as they went. The downward climb was a
greater challenge than James had anticipated. During the

hours in the castle, he and the men had created two long rope ladders, and had added sturdy knots along the lengths of the other ropes to aid climbing. But the going was slow and painstaking, for the ropes were not long enough to reach the ground. The lines, secured to the iron forks, had to be loosened and reattached in different places, while the climbers waited on narrow ledges.

James glanced toward the ground and saw its dark expanse beneath the mist. He looked upward at the castle, perched high overhead, its blazing walls casting a reddish glow into the night sky. Moonlight both helped and hindered them. If they could see their way, then the enemy could see them as well. Only the treacherous mists and darkness protected them.

James knew that the English could discover their escape at any moment and attack them on the cliffside, where they would be most vulnerable. He hoped that the blaze would so distract the enemy that they would neglect to send a patrol around the area until the cliff face was again deserted.

Cold wind whipped his hair into his eyes, and he turned his head to clear his vision. He went down another rung, easing his weight onto the bouncing brace of the rope. The girl's weight was not a burden, though her long legs and her injured arm, strapped tightly, proved awkward to balance. His quiver and bow thumped against his back in the wind, and he paused on the ladder, gripping it firmly with one hand. He rested his other arm and hand around her hips while he caught his breath.

Another strong breeze blew past, and he heard Isobel gasp softly. Her hair unfurled like a banner, weaving a dark curtain with his own. The next gust of wind knocked them roughly against the cliffside. Isobel cried out as her arm slammed against the rock. She buried her face in his shoulder with a ragged whimper.

He turned to shield her from the driving force of the wind, and held still to allow her a moment to recover. She sucked in a breath and raised her head, nodding to him to go on.

"Bonny lass," he said with approval. He glanced down

to find the next rung. " 'Twillna be long now. We're nearly there."

He was amazed to hear Isobel laugh, a frightened doubtful little squeak, but a laugh nonetheless. He half smiled as he resumed his descent.

Isobel knew that she should feel terrified, but she felt strangely secure, wrapped in a cocoon of rope and cloaks, held firm against the outlaw's hard, solid body. She laid her head in the hollow of his shoulder and studied his clean profile, silhouetted against the moon.

She had already discovered that she could not look down at the dark expanse of ground below the cliff. Nor could she look up at the castle, where a hot red light spread into the dark sky; the sight of her burning home hurt far too much. And any glance to right or left, at the others who made their way down ropes, sent chills of fear through her.

Nor could she close her eyes completely—never that, for then the world became an uncertain, frightening place, full of darkness and sharp, unending pain.

So she looked at the outlaw and discovered an odd sort of safety in the midst of danger. His strength held their combined weight with ease, and his long reach and powerful muscles made the awful descent seem effortless.

Isobel was utterly dependent upon his strength, his ability, and his good will. She had no choice but to trust him—for now. She rested her cheek against his shoulder and felt his muscled body shift, solid and reliable and warm, against hers.

James paused on the rope, breathing hard as he summoned the strength to continue. Isobel looked at him.

"How do you fare?" she asked, as he had so often asked her.

He nodded brusquely. "Well enough. We're nearly there." He inhaled deeply, then sank down to the next rung.

She felt a stirring, profound excitement. They hovered between heaven and earth, between night and dawn. Tied to him in a strange intimacy—cheeks touching, breaths mingling, abdomens pressed together, hearts thumping in tandem—Isobel felt protected, and more. Lindsay literally held her life in his hands and risked his own life and safety to help her.

His legs worked beneath her, thighs pushing gently, rhythmically, into her hips. His arms stretched around her to grip the rope as he moved steadily downward.

Finally his feet struck flat on the ground. James released the ladder and stepped away from the massive curtain of rock that towered over them. He supported her in his arms and stood for a moment, his cheek against hers, his breath ragged as he gathered his strength.

She smiled and tightened her good arm around his neck—an impulsive embrace rather than the fearful grip of before. He held her and murmured something that the wind took away.

Then Geordie Shaw leaped to the ground and ran toward them, helping to undo the knots that bound Isobel to James. Within moments, she was lifted away from him to stand on her own. James steadied her with an arm about her waist while he spoke with Geordie. But she was keenly aware of the chill of the wind that separated them.

James looked down, gave her a small, private smile, and touched her cheek. "Brave lass," he murmured, and walked away.

Isobel waited while each man silently reached the ground. But her gaze rested most often on James Lindsay as he and his men helped the others, and then gathered the ropes to hide them, coiled, behind a large boulder.

He came back to her side and drew an arrow from his quiver. Nocking it in the great bow he carried, he shot a single shaft high into the cliffside. The feathered end, pale in the moonlight, trembled in the wind.

"There," he said. "Now they will know who was here."

He turned to Isobel and held out his arms in silence. She stepped into them willingly and he lifted her. While exhaustion settled bone-deep into her body, she rode once more in his arms and tried not to remind herself that he carried her away from Aberlady forever.

"Where are we going?" she asked.

"Into the forest," he said.

She nodded, too weary to ask more. On the morrow, truths would be faced, questions would be asked. But the blessing of the earth was beneath her at last, and the warmth of his arms felt good around her. She wanted to trust James Lindsay for a little while longer, whatever the future would bring.

She closed her eyes as he carried her toward the trees.

Chapter 6

Morning light dispelled the mist as the group advanced through the forest on horseback and on foot. Isobel rode a feather-footed white stallion, its broad back covered with a blanket. Geordie sat behind her, his arms around her waist while he held the reins. As they rode, she looked overhead at the tall, swaying trees, and then glanced at the cluster of men and horses moving along the earthen track.

At dawn, James had led them to the place where the horses had been hidden previously, remarking that he and his men had "borrowed" the warhorses from English soldiers. Isobel did not care if the horses belonged to King Edward himself. In her exhaustion, she was deeply grateful for the chance to ride.

Since several of the garrison had already departed the group to seek out nearby kin, there were mounts enough for all, with some sharing. James rode a huge black stallion, and Eustace a bay; Isobel saw them side by side, ahead of the group, deep in conversation.

For Isobel, most of the morning was a blur of fatigue, pain, and the tedium of riding, all of which she endured in silence. The men showed concern for her, although she noticed that James Lindsay kept his distance from her once the journey began.

She saw him glance toward her often, and heard his brisk order whenever she was thirsty or wanted to stop and rest, as if he somehow knew what she needed. Willing hands were always available to fetch food or water for her, to lift her down or help her remount. But those hands never belonged to James.

The men kept a watchful patrol as they rode, with

their weapons held ready. They stopped just after dawn to catch fish from a burn and cook them. Isobel, however, had so little appetite that she ate only berries and drank cool, fresh water.

Whether riding or resting, the men amiably discussed the lay of the land and the confusing map of the political situation. Isobel noticed that the Border Hawk's outlaws and the survivors of the siege quickly became a band of comrades, united by their bold escape and a shared dislike for the enemy.

But the tentative bond that had formed between Isobel and James seemed to dissolve as they rode deeper into the forest. Isobel became certain, as the day wore on, that James avoided her deliberately. He rarely spoke to her at all, and his quick, frequent glances toward her were cryptic.

He seemed remote and somber. Even his deep blue eyes had hardened to the color of steel. He rode apart from the rest, or beside Eustace or the outlaw Henry Wood, his watchful gaze grim.

She reminded herself that James was a rogue and an outlaw, said to be treacherous. Now that she had entered his world, she told herself, she would probably find out that the rumors were true.

But she missed the feel of his arms around her, and longed for his quiet voice at her ear. She desperately needed the comfort he had shown her earlier. His distant mood, after the easiness that had existed between them, hurt her unexpectedly.

On the cliff, suspended with him between earth and heaven, she had known an exhilarating balance of danger and safekeeping. Now, whenever she heard his voice or caught one of his glances, her heartbeat quickened. He was a brigand and untrustworthy, but he fascinated her.

Isobel sighed, impatient with her thoughts, and turned her head to ease the stiffness in her neck. Her arm ached fiercely, as did her ankle, and she had leaned against Geordie for the last hour or so of the journey.

Even more uncomfortable was her growing hunger, a sensation difficult to ignore now that food was available.

Her stomach had been uncertain earlier, but now she felt ravenous.

The sun climbed higher over the treetops while the group traveled, and translucent beams poured through the leaves. Several yards ahead, James set a steady pace along the forest track. A turn of his head brought a glint of gold to his hair and stirred an odd feeling in her midsection.

After a while, he held up his hand and halted. The others stopped behind him, leather creaking and weaponry jingling softly. James circled his black stallion about and rode toward Eustace, who had halted beside Isobel and Geordie.

"By God's grace, we havena been followed," James told Eustace, his low voice carrying easily in the forest hush. "We can risk a short rest near here if the lady wishes it." He glanced at Isobel, a flash of intense, dark blue.

"I am tired," she said gratefully.

He nodded brusquely. "Remind your men, Sir Eustace, that if any more of them wish to seek friends or kin, now is the time to depart. We will turn south from here and cross the Tweed, and then enter the heart of the Ettrick Forest. Tell them that any man who rides with me may be branded a broken man and a traitor by Scots as well as Southrons."

"Those who wanted to leave have already gone," Eustace said. "The rest will stay."

James nodded. "That grove over there, where the birches are thick, will provide safe cover."

"Good. Lady Isobel needs the respite." Eustace said.

James looked at her again, blue lightning beneath straight brown brows. Without a word, he circled his horse and rode toward the grove.

Quietly and quickly, they followed him into the cover of the birches and dismounted. Geordie helped Isobel settle in a shaded spot beneath the trees and turned away to help Henry Wood and another outlaw, a young Highland man in a wrapped and belted plaid, make a small fire. Then James, Geordie, and a burly outlaw called Patrick went off to hunt small game for the meal, while Aberlady's men established a guard around the grove.

Eustace fetched cold water from a burn in his steel helmet and brought it to Isobel. She thanked him and drank, and then he walked away to stand watch among the trees.

Only the Highlander stayed in the clearing with her, a tall, slender young man, bare-legged but for low, shabby boots and wearing a worn plaid of brown and purple. Isobel relaxed against the tree trunk and watched him as he bent over the fire, cooking flat cakes on a small iron plate that he balanced on two rocks.

He glanced at her and flashed a quick, shy smile. A dimpled smile transformed his lean, serious, young face, and Isobel smiled in return. He blushed and shoved at his blond hair, which slid continually over his eyes despite the sloppy braids he wore to restrain it.

He used his dagger to flip a cake jauntily from the griddle and came toward her, holding the hot cake with a corner of his plaid. He sat down beside her.

"An oatcake for you, Isobel Seton, if you be hungry," he said. He used her full name in the Highland way rather than her title as Lowlanders tended to do. And the Northern English he spoke had the soft, resonant lilt of a speaker of Gaelic. "Take care, now, 'tis hot to the touch," he warned.

"Thank you," she said, and took the thick, hot cake from him, using a fold of her gown to protect her fingers. "I am surprised to see a Highland man among outlaws of the Ettrick Forest in the Lowlands," she said.

He shrugged. "I am a Fraser," he said. "Quentin Fraser, from near Inverness. My kinsman is Sir Simon Fraser, whose name you may know. I came south to fight with him for Scotland."

She nodded. "I've heard that Sir Simon is one of the rebel leaders. How is it you are with James Lindsay now?" she asked.

"I met Jamie when he came north with some of Wallace's men to help Simon around Stirling. I joined him then. Simon asked me to study the lay of the southern lands and to learn the moves of the English armies. Now and again, I travel to wherever Simon is and report to him." He looked intently at her, his eyes bright azure. "I trust you, Isobel Seton of Aberlady, or I wouldna tell you that." He smiled again, and winked, with such charm that Isobel felt immediately befriended.

"My thanks. But how do you know you can trust me?"

Quentin grinned, fleeting and delighted, as if he knew a secret. "Ah, I have the Sight," he said. "I've always had it, and it tells me you're a fine lass and a true seeress."

She smiled, liking him even more. "I have it, too."

He nodded. "I know. The visions and prophecies of Black Isobel are well known in the Lowlands."

She blushed. "But my visions only tell me about war and kings, about strange events in the future that I dinna truly understand. 'Twould be pleasant to know things about ordinary people and help them. Can you do that?"

He nodded. "Sometimes. It just comes to me, like a knowing. I think you could do that easily, for your gift is great, and mine but a wee talent beside it. I have had visions, too, a few. I've seen death for those I love," he said, looking down, brushing dried leaves from his plaid. "And I dinna want to ever see that again."

Isobel sighed. "I've seen death, too," she said quietly. "I usually forget what I see, though. Do you remember?"

"Always," Quentin said grimly. "What would you want to see, if you could, Isobel Seton?"

She broke off a piece of the oatcake to nibble on it. "If I could," she said, swallowing, "I would use my sight to learn why James Lindsay came to Aberlady to find me, and why he is so discontent with me now." She slid him a wry glance. "I trust you, Quentin Fraser, or I wouldna tell you that."

He smiled wanly. "Ah, well, I canna tell you why myself. Jamie has a burden to carry, and he has good reason for whatever he does. But he keeps his thoughts close. No seer could penetrate them. To be truthful, he hasna told any of us why he came to find you. But he was furious that the English would besiege a castle held by a woman, and I know he meant to get you out of there. If there is another reason, I dinna know it." He shrugged. "When he is ready to speak his mind, he will do it."

Isobel watched his fine-cut, youthful profile while she savored the nutty taste of the thick, warm cake. "You follow him when so many have left him," she said after a while.

"I do." Quentin nodded firmly. "I will never believe that he betrayed Wallace. He's a changed man since he returned from English captivity. But he will always have my faith."

"Does your Sight tell you aught about his betrayal?"

He shook his head. "I believe he didna do it. Jamie would trade his own life for a friend. He did that for me, once, and so I owe him loyalty, no matter what is said of him." He rose to his feet. "Another cake, Isobel Seton?"

She refused with soft thanks. Quentin gave her another appealing smile and walked away, stepping between the trees to leave her alone in the little clearing. She watched him go, glad to have found a friend among the outlaws; his smile and easy manner had left a warm glow inside her.

She sighed, looking toward the fire crackling within the circle of stones, and she thought about James Lindsay, and what Quentin had said. Geordie, too, had stubbornly insisted on his hero's innocence, but she had attributed that to his youth. Now the Highlander, a man of about her own age, shared the opinion.

But surely the few followers of the Border Hawk all believed him innocent of treachery. Outside that circle, disturbing tales persisted about him. She had heard the rumors from Father Hugh, a Scotsman and a priest, who would not spread lies.

Unable to make sense of the matter and too exhausted to try, she settled her back against the tree, eased her hand over her aching shoulder, and closed her eyes to rest.

The tantalizing smell of roasting fowl stirred her out of her doze, and she opened her eyes. A few feet away from her, she saw James Lindsay's broad back as he sat by the fire, clothed in the leather hauberk and green tunic. He listened to Henry Wood and laughed softly at something the man said.

James turned to glance over his shoulder and saw that she was awake. He nodded briefly to her, then leaned forward to slice off a portion of meat. This he placed on a bit of bark and handed to the outlaw Patrick, who sat at his other side.

Patrick came toward her. "Here, my lady," he said in a deep, graveled voice, kneeling to offer the steaming white meat. "Jamie said you would be hungry."

"Thank you," she said, glancing at Lindsay's back. He did not turn. Patrick returned to his place by the fire, and Isobel ate hungrily. The meat was charred outside, but inside was moist and delicious. When she finished and licked her fingers, Patrick glanced at her and quickly brought her another portion of meat.

"My thanks," she said. "I have only eaten berries and an oatcake until now. I didna realize I was so hungry."

He nodded. "Your belly wasna ready earlier for heavy food, lass. But now that your hunger has returned, we know you'll recover well."

"We?" She glanced at him while she ate.

"Jamie and us," he answered. He sniffed and wiped his nose on his grimy sleeve. "Jamie watches over you like a hawk watches its fledgling. He says you havena eaten much on this journey."

"He doesna seem to care," she muttered doubtfully, pulling off a bit of steaming flesh. "He lets you and the others do the caring. And I thank you for it," she added.

Patrick leaned forward and lowered his voice. "Och, he willna admit he watches out for your welfare. He wasna pleased wi' you, since you are the prophetess and all."

Isobel cast him a quick frown. He did not see, but pulled off his helmet to scratch his head, his fingers digging into his unkempt brown hair. He spit into the helmet and buffed it with his sleeve. "I know ladies like fine courtesy," he said. "So I'll fetch you some water in a clean helmet, see." He held it out to show her.

"My thanks, Patrick," Isobel said tactfully. "But I think I will go to the burn myself, to wash in privacy."

"I'll show you the way," Patrick said. He helped her

to her feet and supported her with a huge hand at her waist as she limped forward.

Isobel saw James look up as they passed. Quentin glanced up, too, and gave her a dazzling smile. James saw him and frowned sharply.

Isobel smiled at Quentin, smiled at Patrick, and slid a scowl toward James. He glanced away as if he had not seen her, and rubbed his fingers over his whiskered jaw in silence.

Later in the day, as she rode the white stallion in front of Geordie, Isobel felt so tired, so filled with aches and plagued by dizziness that she sometimes thought she could not go on. Yet she said nothing to Geordie of her discomfort, nor did she mention it to anyone else who asked after her welfare.

She had found a moment to tell Eustace that she wanted to part company with the outlaws when they neared Stobo, where Father Hugh had a parish church. Sir Eustace had agreed reluctantly. Isobel decided that he liked the freedom of running with outlaws after weeks trapped in a besieged castle. Isobel, however, wanted rest and peace. Her arm and ankle throbbed mercilessly, and she did not know how she would heal if they kept up this punishing pace.

But some part of her wanted to stay with the Border Hawk in the forest, too. However foolishly, she wanted to be with the compassionate man he had been while tending her wounds—but that man had disappeared completely.

If she had possessed greater strength, clearer thoughts, and better boldness, she would have challenged him to tell her what his intent was concerning her, and why he had grown so cool toward her. But, exhausted and drained, she said nothing to him, and let the stallion carry her deeper into the forest.

She remembered Lindsay's ominous statement that he had come to Aberlady to find her, as if he had some business with her. She felt his intentions hovering over her like storm clouds. The prophetess could not tell if he was her champion or her enemy. She did not have

Quentin's gift for just "knowing" something, and dearly wished she did.

Devastated by her ordeal at Aberlady and scattered in her thoughts without rest, she could answer none of the questions that plagued her. All she truly wanted was a place to lie down and sleep.

The dense forest canopy admitted only a little light, so that the forest path was dim and green. Isobel heard the steady footfalls of the horses, the trills of birds overhead, and the wind soughing through the branches. The sounds were so peaceful, soft, and monotonous that she nearly fell asleep as she rode.

She stirred herself as she leaned back against Geordie and looked around. A long wooded slope rose to one side of the path, covered with trees. Over her shoulder, she saw a bright, silvery flash among the trunks. Dazed and tired, her reactions slow, she did not realize until too late that she had seen the gleam of metal armor.

An instant later she heard the rapid whoosh of an arrow and felt its hard thud as it struck Geordie. He jerked against her, cried out, and fell, suddenly and heavily, to the ground.

Isobel screamed and turned, instinctively reaching out, but Geordie was gone, fallen beneath the hooves of the horse. So fast that she hardly knew what was happening, the men around her began to shout and turn their mounts. She saw Eustace's grim face as he flashed by, saw Henry Wood draw his great bow, saw James turn and ride back, his face furious, his hand reaching behind him for the broadsword at his back.

Another arrow sped through the trees and nicked her horse in its flank. Isobel tried to grab the reins and turn him, but he whinnied and reared up, nearly dumping her to the ground. She clung desperately to the mane with both hands as the horse landed hard on its front feet, jarring her.

With a surge of muscle and power, the warhorse bolted ahead.

Chapter 7

Fierce shouts, the thwack of arrows finding targets, and the ringing clash of steel echoed behind her through the trees. Isobel found the reins with her left hand and yanked desperately. The horse ignored the command and galloped along the track, carrying her toward another part of the forest. Isobel curled forward to shield herself from whipping branches as the stallion swerved left and propelled them through the trees.

Finally the horse slowed and came to a halt among a stand of huge leafy oaks. His fetlocks were immersed in green ferns, his sides heaving and slick. Isobel leaned against his neck, shaking all over, her heart slamming in her chest. Her wounded arm hurt savagely as she tried to turn the horse, pulling hard. The stallion refused to move, though she tugged, cajoled, pressed with her knees, and even begged tearfully.

She bowed wearily over his neck in sheer frustration. In the stillness, she heard the wind shove through the branches and birds chitter. But she heard no sounds of a skirmish.

Lost and in pain, she sat uncertainly on a horse that possessed a stronger will than she did. Unable to command him, she felt too weak to dismount and tend to him properly.

She patted the horse's broad neck, spoke calmly to him, and attempted to turn him again. The stallion moved in a stubborn circle and began to crop a patch of grass beneath a tree.

Isobel sighed and looked around. They were on a long slope thick with trees and bracken, the forest track was out of sight somewhere, and the light had begun to fail.

Increasingly alarmed, Isobel tugged on the reins again. The horse whickered, bowed his head, and simply would not move. She yanked at the reins, rocked on his back, and grew close to losing her temper as she strained to turn him.

"Och, now, lass." She heard a deep, quiet voice, so familiar that she felt a surge of relief. "He's as tired as you are. Give him time, and he'll do what you wish."

She whipped around and saw James Lindsay leaning against a tree, watching her, a bemused look on his face. In the thickening shadows, he seemed to blend into the forest that surrounded him, a long, lean figure in leather and muted green, strong and straight as an oak.

"James! Oh, James!" she burst out. She was so relieved to see him here, and unharmed, that tears welled in her eyes. She dashed her hand over her face as he strode forward. "Where are the others?" she asked. "What happened? Did English attack us?"

"Aye. Our men fought well and chased them off." He reached up to pat the horse's neck, murmuring to him. Then he walked back to examine the horse's flank, where the small cut from the arrow tip bled slightly. "Are you hurt?" he asked her.

"Nay. The horse ran off. I couldna stop him, and then I couldna find the path. I thought I was well and truly lost."

"You're safe now." He went back to the horse's head and patted its wide nose gently, murmuring low.

"How is Geordie?" she asked.

He paused. "He's badly hurt. The arrow went into his back. Eustace offered to take him to Stobo—he says the priest there will help the lad. Henry Wood went with them."

She nodded. "Good. Where are the others?"

"Patrick and Quentin followed the Southrons to learn which patrol they were. I dinna think they were English come from Aberlady, but 'tis possible. Most of your men went with them." He came closer, resting a hand on the horse's neck. "Isobel," he murmured. "Two of Aberlady's garrison were killed. I am sorry. Eustace said they were his cousins."

Isobel gasped. "Thomas and Richard Gibson?"

"Aye." His hand was gentle on the horse, and his gaze was steady on hers. She saw keen regret in his eyes. "Eustace and Henry are taking their bodies to Stobo with Geordie."

She nodded. Tears stung her eyes and she looked away, feeling a piercing sadness. "Thomas and Richard fought well at Aberlady, only to lose their lives after—after escaping."

James's long fingers traced through the horse's mane. "Sometimes life is bitter, lass," he murmured. "We must have faith that the sweetness will return someday."

"Aye," she whispered. His fingers grazed over hers, warm and dry and strong, pressing her hand briefly.

"Eustace said you know this priest in Stobo," he said.

She nodded. "Father Hugh has been priest at Aberlady all my life. He will see that Thomas and Richard are honored, and he'll see to Geordie, too."

"Good." James stepped sideways and leaped up behind her in one quick, lithe movement. His torso was warm and solid against her back, his arms encircled her, and his long thighs pressed hers. When he reached past her to lift the reins, she allowed herself to lean back against his strength.

He tightened the reins and directed the horse to turn. The animal responded easily to his command and carried them down the slope and along the path.

"We'll go back to where I left my horse," he said. "Are you well enough to ride on? 'Twill be dark soon, and the going will be hard after that."

"I can continue." In truth, she felt dizzy and weak, and wondered if she could ride another ten feet. His nearness was reassuring, as was his gentle manner toward her. She could not have borne more coolness from him just now. "Stobo isna far."

"Stobo? We willna go there." His voice vibrated low and mellow at her ear, sending an odd echo deep into her body. "You and I go elsewhere, lass."

"But—surely you arranged to meet Eustace at Stobo," Isobel stammered, turning to look at him.

He shook his head. "Southrons could be patrolling the entire area. 'Tis dangerous enough to go back for my horse. I willna risk another attack by riding to Stobo.

We will go south into the Ettrick Forest, the way we headed before we were ambushed. I will take you to my aunt's house. She lives across the river, in the forest."

Isobel looked at him in alarm. "But I must go to Stobo. Eustace promised to take me there. Now I must ask you to do that. I have nowhere else to go, no home, no kin nearby."

"Have you family at all to take you in?" He spoke brusquely. She half turned, puzzled by his demand, and decided that he, too, had tried to think of somewhere suitable to take her.

"My father is in prison, and my mother is dead," she said quietly. "I dinna have brothers or sisters. But I have Seton uncles in Fife, and cousins in Edinburgh. My mother has a sister in Jedburgh. But I scarcely know them. Still, I suppose you could take me to one of their homes."

"Those places are too far," he said bluntly.

She blinked, stunned by his unexpected refusal. His manner had hardened again, and she did not know why. She frowned. "Stobo is closest," she argued. "Father Hugh will take me in."

"I willna go to Stobo." He had turned to stone again in the space of several heartbeats.

She sighed. "Then take me to Castle Wildshaw," she said. "The constable there will help me, even if you willna."

Tension gathered in the strong hand that circled her waist. "That place is west, beyond the forest, a few hours' ride from here."

"Sir Ralph Leslie is constable there. He will help me. If you willna take me to Stobo, then please escort me to Wildshaw."

"Leslie," he said in a flat tone. "He is your betrothed."

"Aye," she admitted. "How do you know that?"

"I have heard it. Leslie is a Scottish knight who has changed allegiances—what, twice now? Three times?"

She heard the edge in his voice and frowned. "Many Scotsmen have pledged to King Edward. Sir Ralph is a worthy knight who has ties through kin to both England

and Scotland. He says this is a complex war, and he tries to remain neutral."

Lindsay laughed, short and curt. Though she had no real love for Ralph Leslie, Isobel's temper flared. " 'Tis said that you yourself changed—" she began.

"You know naught of my fealty," he snapped. "When do you plan to wed this paragon?"

"Sir Ralph and my father wanted the wedding to take place at Lammastide, a few weeks past. But—"

"And you? When do you want it?"

Never, she thought to herself. "The marriage didna happen because my father was in English captivity, Aberlady was under siege, and Sir Ralph was away searching for my father."

"All good reasons to cancel glad nuptials," James drawled.

She did not like this cold, dark side of him, or the bitterness she heard in his voice. "I dinna understand why you willna help me in this," she said carefully. "It might have to do with the ward and with your loyalty— whatever that may be. But remember that I, too, have loyalties and desires."

"And what are those?" he asked in a low, even tone.

"I want to see my father again," she said. "He may be at Wildshaw even now. Sir Ralph promised me, before the siege had begun, that he would retrieve him from an English dungeon."

"And your loyalty?"

"I am loyal to my father," she said.

He sighed. "Do you favor England or Scotland?"

"I am a Scotswoman," she said, lifting her chin, certain that would answer any question of loyalty.

"Betrothed to a Scotsman with English fealties."

She looked away from him. The matter of her betrothal had confused and tormented her for months. "I will do what my father asks," she said quietly. "And I want to be with him now, if he is free. Surely you understand that."

"I do," he said. "And I imagine that you want to be with your betrothed as well."

She sighed. "I need welcome somewhere, James Lindsay. Those at Wildshaw will provide it. Please take me there."

"I would sooner take you to your grave," he growled.

A shiver ran down her spine. She turned back to look at him. His gaze seemed hard and cold as steel.

"Why do you bear Sir Ralph such vehemence?" she asked.

"Wildshaw," he said calmly, "belongs to me."

She stared at him in surprise. "But the English king made Sir Ralph its captain—Ralph didna take it from you."

"Once it belonged to the Lindsays. I inherited it upon my brother's death." He stared ahead. "The English took it."

"I understand," she said. "I do. I willna trouble you to go there yourself, but I have no other refuge. If you take me in that direction, I can find it myself."

"Nay," he said flatly. "I willna do that."

She turned her head to frown at him, but he stared ahead. Sighing, puzzled, she turned back.

Within moments she saw his black horse tied to a hazel tree. James slid down, mounted the black, and drew up beside her. He had the leather satchel with her spare clothing, which Eustace had carried, tied to the back of his saddle. Without a word, he took up her reins to guide her stallion alongside his own horse.

As they rode along the path, she tried again to persuade him to take her to Stobo. "Father Hugh and Eustace will help me. I will be in their safekeeping and off your hands."

"You are in safekeeping already," he said. "Mine."

"You behave as if you hold me hostage." Sudden apprehension made her voice tremble.

"I do exactly that." Bold words, spoken quietly. His gaze was even and hard, and his grip pulled her reins taut.

Her heart thudded like a wild thing in a cage. She lifted her chin to disguise her panic. "What do you mean? Surely you dinna want to ransom me. I have scant value as an heiress now, with Aberlady destroyed."

"Your value, for me, has naught to do with Aberlady."

"Then what—" She drew in a sudden breath. "King Edward wants me brought to him. That is why you came to Aberlady! You mean to escort me to the English king, and make a profit for yourself in coin and land and privilege!"

"If I intended that," he said, "I would have walked you out the gate of Aberlady and into English keeping, and saved myself the bother of descending a cliff in the night."

"Then what do you want with me?" she demanded. Anger and fear struck through her with hot, quick force. She yanked on the rein. "You canna take me where I dinna want to go!"

He did not relinquish his hold. "Isobel," he said, not unkindly. "For now, I only want to take you where your wounds can be looked after properly."

"And then you will barter me for coin to the English!"

He cocked a brow. "If you prove a wearisome guest," he said, tugging on the rein, "I will give you to them for naught."

"Ah, so you *do* mean to barter me!" She yanked back.

"Possibly," he said. His grip was firm on the leather.

Panic struck through her. "Why? I have done naught to you! You treated me with kindness at first. I dinna understand you!"

"Must you?" he asked, sounding exasperated.

"Aye," she said. Suddenly she wanted to know him, very much; his thoughts, his past, his feelings. Her heart pounded with a heady combination of fear and fascination. "Aye! Why do you do this? What do you want of me?"

He sighed. "We canna stay here, Isobel. Come ahead." He pulled on the rein. She held on to it stubbornly.

"You helped me with a gentle hand when I was injured," she said, the words spilling forth as her temper boiled. "You gave me time in my mother's garden for my farewells. And I was sure that you regretted setting Aberlady afire."

"I did. Let go of the rein."

She would not let go, though it took all of her weight

and strength to hang on to it. "This is unchivalric. I thought you felt some kindness toward me!"

"And I thought you were a gentle, well-bred lass," he muttered in irritation. He pulled on the taut leather strap that linked them in a silent struggle. "Unhand the rein. I dinna want to topple you off. *That* would be unchivalric."

She held her end of the rein though her arm ached to do it. The horse shifted uneasily beneath her. "You wouldna topple me."

"I would." He yanked, and she jerked forward. He relaxed his hold and sighed. "I wouldna," he admitted, but did not release his grip. "You are stubborn as that warhorse. Surely you realize the danger in lingering here for a wee chat."

She rushed on, ignoring his logical point; she felt no need to obey logic just now. Her temper, rarely stirred to this degree, was in full flare. "I wanted to think kindly of you," she said through clenched teeth as she tugged on the rein. "Even though the Border Hawk is said to be a wretched traitor. But all this day, you have treated me coldly. And now you take me hostage and willna say why. When we came down the cliffside together, I thought that the rumors were wrong about you. But now I think they may be right!"

"You do a good deal of thinking," he said, slinging her a grim look. "Come ahead."

"Nay." She glared at him. "What will you gain from keeping me? Tell me why, or I willna budge from this spot. I would rather go with Southron soldiers than go with you. I would rather be lost in this forest than go with you!"

She knew that outburst sounded spoiled and petulant, but it was the best she could do. Confrontation was not her strength. And she had never met a man with his powerful force of presence. She had scant experience with resisting another's will through the strength of her will—until the siege.

But she did not lack determination, and weeks of siege had taught her skills she had hitherto not possessed. She called on those now. She mustered a look of stony fury and held on to the rein out of pure stubbornness, though her arm ached and her body trembled. "What will you gain from this?" she repeated.

His gaze filled with an inner storm, deep and dark. "You, Black Isobel," he said pointedly, "are the only hope I have for gaining someone's freedom. I intend to barter you for a life."

"Barter me?" She gaped at him, barely taking in what he told her. "To whom? For whom?"

"Ralph Leslie holds my cousin at Wildshaw," he said.

She blinked in astonishment. "He holds no one there!"

"He does. I want her back unharmed. I trust that Ralph will trade one woman for another."

"A woman?" she squeaked. "He wouldna hold a woman prisoner. Unlike you!"

James slid her a long look. "He has her. And I will shortly let him know that I have you. You see, then, Lady Isobel," he said smoothly, "we will both get what we want from this. You want to go to Sir Ralph. But it must be on my terms."

"You lack honor," she snapped.

"So they say of me. Come ahead." He pulled on the reins.

She pulled back so hard she thought the stretched leather strip would break between them, thought her arm would come out of its socket. "Why do you do this to me?" she asked, panting. "I have done naught to you! If you have a quarrel with Ralph Leslie, 'tisna my doing. *Let go!*" she burst out in frustration.

He did not. "I dinna bear you a grudge," he said firmly. "But you know well what you have done to me."

"Have I burned your castle or stolen your freedom, as you have done to me?" Her voice rose to a shout.

He held up a hand, palm out, a swift, silencing gesture. "Your words took away what small chance for peace I had in my life. Your words ruined my name and set all this in motion."

She stared at him. "Do you mean one of my—my visions?"

He nodded. "Aye. You know what you said of me."

She blinked in astonishment. "I know naught."

"You know far more than naught," he snapped.

"But I dinna recall what I said. If you have heard the prophecy, then you know my words better than I."

He snorted doubtfully. "Who told you to say what you did of Wallace and of me?"

"Wallace—" She paused, her heart beating fiercely. She had long strived to remember one prediction out of all of them; she knew, now, what he meant. "No one told me what to say. The words just come to me."

"Do you know the damage your words have caused?" he growled.

Isobel saw the thunder in his eyes. "I meant no harm through my visions," she said. The thought pierced her with a deep hurt. "I forget the prophecies as soon as I say them. I am sorry if whatever came from me harmed you and yours. I want my prophecies to help people." She looked up at him with true regret. "Mayhap that will bring you some sense of peace."

"Hardly," he muttered. He yanked so firmly on the leather piece that, in her distraction, she let go. Her horse stepped forward to follow his. She rode in the wake of his silence, like a tethered boat riding through a storm.

"If Ralph does house your lover at Wildshaw," she said after a while, "then let me go there and I will ask him to release her. Then we will both have what we want, without all this fuss of ransom and anger."

"We willna talk more of this now," he said over his shoulder. "I will wait until you are rested and less irritable."

"Irritable! You are the ill-willed one here."

He said nothing, his back to her. The steady footfalls of the horses filled the silence. She watched him for a long time, seeing the wide strength of his back, the power in his arms and thighs, the beautiful strands of gold that threaded his hair—and the invisible iron rod that seemed to form the core of his being.

She remembered his gentle words, his warm touch. All that was irretrievably lost between them. She felt the disappointment of that like a betrayal.

"I thought I could trust you," she said. "I was wrong."

"You willna be the first to say that of me," he replied. He kneed his horse to a canter, drawing her along

behind him. Isobel gripped the horse's mane and glared
at James's back, while she concentrated on keeping her
balance at the pace he set.

Profound weariness, made heavier by fear and anger,
settled like a lead cape over her shoulders. As they rode
on, she grew too exhausted to even think about arguing
with him. She rode in a daze, her body aching with fatigue, her wounds burning, her thoughts and emotions
in a thick muddle.

When James slowed to silently hand her an oatcake
that he took from a pouch at his waist, she said no word
of thanks. She ate woodenly, hardly tasting it.

The sky was almost fully dark as they reached a narrow wooden bridge over a river. The moist air and the
loud, white-capped rush of the water below them revived
her senses, and she guided her own mount across the
bridge. They left the riverbank and rode across a moor,
entering the rim of the forest.

The trees seemed to swallow them in rich darkness.
James slowed their pace, for only silvery strands of
moonlight lit the earthen path. But he went steadily forward, as if he saw through the night, as if he would
know this track blinded.

Isobel frowned at the thought. Her misery—physical,
mental, and emotional—increased as the horses' hooves
thudded onward. She did not want to ride any farther;
she did not want to be held hostage by this infuriating
outlaw; she did not want to feel the deep aches of pain
and fatigue any longer.

She did not even care to gain her freedom in this
moment. All she truly wanted was to rest and, oddly, to
be held and soothed like a child. Her thoughts could
barely go beyond a simple yearning for someone who
cared about her welfare, like her mother or her father,
both gone in different ways. James Lindsay did not seem
willing to offer her comfort ever again.

Tears pooled repeatedly in her eyes, and she dashed
them away. Finally she let them slide silently down her
cheeks, too tired to hold them back any longer. A great,
wet, hiccuping sob escaped from her, and James glanced
at her. He opened his mouth as if to speak, then turned
away, his jaw set tight.

As they reached a fork in the path and turned left, Isobel uttered a small, involuntary cry and slumped forward, collapsing in raw exhaustion. She hardly knew, or cared, if she fell or was lifted down. All she wanted was sleep.

The last sound she heard was James's voice murmuring her name. The last sensation she felt, before she melted into a black void, was the warmth of his hand upon her cheek.

Chapter 8

Kee-kee-kee-er.

Pearled light filtered through the overhead leaves as James opened his eyes. Certain he had heard the cry of a hawk close by, he scanned the clearing in which they had spent the night, but saw nothing overhead or in the trees. He glanced down.

Isobel lay stretched out beside him, wrapped in his cloak. He had dozed with his back against the wide trunk of an oak tree, while a sturdy root, covered by his cloak, served as her pillow and his armrest. She slept deeply, curled warm against his thigh, serene and lovely. But her soft snores created such earthy contrast that James smiled a little.

He remembered ruefully that his older brother had snored like that in the bed they had shared as boys. James had pinched and pushed at him to gain quiet, and his brother often returned a solid, sleepy punch before rolling over.

At the thought of his brother, killed on the bloody, tragic field at Falkirk seven years earlier, James lost the smile and tightened his mouth.

Kee-kee-kee-keer.

He heard, again, the unmistakable cry of a hawk. But it was an agitated kakking and not the drawn-out, clear cry of a hawk in flight. To his practiced falconer's ear, the bird sounded distressed. James sat straighter, careful not to wake Isobel, and looked around the glade again. But he saw no hawks.

Beside him, Isobel blew out a long, loud breath. James patted her shoulder gently. She inhaled and sighed out another snore. He touched the side of her jaw, petal soft yet firm beneath his fingertips, and she turned her head. The shift quieted her breathing. He rested his hand on her shoulder and continued to scan the glade, looking for the hawk.

He had dozed without sleeping deeply, but he felt alert. Years of living as a forest renegade had taught him to rest warily, his weapons close at hand. In the weeks since Wallace had been taken and his own name had become anathema, the ability had served him well.

He leaned back his head to look at the dense texture of the trees, pierced by shafts of light. The forest at dawn had a sleepy silence, and sounds carried clearly. He heard the soft, steady rush of a burn close by, the rustle of ferns as small creatures slipped past, and the whirr of wings among the leaves.

Odd, that. He frowned and glanced about again, his eyes, sharper than most, as keenly attuned to the forest as was his hearing. A handful of larks scattered into the morning sky, a sure sign that a hawk was nearby, even without the kakking he had heard earlier.

If the hawk was a trained bird rather than a wild one, hunters would be nearby. Concerned, he glanced at Isobel and touched her shoulder to wake her, though he knew she needed the sleep. She whimpered and turned. Her body was firm and warm against his leg, and her cheek, soft as a sun-warmed rose, rubbed against his hand.

The sensation plunged through him and whirled in his groin. He withdrew his hand, but several pulsing moments passed before the honest reaction of his body calmed.

The hawk kakked again, somewhere close to the glade. He frowned and shoved his hair back in exasperation. He and Isobel should take to their horses again, and quickly. Hunters could be Scots or English, and eager to take a forest outlaw and a prophetess as a good day's quarry.

He decided to make certain before waking her. As he began to ease away from her, she moaned and turned farther, resting her hand on his thigh.

His body throbbed with the sudden contact. He picked up her hand—delicate and fine-boned in his large fingers—and set it aside. She snuggled against him. He sighed heavily, looking down at her.

Total exhaustion had caused her to collapse last night, he knew. James regretted pushing her stamina, and her stubbornness, so far. He should have made camp long before she fell from her horse. Fortunately, he had caught her before she injured herself further, and he had discovered the little glade where they and the horses could rest safely.

Time had slipped inexorably toward dawn. Now they would be lucky to arrive at his aunt's house before the sun was high. He sighed again, aware that every plan he had made concerning Isobel Seton had unpredictably altered, since the first moment he had sighted Aberlady Castle and found it besieged.

He had expected the prophetess to be a malicious, hard woman. To his dismay, her courage and grace made it difficult for him to coldly remember who she was and what she had done.

Subtle but certain, his body hardened and his heart softened whenever he was near her. He could not easily ignore the charm of her eyes or the graceful sway of her supple figure.

He had never met a truly irresistible woman. The one girl who had caught his young heart had been sweet and good, and had died horribly. In the years that followed, several girls had interested him, but his fascination was easily sated, and his heart remained safe in his own keeping.

The young prophetess enchanted him, distracted him, confused him, and touched off his temper like a flint. And her dazzling smiles, given to Quentin and even to rough-edged Patrick—but not to James—had made him simmer with unaccustomed jealousy.

And last night, her exhausted, lonely sobs had sliced through him. He was not pleased with himself for turning away, for she had collapsed soon afterward.

He shook his head mildly as he watched her, and wondered if he had met the woman he could not resist. Perhaps, together, they sparked one of those rare alchemical integrations of the male and female natures that he had read about in long, postulating theories, years ago.

God only knew what else it could be. He made a sour

grimace as he thought again of the irony: he felt an extraordinary pull to the prophetess of Aberlady.

If he succumbed to the effect she had on him, he would risk his sole chance to save Margaret and to revenge what had been done to his comrade, his kin, and his reputation. But to do that, he needed to keep his reason cold and his emotions colder.

Isobel sighed, and her hair slipped over her pale cheek like a fold of black silk. He brushed her hair back, letting his hand linger over her head; she was finely wrought, delicate and yet strong. Thoughts of pleasure and peace slipped across his mind.

He lifted his hand from her warm, satiny head and fisted it against the cold tree root.

Kee-kee-kee.

James looked up. The hawk sounded quite close. He eased away from Isobel and stood. Then he stepped through undergrowth and between the trees to look around.

The hawk's cry sounded again. Overhead, James saw the upper branches of a large oak tree sway, and he heard the frenzied thrash of wings. He circled the gnarled base, gazing up.

He saw the hawk high up through the leafy cover. Wings flapping, crying intermittently, the bird struggled on its perch. James glimpsed brown leather straps, the bird's jesses, wrapped around the branch.

Quickly, he grabbed hold of a tree limb and hoisted himself up, climbing cautiously, watching the bird. The gray and cream feathers, delicately barred, and the distinctive white slashes over each blazing red-gold eye told him that the bird was a male goshawk, and not yet fully adult.

"There, now," he said quietly as he came closer. "Hush, you bird, hush." He knew that the steady sound of a male voice could calm a trained hawk. As he spoke, he glided upward, keeping his pace slow and careful so as not to cause further alarm.

The bird's jesses—two straps, each several inches long and knotted to slitted leather anklets looped around the legs—had tangled around a branch, probably snagging when the bird perched. James noted with surprise that

the hawk wore no bells on its legs. Perhaps the falconer
had removed the customary bells in order to fly the bird
silently after waterfowl, and the bird had strayed. Had
the bells been attached, the owner might have found his
lost bird already.

As he drew closer, the goshawk bated, violently flinging itself backward off the branch to hang upside down,
wings thrashing. Helplessly caught by its jesses, the bird
could damage its feathers, injure itself, even die.

James straddled a thick tree limb and took off his
waist and sword belts, dropping them to the ground.
Then he unlaced his padded leather tunic, stripped it off,
and removed his woolen tunic after that, letting them
fall as well.

He was careful to make each movement slow while
he slipped off his linen shirt and draped it over his bare
shoulder. He did not want to approach the bird bare-
skinned, for the talons could be vicious, but his shirt
would serve as a trap.

Clad in breeches, hose, and boots, he rose higher in
the tree, murmuring softly and soothingly. Years of raising hawks like this one had taught him to speak in a
gentle, patient tone that was typical to falconers, and he
had developed a relaxed, alert way of moving, a necessary skill for falconry as well as for forest rogues. When
he came close enough, he cautiously extended his hand
toward the goshawk.

The quickest way to retrieve a bird from a tree, he
knew, was to distract and dazzle it with a bright lantern
light. Lacking that, a slow approach would have to do.
The bird was trapped and could not fly away, but James
knew he could scare it literally to death.

As he drew nearer, the goshawk squawked, helpless
where it hung, and beat its wings furiously. Green leaves
spit down to the ground, and the treetop shook. James
paused and waited for the bird to exhaust itself. He had
seen such outbursts in many trained birds and knew it
would not last long.

He narrowed his eyes to examine the bird while it
spent its frenzy. One wing moved unevenly; James
hoped that indicated a sprain rather than a more serious
injury. Or an illness.

"Easy, you bird," he said when the flurrying wings quieted. "Hush, you bonny gos." He slid closer.

Quick and sure, he slipped his hand behind the bird, scooping under the tail to grasp the body firmly between the legs. The surprise of contact sent the goshawk into a limp state of shock, as James expected.

Goshawks taken in the wild had a nervous tendency to fall into a faint when grabbed by a human. Trained birds, which no longer feared humans, did not fall over so readily. But this bird had apparently been free long enough to revert to wildness.

He slipped his dagger from his belt and cut the jesses. The leather was dry, cracked, and filthy; the goshawk must have flown away from its owner weeks ago, he thought.

He gently righted the bird's head, ready to restrain the goshawk quickly, for he did not want to contend with an awake, angry, powerful bird. He held the limp goshawk in one hand and tugged a shirtsleeve over the finely shaped head, deftly trapping the wings and compact body inside. He wound the rest of the shirt around the body and padded the talons as best he could.

With the goshawk cradled in one arm, he looked down. Isobel stood at the base of the tree, staring up at him with her mouth open. She held his tunic in one hand.

"What are you doing?" she called.

"Rescuing a hawk," he answered. He began to make his way down the tree carefully, using the strength of his free arm. In the midst of his descent, the bird stirred, squealed, and began an awkward struggle.

James leaned his weight against a sturdy branch and murmured soothing nonsense, stroking the bird's head and breast as if he held a babe in his arms. All the while, he avoided the vicious, powerful feet. When the exhausted bird quieted, James climbed down, dropped to the ground, and straightened.

Isobel clutched his tunic to her chest, her eyes wide as she stared first at James, and then at the curious bundle he held. He could not help but notice that her eyes were as fine and as pale blue as the clear morning sky.

"You found a hawk?" She blinked at it in disbelief.

"A goshawk. Its jesses were tangled in the tree," he said. She nodded and bent to retrieve his leather hauberk, wincing when she jarred her injured arm, which was still bound to her side. James took the garment from her, and his belts. "How is your wound?" he asked.

"It hurts some," she answered, looking down.

"Then it must hurt a good deal, for you to admit that much," he said. "We should change the bandaging before we travel on."

" 'Tis fine," she said.

He shot her a doubtful glance and walked toward the glade.

"What will you do with the hawk?" she asked, following him.

"I dinna know," he said. "But I couldna leave him there to die." He dropped the garments he carried and sat on a fallen tree trunk, his feet deep in ferns. He held the squawking, trembling hawk in his lap and studied it.

Isobel sat on the trunk with him and leaned toward the bird curiously. "My father had goshawks in his mews. They were gray like that, with the white band over the eye, but much larger."

"Then they were females," he said.

"We released them early in the siege," she said. "Eustace was for eating them, but I asked him to let them go."

James glanced at her. "Was there a male gos in your father's mews? If so, this could be one of Aberlady's birds."

She shook her head. "I dinna remember a smaller goshawk."

"Well, he came from someone's mews," James said. "Settle down, you bird. Let's look at you." Wary of the talons, he began to probe the body gently. "His crop is full enough—his breastbone is well padded—so he's had good hunting while he's been free."

"You are sure it's male? I know little about hawks, though my father kept them. I didna go in the mews often, and I have never been hunting." She leaned closer.

"Watch the talons," he warned. She pulled back. "Size is the best way to tell a male from a female," he explained. "This bird is much smaller than a female goshawk would be at this age. So the males are called tiercels, a third smaller." He stroked the delicate feathering over the head, the only exposed part of the bird. "His feathers have begun to change from the brown of an immature bird to gray, but he's not a full adult yet."

"He's beautiful," she murmured. "And his eyes are as bright as red gold. Can you unwrap him?"

"Not yet. The swaddling helps calm him," James answered. "That orange color in his eyes means he's under two years old. Next spring those irises will be colored red as blood." He held the hawk upright, and the tiercel squawked at him. "Och, lad. He has a stubborn spirit," James added with a chuckle. "He doesna like being tucked in my shirt."

"Will you keep him, or will you release him?"

"I canna let him go just yet. His left wing moves awkwardly, and it feels swollen at the joint. I hope 'tis but a sprain. When he can fly well, I may let him go." He tipped his head and looked at the bird. "Then again, I may keep him. Goshawks are fine hunting birds."

"But he belongs to someone," Isobel said.

He shrugged. "He could have flown a very long way. I think he's been free for a while. His owner will have given him up for dead or lost."

" 'Tis against the law to keep a found trained hawk or falcon," she said, frowning. "Men have been hanged for that."

He met her gaze evenly. "If I am caught, my girl, they will hang me for more than this hawk, and you know it."

Isobel lowered her eyes silently.

James stroked the bird's breast, watching her. "Besides, that is an English hawking law. Scotland doesna have such a rule. Think you that English law should prevail in Scotland?" he asked smoothly. She shook her head, an unconsciously graceful motion. He wished he could believe that she meant it.

James rose and walked over to lay the bird breast-down on the rumpled nest of his cloak. "Well, it hardly matters if I keep him," he said, squatting on his haunches beside the bird, scratching its head while it chittered unhappily at him. "We'll never find the owner.

And I dinna intend to look. I have other matters on my mind."

He picked up his bow as he spoke and carried it to the middle of the glade. Kneeling, he bent the bow in an arch and thrust the ends into the earth.

"What are you doing?" Isobel asked.

"Making him a perch. I canna leave the poor thing cast like that for long. He doesn't like me overmuch as 'tis." He went back to the bird, who rocked and struggled on the cloak. "Isobel, help me, if you will," James said as he knelt down.

"Aye." She knelt beside him, reaching out her left hand to touch the bird's trembling back, her right arm held snug against her body. "What should I do?"

"Can you keep the hawk still, with just the one hand?"

"I think so." She held the bird down.

James reached down to his own ankle and began to unwind one of the leather thongs that bound his thick woolen hose to his leg. When he had freed one long strap and readjusted the stocking, he cut the thong with his dagger, producing two pieces, each less than a foot long.

"Hold him fast," he said. "I'll tie these on as new jesses, and then take him out of the shirt."

She kept her hand on the goshawk's back while James tied the thongs to the bird's leather anklets. He snatched his fingers away a few times to avoid the clenching talons.

"Be careful," he told her as he worked. "He'll foot you quick. And he could crack your fingers with hardly an effort."

Isobel eyed the bird nervously, but did not move her hand. James noted her courage with silent approval. He unwound the linen shirt, then took her slender hand in his to guide it beneath the cloth.

"Hold him here, behind the shoulders. Firmly, now."

While she did, he unlaced the thick leather guard that he wore over his forearm for protection while shooting his bow, and shifted it to cover the back of his hand. Then he picked up one of his discarded belts and wrapped it around his hand to protect his thumb and fingers.

"Lacking a leather gauntlet," he remarked, " 'tis the best I can do. Let go, lass. We'll see if he remembers how to come to the fist."

He wound the makeshift jesses around his fingers. Then he began to slip the shirt off the bird.

Isobel leaped back. The goshawk, freed from the restraining cloth, flapped his wings and rose upward, shrieking furiously.

Chapter 9

"The first rule of hawking," James said, "is to hold fast."

He extended his arm, feeling the tension in his shoulder and chest muscles as he resisted the bird's considerable upward force. The goshawk thrashed and flapped at the limit of the tightened jesses.

James tilted his head to avoid another fierce pass of a wing tip. "Isobel, there is some cooked meat in my pouch over there. Can you get it, and tear it into bits?"

She did so, and came forward cautiously, glancing up at the furious, struggling hawk. She handed the meat to James, who took it in his free hand while Isobel stepped away quickly.

Her gaze, like his, centered on the frenzied bird and the wide, sweeping wings, the flexing talons. James held his arm out patiently, though his muscles ached from the effort of resisting the hawk's strength.

With the other hand he held the food. He would not exert force over the bird. He knew the tiercel was hungry and tired, and he hoped that the appeal of easy food, and the discipline of previous training, would assert itself.

Finally the goshawk raked his wings more slowly and settled on James's offered fist with a decisive flapping. The bird cocked a resentful golden eye toward him.

"Ah," James said, smiling approval. "Here, you stubborn, bonny bird." He transferred the meat to his leather-covered hand. The bird tore at the food immediately. " 'Tis cooked, but 'tis all there is. Take it, aye, and the rest." He watched the bird eat. "Ah, look at him, Isobel," he said impulsively, grinning at her. "He's on the fist faster than I thought."

"He's quiet," Isobel said. "Is he tamed?"

"Hardly. He's just tired, and hurting, and only reluctantly willing to accept me."

"Ah," she said. "Like me."

He flashed a glance at her and gave a grudging laugh. Then the goshawk bated again, flinging himself off the fist to dangle head down, flapping his wings.

"What is it?" Isobel asked, sounding alarmed.

"A bate. 'Tis just temper. He wants us to know he doesna like this. Hawks—particularly gosses—can throw fits over and over, like a spoiled toddler. A falconer needs a good deal of patience to deal with a goshawk." He cocked a brow at the bird. "And this one looks as if he will need that, and more."

The tiercel beat his wings in a fury, then hung motionless. James placed a hand on the breast and gently lifted him back to his fist. The narrow-toed feet clenched fierce as iron through the unpadded protection of the bowguard, and James bit back a wince. The bird roused his chest feathers and hissed.

"Soft, you," James murmured. He went to the bow that he had stuck in the ground and lowered his arm. The tiercel took to the perch with scarce urging, and James quickly secured the leather thongs to the bow.

"He is quite temperamental," Isobel noted, watching.

"Short-winged hawks are of high temper by nature, and more of a challenge to train than long-winged falcons." James shook his head. "Poor bird. He was manned, and lost, and has gone feral again, and now he's had the shock of being trapped and taken. Aye, he's temperamental, and likely to stay that way."

"Mayhap you should let him go," Isobel said. "You shouldna keep a creature who wants to be free." Her eyes sparked with meaning. James returned a somber gaze, though his heart pounded inside until she glanced away.

He raked his fingers through his tangled hair and suddenly felt the chill air over his bare chest and back. He retrieved his woolen tunic from the ground—his linen shirt was soiled with the bird's mutes—and pulled it over his head. While he laced his leather hauberk over the tunic and relatched his belt, he frowned in thought.

The unexpected responsibility of the goshawk would truly throw his plans into chaos. So far, nothing had gone the way he wanted. The sun would be high before they left the glade, and each daylight hour along the forest path brought the risk of being seen. He had no men to fight at his back if they met soldiers. He sighed impatiently and looked at Isobel.

"Are you hungry?" he asked abruptly. She nodded. "We must leave soon," he went on. "But first I want to look after your wounds and find you some food. The gos ate the meat I had saved for breakfast."

"I saw some blackberries beyond that elm tree."

He nodded. "I'll gather some and bring the horses to the stream." He moved away, then looked back at her. "Guard the hawk, if you will, until I get back. If he bates, lift him gently to the perch. Be wary of his feet."

"Will he try to escape?" she asked.

"He is well and truly caught, though he doesna like it." He tipped a brow at her. "And what of you, Lady Isobel?"

"Do you wonder if you have me well and truly caught?" she asked in a spicy tone, her head lifted high.

He nearly chuckled at the unconscious charm in her earnest defiance. But he only shook his head. "I just wondered if I should leave you here unguarded."

"I willna leave—for now. I dinna know this forest, and I can barely control that surly English stallion. And I am hungry." She fisted a hand on her slender hip. "For now, you have two captives."

James returned a frank stare. "And I'll keep you both. Be certain of it." He walked away.

Isobel savored the last few blackberries and sucked the ripe juice from her fingertips. The taste and satisfaction of fresh food was still wondrous after the long hardship of the siege. She sighed and looked at James.

"Shall I fetch more?" he asked from his seat beside her on the fallen tree trunk. Amusement crinkled the skin around his eyes. She noticed the tiny creases there and the golden tips on his dark, thick eyelashes. His eyes were a vibrant, deep blue in the sunlight, like lapis shot with gold.

She shook her head and felt a blush touch her cheeks. "I am full," she murmured.

"Let me look after your arm," he said.

"My arm is fine." The wound ached fiercely, but she was loath to admit it. Her behavior embarrassed her a little. Exhaustion had made her sob like a child and collapse on the horse, and she had likely snored like a soldier after a feast; that, she knew, was a fault of hers. Just now, she had eaten with a ravenous appetite, while James watched with an indulgent look on his face.

She did not want to appear needy or weak to him, and she did not want him to think that she trusted him. At Aberlady, she had put her faith in him, but his rescue had no honor in it. Her anger sparked each time she thought of how he had made her a captive.

"I'm fine," she repeated stubbornly.

"Fine enough to make your cheeks paler than they should be, and so fine that you bite your lip and wince whenever you move. Dinna be a fool. Let me see it."

She sighed. The arm did need attention. She began to loosen the cloth strips that bound her arm to her side. James leaned forward, the morning sun glinting over his hair. He gently pushed down the strap of her dark gray surcoat and peeled back the torn sleeve of the pale gray gown beneath it. When he opened the bandages on her upper arm, Isobel winced sharply.

James glanced at her with concern and took away the last bit of cloth. She peered at her own wound and gasped.

The large punctures in the front and back of her upper arm had clotted, but the surrounding flesh was pink and swollen. The pale flesh of her arm had become a mass of purple bruises. James turned her arm in his hand, and the fierce ache nearly took her breath. After a moment, he nodded.

"This looks bonny," he said.

"Bonny?" she squeaked in dismay.

"There are no streaks of infection. You're fortunate to have only swelling and tenderness. You'll have some deep scars, but there are oils you can put on the skin

for scarring. Let me see your foot." He bent to lift her
ankle and peel back the bandage. The wound stung viciously when he exposed it. She decided not to look.

" 'Tis healing well also," he said. "And you seem able
to walk more easily, though you still limp. I'll clean these
and rebandage them, and my aunt can apply the proper
herbal ointments and remedies to see that the wounds
heal cleanly."

"Is she a healer, your aunt? Where does she live?"

"She understands healing, if more for animals than
humans. Her house is a morning's journey to the south."

"Will you tell your aunt," she said slowly, "that you
intend to hold me for ransom?"

He picked up a cloth that he had soaked in cool water
from the nearby stream, and folded it. His eyes flashed
to hers boldly. "I never said ransom, my lass," he said
softly. "Just a simple trade, one woman for another."

She sucked in a breath in answer, for he pressed the
cold, wet cloth to her arm.

"The cold will help the swelling and ease the pain,"
he said. "Hold it there for a while."

He went to the hawk, who drew in his feathers cautiously as the man came near. James nudged the goshawk's taloned feet with his leather-covered arm. After
several moments, the gos stepped onto his fist with a
flutter of wings. James stood, praising him in a calm,
low tone. He offered a strip of meat, which he laid on
the leather.

"I thought the rabbit meat was gone," Isobel said.

"It is. This is part of a mouse I caught when I got the
berries and the water."

Isobel grimaced. A sparkle of amusement lit James's
eyes. "He needs to eat, too, and he wouldna care for
nuts and berries, even as we wouldna care for his food,"
he said.

"You fed him not long ago."

"Aye," he said. "I'll overfeed him for now, so that
when we travel, he will be fat and full, and less eager to
try to fly his own meals down when he sees larks and
suchlike in the greenwood."

The bird finished the food and clenched his feet, but
he did not bate. He stayed where he perched, as if he

had begun to trust the man who had rescued but also captured him.

Isobel watched, and wished she could have faith in the man again. But he had taken her prisoner, too. "If I were a hawk," she said, "I would bate and bite and foot you until you let me go."

"How fortunate for me that you are a woman, then," James drawled, glancing at her. She blushed.

The tiercel flattened his feathers and squawked. James began to pass his hand in slow, graceful arcs over the bird's head, again and again, while he uttered affectionate phrases in a soft, soothing tone. The hawk watched the moving hand in fascination and seemed to relax.

"What are you doing?" Isobel asked.

"He'll fall into a kind of lazy trance, watching my hand," he explained. "There, you bird, easy," he added quietly. "He will forget that I am his natural enemy, and become comfortable perched on my hand, listening to my voice. Eventually he'll learn that I willna harm him. He'll learn to trust me."

"That," she said, "isna so easy."

"So I hear." He slid her a quick look.

She let it pass. "Do you mean to train him?"

"Aye, I mean to reclaim him. Soft, you gos. There." He swirled his hand in graceful, long loops. The hawk watched, intrigued. Isobel watched, too, feeling herself drawn in by the peaceful, sweeping gestures.

"But he belongs to someone," she said after a while.

"He *did.*" He emphasized the past tense.

"A goshawk is a yeoman's bird," Isobel said. "But knights and barons, even earls and kings, favor goshawks, too. That tiercel could belong to anyone. If his owner is a man of rank, you could suffer for it. You must return him."

"I am an outlaw, my lass. I do what I please." He watched the hawk. She watched his hand, strong and supple and beautifully made. The bird stared at it, too.

Isobel sighed. "Well, he might be from Aberlady's mews," she admitted. "Eustace would know." She came closer, drawn in by the hand, the hawk, and the man. "If you ever let me see Eustace again, that is."

James slid her a look that acknowledged her dry remark. "Come over here beside me, where the gos can see you," he said. "If you stand behind him 'twill make him nervous. And dinna stare at a hawk," he added. "It means danger to them. Wildcats stare before they pounce."

"Ah." She moved to stand at James's right side, still holding the cool, damp cloth to her arm. "My father owned a beautiful goshawk once, a sister to one that King Alexander called his favorite hunting hawk."

James lifted a brow. "My uncle was a royal falconer to King Alexander. Mayhap he raised your father's hawk." He spoke to her in the same voice he used with the bird—low and mellow, almost musical. Shivers cascaded down her back.

"Did you learn hawking from your uncle?" she asked.

"Aye. I fostered with my uncle and aunt in Dunfermline when I was a lad, before I went to a seminary school in Dundee. My uncle taught me much about his art."

"You're a falconer, then." She looked at him in surprise.

"I am but a brigand, named for a hawk, who knows hawks." He leaned forward and set the tiercel on the bow perch, then turned to Isobel. He took the cloth from her hand to wipe his fingers, crammed it in his belt, and leaned forward to refasten the bandages on her arm.

She felt the ache ease as he touched her. Shivers rippled from head to foot as he pulled her sleeve up over her shoulder and wrapped the bandages that bound her arm close to her side. The simple sensations roused by his hands on her were relaxing, even compelling.

She did not want his hands to stop. She felt like the hawk, caught and enthralled. Perhaps she even had the same blithe, silly look on her face.

She cleared her throat. "Let me do that," she said when he knelt to lift the heavy hems of her gown and surcoat.

" 'Twill take but a moment," he said as his fingers slipped beneath and found her ankle. Isobel felt a tender surge of feeling, as if part of her began to melt. She shifted her weight to her right leg and lifted her wounded foot, laying her hand on his head to keep her balance. His sun-warmed hair had a soft, fine texture. Her cheeks flamed suddenly.

"Why do they call you the Border Hawk?" she asked,

groping about for something to say. She felt oddly breathless.

"Mayhap because I strike with swift skill in the forest, taking English prey," he said, his tone dry. "Mayhap because I can see distances clear as crystal. Or mayhap"—he glanced up at her—"I earned the name for my nasty fits of temper."

She pinched back a smile. "Tell me truly."

He shrugged as he wrapped the cloth strips firmly around her foot. "I had another hawk, years back, when I first came to the forest," he said. "She was a goshawk, large and beautiful, a fierce hunter. She hunted grouse with a passion, just as my men and I hunted Southrons. Quarry never escaped us." He set her foot down. Isobel removed her hand from his head. "She was a fine bird."

"You kept her with you in the forest?"

"I made a mews for her in a cave," he said, and turned to crouch beside the tiercel. "She would come out with me nearly every day. If we came across quarry for her, Astolat would fly to it. If we came across my quarry—Southrons—she would perch in a tree or soar overhead. Sometimes she would fly off for a few hours. But she always came back." He smiled faintly, but Isobel saw a bitter sadness in his eyes.

James began to move his hand once again in languid passes over the bird's head. Isobel watched, standing behind him.

An easy peace existed in the little clearing, apart from conflicts of will and temper, of prize and captor. She wanted to preserve that, even if she had to stand there unmoving, just watching the man and the hawk until the sun sank.

"Astolat sounds a remarkable bird," she said. "You must be a gifted falconer to have trained her so well."

"Hawks differ in mood and nature, like people. Astolat was a perfect hawk, intelligent, with an almost canine loyalty. I have never known a better-tempered hawk." He waved his hand, and the goshawk, stared upward, looking enraptured and slightly dim-witted.

"What happened to her?" Isobel watched his fingers glide and felt as beguiled as the tiercel.

"She caught a Southron arrow meant for me," he said quietly.

"I am sorry," she whispered. He nodded. His hand tipped and spiraled like a hawk in flight.

Isobel kept her gaze on the hand that moved in endless, gentle loops over the tiercel's head. All else began to fade from her awareness. Somewhere a bird trilled and a soft wind rushed through the trees.

The restrained grace and power of his hand swept her along in its flight. She listened to his murmuring voice as he spoke to the bird, the same low phrases, over and over.

In a rush of awareness, she suddenly understood what the goshawk knew of the man: a soothing presence, a safe presence, a presence to be trusted.

She wanted to feel that for James Lindsay again, but could not. The thoughts drifted out as quickly as they entered her mind. She watched his hand, listened to his murmurs.

A remembered image came to her suddenly, like a dream recalled, of a man holding a goshawk on his gloved fist, standing beside a hawthorn tree in the rain.

This man.

Isobel's heart began to thump. Months ago, in a vision forgotten until this moment, she had seen James Lindsay with a goshawk. She drew in a breath, and wanted to tell him, and could not. She wanted to take her gaze from his sweeping, gliding hand in the air, and could not.

The sunlit clearing around her began to fade. His hand was all that she saw now. Lights sparkled and glistened at the newborn edges of the field. Isobel felt the darkness slide in, filling her head, replacing the world her eyes saw with another world.

She wanted to cry out, but could not. She wanted him to pull her back, but she could not reach out. Darkness and light mingled and swept in with the power of an ocean wave. She dimly felt herself fall to her knees.

Light swirled into her then, brighter and finer than the glow of fire or sun. It pulsed and shimmered and danced within her mind, brilliant, enthralling, loving, magical.

The images began.

*   *   *

She saw swirling clouds of mist. The veils parted to reveal a green mound and a hawthorn tree. Beyond it rose the soaring walls of a church, its stones dark with rain.

James Lindsay stood beside the tree. He was cloaked and hooded, and held the goshawk on his gloved fist. Isobel felt herself there, too, gliding over the damp grass to stand beside him. He turned to look at her, and she felt his sorrow, deep and dark and endless.

He stepped away. Isobel moved after him, floating on the misted air. But he turned and walked into the mist.

She wanted to follow him, but could not. She felt trapped somehow, as if she wore a chain. She swirled away, and saw another man standing beside the tree.

He was a large man, an armored knight, handsome in a bold way, broad in bone and muscle, taller than any man she had ever seen. His body was powerful beneath a chain mail hauberk and a green cloak. He held a long broadsword upright, his hands folded on the high hilt, as he watched her. His eyes were gray and somehow filled with light.

"Jamie seeks peace," he told her. His voice was deep and kind. "And he seeks forgiveness. But he must grant them to himself, though he resists that."

"Who are you?" she asked.

"A friend," he said. "Be patient with him, Isobel. He will find what he seeks."

She nodded, and looked in the direction that James had gone. But the mist swirled, empty, lonely. She turned back. The huge, handsome knight had vanished.

The mist shifted into darkness again. This time it was a brown murk, cold and filthy, with a vile odor. In the dank shadows, she saw stone walls and a man crouched in a corner.

Her father. His hair was long and straggling, gray and filthy; his beard hid his face, his flesh sagged on the jutting bones of his large frame, but she knew him. She recognized his blue eyes, dulled to a slate color. He covered his head in his shaking hands and curled forward.

She cried out to him, and he looked up. Hope lit up his features—and then the image was gone.

"Father!" she screamed, reaching out. "Father!"

But the darkness flooded into her, sparkling with colored stars, sweeping her away. As it faded to a velvet black depth, she fell forward.

The ground was firm and cool beneath her cheek. She felt the dewy grass between her fingers, smelled its fresh scent and the pungency of wild onion somewhere nearby. The wind and the sun were soft on her face and hands. She heard a lark singing overhead and the soft chirr of the jessed goshawk, a few feet in front of her. She pushed up to prop herself on hands and knees.

"Isobel?" His voice was gentle with concern. She turned toward it. "Isobel, what is it? Are you ill?" James crouched beside her. She felt warmth radiate from him. His hand rested on her shoulder, strong and firm.

"I am fine," she said, a little breathless. "I am fine." She began to stand, rising slowly. His hands supported her as she came up. The breeze pushed her skirt against her legs and the sunlight felt warm and gentle on her face.

"Can you walk?" he asked. She nodded. "Come over here and sit down." His fingers gripped hers, warm, caring, strong. She felt the weight of his other hand at her waist.

She stepped forward and stumbled when her toe caught something, a root, a stone. His hands steadied her.

"Isobel, what is it?" he asked.

She hesitated. "I am blind," she said.

Chapter 10

"Blind?" he whispered.

"Aye." Isobel gave a trembling nod.

James stared at her. Bright sunlight lent her irises a pristine delicacy, but her gaze was flat and unfocused. He lifted a hand and waved it slowly, letting the shadow of his fingers pass over her face. She did not blink.

"Isobel," he said, his voice hushed with shock. "What is it? What is wrong?" He wondered anxiously if she had been injured when the horse ran off with her; he knew head wounds could cause odd effects. "Did you hit your head yesterday?"

She tilted her head slightly as she listened to him. Her eyes stared, their dull gaze aimed somewhere beyond his shoulder. "Nay. The blindness comes over me whenever I have a vision. 'Twill pass."

"When you fell to your knees and cried out, and spoke aloud, you saw a vision?" he asked.

She nodded. "And the blindness always follows."

He raked his fingers through his hair, looked away, looked back at her, trying to piece together cogent understanding in the midst of his alarm and astonishment. "Blind?" he repeated.

"The blindness will pass," she said calmly. She reached out and found his arm, rested her hand there. He gripped her elbow. "I have learned to expect this," she said.

"How long does it last?"

She shrugged. "An hour, an afternoon, sometimes through a full day. It passes each time. I pray 'twill always be so."

"Is there aught wrong with your vision otherwise?"

"Only a little blurring of distances, but that is common enough. My father once had a physician examine my eyes, and he said they were healthy. This only happens during and after the prophecies, and then it goes away of its own will. Father Hugh says 'tis my burden to bear for the gift of the prophecies."

"Mother of God," James said softly. "I didna know."

"Few do," she answered.

He watched her, thinking. Then he realized that she waited for him to speak. "What vision did you see?"

Her brow furrowed. "I saw you."

"Me," he said, suddenly wary. He frowned deeply.

"Aye, and the goshawk," she said. "Beside a hawthorn tree. I am trying to remember—I forget them so quickly. There was another man—a knight—" She paused, as if struggling to recall. "He spoke to me. I was there, too." She shook her head as if confused. "The rest is gone. 'Tis like forgetting a dream upon waking." She bit her lip, looking intensely frustrated. "I am sorry. I try to remember them, but—" She shrugged, shook her head again. Her hair slipped down over her shoulders. Her blank blue eyes held true innocence.

James felt a curious softening sensation in his heart. Logic told him to doubt all of this. But he could not, watching her. He was greatly concerned, and wholly shocked.

"You recall only that much?" he asked.

"Aye. After a vision, I barely remember anything of what I have seen or heard. My father or the priest are often with me to write down what I say. They question me about what I see and what I hear while the vision is upon me, and I can answer them. Father Hugh has recorded all my prophecies, and he understands them better than I do myself. I remember so little of them, and they are often puzzles to me, full of symbols." She sighed, moved her fingers on his arm. "I wish I could remember. Once I did try to make myself recall, and—" She stopped, bit her lip.

"Perhaps 'tis the shock of the blindness that drives all else away," James said.

"That could be. The blindness used to frighten me greatly, although I am more used to it now."

She did not look used to it, James thought. She looked vulnerable, like a frightened child pretending to be brave. Her fingers flexed anxiously on his arm. He pressed her elbow with his own hand to reassure her with touch.

"How long has this been happening?" he asked.

"Since I was thirteen winters, a few times each year," she said. "I have learned to call the prophecies forth by gazing into a bowl of water or into a fire. But just now, it came upon me strangely—so suddenly. That hasna happened since I was young. James—can you recall what I said? Sometimes the images come back to me if I can hear the words I said."

He rubbed his brow, thinking. "You said 'peace and forgiveness,' and something about a friend."

"Ah!" she said. "I saw a knight. He said he was a friend."

"Who was he?"

She shook her head. "I dinna know. I can hardly recall already . . . he was a large man, tall. Was there aught else?"

"You called out 'Father!' I thought you were calling for a priest."

She gasped. "I remember—I saw my father!" Her fingers tightened on his forearm. "He was in a dungeon. He was . . . ill, weakened." She bowed her head. "What if he is hurt, or dead?"

"He is alive," James said quickly. "You saw him alive. Remember that, Isobel."

She nodded. Her face was pale cream in the strong sunlight, and her eyes were transparent blue glass, perfect yet sightless.

"Dear God, Isobel," he murmured. "Dear God." He felt stunned, dizzy, as if he had whirled about blindfolded and faced an unknown direction—a bit like she must feel, he thought. "Tell me what you need of me."

She paused. "For now, I must ask safekeeping of you."

"Aye," he said gruffly. *Anything,* he thought. Suddenly he keenly missed the bond of their gazes, and wanted more contact with her. He touched his fingers to

the curve of her cheek. She tipped her face into the cup
of his palm for an instant, and her eyes drifted shut.

"I promise," he said.

"Thank you," she said. "But then, James Lindsay, you
must let me go." Her tone was light, a mock scold.

Suddenly he did not think that he could ever let her
go. The force and certainty of the feeling astounded him.
Sympathy, he told himself; pity, perhaps. Just that, and
no more.

"Come with me, Isobel," he said gently, and took her
arm to lead her, step by careful step, toward the horses.

Isobel tilted her head as they rode along the forest
track. Sounds seemed louder to her in the blinded state,
scents and tastes were stronger, and her fingers told her
more of texture and shape. The effort needed to sort
through so many sensations at once, without sight to tell
her what she heard or felt or tasted, could be exhausting
and overwhelming. But there were moments when she
felt exhilarated by her awareness of the commonplace.

She knew that James held the gos on his leather-
wrapped fist, for she could hear the creak of the leather
and the scritch-scratch of the bird's talons. She heard
James murmur often to the bird. His deep voice had a
comfortable texture, like warm wool on a cold night.

And she knew that he held the reins of her horse
firmly, for she could feel the tension in the strap. His
leg occasionally brushed hers as they rode, sending quick
leaps of pleasurable sensation through her.

James had ridden close beside her along the way,
speaking kindly, telling her what he knew about the Ettrick Forest. He told her that he had lived in caves in
the Ettrick for almost ten years, and she sensed his respect and love for his adopted home. He was a natural
storyteller, spinning entertaining, exciting tales about his
life as an outlaw and a Scottish rebel.

He described years spent running with Wallace and
his men, engaging in skirmishes and trickery, weighing
strategies and risks. He told of acts of cruelty, and courage, and cleverness. With deft words and the mellow
tones of his voice, he painted images of intelligent, spir-

ited men who believed that freedom should exist in Scotland, and sacrificed much for that end.

But he told her nothing of how he had come to this life, and she did not ask. She listened, and was glad that the earlier conflicts between them seemed to have entered a truce.

"My uncle was partly blind," James said after a while. "He was like that when I fostered with him as a lad."

She tilted her head in interest. "Your uncle the falconer?"

"Aye. He was blinded in the left eye by a trained eagle."

"An eagle! I didna know they could be trained."

"If the falconer is skillful enough, they can. Years ago, Uncle Nigel caught one in the mountains, an eyas straight from the nest, and raised it and trained it. A magnificent bird, though nearly impossible to manage. The bird was feeding on Nigel's fist one day. Birds of prey have a habit of swiping their beaks to clean them, and the eagle swiped against Nigel's head, taking the eye."

"God in heaven! And he trained birds after that?"

"Aye, he continued as royal falconer for years afterward," James said. She heard a note of pride, and a little amusement, in his voice. "He wore his eye patch like a crown. A falconer missing his left eye is most likely to have trained an eagle," he explained. "He had the respect of others just for trying it."

"Does he still keep birds?"

"He died a few years ago," James said quietly. "After King Alexander died, he went into retirement in Dunfermline and made hawking equipment. He kept one old peregrine that had belonged to King Alexander. That bird was over thirty years old when she died."

" 'Tis ancient," Isobel said impulsively. She heard James's soft snort of laughter. "For a falcon or a hawk, I mean."

"Aye, well, I'm more ancient than that," he said wryly. "Though I suppose you are scarce twenty."

She lifted her head. "I will be twenty-six come winter. Most women of my age would be wed, with bairns of their own."

"And you havena done that. Why?"

She shrugged. "I am a poor bargain. Few men would want a blind prophetess for a wife."

He was silent for so long that she tilted her head toward him as if to seek his reply.

"I think you would be a fine bargain," he murmured finally.

"Aye, to win you back what you want," she said sourly. He wanted a certain woman; she marveled at how strong his love must be. A ripple of jealousy went through her.

"The man who gains such a bargain will be fortunate," he said. Her insides swirled, and she felt her cheeks grow hot with a furious blush. His voice, a rich blend of soft and rough, felt as intimate as if he touched her bare skin.

"Sir Ralph is my father's choice for me," she said.

"He isna your choice?"

"He has little interest in me, but great interest in what I possess."

"Already?"

"Prophecy." She tilted her head toward him, though she could not give him the direct stare she wished.

"Ah," he said. "Is that the way of it."

She waited for him to explain his dry comment, but he was silent. Riding beside him, she listened to the muted rhythm of the horses' hooves, the tiercel's faint squawks, and the steady murmur of the forest—rustling leaves, wind, and birdsong.

After a while, she wanted to hear his voice again, as if the tapestry of sounds around her lacked a centerpiece, a focus.

"You said you fostered in Dunfermline, with your uncle."

"Aye, from the time I was ten until I was fifteen," he said easily, as if it pleased him to talk with her.

"I know the place. 'Tis where Saint Margaret is buried, and other Scottish royalty," Isobel said. "I havena been to the abbey myself, but I have heard 'tis beautiful."

"'Tis a great abbey, a holy place. The pilgrimage route goes through there," James said. "But King Edward declared it a den of robbers, since Scottish nobles met there to make plans against the English. So he burned the place down last year. An atrocious deed. His own sister was buried there."

Isobel gasped. "Was the abbey ruined?"

"The church was spared, by grace of God. I have a friend among the monks there. Most of the monks, last year, had no quarters after the great fire."

"And your uncle's house? Was it safe?"

"It burned," he said. "He and his wife retired to a small house in the forest. She lives there now, since his death."

"Your aunt Alice?"

"Aye. Ho, lass, lean left. There's a low branch." James tugged at her good arm, and she ducked as branches swept over her.

"I am causing you a good deal of bother. I am sorry."

"I dinna mind." His tone was gentle.

When the horses began to descend a slope, Isobel leaned back, gripping her mount's mane, until the ground leveled again. She felt the wind blow through her hair, felt the heat of the sun on her face, and heard fainter, higher birdsong.

"We've left the forest," she said.

"Only to cross a moor. We'll enter cover again and follow another forest track soon. The Ettrick Forest is made up of a good deal more than forestland—there are moors, hills, lochs, and burns within its boundaries as well."

The hawk kakked loudly then, and Isobel heard the wild thrashing of wings. "What is it?" she asked.

"Just a bate," James said. Isobel felt the horses stop, while the frenzied whirr of the goshawk's wings continued, slowed, and ceased. "Calm down, lad," James soothed. "Back to the fist, then." After a few moments, the horses stepped forward. "He saw a pair of deer run past. They startled him." Isobel nodded, and they rode on.

"Your hawk needs a name," she said. "Are there rules for naming a hunting bird?"

"Nay, though I have always called my hawks and horses after heroes and ladies from the tales of King Arthur."

She tipped her head curiously. "Why so?"

"When I was a lad, my parents gave me a painted manuscript in French containing many of the Arthurian tales. I read them again and again. I suppose the names stayed in my mind."

"I read them, too, and loved them. My mother owned a copy in English, with beautiful pictures. The priest taught me to read when I was younger, and to write some. I loved to copy my favorite stories out of that volume." She smiled a little, remembering, and turned her head in his direction. "You called your other hawk after Elaine, Lady of Astolat, who died for love of Lancelot, then."

"Aye. 'Twas a prophetic name." His grim tone reminded her of his earlier remark: the bird had been killed by an English arrow. She waited in the darkness that surrounded her, and wondered if he would tell her more, for it clearly sorrowed him. But he said nothing.

She heard leaves rustle, smelled the tang of greenery, and felt the cool and the quiet in the air as they entered the forest again. The pace of the horses slowed. The hawk kakked.

"He does need a name," James said. "What shall it be?"

"Hmm." She frowned. "Arthur, Ector, Gawain, and Tristan all kept hawks or went hunting . . . ah!" She smiled. "Gawain!"

"Gawain the goshawk?" He sounded doubtful.

"It means hawk of May, or hawk of the plain, in the Welsh tongue. Ho, Gawain," she said, speaking toward the hawk. She heard the soft stir of his wings. "It suits him well, I think."

James chuckled. "Better than you know. My aunt Alice keeps a female red-tailed hawk called Ragnell."

Isobel laughed. "Gawain and Ragnell were paired in one of the legends."

"Aye. So the prophetess chose that name, I think." She heard amusement in his voice and imagined a sparkle in his blue eyes.

She smiled toward James. "Sir Gawain promised to wed Lady Ragnell, though she was a hideous old hag," she said. "How can that name suit a beautiful hawk?"

"Believe me, it suits her," James said with wry certainty. "She wants all her will, like the woman in the story. And she is—an unusual-looking bird."

Isobel smiled. "She sounds like an interesting bird. I am eager to meet her."

"Oh, you will meet her."

Isobel sobered instantly. She admonished herself for laughing so freely with him. Regardless of his kind assistance and his patience now, the outlaw had taken her captive.

Of course she would meet the female hawk, she reminded herself bitterly. He meant to take her to his aunt's house and secure her there as his prisoner.

She sighed, and stared into the frustrating blackness that enveloped her, and rode forward into an uncertain future.

Chapter 11

Sunlight streamed down over the forest path. Isobel felt the warmth as the horses stepped into sunny pools and back into cool shadow. She arched her lower back wearily and pushed a hand through her bedraggled hair. Her woolen gown and surcoat had become uncomfortably warm, and she was growing more irritable due to pain, hunger, and fatigue.

And the darkness in her eyes lingered, making her feel as if she balanced precariously on a razored edge, hovering between fear and faith, waiting for her sight to return.

She heard the tiercel bate again, another of several bates during the journey. The horses stopped, and Isobel heard James speak soothingly to the bird. She was sure that the outlaw was as tired and irritable as she was, for lately he had scarcely spoken to her, though he rode close beside her.

Finally the goshawk quieted, and they continued on. Each time she heard the rustle of his wings, Isobel expected to hear the tiresome fury of another bate.

"Do you regret taking on the hawk?" she asked. "He's a difficult bird."

"I couldna leave him where he was," James said. "He needed help. And he canna fly well, as yet."

"Do you regret taking me?" she asked after a moment. "I canna fend for myself just now, either."

"Well," he drawled, "at least you dinna throw tantrums."

She laughed softly and let the horse carry her onward. "Is your aunt's house close now?" she asked after a while.

"Aye," he said. "We'll ride around the base of a slope, and the house is just past that."

Soon James led them off the earthen track to ride between the trees. Isobel cried out in alarm as a branch knocked into her. She put up an arm to shield herself.

She felt the touch of his hand, firm and strong, on her knee. "I'll go ahead to bend the branches out of your way," he said, and moved forward, Isobel's stallion following.

When the horses halted again, Isobel turned toward James. "Are we there?" she asked.

"Just at the edge of the clearing," he answered. "I always stop here at this place and look. 'Tis a welcome sight, this."

"Oh." Disappointment plunged through her, for she could not see what he saw. "It must be lovely."

"Aye." He leaned toward her. She felt the solid press of his shoulder, felt the warmth of his face near hers, heard his soft breathing. "The clearing is just ahead of us," he said. His quiet voice had a rich, sultry depth. "The forest opens suddenly, like a green frame around a painting. The clearing beyond is filled with golden sunlight. The grass is sprinkled with dandelions, and a small stone house sits at the center."

She tipped her head and listened, entranced, easily able to create the picture over the solid darkness in her mind.

"Smoke curls up from a hole in the thatched roof," he went on. "Two tiny windows are open to the air and light, and the door is open, welcoming, with a white cat asleep on the low slate step. A goat wanders through the yard, and under his feet are a few chickens. He ignores them as he nibbles at the flowered turf bench tucked against the side of the house. There is a small garden at the corner, with some vegetables and herbs. The lavender is bright purple, the raspberry canes are green and tangled, and golden honeysuckle grows thick over the fence."

"Ah," she breathed. "How beautiful. So peaceful."

" 'Tis why I come here. For the peace. And to see Alice. You will like her." His shoulder continued to press against hers companionably, underscoring the pleasant sense of ease and security. She let herself lean into him.

"Thank you," she said.

"My uncle used to ask me to describe things for him," James said. "I thought you might like it, too."

"Is Alice waiting for us?" She did not care, just then, that she was a captive. She enjoyed the serenity of the moment. And she craved the comfort offered in the house just ahead. She waited for James to urge her horse forward.

But he tensed, straightening away from her. She thought she heard him swear under his breath. A familiar thumping rhythm sounded in the distance; she recognized the sound of horses.

"Who are they?" she asked in sudden alarm, remembering the skirmish of the day before. "Are they coming this way?"

"Isobel." His voice was hard. "I am going to lead the horses into a stand of birches, and I want you to hide in the bracken. 'Tis deep enough to cover you."

"What—"

"Hush!" he hissed fiercely. He tightened his grip on the reins of her horse and pulled. Branches clawed at her, and a limb snapped her full in the jaw. She cried out and waved her left arm instinctively, panicked, unsure where she was.

Then she felt James's hands like iron around her waist. He hauled her swiftly from her horse, and waded with her through deep fern growth to shove her down into the bracken. He pressed a hand to her head.

"Stay down. Be quiet," he whispered urgently. Then he was gone.

Breathing hard, Isobel lay in the bracken and waited, her face muffled in the crook of her arm. The smells of earth and green were strong around her. Her injured arm throbbed, but she made no sound. She listened with all of her awareness.

She heard the horses snort softly behind her in the cover of trees. The goshawk squealed nearby; James must have tied him to a perch in a tree.

The cantering horses had quieted. Male voices came through the trees, deep but faint. She turned her head under the cover of the ferns. Their soft fingers combed over her skin and their scent filled her nostrils.

Time stretched, stilled. Wildly, suddenly, she feared that James had left her, blind and alone, in the forest.

Then she heard the soft, stealthy thud of footfalls, and she felt him drop down beside her in the ferns. With great relief, she turned toward him and opened her mouth to speak.

"Hush!" he whispered, touching a finger to her lips. She felt him stretch out close beside her. Then he pulled her back against his chest, so close that they lay spooned together, with Isobel lying on her left side. The length of his body pressed hard against her, head to foot, his arms firm around her. He placed the palm of his hand over her mouth, and she gasped in surprise.

"Be silent," he whispered. She felt his steel-hard grip and the heavy thump of his heart through her back. Unable to see, scarcely able to move, she panicked. She struggled, kicked out, and squealed.

James locked a leg over hers to still the kicks. Isobel gathered breath to scream. He tightened his hand over her mouth. She bit the finger that rested across her lips.

James uttered a soft oath. "Be still and be silent," he growled. "Promise me that, or I willna let go, though you bite off my finger."

She nodded desperately. He lifted his hand from her mouth, but kept his arms tightly about her. Isobel felt like a wild thing caught in a trap. How could she have been so wrong about him, she thought. How could she have trusted him? She twisted again. He yanked tighter, and she stilled, breath heaving.

"Soft, you," he whispered. "I willna harm you." His embrace relaxed a bit. "But dinna make a sound."

Isobel elbowed him heartily in the breastbone, though it pained her injured arm to do it. He grunted, giving her small satisfaction. Little short of a miracle could appease the anger she felt toward him now. She could not trust him. And by his actions, he clearly did not trust her either.

That thought sobered her suddenly. She let herself go slack in his arms. After a moment, she felt James lift his head to look around.

Isobel raised her head, too, wanting to hear more clearly. James pushed her head down. "Riders are coming into the clearing," he whispered.

The cadence of horses' hooves vibrated the earth beneath her. Then she heard the muffled thuds of a single horse moving forward. "How many are there?" she whispered.

"Four," he hissed back. "One of them is crossing the yard."

"Are they Scots?"

"Their armor is too fine. Few Scotsmen could afford such trappings. The Scots dinna think kindly of me just now either, so we'll stay hidden." His voice was a soft breath of air. None but she could have heard it.

"What does the leader look like?" she whispered.

"He has a fine dappled horse and good chain mail. Hush."

She heard a deep, smooth male voice give a polite greeting, and she heard a woman's reply, gruff and quick. As she lay in James's arms, she tried to listen to what the knight said to Alice, but much of what they said was not audible.

Isobel found herself distracted by the hard wrap of James's arms around her, the firm length of his body behind hers, the soft rhythm of his breath at her ear.

She scowled and tried to concentrate.

"I want to know where he is, madame." The knight's voice was raised in anger. Isobel frowned; the voice was familiar.

"I havena seen the lad in months," Isobel heard Alice reply. Her voice was earthy, full, and dauntless somehow. "I live alone here, and no one bothers me—but for you. Begone from here."

"Surely he has come to you for help recently," the man said. "Tell me where he is!" His voice was louder now, demanding.

Isobel gasped. James clapped his fingers over her mouth. She lay enclosed in his arms, tempted to struggle away from the forest brigand who held her and flee to sure safety.

She waited for Sir Ralph Leslie to speak again.

*   *   *

James pulled Isobel closer and pressed the palm of his hand over her soft lips. A moment ago, she had gasped out as if in surprise. He glanced down. Her blue eyes had a startled look, wide open, yet she stared at nothing. *Nothing.* Her blindness still alarmed him. He had to keep her safe and hidden from Ralph Leslie. Her expression told him that she had already recognized the voice of her betrothed.

James kept his firm hold on her, and watched Alice step forward. His aunt fisted her hands on wide hips beneath her brown kirtle and stared boldly at Leslie. Taller than most men, Alice Crawford was not easily intimidated.

"What do you want with James Lindsay?" she demanded.

"He's wanted for crimes against King Edward and he killed several Englishmen."

"I know that," Alice snapped impatiently.

"Surely you know that William Wallace was taken last month, and executed in London on charges of treason."

"I heard. The Southrons are heartless bastards," she said bluntly. "God rest his soul. Will Wallace never did treason in his life. What of Jamie, then?"

"James Lindsay betrayed Wallace."

"Never!" Alice cried.

"I have proof," Leslie said.

"I'll never believe it," Alice said stoutly. "Why do you spread such a foul tale? You, a Scotsman?"

"If the Scots find him, they will cut him down like a beast. If the English find him, they will hang him—and worse." Leslie leaned closer. "But I can help your nephew, Dame Crawford. The charges against him can be remanded by King Edward. Lindsay knows that the king may see fit to grant him a reward for Wallace's capture."

James felt Isobel grow still as a stone in his arms. He was certain that she had heard. He turned his attention to the clearing.

"Are you one of those who turn their loyalty with the wind?" Alice asked in a suspicious tone.

"I am merely a practical man, dame."

"Then show your good sense and get out of my yard!"

"Peace, woman. I came here for another reason."

"Then speak," she snapped.

He lifted his left arm to display the black armband wrapped around his chain-mail sleeve. "I am in mourning."

"Forgive me. I didna know."

"I have lost my betrothed. Two days past, there was a fire at a castle in Midlothian. My beloved Lady Isobel Seton was inside with her garrison."

Isobel gasped and twisted against James, as if she was desperate to escape and go to her lover. James dragged her close, more roughly than he meant to do. Her hip pressed against his groin, her breast was soft beneath his arm, and her lips were moist and warm against his palm.

A sudden, unexpected lust flared in him. James drew a ragged breath, his heart hammering in his chest.

He had spent a few years in a monastery, and even more as a renegade; he thought he could master his body and his emotions. But desire still surged through him like fire.

He felt her tremble, and knew he had frightened her. That acted like a dousing of cold water, and he lessened his hold.

"I willna hurt you," he murmured. "But dinna think to call out to your lover." The word tasted bitter on his tongue. He held her down and raised his head to listen once again to the conversation in the clearing.

"I tried to save Lady Isobel from the fire, but I was too late," Leslie told Alice. "I ran into the flames without fear for my own life, so great was my urge to find her. Love makes a courageous heart, madame."

James felt a chill run through him. Ralph Leslie spoke bold lies, but his words stirred old nightmares. James closed his eyes against remorse and an empty, hollow pain.

When he looked again, his aunt had clasped her hands over her wide bosom, absorbed in Leslie's story. James scowled. Alice, tough as she looked, had a sentimental core that melted like butter over the scarcest flame.

"Isobel died in the inferno." Leslie lowered his head.

"Poor lady!" Alice cried.

In his arms, Isobel squirmed. He felt her throat shift

as she swallowed, heard her muffled wince of pain—or was it a smothered cry for help?

"She was a beautiful woman, and a gifted prophetess."

"Black Isobel?" Alice asked hesitantly. "The prophetess?"

"Aye, the same. Madame, someone escaped the fire. An arrow protruded from the cliff side, white feathered like those the Border Hawk uses. If he killed my Isobel, I will kill him with my own hands."

"A white-tipped arrow isna proof that Jamie was there. And your beloved might have escaped the fire."

"That would gladden my heart," Leslie said. "If you see your nephew, madame, give him a message from me."

"He doesna come here."

"Then you will have to find him and tell him that I have Margaret Crawford in my keeping."

"Margaret!" Alice burst out. "She is my niece! Is she safe? If you harm her—"

"She is my guest, never fret. Now you will be sure to find Lindsay to tell him where she is. I am sure he is concerned."

"Jamie will bring a host of men upon your walls—"

"Margaret is safe in my care. But tell Lindsay that if he wants to see her again, he must come to Wildshaw Castle, where I am constable, to escort her home."

James fisted his hand, white-knuckled, against Isobel's waist as he listened to Leslie's mild words, couching a strong threat to both Margaret and the Border Hawk. Isobel stirred in his arms. He tightened his hold around her waist and over her mouth to still her.

"You hold Wildshaw?" Alice asked, her voice tense.

"Aye. King Edward put it in my command recently," Leslie said. "Deliver my message, Dame Crawford. I am sure you have some contact who knows where the outlaw is. I will return in a few days. I hope you will have some news for me." He circled his horse. "Good day, madame."

He and his men rode out of the yard. Alice watched them, her hands clapped over her mouth, her cheeks flaming red. Then she turned and ran into her house.

James felt Isobel struggle in his arms. "He's gone,"

he growled. Then he felt a rapid pulsing in the earth
beneath him. "Riders!" he hissed, and flattened, belly
down, in the bracken. He pushed Isobel onto her back
to flatten her, too, and shielded her body with his, half
resting his torso over hers, pressing his hand over her
mouth.

High and thick, the ferns enclosed them in a verdant
cave. James smelled the rich, green tang of the fronds,
and inhaled the warm sweetness of Isobel, his face close
to hers, half buried in her hair. Her lean body was a
firm cushion beneath his.

They lay for endless moments, breathing rapidly.
James closed his eyes, and listened with his entire being,
feeling the hoofbeats in the earth, hearing the jingle of
armor and weapons.

The riders came so close to them that the ferns quivered as the horses passed through. A clod of earth, torn
loose, fell on James's back. Isobel trembled beneath him.

Suddenly she twisted her head, slipping away from the
cover of his hand. A small cry escaped her mouth.

In sudden desperation, James scooped his hand along
her jaw and turned her head. He covered her lips with
his, silencing her, hard, swift, and complete.

Isobel went still beneath him. With his mouth pressed
to hers, James breathed with her, moist and slow, while
the thunder of hoofbeats surrounded them.

Her lips moved beneath his hesitantly, almost poi-
gnantly. A deep thrill spiraled through his body. James
lay still, his lips motionless, but softening upon hers until
his blood rushed.

He lifted his mouth away, stunned by the force that
had poured through him. His heart pounded wildly—
with fear, with desire, with an intense craving to taste
her again. He glanced at her and saw that her eyes,
gorgeous in the green glow of the ferny cave, were filled
with tears.

"Isobel—" Gently, he slipped his fingers into the tousled silk of her hair and touched his lips to hers once
again. This time, he meant it for a true kiss, and no act
of desperation.

Tender and sweet, her lips were sun-warmed honey
beneath his. The slow, exquisite kiss took him over, stole

his breath and his reason, and changed the beat of his heart.

A moment later, he realized that the riders had gone, though he was not sure when that had happened. He separated his lips from hers reluctantly, and lifted his head to listen.

Silence.

He glanced at Isobel. She stared at him, her eyes glistening, keen on his, filled with awareness.

Filled with sight.

He touched her cheek with his finger, and his heart thundered in his chest.

"God in heaven. You can see," he whispered.

"Aye," she said softly. "Just now." She laughed airily. "It came back when you kissed me."

James stared. "How—" He let out a stunned breath. "Does it always need a—a kiss?" He thought he sounded like a halfwit.

"I have never tried kissing as a cure." She laughed again, sounding delighted. "But it worked like a miracle."

James blinked in disbelief, then shook his head. "I dinna understand any of this. I truly dinna," he muttered, and rose to his knees in the ferns—nearly bolted upright, for the import of what had happened hit him like a blow.

He frowned as he scanned the surrounding, deserted forest. Only in a collection of saint's tales, or in a *roman d'aventure,* could a chaste kiss heal miraculously. But that had been no chaste kiss; his body still throbbed, his blood still surged.

By the Rood, he thought. This was not some epic tale. He was a brigand, not a hero. But he could not shake the effects of that stunning, impulsive kiss, in his body or in his heart. He wanted to take her into his arms and feel that sweeping power once again.

Isobel's gaze fastened calmly and sweetly on him. He was glad to have the contact of their eyes again. He had missed it. But the look of adoration in her eyes made him distinctly uncomfortable.

He preferred the safer ground of enemies, of distrust, of practical matters like hostages and strategies. He did not know what to do with visions, with magic and miracles. With love.

Not that, he warned himself. Surely not that. Not with the prophetess, of all women. He shoved a hand roughly through his hair. Once again, Black Isobel had brought something unexpected into his life. He did not know what to think of her. He did not know what to feel about her.

But he knew he wanted to touch her again, kiss her, immerse his hardened heart in her gentle nature. He even wanted that adoration from her. But he knew he did not deserve it.

He scowled and looked away. "The riders are gone now. 'Tis safe to leave." Aye, safer than staying here and yearning after a lass, he thought sourly. "I'll fetch the goshawk and the horses. Stay here." He stood.

She rolled to her side and sat up. "James Lindsay."

He looked down. She rose out of the ferns like a faerie queen, with the green fronds clinging to her gown and her hair. He felt an odd sensation in the region of his heart.

"Aye?" he asked softly.

"Thank you," she whispered. "For the kiss."

He sighed. "Your sight would have returned soon or late, as you said. But I am glad . . . to have been of some help."

She watched him. He thought how innocent she was, yet how mysterious, with her strange wisdom, with her beautiful eyes and her sweet mouth.

He wished he were free to love her. He sometimes wondered what it would be like to live a peaceful life. But he would never know. Danger lurked around him. He could not yearn after peace, or love, or black-haired prophetesses.

She began to gain her feet. James hesitated, then reached out to help her, steeling himself against the pleasure of touching her. He let go and stepped away.

"James," she said. "Ralph does have Margaret."

"Aye," he said gruffly. "And he holds her to trap me."

"But he said that you murdered several men. He said

that you promised to betray Wallace for reward. But—"
She paused. "That canna be true."

He looked at her for the length of a heartbeat, of
another. He saw the faith in her eyes, and knew what
she wanted to hear. And he knew that his words would
hurt her.

"Aye," he said. " 'Tis true."

He turned away, so that he would not see the newborn
trust shatter in her beautiful eyes.

Chapter 12

Isobel looked eagerly around as she and James rode forward. The clearing was a sunlit jewel, with the small stone house set at its center, as cozy and welcoming as she had imagined from James's description.

The blindness, when it cleared, often left her with a kind of visual hunger. She gazed around avidly and looked at James, who rode ahead of her, the reins of her horse held in his hand.

His posture was powerful and agile as he sat the black stallion. The goshawk on his fist was calm, his feathers delicately barred, his eye blazing as he turned his head.

James glanced over his shoulder at her and looked away.

Isobel felt a rising blush heat her throat and cheeks. The echo of that stunning, breath-robbing kiss rushed through her again. She would never forget how the darkness had vanished when the kiss had turned tender and profound.

She had felt so full of relief and gratitude in that moment that she had wanted to kiss him again, resoundingly. She had, quite simply, adored him. But he had turned away, remote once again—and then he had admitted to treachery.

Isobel felt as if she had been struck through the heart. The arrow that had slammed into her arm was a puny thorn compared to the stabbing force of his words.

She watched him now, the proud lift of his head, the strong carriage of his wide shoulders. And she could not believe him capable of such an atrocious crime.

Confusion flooded through her. She had learned that Sir Ralph Leslie was not the staunch knight her father thought him to be. He did indeed hold a woman hostage, and he had lied about his attempt to rescue Isobel to gain Alice's sympathy.

If he believed her dead, his grief did not seem genuine. Isobel scowled. Now she could not trust Ralph any more than she could trust James—but she preferred the outlaw to the knight.

The tiercel fluttered his wings suddenly and squawked. James hushed the bird and halted both horses.

Isobel looked ahead and saw a woman step out of the doorway of the house. Gowned in earthy brown with a snowy headdress, she ducked her head slightly to clear the lintel. She was tall and large, with a warriorlike frame and a cumbersome bosom. She fisted her hands on her broad hips and stared.

"Greetings, aunt." James swung down from his horse.

His aunt stepped toward him and grabbed him in a fierce hug. She stepped back, tears glazing her eyes. "Come inside! They are searching for you!" She looked at Isobel. "Lord save us! Is this the prophetess?"

"Aye," James said. "She is quite alive."

"You heard what the knight said?" Alice stared at him.

"Most of it. We were hiding in the fern brake." James balanced the goshawk on the makeshift leather covering on his fist, and turned to help Isobel dismount. He lifted her down and let go of her quickly. She turned to face his formidable aunt.

"What a sorry pair of travelers," Alice said, shaking her head. "And where did you find that gos?"

" 'Tis a long tale, Alice," James said wearily.

"And I shall hear it, too," Alice said briskly. She reached out a hand toward Isobel. "Tch, look at you, poor lass. Pale as a dove, you are, and just as bonny." Isobel was gathered under the warm circle of Alice's arm and ushered toward the door. "Och, is your arm wounded, then? And you're limping, too." Alice turned to look at James. "How did it happen?"

"Arrow shot," James said as he walked behind them. "Arm and foot, both." Isobel caught his sober glance, and realized he would not mention her blindness.

Alice gaped at him. "Lord save us! An arrow-shot

lady, a raggedy hawk, and Scots and Southrons out
searching for you both." She shook her head. "This lass
is so weary she can hardly stand."

" 'Tis why I brought her here. I knew you would take
us in—without *too* many questions."

"And you ought to be questioned, you great brigand!"
Alice burst out. "How could you allow a lady to be so
mistreated?" She turned a scowl on the goshawk. "Is
that gos trained? He has a wild look to him."

"He's part wild," James said.

"Then be wary of Ragnell if you bring him inside.
You'd best put him in the mews when you look to those
stolen horses. I know English horseflesh when I see it,"
she added crisply.

James hid a smile. "Aye, Alice."

"And dinna smile so at me. I lied for you this day,
laddie, about never seeing you, and I pretended that I
didna know Margaret had been taken into custody. 'Tis
the only sin I commit, such wee lies for you. Pray heavenly forgiveness for me, will you."

"I will," he said. Isobel saw his affectionate smile.

Alice grunted in gruff answer and escorted Isobel inside the little house. The enveloping dimness was relieved only by the glow of a fire in the floor hearth.
Alice led Isobel to a flat-topped wooden chest, where
she sat.

As James crossed the threshold, Isobel heard a shriek
and the rapid flutter of wings. In a dark corner of the
room, a hawk on a tall perch fell backward in a resound-
ing bate.

On James's fist, the tiercel did the same, as if the other
hawk had frightened the wits out of him. James extended
his arm to give the goshawk space for his tantrum.

"Benedicite," Alice said. "That gos has startled her,
and I just got her calmed down from the last visitors."
She bustled toward the perch and spoke soothingly to
the agitated bird.

Isobel sat and watched, blinking from one hawk to the
other, from one owner to the other. Alice's bird was a
large female red-tailed hawk, brown with a bright russet
tail. The tiercel was smaller, but his fit was equally tem-

pestuous. Both Alice and James waited with supreme patience until their bating hawks slowed.

When the tiercel calmed, James lifted him back to his fist. Isobel glanced at the female, who still hung upside down from her jesses, gradually slowing her wings to an occasional twitch.

"Ragnell is making this into a ceremony," James remarked.

"She should have been a mummer, for she loves to perform." Alice heaved the hawk onto the perch. "Och, you spoiled bird," she murmured affectionately, stroking the puffed breast feathers. "Useless, bonny bird."

Ragnell chirred to her mistress and clenched the wooden perch with her feet—or what she had of them. Isobel saw with surprise that the lower part of the bird's left leg was made of silver. The metal foot, strapped on her leg, was shaped into a perfect set of talons that fit over the perch.

"She's missing a foot?" she asked in surprise.

"Since she was a brancher," Alice said. " 'Tis why she is so spoiled, see. We coddled her, and now she rules us."

James stepped into the house cautiously, balancing the goshawk. "Hush, Lady Ragnell. I've brought a friend."

"Aye, be polite, you silly bird," Alice said to her hawk. "I dinna want to hood you, though 'twill calm you. Gentle, now." She spoke to Ragnell for a few moments, then turned to fix James with an intent stare.

"Ho," James said, holding up his hand. "I know that look."

"Aye, I want the truth," Alice said. "Why is Sir Ralph Leslie looking for you? Does he hold Margaret for ransom now?"

James shrugged. "The English want me, and Leslie has joined them. 'Tis widely known that I attacked the party of men who took Wallace. And you know that Leslie was with those who took Margaret and me to Carlisle last spring." He glanced at Isobel, as if explaining in part to her. "When I escaped the English guard weeks ago, Leslie kept Margaret in his custody."

" 'Twas enough that they killed my Tom," Alice said quietly. "I canna bear to lose my niece, too. She insisted on joining her male kin in the forest and fighting with them, but I hoped they would release her when they learned she was a woman. I hope you mean to go after her, Jamie. Naught would please me more." She peered at him. "But now tell me how it is that you have the prophetess, when Leslie thinks her dead?"

"The Southrons besieged her castle, so I took her out of there," James said. "We had to go down the cliff side."

"After setting the castle on fire," Isobel said.

Alice gasped. "This is a grim tale indeed!"

"And gets worse," James said. "Alice, we need your help. The lass needs care and rest."

"Sir Ralph will want to know that she is alive."

"Oh, he will find out," James said grimly.

"He dearly loves the lass. I'm certain of that, at least."

"Aye," James said. "I believe he wants the lady."

Something in his low, quiet voice sent shivers through Isobel. She wished, suddenly, that James was the one who wanted her. A swift, intense memory of shared kisses beneath the fern fronds rushed through her. She drew in a breath and turned away.

"But Leslie willna have her," James continued, looking at Isobel, "until we have Margaret back."

"You mean to barter her for Margaret?" Alice asked.

"I had that in mind."

Alice frowned, hands on hips. "Aye, if he wants her, and she wants him, and we want Margaret, who loses in the trade?"

"Who, indeed?" James murmured, his gaze steady on Isobel.

"Let me go to Wildshaw and ask him to release Margaret," Isobel offered wearily. "I must see my father. He may be at Wildshaw. I must find out."

"Nay," James said.

"I will go there," she said, summoning boldness.

"Is that a prediction?" he inquired softly.

Alice stepped between them. "Let this go for now. Isobel has been too long in the hands of ruffians. She's exhausted. You are both weary."

James nodded as he watched Isobel. She sighed and pushed her fingers through her tangled hair. She curled forward and buried her face in her hand. "I am tired," she admitted.

James turned toward the door. "I'll take the gos to the cave, and I'll tend to the horses."

"Good. Ragnell willna tolerate that gos in the house," Alice said. "She looks ready to bate again." As if she understood, Ragnell uttered a squawk and lifted her wings. "I wonder what has gotten into her."

"We named the gos Gawain," James said. "Mayhap she knows she's met her match, and she doesna like it."

"Hah! She'll never meet her equal," Alice said.

"We all do, Alice," James said. "Soon or late, we meet the one who will do our heart in." He inclined his head briefly to Isobel, turned, and left the house.

Isobel stared after him, her heart pounding.

"Benedicite," Alice said softly. "Will you look at that."

"She snores, your prophetess," Alice observed. "Near as loud as Nigel did. He could shake the bed curtains with his snores, that man."

James laughed softly and swallowed ale from a wooden cup. He looked at his aunt, who sat beside him on the bench near the hearth fire. Her thick fingers wielded a needle as she repaired a rent in Isobel's gown.

The firelight flickered over her face, which creased in a frown. "You and Margaret are all I have left in this world," she said. "Nigel has been gone four years, and our two oldest sons died at Stirling, seven years back. Now young Tom, last spring." She stopped and bit her lower lip.

"I know it has been hard for you," James said softly.

"You must get Margaret back, Jamie."

"I will."

The needle flashed. "I hoped you might marry our Margaret someday. You are cousins by marriage only. She is a good lass."

"Margaret," James said, "has a will like an ox."

Alice chuckled. "Tom said that of her once," she said. " 'Margaret has the will of an ox, and a rump to match, and I dinna want to play with her.' Och, I beat him

about his own rump with my broom when I heard that!"
She laughed again, and James chuckled with her.

She stitched the cloth, and James finished his ale.
Then he heard an audible, wet sniff and looked up to
see his aunt blinking back tears. He sighed.

"Alice—"

"I am fine, lad," she said. "So long as I have you and
Margaret, I am fine." but a shadow passed over her eyes.

James nodded, aware that his aunt deeply mourned
the loss of her husband and all three of her sons to the
cause of Scotland. But she loved James, her sister's son,
and Margaret, her husband's niece, as if they were her
own children.

Something warm shoved against James's leg. He
reached down to pet the large white cat. "Ho, Cosmo,"
James murmured as he stroked the long back. "Have
you been out catching mice for Lady Ragnell? Mayhap
you'll find a few extra for Gawain."

"He only brings mice to Ragnell because he is terrified
of her and tries to appease her," Alice said. "You'll have
to catch mice yourself for that gos of yours. Sparrows,
too. Gosses love sparrows." She glanced up. "Cosmo,
come away from the bed. You'll wake the lass. Shoo!"
She waved at the cat, who turned and settled by the
hearthstones.

James glanced toward Alice's curtained box bed built
into the north wall of the main room, where Isobel still
slept, and would likely slumber until morning. Perhaps
then she would be rested enough that he could finally
ask questions of her.

By the time he had returned to the house after tending
to the hawk and the horses, Isobel was asleep. Alice
had treated the girl's wounds with herbal ointments, had
prepared a bath for her, and had given her a supper of
porridge. While James ate, Alice refreshed the remaining bathwater with a hot bucketful, and James had
stripped and stepped into its luxury.

The water was still scented with lavender and foamed
with the herbal soap that Isobel had used. James had
scrubbed his hair and shaved his unkempt beard, ignoring thoughts of Isobel's cream-skinned body, slick and
nude, sharing the same water.

He forced himself to think about other, simpler matters. He was used to bathing in a cold pool near his forest home. But the warmth and fragrance of the heated water eased his weariness as little else could.

After changing into a tunic and trews of brown serge—the clothing had belonged to his tall, large-boned cousin Tom—he had settled by the fire to explain to his aunt what had happened since he had escaped English custody several weeks before. Alice had listened quietly, and offered steadfast praise for his attempt to save Wallace—though he viewed it as a failure—and the rescue of the besieged inhabitants of Aberlady Castle.

Alice had scolded him regarding Isobel's condition, but James knew that she expressed only fleeting disapproval. No matter what he did, his aunt believed in his integrity.

He was glad that someone did.

Now, as the night deepened to true darkness, they sat quietly together. He associated peaceful moments with Alice's warm hearth, either here in the forest house, or years ago in the Crawford home in Dunfermline.

"She does snore, that one," Alice commented, looking up from her sewing. "Listen to her."

James hid a smile. He found the soft snores emanating from behind the curtain scarcely audible. But Alice had lived in near isolation for a long while, with only her animals for company; she had grown unused to human noise.

"If you tilt her head, she'll quiet," he said.

Alice gave him a sharp glance. "And how do you know that?"

"We slept in the forest last night. I learned it then."

"Ah, I did notice how gently you spoke to her, and how careful you were of her comfort." Her brown eyes twinkled suddenly. "What about our Margaret, eh?"

"Och. 'Tisna the way of it. For either lass," James said sternly. "Isobel is in my safekeeping."

"If that is what you want to call it." Alice stitched the cloth. "How long do you intend to keep her?"

"I'll send word to Leslie soon."

"I think you dinna want to let her go," Alice said softly.

He pressed his lips. "She is far more trouble than you can imagine. I just didna expect her to be injured. She needs some time to recover," he finished lamely. He could not explain to his aunt the tangle that formed his feelings toward the prophetess. He could hardly sort through the threads himself.

"Black Isobel is younger than I would have thought. So young, such a gentle girl, to make such dire and accurate predictions."

"Aye." James leaned forward, fingers spread toward the warmth of the hearth. "She foretold Will's betrayal and his execution, and her prediction laid the blame on me. The hawk of the forest. The Border Hawk. Why, Alice? Who told her to say what she did about Will, and about me?"

"Mayhap she is a genuine prophet," Alice suggested.

"She may be," he said softly, remembering what he had witnessed in the forest. "She may be. But some there are who would have done anything to stop Wallace—and to stop those of us who still fight for Scotland's independence."

"You think Isobel knows who these men might be," she said.

"I wonder if she can name them. Sir Ralph Leslie, for one. But she might know of others who were after Wallace."

"Sir Ralph wears a black armband for Isobel. He loves her."

"I doubt his sincerity," James said. "And he can love and still commit murderous deeds. I have been purposely blamed for Will's betrayal. If there is a scheme, I will learn the truth."

Alice nodded. "You must vindicate your name."

He shook his head. " 'Tis too late for that. I owe this to Will," he said quietly. "Just that."

"Leslie said that he has proof that you betrayed Will. What did he mean? 'Tis surely a lie."

James sighed. He knew that he should tell Alice the truth. But he hesitated, fearing that she would no longer revere him once she learned what he had done. He said nothing.

"Jamie," Alice said quietly. "I would never believe treachery of you. I want you to know that."

James could not trust himself to speak. The silence lingered. " 'Tis late," he finally said. "I must see to the goshawk. He has been in the mews too long without me. I had to hood him to quiet him. With luck, he has slept and hasna bated."

"I hope you mean to get some sleep, too, and not stay up the night watching that hawk to train him."

"I'll sleep," he said. "I will begin his training in the morn."

"You swore never to take on another hawk."

"I found this one hanging in a tree by his jesses. I could hardly leave him, but I'll keep him only until he recovers."

"Aye, well," Alice said philosophically, "mayhap he's a wee gift from the Lord."

"Or a wee trial," James answered, picking up a lighted candle from two fat ones that sat glowing on a shelf.

"You've had too many trials, Jamie. 'Tis time the Lord gave you a gift."

"The Lord doesna seem to agree," he said sourly, and opened the door to step out into the night.

Chapter 13

The goshawk's gaze was captured by the bright candle flame as James crossed the dark cave. Years ago he had sometimes used the tiny, wedge-shaped cave as a mews for Astolat and Ragnell. He set the candle on a natural alcove in the dark stone wall, and angled it so that the hawk could see it. Then he bent down to check the fire in the small iron brazier set in one corner; he had set the peat coals glowing earlier, when he had first brought the hawk to the cave, and the fire was steady now. He knew the hawk would benefit more from warmth and dryness than from cold and damp.

James opened a wooden chest tucked in the farthest angle of the cave. He sifted through an assortment of hawking gear—leather gloves, pouches, straps, brass fastenings, ankle bells, and tiny leather hoods. He chose a particular glove and slipped it on his left hand.

The fit was still perfect, though he had not worn it for years. He flexed his fingers inside the padded lining and adjusted the long gauntlet over his forearm. The leather needed oiling, but otherwise it was in good condition.

He had never intended to wear this glove again, much less to handle a hawk of his own. The glove felt heavy and stiff at first, but soon the worn leather warmed and molded comfortably to his hand.

He looked at the old stain that darkened the palm of the glove. The scrubbed spot was still faintly visible, made by Astolat's blood as she had died in his hand.

The glove stirred other memories of that cursed day when tragedy had struck him again and again before the setting of the sun. James felt the dense weight of that old, congealed sadness, like a burden he could never quite release.

But he shoved the thoughts away, gathered jesses and a pouch, and turned to approach the goshawk, which blinked past him, still entranced by the golden flame. James smiled ruefully.

The half-wild tiercel was handsome, but none too bright. The bird was not likely to enthrall his new master as Astolat had done. She had been a brilliant hunter and a rare, loyal creature; James was sure he would never see her ilk again.

He would keep Gawain until the tiercel recovered, and then he would let him go without regret. James did not want a hawk to hand. The beautiful, difficult creatures complicated life far too much, requiring time and attention he could not give.

"Ho, you gos," he said softly. The goshawk's lids moved like lightning as he watched the flame with utter fascination. James reached out his gloved hand, murmuring to the bird.

As he spoke, he detached the thongs from the tiercel's bracelets and reattached a pair of jesses that had belonged to Astolat. He wrapped the leather straps around his smallest gloved fingers, and nudged his covered fist against the backs of the thin, muscular golden legs.

Gawain must have been thoroughly trained once, James thought. With scarcely a hesitation, the goshawk stepped back and perched on James's fist, his talons flexing firmly on the glove just over the wrist and base of the thumb.

"Good lad," James said. He offered the bird some raw, sliced meat that he had left in the mews earlier, when he had first put the hawk here. "You do remember something of your training. Or else you are just too tired to bate." He sighed, gave the bird more of the meat, and put the rest in the pouch at his belt. Gawain ate quickly and eagerly.

"I dinna have need of a hawk, lad," James said, "but I'll keep you so long as you need care. You'll have to be trained, though, for your manners are poor." He stroked the back feathers softly, knowing that gentle contact would soothe the bird. Yet he was aware that

an abundance of human touching would flatten the
feathers and make them heavy.

When the hawk was done with the meal, James turned
and carried him toward the candle, and blew it out. The
goshawk stirred on his fist, and then quieted, lulled by
the darkness that was relieved only by the red glow of
the brazier. James knew the young hawk was tired, and
perhaps in pain from what appeared to be a sprained
wing.

"So, Sir Gawain, the manning begins," James said, the
words floating low and gentle in the darkness. "I am
your source of food now. I am your captor, and I am
your freedom. You will learn to know my voice like the
beat of your own heart." He smoothed his finger pads
over the breast feathers as he spoke.

Isobel drifted into his thoughts like a summer mist,
softening his mood. He was her captor as well. With the
bird, he must work toward an exchange of wary trust
between master and hawk. That was all he could ask for
with such a wild, elemental creature.

The woman was already gentled, with a fine and delicate character, but James craved the gift of her trust.
Still, he thought he would never have it of her; the tension between them was too great. And he would keep
the hawk longer than he would keep Isobel.

He drew breath, watching the hawk, and began to sing
softly, repeating the notes in a haunting, airy pattern.

"Ky-ri-e e-le-i-son. Ky-ri-e e-le-i-son."

Threads of moonlight slipped through the entrance,
which was shielded by tree branches and vines. In the
thin light, James saw the goshawk tip his head curiously
to listen. He sang the phrase again.

"Ky-ri-e e-le-i-son. Ky-ri-e e-le-i-son."

He had thought about the call he would use for this
bird during the hours he had ridden beside Isobel in the
forest. Somehow this one fit. The melody had an elusive
serenity, the notes rising and vanishing like the graceful,
soaring flight of a hawk.

He hummed it again, soft and low. Steady repetition
would teach the hawk to recognize the phrase as his
master's call. He talked to the bird, his tone patient,
quiet. James sang, and murmured, and walked the bird

around the dark mews, forcing the hawk to stay awake, and keeping himself alert, in order to achieve taming as quickly as possible. He knew that as long as the tiercel continued to bate and throw fits of fury due to wildness, the wing would never heal properly, and new injuries could occur. Although he intended to release the goshawk later, he knew that he must reclaim him for now.

And all the while, as he walked and stroked and sang to the bird, he thought about faith. He wanted faith and trust from the goshawk. He had it freely from Alice, no matter what he did. And he had sensed it, fleetingly, from Isobel, and tasted it like honey on her lips.

He craved more from her, but knew she had changed her mind about him again. He had seen trust flicker within her like a flame, now bright, now fading.

But when he had admitted to her that, indeed, he had taken part in Wallace's betrayal, he had watched the spark of faith disappear utterly in her eyes.

He could not blame her. He had lost faith in himself.

In the darkness of the curtained bed, Isobel awoke to quiet, comfortable sounds: Alice hummed at some task, the fire crackled, Ragnell chirred, and rain pattered on the roof. She pulled the covers high and peered out through the curtains.

"There you are!" Alice stood by the table, kneading a large mound of pale dough.

"Greetings, Dame Crawford," Isobel said hoarsely.

"Just Alice," the woman corrected her. She grinned. "You have slept nearly two full days! Good rest heals, though."

Isobel blinked in amazement. "Two days? I remember waking a few times to eat and get up."

"But you could scarcely speak, you were so tired." Alice smiled. "If you want to get up now, we must get some food into you for strength." Alice worked as she talked, her sleeves pushed up, her hands capable as she punched and folded the dough.

Isobel glanced around the room. "Where is—"

"Jamie's with his gos. Gawain, he says you call it." Alice laughed. "He asked me to bake bread for the tiercel, so I've been at that task most of the afternoon."

"Bread for the hawk? I didna think they ate bread."

"They dinna. 'Tis for something else. Jamie knows I have the way of making bread, though few Scots do. But milled wheat is hard to find, with the Southrons harassing all Scotland and denying us their goods in trade." She worked the dough while she spoke. " 'Tis muckle hard to buy wheat from them, and Scottish wheat is a sparse crop. Jamie brings me milled wheat when he can get it. He brought me some two weeks past, and so I said aye, I could bake bread today. And if he stole this flour from the English, I dinna want to know."

"Stole it?"

"Och, he is an outlaw." Alice shrugged. "And he doesna care for Southrons. A few times, he and his men took supplies from Southron packhorses being led through the forest, and gave the wheat and other goods round the countryside.

"You see," she continued, "there are many Scots with empty larders and fields, and even homeless, because of the Southrons who come through the Lowlands, stealing and burning. Jamie says we are owed goods back in trade." She shaped a few fat, round loaves. "This is a good, chewy bread I make. I use wheat, barley, and oats in the flour, and bere hops to rise it. You had best eat your fill of it, lass. You are all bones."

Isobel blushed and glanced at her thin forearms and the ribbed shadows along her breastbone. "I am hungry," she said.

"Good. I'll feed you well. First you'll want to dress. Your gown and surcoat are mended and freshened, and folded by your feet." Alice set the loaves aside and covered them with a cloth. "Let me help you, since you have but one arm to use."

Within a short time, Isobel was bathed, dressed, and seated by the table with her right arm snug in a sling, and her left hand holding a cup of warm spiced wine. Alice set a bowl of hot porridge on the table and stuck a wooden spoon in it.

"When the bread is baked, we'll take some to Jamie. Eat."

Isobel ate. Alice carried the loaves outside to a stone bread oven behind the house. When she returned, she refilled the porridge bowl. Isobel finished nearly all of that helping, too.

"Good lass," Alice said. "You're tall, but slim as a reed. Jamie said you hardly ate for weeks, due to the siege."

Isobel nodded, and answered Alice's questions about the ordeal at Aberlady Castle. Hearing thunder, she glanced toward the windows, tiny openings covered in oiled parchment that let in a faint grayish light. Rain battered the roof and the door.

" 'Tis a soft rain," Alice said. "But we will get wet when we take the bread to Jamie."

"Where is he?"

" 'Tisna far, a walk through the greenwood and up a long slope to a cave," Alice said. "He set it up for a mews long ago, and he took the goshawk there. Can you walk on that ankle?"

Isobel stretched her foot. "It feels much better. I can walk well enough." Hearing a flutter of wings, she glanced up.

Ragnell left her perch and flew across the room, landing on the back of a chair. Her silver leg and claw foot thumped down as she found her balance. The large bird fixed Isobel with a gleaming rust-red eye.

"She isna leashed to the perch?" Isobel asked.

"Ragnell flies where she pleases," Alice said. "She is free to come and go, even outside." She smiled. "She willna go far. She canna live on her own out there, one-legged and spoiled to the fist as she is, and she knows it."

"What happened to her leg?" Isobel asked.

"Ragnell was given to my husband as a wounded eyas—that is, an infant bird taken from the nest to be trained. Nigel was a royal falconer," Alice said as she poured steaming, spice-scented wine into Isobel's cup, and a second cup for herself.

Isobel nodded. "I know. Jamie told me about him."

Alice picked up a leather glove and slipped it on, raising her hand. With a rapid fluttering, Ragnell crossed the room, wings spread, to land on her mistress's fist. "Ragnell had been attacked by a jealous merlin in another man's mews. Nigel thought she would die, but she was a fierce wee hawk."

Alice produced a bit of raw meat from a dish by the hearth and fed the bird a morsel, wiping her fingers on a cloth. "Her wounded foot turned black and fell off. Nigel made her a false one, and then others as she grew larger. She learned to fly and perch wearing the silver foot. She even learned to fly at quarry, though she doesna prefer that. She's spoiled to the fist and only feeds there. Och, my lazy, silly bird," she cooed.

Ragnell kakked and stretched down to clean her beak sideways on the glove. She opened her tail wide, shot a wet mute across the floor, and blinked at Isobel.

Alice made a disparaging sound. "She wants you to know she's queen here. Nay, dinna—I'll clean it up. Lady Ragnell has trained me for her handmaiden. 'Tis the price I pay for such noble company, I suppose. We're alone here, Ragnell and I, but for the cat, the goat, and the chickens. Ragnell's made a mewling servant of the cat, too, but so far the goat ignores her."

"It must be pleasant to live alone, with no one to answer to but yourself," Isobel said.

" 'Tis lonely, lass."

"Sometimes I think living alone would be like paradise. I have always obeyed someone—my father, my priest. Now my betrothed will want the same obeisance from me. Mayhap I should go into the forest and live as an anchoress."

"You dinna look like you would be content as a religious hermitess."

"You have found contentment alone. Mayhap I shall, too."

Alice shrugged and stroked the bird. "I dinna choose to be alone, lass. My sons and my husband are dead, all gone fighting for Scotland." Isobel saw Alice's eyes pinken with unshed tears. She sighed, shook her head. "All I have is Jamie, and Margaret, and this arrogant bird." She cooed at Ragnell. "I hope one day that James will wed Margaret. They're cousins, but only by marriage."

"Jamie would do anything for you," Isobel said softly, feeling a deep inner tug as she realized that James loved this Margaret so well that he would risk all to gain her back.

Alice smiled. "He is like one of my own sons, though he's a brigand and a rogue."

"Alice, is he a traitor?" Isobel asked. The question had troubled her ever since James had implied that he was.

Alice shook her head. "Nay. He doesna have that in him."

"Ralph claims there is proof of it."

"There canna be." She frowned. "But Jamie looks haunted, as if he keeps a secret to himself. But then, he has carried a heavy burden ever since Wildshaw was taken by the English."

"What do you mean?" Isobel asked.

"He has many deaths on his conscience."

Isobel frowned. "Do you mean those he killed in battle?"

"Such deeds bother him, but he is a warrior, and nae the priest his father wanted him to be. Battle deaths are deemed righteous deaths by the Church, and I am sure he confesses those and is absolved. But what sits upon Jamie's shoulders like a yoke are the deaths of . . . those he loved, though he didna cause their deaths." Alice got to her feet to set the bird on a perch. She took off her glove and turned. "That bread will be done now," she said crisply. "Come outside with me, lass."

She lifted a cloak from a wall peg and threw it around her shoulders, then held out Isobel's own cloak and waited while she came forward to put it on.

"We'll take the bread to Jamie and his gos," Alice said. "And we'll hope that the rain will keep Sir Ralph away for now."

Isobel followed Alice out into an increasing rain, her heart thumping wildly as she anticipated seeing James again. And she wondered what would happen after that. Would he insist on keeping her captive—or would he let her go? She wondered if she should try to escape.

For now, she thought, as she walked through the wet grass, she had no choice but to stay with Alice and James. She hardly limped at all, and soon her foot would be strong enough for the long trek through the forest to Wildshaw Castle.

As she passed between the trees, cool raindrops sprinkled over her cheeks and hair, and the damp breeze filled each breath. She inhaled deeply and sensed the freedom, somehow, in the scent.

Most of her life had been spent inside castle walls, effectively imprisoned by the will of those who would protect her. For the first time in her life, she tasted freedom and independence, and craved more.

Yet, ironically, she was still a captive.

Chapter 14

Isobel clutched a loaf of hot bread, wrapped in coarse cloth, and savored its warmth as she followed Alice through the murky rain. They climbed up a long, rocky slope and halted near the top. A massive rock face soared beyond the earthen crest of the hill, a bleak stone surface covered with scrub and vines.

Alice walked toward the craggy rock. At first glance, Isobel saw several deep crevices. Alice edged along between the rock and huge clumps of prickly gorse.

Isobel, following, saw that one of the deep shadows was actually a narrow opening, obscured by thick green growth. Alice put a finger to her lips as they approached the cave.

From out of the rock came an unexpected sound. Mellifluous and deep, a singer created a resonant, low harmony with the silvery patter of the rain. Isobel looked at Alice in amazement.

"Jamie sang with the Benedictines at Dunfermline, in a choir the angels themselves would have praised," Alice murmured proudly. "When he was a lad, he sang alone for King Alexander. Now he sings to his hawk, I think." She called out his name.

The chanting stopped. "Come in, Alice," James said.

Alice turned sideways to squeeze her bulk through the small opening. Isobel followed her into darkness. The cave was narrow at the entrance, and widened somewhat toward the back. Gray light filtered through the opening, and a glowing brazier gave out a dry heat. A wooden perch stood on the floor, which was covered in sand and earth to absorb the bird's mutes.

James sat on a long bench, his back leaned against the
dark stone wall. The goshawk perched on his gloved fist.

"Alice," James said softly. He and the goshawk both
fixed their bright gazes on Isobel. "Lady Isobel," James
said. She nodded.

"We brought the bread," Alice said.

"Fresh baked, still hot?" James asked, sitting up. Isobel noticed he kept his voice soft and low for the bird's
benefit. She perceived, too, the undercurrent of fatigue
in his slumped shoulders and in the shadows beneath his
eyes. The goshawk stirred restively, and James shushed
him.

"Certes, hot, or 'twould be of little use to the bird,"
Alice said. "And here's a loaf for yourself." She came
close to James to set a wrapped loaf on the bench.

The goshawk bated, throwing himself from James's
fist, flapping his wings and kakking. James extended his
arm with a resigned expression while the bird beat the
air furiously.

" 'Twillna last long," he told them. "He is exhausted."

"As are you," Alice said sternly. "Have you slept at
all these two days?"

He shrugged. The goshawk stilled, and James lifted
him back to the fist. "Some."

"Hmph," she said. "You will kill yourself for that
bird. I thought Ragnell was queen of the ruined birds,
but that tiercel is almost worse."

"He isna as bad as you think," James said.

She grunted doubtfully. "Well, Nigel taught you well.
If anyone can reclaim that gone-to-wild gos, 'tis you."

Gawain flapped his wings in agitation and opened his
beak repeatedly to squawk.

"What is bothering him?" Isobel asked.

"Alice makes him nervous," James said.

"Aye, he sees me and remembers that great fright
Ragnell gave him yesterday," Alice said. "Gosses do
learn quick, but they can be stupid, just the same—there,
Gawain, go easy, the rude lady red-tail isna with me,"
she told the hawk. "Och, there he goes again." Gawain
batted his wings, and James held him out patiently. "I
willna stay and ruffle him further. Do you need anything
more, Jamie? We'll be back to bring more food later."

"I want Lady Isobel to stay here," James said.

"Stay?" Isobel asked. "Here?"

"I need help tending the bird, and Alice canna come near him." He gave his attention to the hawk. Isobel and Alice watched until the bird finally settled down. James put him on the fist and fed him a strip of raw meat. "There, that's for going back to the fist, laddie," he said. He looked at Isobel. "Are you stronger? You walked up here, so your foot must be better. Can you help me with Gawain?"

His quiet voice, as compelling as his gaze, sent curious shivers through her, and a hot blush rose in her cheeks. Her heartbeat grew heavy, suddenly, as if in anticipation. "I am well enough," she said.

"She slept all this time, so she's rested," Alice said. "If you have any wit left, Jamie—which I misdoubt after so long without sleep—you will let her watch that gos for you while you nap. I'll be back." She went to the cave opening, squeezed out with a mutter and a grunt, and was gone.

Isobel lifted the wrapped, warm loaf that she held in her hands. "Shall we feed this bread to him?"

"He isna going to eat it. Come here." He patted the bench. "Sit beside me. The bird will have another fit if he canna see you clear."

She sat where he indicated. Her left shoulder brushed against his arm. With his free hand, James withdrew his dirk from the sheath at his belt and handed it to her. "Cut the loaf in two," he directed.

She did so, a bit awkwardly, with her left hand. Hot steam rose into the air between them, and she closed her eyes briefly, smiling as she inhaled the comforting smell of fresh bread.

"Are you hungry?" James sounded amused. "We'll share my loaf later. Cut one half, slicing partway through. Aye, good. Now slide the split bread over his left wing."

Isobel hesitated. "You want me to put the bread on his wing?" she asked, incredulous.

"Aye. He has a sprained wing. See the way it droops at the top? When he spreads his wings, he doesna lift that one quite so high. His bates are making the sprain worse. The damp heat from hot bread is a good, simple treatment."

"Ah." Isobel lifted the cut loaf toward the bird. Gawain screeched, striking out with his talons. Isobel snatched her hand away and nearly dropped the bread. "I make him nervous, too. Should I go?"

" 'Twasna you that alarmed him. He is used to your voice and face. But he doesna know if the bread is friend or foe."

Isobel chuckled. James smiled, a quick dazzle that set her heart to thumping. He turned to murmur gently to the hawk. Then he rose to his feet, carrying the hawk, and took an object from among a tangle of leather things on top of a small wooden chest. He returned to sit beside her.

"Hush, now," James said to Gawain. With deft, quick fingers, he dropped a leather hood over the hawk's head.

Gawain fluttered his wings, stretched his neck as if to protest the hood, and became utterly still and silent.

Isobel gasped. "Nay," she whispered. "You blind him with the hood—" She reached out.

"Careful!" James grabbed her fingers. She lowered her hand. James sighed. "Look, he isna troubled by it at all."

The goshawk did seem content. Isobel told herself that she was foolish to react with alarm over blindfolding the bird.

"He doesna fight it," she said, watching the tiercel.

"Hawks are quieted by darkness, so hoods help to calm them," James explained. "Gawain has obviously been hooded before." He glanced at her. " 'Tisna cruel, Isobel."

"I know," she murmured. " 'Tis necessary sometimes."

"Aye. We canna tend to his shoulder unless he's calm. I wouldna mistreat a bird. They only accept gentleness and patience. These creatures canna be forced."

She felt her cheeks warm under his gaze. She wondered if his quiet, affectionate tone was meant for the bird's benefit, or was directed at her. "You've been kind. For a brigand," she said.

His eyes twinkled. "I've learned well from hawks."

"Aye, you have." She smothered a smile. James

looked at the goshawk, scratching the bird's puffed-out breast with a fingertip.

True, she thought. His calm, patient manner, his low, soothing voice, even the agile way he moved had all been influenced by years of caring for hawks. Her father's falconers, and her father, too, had that same way about them, of purposefully gentled strength. She watched as James adjusted the tiny strap of the hawk's hood with long, nimble fingers. All the while, he murmured soothing phrases to the hawk.

"My father sometimes said that falconers would make excellent mothers," she said.

He huffed a low laugh. "Aye. 'Tis like mothering, in a way. We must care for a young thing with endless patience, and we often must put its needs before our own."

He began to hum the chant again. The notes rose and fell in mellow nuances. Isobel leaned her head back against the rock wall and listened, succumbing to his deliberate magic.

On another day, he had waved his hand in languid patterns over the hawk's head, seducing her into this same dreamlike state. Now he wove the spell with his beautiful voice. As the hawk surrendered, so did she.

"Ah," James whispered after a while. "He is calm. Place the bread over the top of his wing, if you will."

If he had asked her to set the loaf on her own hand, she might have done it without question. She stirred herself out of her reverie and raised the bread toward the bird.

James lifted his free hand to guide her, his long fingers gentle on hers. Together they eased the warm bread over the joint of the bird's wing and shoulder. Gawain shifted a little beneath their combined touch.

"Easy, bonny gos," James said softly. Isobel kept her hand on the bread and James let his hand rest over hers. Steamy heat gathered between their fingers.

He sang the *kyrie* again. The melodic drone thrummed through her body, as soothing as the heat and the gentle pressure of his fingers over hers.

She closed her eyes. When he stopped, she looked up at him in the silence. He leaned back against the wall

and flexed his fingers over hers. Then he lifted his hand
away. She missed its comfort as she continued to hold
the warm bread compress on the bird's wing.

"You have a beautiful voice," she said. "Like spiced
wine, warm and cozy somehow. Your aunt said you sang
for a king."

"I did, as a lad. I was in the choir at Dunfermline. I
sang hymns when King Alexander came to mass. No
terror could quite compare to that," he said wryly.
"Knees knocking, hands shaking, a ten-year-old lad standing alone before a king and his court. Later, when I went
to the seminary school in Dundee, I sang in the monks'
choir there. My singing voice survived the journey into
manhood, as it happened." He smiled.

"Seminary? Did you study to be a priest?"

"My father wanted that," he said. "But 'twas at Dundee that I met William Wallace and John Blair, who
became a Benedictine, though he still fought at Wallace's side and acted as his confessor. When Wallace left
Dundee and became a rebel, I stayed at the school, hearing more and more stories of his deeds. I stole away one
night and went to join him. I was sixteen."

"Was your father angry?"

"My father," he said, "was a rebel himself, hiding out
from the English because he refused to sign an oath of
fealty to the English king. They killed him a few years
later." He watched the bird and murmured to it. Then
he glanced at Isobel. "My older brother, who had inherited our father's castle, died at Falkirk. Shortly after
that, the English took Wildshaw by treachery and fire."

"And they have kept it ever since?" she asked.

"Ever since."

"You couldna win it back?"

"Nay," he said, so quietly she hardly heard him. "I
couldna." He reached up to adjust the bread on the
bird's wing, his fingers dry and warm as they glided over
hers. She saw that he meant to take over the task of
balancing the bread, and she lifted her hand away to
rest it in her lap.

She wanted to hear more about his life as a rebel and
how he had lost Wildshaw, but she sensed that he did
not want to talk about it beyond what he had said. "You

have spent half your life fighting and hiding," she observed.

He smiled ruefully. "I suppose I have." He began to sing the *kyrie* again, low and mellifluous, sending wonderful shivers through her.

"Why do you sing that phrase, over and over?" she asked. "Does it remind you of the past?"

"I'm teaching Gawain to recognize it as the call I will use for him. Later I'll whistle it, so he will know it in different ways. Then I will add food to the routine, feeding him each time he hears the phrase. When he learns to trust me, he'll come quickly, without fear of threat."

"Ah," Isobel said. "I thought you sang it because you still longed for the peace of the monkish life."

"Sometimes I do think about that peace," he said quietly.

They sat watching the hawk, and James hummed the melody again. Gawain tipped his hooded head as if he listened avidly and tried to work out a puzzle. Isobel felt a bubbling urge to laugh. The goshawk looked comical with the small leather hood over his head, like a hat fallen down over his eyes, the loaf of bread perched absurdly on his wing. She giggled.

"He looks like a king's jester, or a mummer in a Yuletide play," she said.

James smiled. "He does look silly." Then he shook his head slightly. "I never thought to be sitting here again, going without sleep and nursing a hawk."

"You have stayed awake these last two days?"

"I have dozed some." He yawned and jiggled the goshawk, whose head had begun to droop. "But whenever Sir Gawain starts to sleep, I try to wake him up."

Isobel studied James's face in the flickering light of the glowing brazier. His eyes were weary, surrounded by shadows, and he was pale with fatigue. She noticed the shape of his lower lip, slightly full and moist, the creases beside his mouth, the dark sand of his day-old beard, which softened the edges of his jaw.

"Why do you force yourself to do this?" she asked softly.

" 'Tis the quickest way to tame a hawk."

"But hardest on the falconer and the bird," she said.

"When I was small, my father would carry new hawks or falcons throughout the day, and set them in darkness at night, keeping them close to him for a week or two. My mother objected to the birds sitting on his fist at mealtimes, and didna like having them sleep on a perch in their bedchamber. But he insisted that it took time to train each one properly."

"Time," James said, "is what I dinna have. I didna plan on taming a hawk."

She scowled. "You only planned to abduct a prophetess."

"True." He looked at her intently. Then he lifted the bread. " 'Tis still warm. We will keep it there until it cools."

"Can we eat the other half?" she asked plaintively.

James chuckled. "Aye, we'll share." She tore the remainder of the loaf apart and handed James the larger portion, and they ate in silence.

"I'm glad you are here," James murmured when they were done.

"Aye?" she asked, feeling shy.

"Aye. You keep me awake, and I'll keep him awake."

"Oh." She had almost hoped to hear something else from him. She glanced up and saw the curve and gentle swell of his lips, and vividly recalled the feel of his lips on hers. Reminding herself to be wary of this man suddenly became a challenge.

"Talk to me, Isobel," he said, leaning his head against the wall with a sigh. "I am as sleepy as this bedecked hawk."

She began to tell him about her father's mews, and he asked interested questions, his voice hoarse with fatigue. The hawk drooped his head, and James wiggled his fist to stir him. Then he asked about her childhood and her life at Aberlady.

She spoke quietly while James listened, holding the bread on the bird's wing. He lifted his left foot to the bench so that he could rest his forearm, with the bird, on his knee.

"So after your mother died, your father and the priest have been the only ones to witness your prophecies?" he asked.

"And lately Sir Ralph," she said. "My father invited him to watch the sessions when 'twas agreed we would wed. He wanted Ralph to know what to do."

"What to do when the blindness comes?"

"What to do during the visions. My father and the priest talk to me and ask me questions. And Father Hugh writes down whatever I say. I canna recall it, usually."

He slid her a penetrating glance. "You recall naught?"

"Very little," she answered, "as you have seen yourself."

His straight brows pulled together. "Who was with you when you prophesied about Wallace?"

"Those three."

"And the priest recorded everything that you said?"

"Aye," she said. "He presented some of it to his parish after that, and sent a copy to the Guardians of the Realm. But he didna reveal all that I had said about Wallace right away. He and my father knew 'twould cause distress. So they kept it to themselves for a while, and let it out, finally, a week before it happened." She shook her head and sighed. "How were they to know 'twould happen so soon after that?"

"How, indeed." She frowned at his cynical tone and looked up. James fixed her with a glance from the corner of his eye. "Do you know what you said about Wallace?" he asked. "Do you know what you said about me, Isobel?"

She looked away, feeling uncomfortable. "I know some of what I said that day. That bread must be cool now," she said, a little sharply. "What else should we do for the hawk?"

She did not want to talk about the prophecies. She liked the peacefulness of the warm, dark cave, and she liked James's soothing voice and his gentle mood. To speak of the predictions only created tension between them. She felt the strain already.

James removed the compress and brushed the crumbs from the goshawk's feathers. "I thought you forgot all of what you saw."

He was a stubborn, intelligent man, and Isobel knew that he was not going to be distracted. She got to her feet and went to stand before the brazier, holding out her hands to its warmth.

"That one time," she said, "I did my best to remember. I made Father Hugh read me every word of it, though he tells me 'tis best if I dinna know what I foretell. He and my father, and Sir Ralph, too, were upset with me for asking about that vision."

"Why?" James asked. He spoke harshly, and the hawk ruffled his feathers in response. "Why do they want to keep you from knowing?" he asked, more softly.

She shrugged. "My father says 'tis too much responsibility for me. And Father Hugh says the visions are too erudite for one of my small education and feeble female mind."

James huffed, a skeptical sound. "You have a distinctly female way of looking at the world, aye. But 'tis hardly a feeble mind. Just the opposite, I would say."

She nodded, flustered by his compliment. She looked into the bright heart of the brazier. "Father Hugh interprets the visions carefully to understand the symbolism. He says there is much deep meaning in them. He believes that the prophecies come from God, in the language of the patriarchs, and must be studied with care." She shrugged. "He is preparing a book of the prophecies, though I have asked him not to do that. But he says he will gain much respect through them."

"Let us hope he intends to share the honors with the prophetess," James muttered. "Tell me the rest."

"After that day, I tried to recall the visions myself, but only parts came to me. I begged my father to tell me what I had said. But I didna trust—" She stopped.

James sat forward. "Didna trust whom?"

She lowered her head. "I didna trust any of them to tell me the truth about my words," she murmured. "And I wanted to know."

"Why would they lie to you?" His voice was a sea of gentleness. She wanted to sink into its rhythm and warmth.

"My father and the priest have always protected me, and so they kept secrets from me. When I was younger, my father felt that he should guard me from the outside world. But even when I grew older, he did not relax his protection."

"Have you always seen visions?" he asked.

"They began when I was thirteen," she said. "I suffered a serious fever for several days and nearly died. Afterward, I lost my sight for a month. During the worst of the fever, in a kind of delirium, I described a battle between English and Scots that hadna yet taken place. My parents and the priest were with me, for Father Hugh had come to give me the last rites."

James watched her steadily. "Dear God," he murmured. "And did the battle come about?"

"A few days after the vision, it happened just as I had said. Father Hugh told my parents that my prophesy was a gift from heaven, bestowed by the angels when I lay on the brink of death. He told my father that such a gift must be used. He said the angels could speak through me to benefit all of Scotland."

James sighed. "And then the priest and your father discovered that they had a way of predicting the war."

She shrugged. "I dinna know if they thought that. They told me little. I did as they asked."

"Of course. You were but a lass," James said.

"My father and the priest, and my mother, too, seemed to truly cherish me once I became a prophetess. I was suddenly more than just a tall, awkward, timid lass to be wed off to some eligible knight. So I did what I could to please them. The visions came easily enough, but the blindness and the forgetfulness were horrible to endure." She looked away, bit her lip. "Father Hugh says 'tis the price I must pay for the gift."

James sat silently, watching her. "Ah, lass," he said, sounding sad, as if he felt her pain himself. "You are a rebel, and a warrior, and dinna even know it."

She tipped her head. "What do you mean?"

"You endure much," he said softly. "And you fight in your own way."

"How so?"

"Your blindness and forgetfulness are like a battle within yourself—a protest at being forced by others to prophesy."

Isobel felt a weight turn inside her gut as she realized the truth of his words. She stared at him. "My God," she whispered, shocked. "Can it be so?"

James sighed. "Isobel," he murmured. "Come here."
He patted the bench. She did not move. "I would come
to you, lass," he murmured, "but I am so tired I dinna
think my knees will hold me upright."

Still she did not move, watching him, partly entranced
by his gaze and voice, and partly caught by the stunning
truth he had revealed to her.

"Come here," he whispered again, and held out a
hand.

Chapter 15

Isobel sat beside him, and James touched her hand. The quick, soft brush of his fingertips seemed to caress her entire being. She trembled inside as she looked up at him.

"Do you think the blindness and the forgetfulness could leave me, then?" she asked.

"They might, if you ever found peace with your gift," he said. "In the seminary, we studied the intricate symbolism that exists throughout life, the reflection of the heavenly and earthly realms in objects, in thoughts, in everything. Your blindness is like a symbol of some sort. I think it reflects a struggle inside yourself."

"Father Hugh saw that, too. But he said it reflects my unworthiness to know the full truth of God."

He grimaced. "I doubt it. The blindness may not come from the hand of God at all, but from your own fears. I have heard of cases of blindness where it goes away on its own, when 'twas thought hopeless. My uncle, who was blind in one eye, once had a bout of blindness in the other eye. A sensible wise woman brought him herbal medicines and told him that his sight would improve only when he stopped being afraid of the blindness in the eye that he had lost. He thought about what she said. A week later, his sight was restored—quite miraculously."

She frowned, considering that. "But I dinna fear the visions."

"You might fear the insistence from others that you prophesy again and again." He shrugged.

She rubbed her fingers over her eyes. "Dear God. I think you could be right."

He leaned his head against the rock wall. "Sometimes it needs another to show us truths about ourselves," he said softly.

"There are many forms of blindness," she agreed.

"True," he said. "Tell me—why did you try to recall your prediction about Wallace?"

She sighed. The hawk chittered and shifted on James's fist. "I am able to understand my visions," she began. "I see their meaning clearly when they come to me, but then I forget it. My father and the priest think the symbolic meanings are beyond my intelligence. But I know what I see. That day, I knew I had to remember what I saw."

"Why?" he asked again.

"I wanted to warn Wallace," she said. "I never doubt the truth of my visions. That much I have learned. What is harder to know is the exact meaning of what I see."

He watched her. "Did you warn Wallace?"

"I wrote a note with my own hand, and begged my father to deliver it." She twisted her hands together. "He said he would. But the three of them—my father, the priest, and Sir Ralph—acted strangely about that vision. The images I remembered alarmed me. I knew that Wallace would come to a dishonorable fate, and a horrible end." She sighed. "But my note to him was sent in vain. He died, and just as I foresaw." She felt the quick sting of gathering tears.

"If he received your note, he would have been grateful to you. He respected prophecy—he had dreams of his own that foretold events, and he mentioned your prophecies once or twice. But I doubt Will would have needed a warning."

"I couldna bear to know such a thing about a man and keep silent about it." She frowned at him through a glaze of tears. A drop spilled down.

James touched his thumb to her cheek, and his hand drifted down to cup her shoulder. She was glad of the warmth and weight of his touch, for she felt forlorn and remorseful.

"We both tried to help him," he said.

"We?" she whispered. She leaned the side of her head

against the rock wall, as he did. His eyes were but a hand span from hers.

"Regardless of what else I have done, I tried to help Wallace the night he was taken. My attempt came to naught but trouble."

"How?" she asked.

"I hid among the trees and shot one arrow after another at those who beat him and took him. I killed several guards," he said. "I dinna know how many. I thought to reduce their numbers so that I could get to him myself, or provide him a chance to get away. I was half-mad with rage and guilt, I think."

"Guilt?"

He sighed. "What you did, what I did, both came to naught."

She rested her hand on his arm. "You did help him."

He slid her a glance. "Isobel, he is dead."

"James, did Wallace see you there, fighting for him?"

"I think so," he said slowly.

"Then he knew you tried to save him."

His eyelids lowered pensively. He nodded. "Aye, but—"

"You helped him, James," she said firmly. "He knew that he wasna alone. That must have seemed like a blessing to him."

"I hadna thought of that." He watched her for a moment. She rested her head against the wall, as he did, and returned his gaze.

Then he shifted forward, and touched his lips to hers.

Isobel tilted her head backward, drinking in the soft, warm kiss. The brush of his mouth on hers brought a delicious shock that burst in her center and blossomed outward.

He moved back and gazed at her. The goshawk perched on his fist made tiny noises in his throat.

She stared up at James. "What—what was that for?"

He smiled a little. "A gesture of thanks. 'Twas you who took the blindness from me this time," he said.

"Blindness?" she asked.

"The scales from my eyes, as it were." His mouth quirked in a sad, fleeting smile. "Mayhap I did help Will in some small way. You canna know how much it means to me to think that."

Her heart thumped. "I owe you a—a gesture of thanks as well, for interpreting the symbolism of my blindness as you did."

He looked at her, his eyes crinkling in a private smile.

She leaned forward, drifting her eyes shut, waiting, hoping for the divine touch of his mouth to hers once again.

He slid toward her, his breath soft on her cheek. She waited, eyes closed, heart pounding. He let out a breath, and then his finger touched her lips and lifted.

"Nay," he whispered.

She opened her eyes wide, startled.

"Nay, lass," he murmured. "I canna be trusted."

"I trust you, Jamie," she whispered, her gaze full of him, taking in his deep eyes in the warm, dim light, the red-gold sheen on his hair, the full curve of his lower lip.

"But if I so much as touch you," he said, his voice like a caress, "I will be guilty of more than taking a woman hostage."

Her heartbeat increased to thunder. She reached up and cupped her palm against his cheek. His face was warm and prickly against her skin. "And if I touch you?" she asked softly.

He closed his eyes. "Dinna do that, lass," he whispered.

Before, she had been taken in by the rhythmic grace of his moving hand as he entranced the hawk, and the thrum of his voice as he sang. Now it was the solid, steady thump of his heart, sensed in the pulse that beat against the heel of her hand, that pulled her toward him. She could not stop herself.

She closed her eyes and touched the strong shape of his jaw, with its grainy texture of beard. She slid her fingertips downward and felt the outline of his mouth, felt the warmth of his breath over her fingers.

"Isobel," he whispered. She felt his mouth moving on her fingers. She sucked in a breath.

James sighed out, a low groan. He dipped toward her and pressed his mouth to hers, hungry and hard, kissing her as he had under the cover of the ferns. Rich and full, the kiss delved deep inside of her, overturning her like a wave might take a boat. She was lost, drifting, anchored only by his mouth, by his breath, by the touch of his hand upon her cheek.

His fingers slipped inside the curtain of her hair. He tugged gently, angling her head, opening his mouth over hers, his lips moving in a delectable rhythm, rising and falling, opening and closing.

Isobel tipped back her head and gave in to the shivers that plunged and swirled within her. She followed the rhythm he set, her lips moving in harmony with his.

The hawk shifted and squawked. James lifted his mouth away and sat back. He murmured something low—Isobel thought it sounded like an oath—and turned toward the hawk, resting his gloved fist on his upraised knee. He ran his fingers through his thick hair in an exasperated gesture.

Isobel folded her good arm around her waist, heart still thumping. She felt heat seep into her cheeks and endured a sudden agony of shame at her unsuitable boldness. She lowered her head.

"I was foolish," she whispered, not looking at him.

"You?" He shook his head. " 'Twas my foolishness, lass. None of this is happening as I planned. None of it—the besieged castle, the hawk, you—"

"Me?"

"Especially you," he said wryly. "I thought the prophetess would be easy enough to manage. A woman who didna care for me, nor I for her. I would steal her away in a sack, hide her in a cave, send a message to Ralph, and have Margaret back again."

She ducked her head, her hair sliding down. She covered her eyes with her hand. "That is all you want of me," she whispered. "You will use me as a means to get back Margaret."

He laughed, a bitter sound, lacking humor. "All I want of you?" He sighed, shook his head. "I want far more than that of you, and God help me for thinking it."

She raised her head. He did not look at her. A storm rose within her, stirred by his hurtful rejection. He had pulled her toward him with that powerful kiss, and now he sought to push her away. "If Ralph came here this moment and offered Margaret in exchange for me, you would be glad of it. 'Tis what you want."

"I would be tempted to keep you and let Margaret fend for herself," he muttered. "She could do it well enough, I think."

"Keep me?" She huffed impatiently. "Keep me? Do you think I am some prize hawk to be mewed?"

"That," he said, "isna what I meant."

"That," she snapped, "is what I took as your meaning. And how can you be so disloyal to your Margaret?" Her voice rose.

The goshawk flattened his feathers and lifted his wings at Isobel's sharp tone. James sighed, rubbed his hand over his jaw, and began to murmur to the hawk, scratching the thick breast feathers.

Isobel sat and watched, scowling, as a tumult of thoughts and emotions assaulted her. Her initial flash of fury was followed by a confusing blend of resentment and embarrassment, underscored by a strong attraction to him.

"Ho, Gawain," James said softly. "Look at you, we forgot about your hood." He reached up and plucked the hood free from the hawk's head. Gawain blinked, his eyes reddish in the glowing, dim light.

"There, now he can see again," James commented. Isobel glanced toward the bird and nodded silently. James glanced at her. "And we didna even have to kiss him," he added.

Isobel laughed reluctantly. James chuckled and leaned back against the wall, watching her.

"I owe you an apology," he said.

"Aye, several," she said, her tone spicy.

"I do ask your pardon on one matter, at least," he murmured. "I doubted your visions, Isobel. I doubted the sincerity of your purpose—I was sure you were part of some Southron conspiracy. But now I know that you had naught to do with Will's betrayal yourself." He looked away. "And I know you didna set the blame on me and ruin my name with malicious intent."

She blinked at him. "You thought me so evil-minded?"

He shrugged. "Aye. But I didna know you then."

"Just as I didna know you, when I thought you a traitor."

"Ah, but I am," he said tightly. "That I am." The words were bitter and hard.

Isobel touched the back of his hand, where it rested on his thigh. "I canna believe that."

He uttered a curt laugh. "You have been talking to Alice."

"Some," she said. "But 'tis my own feeling. Tell me why you call yourself a traitor."

He shook his head and leaned against the wall. "Nay," he whispered. "I willna tell you, or anyone, that foul tale."

"Jamie, please," she whispered.

He shook his head. "You wouldna like to hear it."

"I would."

"I am tired and I dinna want to tell it," he said bluntly.

She watched him, silent and unmoving as the rock behind him. "Then tell me what I predicted about you."

He opened his eyes, frowned at her. "You know."

She shook her head. "Father Hugh told me what I said about Wallace. And that 'twas a bit different than I recalled." She frowned. "Mayhap he wrote it down inaccurately. But he never told me what I said about you. I only heard, later, that I had predicted that the Border Hawk would take down Wallace. James, what was the prophecy that went about?"

He closed his eyes. " 'The hawk of the tower and the hawk of the forest fly together to take the eagle,' " he began in a low, quiet tone. His voice seemed to reverberate around the small cave. " 'The hawk of the forest is laird of the wind. He will betray his brother the eagle in his nest at night. He will loose the white feather and flee through heather and greenwood. And the eagle will lose his heart.' "

Isobel lowered her eyelids, her hand at rest on his forearm. "Aye, now I recall those words, or something like them," she said. "Wallace was the eagle."

"He was much like an eagle."

"As you are much like a hawk. But how did your

name become involved? I didna say James Lindsay or
Border Hawk in my prophesy."

"The English have called me the Border Hawk for
years," he said. "I live in the forests. I ran with Wallace,
at his side. And I fletch my arrows with white goose
feathers."

"And the hawk of the tower?" she asked.

" 'Hawk of the tower' is a term falconers use to describe the high flight of a hawk just before the dive for
the quarry. So hawk of the tower could refer to me, also,
you see, if the eagle was the quarry here."

She nodded. "And the laird of the wind?" she asked.

He shrugged. "That one I dinna understand. But word
went round fairly quickly that the Border Hawk had
betrayed Wallace."

"Dear God, Jamie," she whispered, stunned by what
she had learned, shocked at her part in it. "I didna mean
to put the blame on you. I never even heard your name
until weeks ago. I am sorry if the prophecy fit you." She
bit her lip as regret flooded through her.

"I know. But I had a hand in what happened to Will."

"How?" she whispered. "You tried to save him."

He shook his head as if to silence her. He turned his
hand over, where her hand rested on his arm, and folded
his fingers over hers. "What is done, is done," he murmured. "Dinna fret over this. 'Tis my matter. I dinna
hold a grudge against you for your prophecy. I regret
the loss of a friend far more than the loss of my name."

Isobel sighed miserably. "Jamie—"

The hawk squawked on his fist, and James jiggled his
hand gently. "Soft, you bird." He glanced at her. "Isobel, I know you might be angry with me, but I still must
ask you to help me keep awake. Just through this night,
and through the morrow, and then we will have our
hawk trained."

"I am not angry." She glanced up at him. His eyes
were midnight-blue in the flickering light inside the cave,
and deeply shadowed beneath. She felt the slow current
of his fatigue, as if it flowed between them. "But—our
hawk? Will you let me hold him, then, so that you can
rest?"

He considered that. "I suppose I could. Hawks are

solitary creatures, but they often accept both falconer and owner at the same time."

"Let me try. He doesna seem to mind my voice, or my presence. Well, Gawain?" She looked at the hawk. "What do you think, laddie?"

The bird tipped his head at her, his bronze eyes glowing.

"We can find out," James said. "In that chest over there are gloves and suchlike. Go through it, if you will, and find a glove to fit your left hand."

Isobel got up and went to the little chest, sifting through its contents until she found a worn, thick leather glove. She slipped it on, stretching her fingers inside its padding. The glove was large, nearly reaching her elbow, and heavy, made of stout leather with thick cloth padding inside. She returned to the bench and sat beside James.

"Sit this way," he said, and circled his right arm around her shoulders to bring her close, so that her shoulder was supported against his chest. With his direction, she raised her left arm to echo the line of his arm, her wrist cocked and offered as a perch.

"Sir Gawain, will you accept a master and a mistress both?" James asked softly. The close, low murmur of his voice nearly melted her bones.

The bird blinked dumbly at them. Isobel held her left arm up and held her breath. The hawk watched them for a moment.

Then he stretched his wings and went into a furious bate.

The hawk sat quietly on her fist at last. Isobel shifted softly, so as not to wake James, who dozed beside her, after a long while spent convincing the hawk to calm down and accept the woman's hand as another perch. Isobel propped her left elbow on James's bent arm, and watched Gawain.

He looked at her, his eyes shining in the low light of the brazier. He dipped his head to tuck it toward his shoulder sleepily.

"Ho, bird," she said into the silence. Gawain lifted his head to look at her. "Ho, there. Jamie said to keep you awake. But then he fell asleep himself, though I dinna think he planned to do that,'' she murmured. "Those were mighty bates you threw for us, Sir Gawain. I am impressed. How is your shoulder?"

She reached out with a fingertip and tickled his breast feathers as she had seen James do. The speckled white and gray feathers were divinely soft and warm underneath. Gawain chirred, and she felt the rapid vibration of his heart in his chest.

Not long ago, she had been surprised when, after a sequence of bates and another treatment of warm bread on his wing joint, Gawain had finally stepped onto Isobel's offered fist. He behaved as if he had always done it, puffing his feathers and blinking at her calmly.

Recently, though, the bird had grown more restive, lifting his wings and flattening his feathers. The grip of his talons on her fist was stronger, and she sensed his increasing anxiety. Isobel plucked a bit of raw meat from the pouch James wore, laid it on her thumb, and watched the bird dip to eat it. All the while, she hoped he would not bate or try to foot her, while she sat with him.

On impulse, she drew a breath and began to sing the *kyrie*. Although she lacked James's gift for true notes, the sound was pleasing and serene as it echoed around the cave.

The bird, finishing his food, cocked his head curiously. His eyelids came together like lightning flashes, and he stilled.

Isobel smiled and looked at James, but he only shifted and tipped his head toward hers in his sleep. Isobel rested her brow against his head, his hair a thick cushion, his breath soft on her cheek.

"Oh, Jamie," she whispered. "Look at our bonny gos. He has decided to trust both of us. And here you are asleep, and didna even see it."

Gawain roused his feathers, turning himself into a puffball, as if he was content to sit the fist without protest.

Isobel held the hawk and let James sleep while she waited for dawn. As light began to stream through the cave entrance, she suddenly realized that she was a few steps away from freedom.

Beside her, James slept soundly, his breaths long and full, his body utterly relaxed. He would not know if she quietly got up, set the bird on a perch, and slipped out the opening. She could be on the way to Wildshaw before he ever woke.

The faint morning light began to glow like a pearl. If she was going to escape captivity, she would have to do it now.

She eased her left arm away from James. Gawain blinked at her and sat calmly, despite the movement she made. The simple trust and reliance in the bird's gaze and posture stopped her.

She glanced at James and saw on his strong, beautiful face a true vulnerability, a state of faith. He trusted her enough to sleep beside her. He trusted her with the care of his tempestuous, frustrating, fragile hawk. And although he was a secretive, quiet man, he had begun to share some of his innermost thoughts with her.

She remembered what the lad Geordie had told her— that James needed someone to trust him, someone to have faith in him again. She had begun to do just that, as had the goshawk. If she left now, in stealth, she would feel as if she had betrayed James. Her heart told her to stay, when her head said she should leave and seek certain protection.

Dawn bloomed outside, and Isobel sat quietly with the hawk and the man, and heeded the whisper of her heart.

Chapter 16

A cool breeze whispered through his hair. James drank in the refreshing early morning air as he stood by the cave opening, leaning one shoulder against the rock wall. He murmured to the hawk, which sat once more on his fist, then returned his gaze to the forest treetops beyond the cave.

He glanced behind him. Isobel slept, stretched out on the bench, her cloak over her. James had eased her there when her head drooped after their breakfast of bread and ale. He returned his gaze to the vast, textured expanse of soft green treetops. The pale, early sky was filled with clouds that would bring more rain before long.

Far off in the forest below, he saw a flash of movement. He narrowed his eyes, stepping forward for a better view. The hawk fluttered his wings, sensing the wind as it blew through the opening.

"You'll soon be out there," James murmured. "I promise."

"He longs to be free," Isobel said behind him.

James glanced over his shoulder to see her sitting up. "He'll fly soon enough. I thought you were asleep."

She smiled wanly in answer, and came forward to stand near the entrance as he did. She cupped her left hand over her injured arm and rubbed slowly, as if she soothed pain.

As she looked out the doorway, the light gave her face a delicate clarity, and set a sparkle in her blue eyes. James drew in his breath in awe as he watched her. Her face was pale and lovely, and her hair flowed smoothly down her back, sheened like polished jet. He longed to touch its silkiness.

He wanted far more than that, but such impulses were dangerous. He reminded himself that he must practice better wisdom—or at least common sense—regarding the prophetess.

Last night he had succumbed to an overwhelming desire to touch her, and would have been willing to take it beyond a simple kiss. He had shown neither good judgment nor discipline, but he would not let that happen again.

"Look below, there," he said, pointing toward the forest. "Two runners, coming along the path." Isobel leaned forward, and James looked over her shoulder, holding the hawk up on his fist.

"I dinna see them," she said, squinting.

His sharp vision often showed him details that others did not see. "Wait," he said. He watched the figures run through the forest, blond and dark heads bobbing as they came onward.

"Ah," she said at last as the two men cleared the forest and began to mount the slope that led to the cave. She looked up at James, her eyes wide. "Quentin and Patrick?"

"Aye, back from Stobo. Alice must have told them that we were up here."

"What will you do now that they are back?"

"I have a task to attend," he said.

Her eyes, large and sad, questioned him silently.

" 'Tis time to send a message to Wildshaw, and time to barter one woman for another." Suddenly he could no longer look into those wide eyes, filled with gentle light. He turned to stare out the doorway.

Isobel sighed, a whisper of sound. He felt its echo in himself. She gazed down at the long slope as Quentin and Patrick began to climb. "Your Margaret is a blessed lady, to be loved so well," she murmured.

"My Margaret? A blessed lady?" he asked, dumbfounded.

"I, on the other hand," she said stepping forward, "dinna have such a blessing. Quentin! Patrick!" She waved.

James had no chance to ask her what she meant, or to explain about Margaret. Quentin and Patrick edged past the clustered gorse and stepped into the cave. Isobel greeted them with a smile. Quentin winked at her, and Patrick turned red-cheeked.

Gawain, on the fist, lifted his wings as if ready to launch into a bate. James murmured to him and scratched his feet gently, and the bird calmed.

"What word of Geordie?" James asked. "Is he recovering?"

"Aye, he'll be fine," Patrick said, his breath heaving after his climb. He was not as tall as James, but his barrel chest and heavy limbs and features made him seem large. He fisted huge hands on his hips and looked at the hawk. "Jamie, we have trouble. . . . What are you doing with a goshawk?" he asked, sounding astonished.

"Training him. What trouble?"

"We came through the forest just after dawn," Quentin said. "We were chased by a Southron patrol of about ten men. Henry and Eustace were with us. Both were caught by arrows. We took them to Alice Crawford's house. She told us you were here."

"Are they badly hurt?"

He shook his head. "Both will be fine. Alice sent you some food—Patrick has it in that sack. And this sack," Quentin said, handing James a bulky cloth bundle, "is for the bird. Alice said you would have a hungry hawk here. She sent meat for him."

"Aye, thanks," James said. He turned to Isobel. "Gather your cloak and the food, if you will. We must leave here."

"Leave?" she asked.

"Aye. Hurry." James turned to Quentin and Patrick. "Go back to Alice's house and guard it well. If those were Ralph Leslie's men, they will return. Alice and the others will need protection."

He went to the back of the cave and returned with his bow and sword. With Patrick's help, he looped the quiver on his belt, slung the bow over his back, and slid the long broadsword into the sheath between his shoulders. James then gathered a few hawking items—a hood, jesses, Isobel's glove—and shoved them into a large pouch at his belt.

He fed Gawain a chunk of fresh meat from the bag Alice had sent, and turned to help Isobel put her cloak over her shoulders. She picked up the bundle of wrapped food.

"Do we go back to Alice's house?" she asked.

He shook his head, took her elbow, and turned to Quentin and Patrick. "Lads, go down and see that Alice and the others are safe. I will take Isobel up to Aird Craig."

She turned to him, her look questioning. He did not glance at her, but tightened his grip on her arm.

"Leslie's men willna find you up there so easily," Quentin said, nodding. "Jamie—you mean to hide the lass there?"

"I do," James said. He met Quentin's frown.

"Ah," Quentin said after a moment. "I thought as much. You think to trade Isobel for Margaret."

"What?" Patrick asked. "Trade her for Margaret? 'Tisna an honorable thing, Jamie, holding women like this."

"Tell that to Leslie, who keeps Margaret against her will," James said. "But I think he will trade her for his betrothed."

"Eagerly," Quentin drawled. " 'Tis a wonder he's kept Margaret this long. That lass can be a trial."

"I canna imagine anyone keeping Margaret against her will," Patrick said. "She's a clever lass, and has the strength of two or three men."

"You ought to know," Quentin drawled. "She was after you often enough. And I saw you go off into the greenwood with Margaret a time or two, laddie." He wiggled a brow.

Patrick blushed a deep red. "Aye, but she were never after me. She were after Jamie."

" 'Tis both of you she favors—Quentin for his bonny face, and Patrick for his, ah . . . ." James seemed at a loss for words.

"For my courtesy," Patrick supplied. "And I'd favor that lass quick enough, I would." He grinned.

"Watch how you speak of my cousin," James warned.

"And if you truly favor the lass, you'll want to help me reclaim her."

"Aye, bold as she is, she needs our help," Quentin said.

"Then meet me on the height this even." James led Isobel through the cave opening as he spoke. "I will have a message prepared for Ralph Leslie, which I'll want you to deliver." He nodded to them and slid through the crevice, hawk in hand.

"That," James said, pointing westward, "is the Craig."

He glanced at Isobel as he stood beside her on a hill-top overlooking the forest. They had already walked a good distance from the cave in relative silence. Now, as they stood side by side, the wind whipped at their cloaks and hair. Two grouse flew overhead, and the bird on James's fist suddenly pitched off the fist in a wild bate.

James sighed and extended his arm. "We may have to begin again with this laddie," he muttered. He did not want to stand out in the open for long, but while the bird fussed, he pointed toward the enormous crag that rose high above the forest, dominating its western side.

" 'Tis called Aird Craig—the high crag," he said. Jutting out the side of a mountain, whose high slopes were pale blue in the morning light, the rough, rugged sides and flattened top of the crag were swathed in a thick cover of trees, as if a rumpled green tapestry had been tossed over it. Along one steep side, a towering expanse of gray rock was split by a foaming white waterfall. The long white tail of water tumbled into a wide burn that skimmed past the base of the crag.

Isobel tipped her head to stare upward. "Do you live up there?" she asked.

"Aye, near the top," James said. Gawain calmed, and he lifted the bird gently back to the fist. "There are caves throughout the interior, like a honeycomb. At the summit—see up there, through the trees—is a ruin of an ancient stone tower."

"Ah. So the Border Hawk has an eyrie."

He shrugged. "So to speak. 'Tis a good place. The Craig is nearly impossible to climb without ropes and iron hooks. The only other access is to go up the mountain behind the crag, a steep and dangerous route." He glanced down at her. "But my men and I have found an easier way to the top, and so we've used the crag as a refuge for years."

She frowned, her expression doubtful. "Must we climb up to this eyrie of yours?"

"Well, we lack the wings to fly," he said dryly. "I hope your foot is well enough for a long walk. Come ahead." He took her elbow and urged her forward. As they walked along the ridge of the hill, passing behind a screen of birches and gorse, James heard the faint, dull roar of the waterfall.

He glanced down and saw Isobel scowling as she walked beside him. "We have been climbing and walking about for days," she grumbled. "Through forests, up hills, down cliffs. And now you want me to climb that monstrous crag."

James hid a smile. " 'Tisna so bad as it looks."

"I dinna want to climb a mountain," she said, and stopped walking. "I dinna have to go up there with you."

He halted beside her. "Nay?"

"Nay." She fisted her free hand on her hip, her right arm still in a sling, and looked up at him. "I could walk back to Alice's house. I could even walk to Wildshaw myself, if I want."

"And do you want to do that?" he asked carefully.

She tipped her head. "Would you stop me if I did?"

He felt tension spring and begin to thrum between them. He sensed that she waited for something. He was not certain why she had set such a dare so blatantly before him, for it seemed unlike her. Nor did he know what she wanted to hear from him.

He turned away to survey the thicket of the forest. "You must be wondering if I intend to force you to stay with me."

She stood beside him and looked out over the forest. The wind lifted the glorious length of her hair, released it. "You know that I dinna care to be a hostage, James Lindsay," she said. She turned to gaze at him. "I should walk away now, and take freedom for myself. What would you do if I wanted that?"

Silence hung between them, thick as the overhead clouds. His heart thumped in rapid tandem with his thoughts. Without a hostage, he had no chance of gaining Margaret, and less chance of exacting revenge on Leslie for the deeds that had brought him—and Wallace, and the cause of Scotland—to such a sorry state.

If he continued to force Isobel into captivity, he would lose the trust she was beginning to show him; and he would lose what scant respect he had for himself. But if he let Isobel go as she wished, he would lose her entirely.

That unexpected thought struck him like a blow. He frowned deeply and stared out at the forest without reply. He understood her desire for freedom. He had been a close comrade of the greatest rebel leader in Scotland; he had spent time himself in a dungeon; and he had lost his inheritance and his legal freedom through unfair means. He understood better than most the gut-based human need for liberty.

Despite that, he had taken Isobel hostage in his passion to avenge the wrongs done to him and to his. And he could not ignore the irony of the jessed hawk on his fist. He forced a wild thing into captivity and denied Isobel her freedom. Her resistance should hardly surprise him.

He sighed. The wind stirred his hair and his cloak and ruffled the bird's feathers. That gentle power was strong enough to blow a little sense into his wounded, blinded heart.

"Aye," he agreed. "You deserve your freedom."

She nodded beside him. "You canna keep me."

"I canna," he said tautly.

"When I was blind," she said quietly, "you gave me a promise of safekeeping. I am grateful for that. But you made me another promise. You agreed to let me go after my sight returned."

He closed his eyes for an instant. "Aye," he said. "I did agree to that." Fool, he told himself; he had been a fool, to speak from his heart that day. If he said her nay now, he would have no honor in her regard. She would never trust him. Ever.

"Go, then," he said woodenly.

Rain began to fall, tiny, misted drops. James waited. But Isobel did not walk away.

"Are you leaving, then?" he asked.

"I might." The wind buffeted between them. Still she did not move. She slid a glance at him. "Is Wildshaw to the west or to the east from here?" she asked in a small voice.

He nearly laughed. "West," he said. "Beyond the Craig."

"I will ask Ralph to release Margaret."

"He willna do it."

"Then I will release her myself." She lifted her chin.

"Ah," he said, flattening another smile—what was it about her that she could so innocently charm a smile from him, and hurt him, all at once? "Ah, now, that I would like to see. A pair, you two would be. But if 'twere so easy, lass, Margaret would have walked out already."

"You think well of her."

He shrugged. "She's a good lass. I want her safe."

"You love her." Isobel's low voice hardly carried on the wind.

"I love her, in my way," he said. His heart was suddenly slamming in his chest. "But I dinna love her as you love Ralph Leslie. You have promised yourself to him in marriage."

The wind ruffled the dark, sheened curtain of her hair, but she stood motionless. "My father wanted the match. I agreed. A betrothal doesna always mean a promise of love."

"But you are eager to get to Wildshaw, and eager to get away from me."

"My father may be at Wildshaw. And I dinna much like being held for ransom," she said. "But I am not eager to get away from you, if that is what you think," she added softly.

"Ah," he said. He paused, listening to the lift of the wind, the rush of the waterfall far ahead. "Margaret," he said after a moment, "isna my betrothed—if that is what *you* think."

"But you are willing to risk a great deal to get her back. Clearly you love her. I think 'tis—'tis admirable."

He smiled a little. "Margaret Crawford loves me in her way, I suppose, as I care for her in mine. But that lass wouldna wed me if I begged her on my knees. Which I would never do."

Her eyes, in that moment, were a silvery blue, as if they had taken on the grayness of the overcast sky. "I thought she was your lover."

He made a wry face. "By the saints, nay. She is like my sister." He considered that. "Even like a brother, at times."

"Aye?" Her eyes seemed to lighten. "I should like to meet her one day."

"You might." Gawain shifted on the fist, cheeping and squawking, threatening to bate again.

"What bothers him?" Isobel asked.

"He is a wild thing," James said. "With all this moving about, we may have lost the ground we gained toward manning him." He sighed and plucked the small hood from the pouch at his belt, and dropped it deftly over the bird's head. Isobel began to protest. "He could bate all the way up the crag and hurt himself, or make the ascent difficult for us," James told her. "The hood will quiet him, at least. But we might have to start over with his training."

We. They had worked together to man the hawk. An idea struck James with strong force. A risk, but he must take it.

"Isobel, grant me one favor."

She paused. "Ask it, then," she said warily.

"You dinna wish to be the hostage of a forest outlaw. You want to be reunited with your father, and be safe with the constable at Wildshaw." He glanced at her. "Even if you dinna love the man, you feel safer with him than with an outlaw."

"I . . . I might feel that," she said hesitantly.

"And I want Margaret safe. Mayhap we can help each other."

"How?" Her voice was a low whisper.

"I promise you will have what you want. All I ask is a little part of your time."

"My time?" she asked cautiously.

"Aye. Give me a few days to send a message to Leslie

and ask for Margaret in trade for you. Wait on the Craig with me until she is returned to my safekeeping."

"You want me to remain your hostage?" She stared at him.

"My guest," he said quietly. "My—my friend. I ask for your help. And that is all I will ask of you."

She said nothing. The wind rippled the length of her hair, and the same wind lifted his hair from his shoulders. James looked away, feeling suddenly, horribly vulnerable. She could easily refuse him and walk away. And he would have to let her go, and watch his hopes shatter. To force her to be his hostage now would condemn him as the worst of rogues in her eyes.

Her silence lingered, twisting in him. He glanced at her. "I want to rescue Margaret without wasting more lives," he said. "But I willna keep you if you dinna want to stay."

She let out a low breath and looked toward the forest, then glanced toward the great crag on the other side. "You want me to act as an accomplice in your scheme," she finally said.

"Aye, I suppose so." He smiled bitterly. "Leslie need never know the truth. He will always believe that you were kept in fear of your life."

"He would kill you for that reason," she said softly.

"He means to kill me regardless."

She stared at him. The wind blew through her hair, whipping over her shoulder and the side of her face. James reached out and sifted the strands back.

"What do you say, Black Isobel?" he asked.

"Why did you decide to let me go, if I want that?"

He shrugged. " 'Tis unchivalric to hold a woman for ransom," he said lightly. "If I hear a lesson repeated often enough, I will learn it."

"You once said I was your only hope of gaining what you wanted—rescuing Margaret."

"My only hope," he murmured. "Aye. But I find that I canna jess you after all, as I can Gawain. And so I must humbly beg a boon of you, and wait upon your good will." He kept his tone light, though he felt only tension inside, waiting for her answer. He had impulsively gambled everything in the last few moments, his wager placed on her trust and regard for him.

She tipped her head as if to assess him. "I have seen little humility in you. What changed your mind on this matter?"

"You," he said quietly.

She bit her lower lip and glanced away.

"I willna keep you against your will." He paused. "But if you feel that you canna trust the Border Hawk—" He shrugged. "Then I understand. Wildshaw Castle is that way." He indicated the direction.

She turned her back on where he pointed. "Show me your Craig," she said. "I will give you a few days."

His heart gave a wild surge, but he calmly inclined his head in thanks. "A few days, then."

"If you treat me kindly," she added.

"Ah, well," he said, turning to walk ahead. "That much I can do, I suppose. I have learned well from hawks."

"I know," she said as she followed behind him.

Chapter 17

"Take off your shoes," James said, raising his voice so that Isobel could hear him over the pounding din of the waterfall.

Isobel blinked up at him. "My shoes? Must we scale the cliff in bare feet?"

The crag towered over them, surging upward on the far bank of a wide stream. Isobel stood with James on the other side of the burn. A short distance away, the long, narrow waterfall plunged into the burn with considerable force. The water churned and spilled over rocks to speed past their feet.

"Take off your shoes, and your hose, too," James said. He set the hawk on a branch so that he could pull off his own boots and hosen. Then he retrieved the hawk and stepped into the burn. The water rushed and swirled around his bare, muscular calves. He held out a hand to her.

"Hurry, Isobel," he said.

She scowled at him, and then sat to awkwardly pull off her hose and her low, soft boots with her left hand. She crammed them into her belt and stood, lifting the hem of her gown and tucking it under her right arm.

The water was so cold that she gasped aloud as she stepped gingerly into the rushing burn, soon knee-deep in the current.

James took her hand in a firm grip and guided her carefully over the slippery stones that littered the streambed. When they reached the opposite bank, he helped her step out, then leaped onto the bank beside her.

Isobel looked up at the soaring crag. "Have you a rope?" she asked, dreading the climb.

"Nay. Come on," he said, and led her toward the waterfall.

Frowning in doubt, she followed, picking her way barefooted over mossy rocks and tufted grass, walking carefully past a prickly clump of gorse bushes.

James led her so close to the waterfall that the spray dampened her skin and gown and slicked her hair against her brow. She wiped her sleeved arm over the moisture on her face and kept behind him. Holding the hawk, James stepped behind the rushing foam of the fall so quickly that she blinked. Isobel peered after him.

His arm thrust out and grabbed her hand, and he pulled her through a beating rush of water to stand behind the fall.

The light there was almost totally diminished, and the sound was deafening. She saw the outline of his head and shoulders, saw the dark depth of his eyes. He sluiced water from his brow, pushed back his wet hair and turned with a quick gesture for her to follow.

Again he disappeared, slipping into shadows with the quick grace of a wildcat. Isobel moved hesitantly into the darkness and saw the pale shape of his hand waving her forward. He had gone into a crevice. She stepped inside. All was blackness, and the stone beneath her bare feet felt slick and cold.

Isobel put out a hand, panicking suddenly. The darkness was too complete, too much like blindness. The roar of the waterfall behind her had dulled somewhat inside the tiny space, and she called out, bumping her head on the low ceiling. "Jamie!"

Ahead of her, a dim golden light flared, highlighting a narrow passage. She stepped forward. The floor sloped upward at a steep angle, and she placed her right hand on the uneven rock wall for balance. She ducked her head and shoulders to avoid hitting the ceiling of the tunnel.

"Jamie!" she called. The sound echoed.

"Here," he answered. The light flickered, bloomed brighter as Isobel followed the twisting tunnel.

He waited farther along in the passage, holding a thick

pine splint, sparking and burning, in one hand, the hooded hawk resting on his gloved fist. He had pulled on his hose and boots, and stood with his head and shoulders tucked down beneath the low ceiling of the tunnel.

"We keep a flint and torches here," he said. "Put your shoes on now. 'Tis a long walk, but far better than a climb up the cliff side."

Isobel sat, yanked on her stockings and gartered them, then pulled on her boots. She followed James as he loped up the incline. The space was long and narrow, a rounded scooping of the pinkish sandstone, as if some stone-devouring dragon had carved an entrance into a deep lair.

"Is this a secret passage into the crag?" she asked.

"I surely hope 'tis a secret," he drawled. "We've been using it for years. The tunnel seems to be as ancient as the tower that sits high on the crag. Wallace and I, and Patrick, discovered the cave and the tunnel years ago, when we were running from a Southron patrol and leaped into the waterfall to hide. Until that day, the only way to reach the top of the crag was to scale the side, or take a long, difficult route over the mountain."

"Who knows about this?" she asked as she followed him.

"Only those who have stayed close to me," he said. "Quentin, Patrick, Geordie, Margaret, a few others. Most of those who knew about it are dead now." He walked on for several moments before he spoke again. "As for the rest, pray God they never tell the English."

"The rest?"

"Nearly a hundred men followed my lead at one time," he said. "Though less than twenty knew about this place." He walked on.

"Do the Southrons know that you live up here?" she asked.

"They know that the Border Hawk hides on the crag, but they dinna know how I come and go from here. Now that I have shown you—" He stopped, and turned. The fire shone brightly on his face. He looked rugged, strong, and unyielding in its light. "Give me your solemn promise to never reveal this passageway."

"I—I promise," she stammered. "Upon my heart, I promise."

"Ah, then," he said, watching her. "Will you risk your heart?" His voice was quiet but strong in the confined space.

She nodded. "I will."

His gaze did not waver. "Then I will hold you to it," he said. "Upon your heart." He turned to walk on. The torchlight poured gold over his hair and his powerful back and shoulders, slung with bow and sword.

Isobel watched him, and felt an intense yearning. The feeling was unlike any she had ever known, as if, in those few words spoken between them, she had made a deeper promise than he had asked of her. As if she had indeed pledged her heart, not for the sake of this secret tunnel, but for the man who hid here.

She slowed and stopped, watching his back ahead of her. The feeling was wrenching, so powerful that she nearly fell to her knees. She leaned against the cold, raw-cut rock of the tunnel and placed her hand over her mouth.

The stunning, sudden memory of a vision flooded into her mind. She remembered the misty image of a church, a rain-soaked yard, and a hawthorn tree. A man stood there, cloaked and hooded like a pilgrim, a hawk on his gloved fist. He turned, and she saw his face. James. And she saw herself nearby, reaching out.

With an almost physical shock, she remembered that she had seen those images another time, months ago, the day she had seen Wallace's death. But what did they mean—the hawthorn tree, the pilgrim, the hawk? Why did she see James and herself together by that tree? She could answer none of those questions, but the image was vivid in her mind.

James turned. "What is it?" he asked.

"Naught," she answered, straightening away from the wall. "Naught." She came forward.

"You are pale as the moon," he said coming toward her.

She shook her head. "I am fine. How much farther?"

He handed her the torch, since he had one hand occupied with the quiet, hooded hawk, and took her elbow to lead her upward. " 'Tis a long, steady climb," he said. "We estimated it once to be half a league, winding through the inside of the crag."

"Was this cut by hand?" She stared at the narrow tunnel, with its low ceiling, curved floor, and rough walls, reddish rock gleaming in the torchlight. As she scanned the raw, glimmering rock, the memory of her strange vision began to fade.

"Much of this was tunneled by ancient men, I think, for there are deep, old chisel marks. But 'twas begun by the hand of God," he said. "Throughout the crag, we found numerous caves, connected by crevices large enough to be used as tunnels. 'Tis as open, in some places, as a dovecote. There are even wells and a spring inside the crag."

"So much water? How can that be, up this high?"

"The spring thaws funnel off the mountain, I suppose," he said. "I'll show you one of the springs when we get higher." He took the torch.

They resumed walking. The climb did not proceed steadily upward, nor was the tunnel of uniform dimension. Its narrow, snaking path turned, ascended, dipped, and flattened as the width and height changed, so that at times they had to bend down. As they went higher inside the crag, Isobel saw a few small caves off the tunnel, hardly large enough for a man to stand up inside. James passed those without comment. Farther on, she saw the opening of another larger cave.

"Do you live in these caves?" she asked.

"We have used them as hideaways," he said, "but we live on the summit." He walked past. The torchlight sputtered as they turned a sharp angle in the tunnel, both of them bending their heads to avoid the low ceiling, which had dipped again.

Then the tunnel split into two arms. Isobel heard the sound of trickling water, its echo magnified by stone.

"There is a spring to the right," James said. "For now, we go this way." He turned left, and followed a steep incline, his stride long. Finally, when Isobel yearned for a rest, James turned a corner, ducked beneath an overhang, and beckoned.

She stepped forward and saw a steep flight of steps,

stone slabs layered one over another soaring upward. Above was the pale glow of daylight.

James took the steps two at a time. Isobel came slowly, holding her skirts, wary of the height and the uneven steps. Though she was long-legged, the stairs seemed cut for giants.

They emerged onto a grassy surface, bathed in gray light, the wind fresh and full. Isobel looked around, and James walked ahead, disappearing around the end of a stone wall.

The huge, curving wall surrounded the grassy area. Blocks and slabs, apparently cut from the same rosy sandstone that formed the core of the crag, were carefully layered without mortar and rose to a remarkable height. Isobel saw several tiny window openings and, in the base, one rectangular door with a flat overhead lintel.

She walked around the inner yard, a circular space defined by the walls. One section of the wall had fallen, revealing the double wall construction of the circular tower. Inside, the space between the walls was divided by floors and interior cells.

James came back toward her, still holding the hawk, but without the torch. "This is a broch," he said. "An ancient fortress, abandoned ages ago, built by a people who, 'tis said, have vanished from Scotland."

"They must have been a race of giants, judging by this place," she said.

He smiled a little. "No one knows. Sometimes such towers form the foundation of later castles, but the summit of Aird Craig was too difficult to attain, and so 'twas abandoned."

"No one knew about the passageway," she said.

" 'Twould seem so," he answered.

"The secret must have died with someone, to be lost like that," she said. He nodded. Overhead, the sky darkened to a pewter sheen, and a few drops of rain touched her cheeks. James reached out and took her hand.

"This way," he said, and strode around the inner, curving base of the wall, pulling her along beside him.

James turned where the wall had collapsed into rubble, and stepped over some broken blocks. He entered the hollow core formed by the inner and outer walls, and Isobel followed.

A staircase, built of the same layered sandstone as the other stairs, rose up along the inside wall. They mounted that, and stepped out onto a gallery, where several windows cut into the interior wall overlooked the courtyard. Isobel noticed small chambers built from the space between the double walls.

James entered one of these cells. Light from the doorway filled the small, windowless room. A stone bench lined one wall, and three wooden perch stands were placed on the floor. He set Gawain on one of the perches.

"This was a mews for my other goshawk," he said.

"Astolat?" Isobel asked.

He nodded, stroking Gawain's back. The bird was still hooded. "We'll let him rest," James said. "But not for long, or he'll go feral again. Come with me."

Isobel followed him out of the little cell and up another flight of steps to a higher gallery. They crossed the threshold of another chamber, this one placed against the inner wall. A small, square window shed some light into the room, illuminating a stone slab bench, table, and a bed, supplied with a mattress and fur coverings. The room was austere; blankets on the bed and a small stone hearth in the corner were the only notes of comfort.

"Is this the chamber you use for yourself?" she asked.

"Aye."

"Grand for a brigand," she remarked, wandering forward, touching the walls and the massive stone frame of the bed. "I thought outlaws only lived in caves, or hollow trees, or out in the open."

"Some of us live in coziness and luxury, inside abandoned fortresses," he answered. "But none of us have true homes." Isobel heard the sad, low note in his voice. "An adjoining chamber is there," he went on. He pointed to a small door in a dividing wall. "You may use that, if you like."

Her footsteps echoed on the stone floor as she crossed the room and peered through the doorway. The adjoin-

ing chamber was a twin to the first, with a courtyard
view and stone furniture, although it lacked bedding.

The space, as stark as its twin, was peaceful in its
simplicity. Isobel sat on the bench beneath the window,
and looked out over the courtyard. Rain pattered over
the stones and the grass below. She shivered, grateful to
be in a dry place.

"I'll make a fire—there is a hearth in my chamber.
And we have stores of goods and food tucked away, so
you will be comfortable," James said. "While you stay."

She nodded silently. Fatigue and hunger had finally
sapped her strength. As he left she leaned her head beside the window, watching the rain thicken to a
downpour.

She sighed, and closed her eyes, and wondered how
she could have agreed to this. Enclosed in a stout tower
high on an inaccessible crag, she was more firmly imprisoned now than she had ever been.

Her only chance for freedom rested with the outlaw.
And her only hope existed in the trust she had placed
in him.

"The rain has stopped," Isobel said.

James nodded, barely looking up from the hawk,
which was involved in yet another bate. He and Isobel
sat in James's chamber, sheltered from the rain which
had continued while they had eaten a meal of the bread
and cheese that Alice had sent, along with a flask of red
wine taken from James's own stores. A small fire crackled on the hearth, filling the room with warmth.

James sighed and watched the hawk as he beat his
wings. Once unhooded, Gawain had flung himself from
the fist repeatedly, as if working off his anger at being
transported yet again. James had begun to despair of
ever training the hawk.

"He's been ruined, this gos," he said. "Whoever had
him before spoiled him utterly."

"Then he couldna have come out of my father's
mews," Isobel remarked, coming closer. "My father
raised hawks properly."

When the wing beats stopped, James scooped the
panting bird back to his fist. "I canna right damage done

by a poor falconer. There isna enough patience in the world for that."

"If anyone has the patience, 'tis you," Isobel murmured.

He buffed a humorless laugh. "I know when 'tis hopeless."

" 'Tisna hopeless." She reached out to smooth a fingertip over the bird's back. "Ho, Sir Gawain, tell the man you can be reclaimed. Aye, tell him."

James looked at her with a sense of surprise. "I thought you wanted me to set him free," he said.

"I do, when the time comes. But you said yourself that his wing must heal before you can let him go."

"Aye." He reached into the pouch at his waist and pulled out a gray feather, lost by Gawain in his tantrums. He used the feather to stroke the bird's breast and legs.

Gawain glared at them both, his bronze eyes resentful. He perched with his wings hunched forward, wingtips touching James's fist, his talons flexing restively.

"He's hungry," James said. "See how his talons clench. And he's exhausted, too, and yet willna sit the fist quietly for me." He shook his head and reached inside his hawking pouch to pluck a bit of raw meat from inside a cloth, which he fed to Gawain. "He just willna take to the fist reliably. And look at him. He is as bedraggled as when I got him out of the tree. He's twisted his tail feathers with all these bates. Now they will have to be straightened—and that isna a merry process, let me tell you," he said sourly.

"Let it go until later," Isobel said quietly, watching him. "You are as exhausted as he is. Just feed him and let him sleep, and rest yourself. Then start afresh with his training."

James sighed. "Aye, I am tired. But I have to train the hawk—I canna let him behave wildly, and I canna let him go with a weak wing. He has to be able to hunt or he will die."

" 'Tis honorable of you to rescue the hawk, and try to man him for his own well-being."

James lifted a brow, surprised and inwardly pleased by her compliment, and by the unmistakable sympathy he sensed in her voice. But he gave her a wry look, hesitant to reveal how much her quiet support meant to him. "Honorable? This, from the lass who thinks me a wretched traitor?"

"I think you are much like that goshawk, Jamie Lindsay," she said softly. Her eyes glimmered in the shadows. He thought their color was very like the rain, just then.

"Foul-tempered and bedraggled?" he drawled.

A smile played at a corner of her mouth. "Aye, that, too."

Despite discouragement and aching fatigue, he felt his glum mood lighten at her kind tone. He was glad to know that he pleased her, that she had some faith and respect for him. And he liked the humor that sparked pleasantly between them.

She sat on the stone bench beside him. "But there's more. Both of you are wild, and strong, and stubborn. And neither of you will ever give in. I can see that."

He slid her a long look. "I seldom relent in any matter, but this goshawk comes close to defeating me."

"Never," she said softly. "Naught will ever defeat you."

He drew his brows together. A soft light glowed in her remarkable eyes, a glint of admiration. He had seen that before, when they had shared a sweet, lingering kiss among the ferns. He was grateful for the renewal of her trust, but he felt discomfited by it, too. He did not truly deserve it.

"Oh, I am often defeated," he drawled. "I just dinna show my displeasure over it. Unlike this rude laddie."

Isobel tilted her head to stare at him. Her gaze was affectionate, gentle, and pierced him deeply. James felt his blood begin to surge. He wanted to touch her, wanted to sip some of the sweetness he sensed in her lips, in her eyes.

Fatigue blurred his thoughts, blurred the edges of years of self-discipline. If he stayed here with her, he would surely do something he would later regret.

"Come outside," he said, standing. "I will show you the Craig."

Chapter 18

The wind pushed at her hair. Isobel captured her thick tresses in one hand, taming the mass with a twisting motion. She wished she had the use of two hands to braid it, for the wind on top of the crag was fierce, beating her hair about her head, whipping her skirts against her legs.

She stood on the summit and looked out over a view as glorious as any she had ever seen. After the rain, the sky brightened, but clouds still rolled, large and dove-gray, overhead. The forest below was a deep green, muted under transparent veils of mist.

All around stretched an expanse of texture and pattern, made up of hills and forestland, of lochs like slices of silver and rivers like shining ribbons.

Isobel turned to look at Jamie. He stood beside her, the hawk on his gloved fist. " 'Tis beautiful up here," she said in awe. "I have never been so high up before."

"The view extends for miles when it's clearer." He raised his free hand to point. "Over there are the low hills of the Borderlands, round and green. And there"—he shifted his arm to indicate a gentle, meandering river—"the Yarrow Water, which flows to meet the Ettrick Water. And all around us, the forest itself. Just there, beyond that long, rocky hill, is the clearing and Alice's house. On bright days, to the east, we can even see the three peaks of the Eildon hills."

She looked west. "Can you see Wildshaw Castle from here?"

He stood silently beside her. The hawk chirred and lifted his wings, and Jamie soothed him with a quick, low word. "We canna see the castle," he said quietly.

" 'Tis beyond the edge of the forest, past that round hill over there. Wildshaw overlooks a river valley on the other side of the hill."

"It must be very beautiful there."

" 'Tis, aye." A muscle beat in his cheek briefly.

"You can see much of what goes on in the forest from here, then," she said. "That must be useful for a forest brigand."

"Certes," he agreed. "We see Southron soldiers riding through the forests and over the hills. We have seen patrols riding to and from Wildshaw, and from other castles nearby. We know when soldiers are in the forest. And we can see them easily when they ride along the riverbanks."

"Then you know your foes before you have to face them," she said. "The Southrons must hate the fact that you are safely up here, and they canna get to you."

"They would give much to take the Border Hawk out of his eyrie, I think." He glanced at her. "In a way, watching from this height is like looking into the future. From up here, we can predict who we will meet down in the forest, how many, from what direction. We can choose our skirmishes. We just canna foresee the outcome."

" 'Tis a more practical way to know your future than I can offer you," she murmured. "Watching from up here has helped to protect you all these years."

He shrugged, nodded. "I have been fortunate I suppose. When I was captured for the first time by Southrons several months ago, 'twas elsewhere. 'Twouldna have happened in this part of the Ettrick."

Isobel gazed at his strong profile, and at the beautiful form of the hawk on his fist. "Where were you taken?"

"We were west of here, just past Wildshaw, traveling to meet up with another band of men loyal to Wallace. We were ambushed by a Southron patrol." He drew a long breath. "Several of my men were killed. My cousin Tom Crawford—Alice's youngest son—died fighting beside me. Margaret was taken with us."

"She was with you that day?"

"Aye. She was often with us. The lass is willing and strong, and fearless. I wouldna refuse a good bow arm just because it belonged to a female. But the day was ill-fated. We were taken to Carlisle—those of us who survived the ambush. I was held there until summer. And Margaret was taken into Leslie's custody. He was there, and sympathetic to the English."

"Was that when you lost possession of Wildshaw—when you were taken by the English?"

He shook his head. "They took the castle seven years ago, after my brother, the laird, died on the field at Falkirk. Wildshaw is mine by right. But the English king added my name to a list of dispossessed barons and had me declared an outlaw for refusing to sign an oath of fealty."

"As if Edward Longshanks has the right to demand fealty, or to take land from Scotsmen and reassign it," she commented.

He lifted a brow. "This, from a lass who means to wed a Scotsman lately gone over to the English?"

"This from a lass who knows what is fair, and what isna," she retorted. "Marriage willna change that."

He nodded once, as if in approval. "King Edward's commanders have installed a garrison of over a hundred at Wildshaw. They keep the castle stocked with supplies and war machines to aid them in fighting in the Borderlands."

"You canna gain it back, as laird of Wildshaw?" she asked.

"I tried," he said. "It came to naught but sorrow."

She remembered standing in the bleak, threatened garden at Aberlady, cradling a white rose while James told her that he, too, had lost a castle—and loved ones—to a fire caused by the English. And she recalled Alice's comment that he carried a heavy inner burden since he had lost Wildshaw.

"What happened, Jamie?" she asked quietly.

He stared out over the misty forest, and sighed. With a knuckle, he gently stroked Gawain's breast feathers and murmured to the bird.

Isobel waited patiently. She knew he had heard her question, and thought about his answer. But she wondered if he would choose to tell her.

"Astolat and I used to come up here," he finally said.

"I would watch for Southrons, and she would watch for grouse, for larks, for partridge. If I released her to fly at quarry, she would bring it back to me each time. If I didna set her to flight, she would perch calmly, even if a tempting bit of bird went past."

"She was a remarkable hawk, you said."

"Aye," he said. He looked around, his eyes narrowed as they scanned the forest. The wind lifted his hair from his shoulders. "From up here, I could always see who went through the forest to Wildshaw. I was already spending most of my time with Wallace and others, while my brother held Wildshaw. But that day, 'twas shortly after Falkirk. My brother had been killed, with two of my cousins—Alice's sons. After the battle, I had gone home to Wildshaw, and then spent a day or so with Alice. I left her house, and came to the Craig to tend to . . . some matters of rebellion. I hadna been home for days.

"That morning," he continued, "I saw Southrons riding through the forest, a large group, fitted for war. I went down with a patrol. We split up to scout the situation, and realized that they were headed for Wildshaw. Astolat was with me."

Gawain shifted restively on his fist, flapping his wings. James paused to whisper to him, and Isobel noticed that James's patient tone prevented a bate. She waited for him to speak again.

"Astolat saw my attacker before I did," he said. "She raised her wings as she sat on my fist, and took the arrow that had been aimed at me." He paused. "Straight into her breast."

Isobel caught her breath in sympathy. "Did she act apurpose?" she asked, amazed.

"I doubt it. Hawks are too wild for that. But she was always different, that gos. Later, my men were convinced that she sacrificed herself to protect my life."

"A hard loss to bear," she said. "You loved her."

"I did, in a way. She was more strong-willed and loyal than many people I have known. But for one man," he murmured, "and one lass, long ago."

She was certain that he spoke of William Wallace, but she wondered about the girl. His quiet voice gentled when he mentioned her. An empty ache bloomed inside Isobel. She realized with mild surprise that she felt jealousy—toward the hawk he had loved so well and toward the unknown girl.

"Loyalty is important to you," she murmured.

" 'Tis essential to me," he said bluntly.

She nodded. "Did you love the lass?"

"I did," he said. "In a way. We were both young, and didna know much of love, or of each other. But I was fond of her. I admired her kind nature. And she had a fine laugh." He smiled, rueful and fleeting. "We were betrothed, had been for years on my father's wish. When I gave up the seminary, he decided that I needed marriage to settle me. But the wars, and my commitment to Wallace, delayed the marriage."

Silence lengthened between them. The goshawk chittered.

"Elizabeth was as loyal as Astolat," he said. "Sweet lass, she died unfairly, shortly after Astolat was killed." He spoke with a new edge to his voice. The air between them seemed heavier, as if weighted with regret or sorrow. Beyond the stern beauty of his features, Isobel saw the glimmer of deep hurt in his eyes. "She was at Wildshaw with her old nurse. Elizabeth sometimes acted as chatelaine, since my mother and father were dead, and my brother and I were often absent."

"She was there when Wildshaw was taken?" Isobel asked in a stunned whisper.

"Aye." He stared out over the forest, his chin high, his face set hard. "An English arrow took Astolat in the morning. By afternoon, Elizabeth was gone as well, in a fire set by the English with flaming arrows. They marched through the burning gates of Wildshaw Castle and killed those they didna take prisoner. One man survived to escape. He found us, and told me how Elizabeth had died." He closed his eyes, turned his head.

"Jamie, dear God." The truth of what he had endured that day slammed through her. "You witnessed the fire?" She gazed at him in horror and sympathy.

"Aye, and heard the screams within. But we didna sit idly by," he said. "We took as many Southron lives as we could, though there were close to two hundred armed

and horsed men against seventy on foot. We had just
suffered a great loss to the English at Falkirk. We lacked
the spirit to win."

"Do you know who was responsible for the attack?"

"Only in part," he said. "But I know that Ralph Leslie
was with the English commander."

"I didna think he was a Southron sympathizer then."

"He has changed allegiance often. I am sure he was
there. He was with the party that captured Margaret and
I last spring, and I recognized him from Wildshaw. Some
of the faces from that day, years ago, are seared into my
memory," he said huskily.

"You have a bitter quarrel against the English," she
said. "Against Ralph."

"I do," he agreed. He closed his eyes. "I tried to get
through the gate to save her. I would have walked
through fire for her—for any one of them in that castle—
I swear it," he said fiercely. "But I was wounded, and
dragged back by my men."

Isobel gasped. " 'Tis what Ralph told Alice he did for
me, at Aberlady! Jamie—he must have been there, at
Wildshaw. He must have seen you do that, to think up
such a deed for himself!"

"Aye," he ground out.

She heard the anger and the pain in his voice. "Ralph
lied, but you had the true courage to try to save your
love that day."

He stared out over the forest and did not speak. She
saw a muscle twitch in the angle of his jaw, saw a flush
spread in his cheek. Sympathy washed through her, and
she stepped closer, pressing her hand on his hard-
wrought forearm.

"James," she said. "What happened at Wildshaw was
inevitable. You couldna have saved her. You would have
died, too." She rubbed her fingers over his arm. "I am
sorry that it happened. But I . . . I am glad that you
didna die that day."

Something flickered across his features. He glanced at
her swiftly, and away. "I avenged her death," he said
fiercely. "Without mercy. For weeks afterward. For
months." He drew a long breath. "I may still be aveng-
ing it, even now. But those bloody deeds did naught to

appease what I felt. Every Southron I killed only added to the—to the hollowness I felt inside."

Isobel slipped her hand down to touch his. He grabbed her fingers swiftly, almost desperately, and squeezed them. "Jamie, such suffering must be impossible to ease," she said. "Revenge canna quench so much hurt and anger."

"Neither can prayer," he said bitterly. His fingers gripped hers. "Naught mends that sort of rip in the soul. I may never find peace. But I didna wallow in the hurt. I grew stronger. I grew cold inside, and went after Southrons with a ferocity I didna have before. The Border Hawk became a name that every English soldier knew, and feared. They vowed to capture me, and couldna, for years."

She rubbed her thumb over his. "And they want you still."

"They had me once, at Carlisle in the spring," he said. His voice was so near a growl that she glanced up at him. "And they nearly took my soul. But I will make up for that."

"What do you mean?" she asked in a whisper.

He shook his head and let go of her hand, and lifted a finger to stroke the goshawk's feet. "I swore that I would never keep another hawk," he murmured. "I thought a hawk would only remind me of what I had lost."

"But this silly, wee hawk needs you," Isobel said.

He smiled ruefully. Isobel watched him, glad that he had opened up some of his life to her. But he kept the innermost doors closed, hiding what she feared was the darkest part of his life—that time from the moment he had been taken by the English until now.

She knew, from his mood, that he would answer no questions related to the events that had caused him to be named a traitor. But the more she learned about him, the deeper her compassion became. James would never be able to convince her that he was a true traitor.

"So after Wildshaw was taken, you stayed on the Craig, and continued to run with Wallace?" she asked.

He nodded. "Men came to join me in the forest, Wildshaw's tenants and others, made homeless by Southron

attacks. We ran with Wallace, but we also acted on our
own. Will and I would meet to discuss plans. Ours was
an unsophisticated band—most of the men had naught
but the clothes on their backs and the weapons in their
hands. We lacked the might of the Southrons, but we
had cleverness. We struck as the English went through
the forest, but there were always more to replace the
soldiers we eliminated."

Isobel looked out over the wide vista of forest and
hills as she listened. A movement caught her eye—a
hawk, circling over the trees, rising higher, riding the
wind with an easy grace. As she watched, it swooped
down, disappearing into the forest, intent on quarry.

"One day you will be able to gain back your home
and all that belongs to you," she murmured.

"I hope that isna a prophecy."

She frowned. "Why do you say that?"

"If I regained Wildshaw, I would have to destroy it."

She stared at him. "Are you so bitter, Jamie Lindsay?"

"Hardened of heart," he said. "Scotland lacks the armies and the supplies needed to keep her castles garrisoned against English attack. We can defend only the
most important strongholds—those that are called the
strengths of Scotland. So we must render the rest useless
to the enemy. Aberlady wasna a major castle, and neither is Wildshaw."

"But both were homes," she said. "Homes to their
lairds. And Wildshaw could be that again."

"Of what am I laird?" James made a wide sweep with
his free hand, encompassing the forest, the hills, the sky.
"Of a castle that I havena set foot inside for years? Of
a forest filled with Scottish deer that an English king
claims for his own? Of tenants who have been cast out
of their homes?" He let out a blasting sigh. "I am laird
of naught, lass. I am a brigand, an outlaw, a broken
man."

"You are far more," she said. "You have respect here.
You are a legend in this forest."

He shook his head. "I have lost all claim to that. I am
laird of naught but a mistrusted name and a fading
cause. Naught that can be kept, or measured, or pro-

tected. Like the wind." He waved his hand impatiently. "Impossible to hold."

She looked at him, startled. "Laird of the wind."

A frown creased his brow. "What?"

"Laird of the wind." She gestured around the crag, an echo of his sweep. "You have dominion over this high, windy place," she said. "And more, you command your own freedom. The Southrons canna get to you here. They canna force you to surrender or to say a false oath. You have a freedom that they can never possess, weighted down as they are by armor and weapons, by castles and greed, by the anger of their king. You fight for liberty, and you have given up much for that. But you have gained freedom for yourself, and made progress toward gaining it for others."

He stared at her. "Laird of the wind. Your prophecy."

She nodded. "Aye. I just realized what it means. The hawk of the forest, the laird of the wind—a free man, a man who willna bow down, who rises above the rest— like that hawk you hold, or like that other hawk there, flying above the forest."

She saw his eyes crinkle, his cheek pulse with tension, as if he thought deeply, and held back his secrets. "So 'tis me in your prophecy, after all."

"I think so. But if I named you a traitor, I was wrong. I know you now. You are a man of honor."

He regarded her steadily, intently. "Nay, lass. You think of me as a hero, a champion who saves maidens, who saves the liberty of Scotland, who . . . kisses the blindness from your eyes."

"You are," she insisted. "Those who say you are a traitor dinna know you. You are noble in the heart, where honor dwells."

He frowned. "Nay. I am the man you called a wretched traitor. I am the man who took you from your castle, who made you a hostage, and who now asks you to deceive your betrothed in a scheme of ransom."

You are the man who took my heart, she thought impulsively, but bit back the words before she was foolish enough to say them. "Aye," she said. "You are that man. And I think you are honorable." She lifted her chin stubbornly.

"Are you so certain, Black Isobel?" His quiet voice was powerful enough to be heard over the wind that rushed past them.

"I am," she said. "I stayed with you because I believe that you didna commit treachery. Because I have faith in you."

He glanced at her, his eyes a dark, penetrating blue. "You have faith in me," he repeated slowly, as if he tried to understand the words. The wind whipped around him, but he stood still. The hawk chirred and blinked at both of them, but James did not take his gaze from hers.

"Aye." She leaned toward him. "I do have faith in you," she said as fiercely as she could muster. "Alice does. Your men do. Are you so blind to your own honor that you canna see that? There isna one of us who believes you a traitor. Not one, though you insist we should."

He looked down at her, his eyes as dark as sapphires. "None of you know the truth," he said simply.

"Then tell me." She cupped her hand over his arm.

He watched her silently. His hair blew over his cheek, fluttering like a dark golden banner. He shook it away, and she saw that he shook his head in refusal.

"You trusted me enough to tell me some of what haunts you," she said. "Trust me for the rest."

He smiled, slow and sad, and lifted a hand to trace the curve of her jaw with his fingertips. His thumb brushed the corner of her mouth. She closed her eyes briefly as the sensation streamed through her. He leaned close, his hand warm against her cheek, his face nearly touching hers. She felt his fingers shape her cheek, slide down along her neck, cup the back of her head.

"I trust you well, lass, and I dinna do that easily," he murmured. "But if I told you, your faith would vanish. And I want your trust. I need it." His mouth was so close to hers that she tilted back her head. "God, I need it," he whispered.

His lips covered hers in a kiss more stirring, more hungered than any he had shared with her before. With one arm, he pulled her to him, delving his fingers into the windblown mass of her hair as his mouth slanted over hers.

Isobel leaned back in his embrace and circled her arm around his waist, tipping her head to open to the deepening kiss. The wind rocked against her, and his arm held her steady while his lips caressed hers, softening, hardening, coaxing. She felt as if the world tilted and the wind lifted her.

Then Gawain leaped off of James's outstretched hand like a frog leaving a sunny rock. But his jesses caught him, as always, and he battered wildly against the wind. His wing tips brushed rapidly against her arm. Isobel broke away from James and leaped back with a startled cry.

James looked sternly at the hawk. With a deft flick of his gloved wrist, he turned his arm to accommodate the tiercel, which grasped the jesses with his talons and clambered back onto the fist, squawking. James shook his head in disgust, but he spoke gently to the bird and sang a few notes of the *kyrie* until the bird settled, blinking wide, feet firmly planted on the glove.

James smiled at Isobel, a wry twist of his mouth. "This dim-witted hawk has more sense than I do, I think. I must ask your pardon once again."

Breathless and reeling from the shimmering strength of what had passed between them, Isobel touched his arm. "Dinna beg pardon of me. I was part of that, too," she murmured.

"You have placed yourself in my care, and are about to be sent off to your betrothed. That kiss lacked honor. I willna give Ralph Leslie more reason to seek my head. Nor will I give you reason to regret . . . what passes between us."

She tilted her head to look up at him. "Ah, then," she breathed. "See, you are a man of honor."

He took her hand tightly, as if he would never let go. Then he turned to scan the forest and the sky with keen, brilliant blue eyes. "Do you see the hawk out there?" he asked.

"Aye—there 'tis, to the west."

" 'Tis a red-tailed hawk," he said. "And a large one. A female, I would guess. 'Tisna wild, but a hunting bird. There must be a hunting party down there."

"Look at her. So beautiful!" The hawk soared over

the trees, circled, banked, and sank into the forest. "Soon Sir Gawain will fly like that."

James tilted a doubtful brow as he looked at the gos-hawk on his fist. The bird fluttered his wings and roused his breast feathers. "This sorry gos may never fly for us, or for any owner. We may have to give in to his stub-born nature and let him go when his wing is healed." He narrowed his eyes. "There, through the trees—do you see the riders?"

She shaded her eyes. "Where? Oh—I see a flash of light. What is it?"

"Armor," he said. "Soldiers, coming along the path from Wildshaw." James tugged on her hand. "Come on. We canna risk being sighted up here. If we can see them, they might be able to see us. And there is something I want to show you."

She followed, her hand captured in his, her heart beating like a wild thing, and realized that she did not ever want to leave the crag, or let go of the outlaw who lived there.

And she knew for certain that she did not want to be sent into the cold arms of another man.

Chapter 19

James led Isobel along the length of the promontory, away from the outermost projection with its towering stone broch. She followed him toward the mountain that rose up, solid and dark, on the eastern side. His long steps hurried her along as he led her behind an outcropping formed by a rock slide that must have spilled off the mountain long ago.

"This way," James said. "Go careful, now."

He preceded her down a narrow, sloped path edged with scrub and gorse. A plateau jutted out below the upper level of the crag, tucked in the juncture where the crag split from the mountainside.

A few runnels creased the slope, filled with water from the day's rain. The narrow streams trickled toward the plateau and disappeared behind a thick cluster of gorse.

"Look down here," James said, dropping to his haunches beside the rough green hedge. Isobel leaned forward.

The rocks behind the gorse were jumbled and cracked, a pile of stone broken by the hand of nature. One wide gap opened directly into the crag, and the rills poured over the rounded edge of the gap, forming a thin, delicate fall of water.

Isobel heard the echo of water hitting stone. She peered into the opening and saw flickering reflections of daylight.

"What's down there?" she asked.

"A cave and a spring," he answered. "Can you climb down that ladder with one hand?" He pointed toward the wooden ladder, which leaned against the opening and went down into the gap.

Isobel nodded. James sat on the edge of the hole and caught the side of the ladder, descending it carefully, since he gripped the hawk's jesses in one hand. Gawain flapped his wings and squawked, but maintained enough composure to permit James to drop to the floor of the cave without trouble. James looked at Isobel and held up his hand.

The ladder was ten feet high or so. Isobel sat on the edge of the gap, set her feet on a rung, and grasped the side. She used her injured arm to balance herself as she went down. Then she felt James's hand at her waist, and within moments set foot on the stone floor.

"Step careful now, 'tis wet," he said. His voice had a muted echo. Isobel turned and caught her breath in wonder.

Soft daylight, damp air, and the rushing sound of water filled her senses. Water sparkled as it poured over the rim of the gap, collected in glistening puddles on the uneven floor, and finally spilled into a deep, wide pool.

Along one wall, water cascaded from the rock itself, issuing in foamy surges and clear trickles from crevices in the stone, running down to splash into the same large pool. Another wall had a doorway that looked out on the underground tunnel.

Isobel turned in astonishment. James smiled at her, tipping his head to watch as she spun around. "The shallow end of that pool," he said, "is warm as a bath on days when sunlight shines directly on it. This cave is on the south side of the crag, and so the sun can be strong at times here. The other side of the pool is deeper, and in shadow, and can be quite cold. But we sometimes use hot stones to take the chill from the water."

"This is a miraculous place," Isobel said. "Incredible. I dinna know such things existed—underground pools and falls!"

"Aye, though they are rare. 'Tis often said that springs and pools like this have healing powers. Although I havena heard legends about the Craig. Only my men and I know this place is here, though—the secrets of this crag were lost ages ago."

She nodded, and looked up at the falling water. "Does the water run down like that because of the rain?"

"The rain increases the flow from the outside, but there is always a small stream coming down from the mountain. And the spring in the cave wall comes from somewhere within the mountain. In summer especially, and on warm days, 'tis a bit of paradise to be here."

"Oh, aye," Isobel said, lifting her skirts to walk around the rim of the large pool, which looked like a luxurious tub for a giant, scooped out of sandstone. "Paradise indeed."

James knelt beside one of the puddles, and extended his arm, allowing Gawain to come close to the water.

"Will he drink?" Isobel asked.

"Nay," James said. "Hawks dinna drink unless they are ill. But bathing is good for their feathers and their health. Aye, laddie, try it," he urged gently as the hawk bent down and pecked suspiciously at the water.

The tiercel dipped a talon into the wetness, bit at the gleaming surface again, and then stepped off the fist. He plopped into the water, stretching his wings and widening his tail feathers.

Isobel laughed, the quick trill echoing around the basin of the watery cave. "He likes it."

James smiled up at her. "He might be a useless hawk, but at least he'll be clean." Isobel laughed again. Gawain splashed and uttered a few cheeps and pips as if he were a fledgling in the nest. Isobel and James laughed together, the sounds rising up in a sweet, harmonic echo.

She glanced from the hawk to the man, and felt her heart open like a rose budding in the sun. James did not look at her, and she was glad. He would not see the glow of her feelings, which she could scarcely hide.

If he felt the same joy that rushed through her—made up of this moment's laughter, and of deeper, less definable feelings—then she was sure he would do his best to resist them.

He watched the hawk splash childlike in the puddle. "You can bathe here, too," he said.

"In the puddle, with the hawk?" She blinked at him.

He smiled. "In the pool. You need to strengthen and ease your arm, and the water here will help."

No one had ever showed her such tender concern,

even at home during her bouts of blindness. "I do like water," she admitted. "But that pool looks quite cold."

"Aye. We'll warm the water with stones heated in the fire, so you can have a long soak."

" 'Twould be lovely," she said. "I did wonder if you would recommend a hot loaf of bread for my arm."

He grinned. "How does it feel now, lass?"

She flexed her arm slightly and winced at the searing ache. "The pain is better unless I try to move it. Alice suggested hot poultices to draw the stiffness out. She was going to start those for me."

"When Quentin and Patrick come back, I will ask one of them to fetch the poultice." He frowned, eyeing her arm. "Have you tended to your wound at all today?"

She shook her head. "I havena had the chance."

"I will help you clean and bandage it before you go to sleep. If you want," he added.

She stared up at him, realizing that she would be alone with James when night came, sleeping in a room adjacent to his. The thought of him touching her—indeed, the thought of him peeling away her clothing as he had done before to look at the wound—made her draw in her breath as she gazed at him.

She nodded slowly, wordlessly, stunned by how much he seemed to care about her well-being. The man who had taken her hostage was, at heart, a compassionate man, as she had first thought when he had tended her wounds at Aberlady Castle.

While the hawk dabbled in the puddle, James drew off his heavy glove with languid ease, and stepped toward Isobel. He took her forearm, rounding his long fingers over her wrist and lifting away the sling.

Isobel watched him, her eyes wide, her breath quickening, as he supported her arm in both of his hands and slowly, gently turned it.

"Push against my hand," he instructed her. She did, tentatively. "Now pull up," he said, placing the weight of his hand on her forearm. She did, and winced. "Good. The muscles still have their strength, I think," he said. "I was concerned that the broadhead might have caused permanent damage. As you use the arm, 'twill get stronger. But rest it for now." He replaced the cloth sling.

As he withdrew his hand, his fingers grazed against hers, and she drew in her breath. James tugged on her fingers to pull her forward a step. He brushed away a drift of her dark hair, which had fallen over her shoulder.

"Is this why you are called Black Isobel?" he murmured.

"Aye. Did you think 'twas for my black temperament?" she teased, remembering when she had asked him about his name. His quick smile lifted a corner of his lip.

Her hair slipped down over her shoulder again. "I do like to keep my hair braided back, and under a veil," she went on, searching for something to say. His steady gaze and the press of his fingers on hers made her heart beat at a frantic pace. "But I lack a veil and a comb. Alice braided my hair, but I canna do it myself with but one arm." She turned her head to shake the mass over her shoulders. "The wind has made a wild tangle of it."

He touched the crown of her head. "I can braid it, if you dinna mind a clumsy hand at the task. Turn, now." He urged her around with a little push.

His fingers soothed through her hair, lifting, tugging gently, grazing against her neck and shoulders as he made a thick plait. Deep shivers traced through her from head to foot, pooling and swirling in her breasts and abdomen.

The heat of his body encompassed her inside the intimate, damp space of the cave. Her heart thundered within her, echoing the plunging sound of the water. She did not move, hesitant to disturb the sparkling web of sensation around her, formed by his touch and his presence.

His hands worked onward, smoothing, tucking, creating cascades of luxurious sensation in her. " 'Tis a sorry sort of braid, but 'twill do," he finally said.

She half turned her head. "Your hand isna clumsy," she murmured. "You have a gentle, deft hand."

"I've learned well from hawks," he murmured.

"You have," she agreed, closing her eyes briefly.

He smoothed her hair over her ear, and his thumb

caressed a path down the slope of her neck, sending wondrous tremors through her. She wanted to turn in his arms and feel his lips press hers again. Her body pounded with an urgent, startling need. But she stood still, trembling, waiting.

"Ah, lass," he murmured softly, and lifted his hands away. "I will regret sending you to your betrothed, I think."

"Will you?" she asked, breathless.

He sighed out. "But you must go back—for your father, and for Margaret." He paused. "And Ralph Leslie will want to see you again."

She bowed her head, feeling as if a sad weight descended upon her shoulders. "I dinna go back just for Sir Ralph." She heard his indrawn breath, and rushed on. "I think that he only means to use me—for the prophecies."

"The others used you, too, lass. They kept you away from the world, and cared more about the prophetess than the lass."

"I know that now," she murmured. She glanced over her shoulder at him. "I think you may be the only one who cares about . . . about *me*. You have shown me kindness and patience."

He sighed. "I meant to use you, too, as a barter for Margaret. I still intend to do that. Dinna be so quick to think me a champion or a saint. I am a rogue, and that I will stay."

"But—" She frowned as she tried to put the words together. "But you never forced me to your will, as a true rogue would have done. And when I insisted on my freedom, you were willing to give it to me, even though 'twould deprive you of what you wanted. And you—you—"

"What?" His voice was so gentle she thought she would melt into its warmth. She wanted to turn around, and yet kept her back to him, her head bowed, her hands tucked across her waist protectively. But she spilled her thoughts and feelings like the water that poured over the rim of the cave.

"You asked me to help you, as a friend," she said. "I

valued that, Jamie. So much, you canna know," she added in a whisper. "I have had few friends."

"Ah," he said. "And so you dinna want to go to Ralph. You want to stay here with me."

She nodded, a little trembling shake. She waited through his silence, her heart pounding heavily. What she wanted in her life, what she needed, suddenly crystallized in her mind, as if she had indeed been blind inside, for a very long time, and now saw a promising ray of light.

But she did not have the courage to tell him what she felt. She did not want to leave him, and could not say that out loud. And she hesitated to name the true reason for that urge, even in her own thoughts. She closed her eyes.

He touched her hair at the bared nape of her neck, his fingers threading through the tendrils. "Isobel," he said.

She savored the sultry way he said her name, as if he breathed it, breathed her. "Aye?" she asked.

"I have been a fool," he said. He touched her shoulder and turned her slowly.

Her heart pounded hard as she looked up at him. "A fool?"

He nodded, folding his arms over his chest, tilting his head to look at her. "I should have kept you a hostage."

A keen sense of disappointment shot through her. "Oh."

With thumb and finger, he reached out and lifted her chin. "I should never have let you become a friend." Isobel watched him, silent, enthralled. "Now I canna easily give you up."

"You dinna have to give me up," she murmured.

His thumb brushed the edge of her jaw. "I must," he whispered.

She drew a breath, leaned toward him. "Jamie—"

"Och!" A voice hovered above them. "Look at that, would you, Quentin. Margaret willna like that."

Isobel jumped as if she had been stung. James shifted a hand to her shoulder as they both looked upward.

Quentin and Patrick peered down at them from the overhead gap, with sheepish, delighted grins on their faces. "Aye," Quentin said to Patrick. "She willna like it at all."

"Och, then we willna tell her," Patrick said helpfully. "Can we come down there, or do you two want to be alone?"

Isobel felt a deep, hot flush spread over her cheeks and throat. She looked up and saw Quentin wink at her. Patrick still grinned. James scowled at both of them.

"We'll come up," James said. "I hope you two ruffians brought something for supper."

Patrick held up a brace of rabbits. "Two for us, and one for that surly gos of yours."

James glanced at Isobel, and frowned as he pulled on his hawking glove. Without a word, he bent down to the goshawk and patiently coaxed him out of the puddle.

Isobel waited for him, noticing the bright, telling blush that stained the outlaw's cheeks.

" 'Twould be more than foolish to walk up to the yett of Wildshaw Castle and call out that we've a message from the Border Hawk," Patrick grumbled, his mouth full of roasted meat. He wiped his chin on his sleeve and shifted his legs, crossed on the stone floor of James's small bedchamber inside the broch wall. "We would be taken hostage ourselves—or slain on the spot."

"We willna approach the gate of Wildshaw Castle," James said, seated on the floor with them, his back leaned against his bed. "We can conduct the whole of this business in Stobo."

"Aye," Quentin said. "The priest there, Father Hugh, says he knows both Ralph Leslie and Black Isobel."

"Exactly," James said. "I want you to go back there. Ask him to convey the glad news to Sir Ralph Leslie that Lady Isobel is alive, for Leslie believes she died at Aberlady. And ask him to deliver our demands as well."

"And just what are your demands?" Isobel asked.

James glanced at her. She sat on the stone bench by the window, a few feet away. Faint moonlight cascaded through the narrow opening and over her face. The long, fluid lines of her body were highlighted by the glow of the fire that burned in the small stone hearth.

"We will request that Leslie meet us at the village

church in Stobo, after mass Sunday next," he said. "I
believe 'tis the feast day of Saint Ursula."

"How fitting," she murmured.

"Fitting? Why?" Patrick asked.

"Saint Ursula, the patroness of virgins," Isobel said
"ran away from an impending marriage that she protested. She took her female companions with her. Eleven
thousand of them."

"Och," Patrick grunted. "At least we only have to
look after two lassies."

"Tell Father Hugh," James said, "that we will meet Leslie before mass on Sunday, in the presence of many others,
since the villagers will be gathered outside the church after
mass. Isobel will wait for him inside the church. He must
bring three men only in escort, and he must send Margaret into the church alone. We will permit Isobel to go
out to him when Margaret is safely in our hands."

"You will claim sanctuary, then," Isobel said. "The
safety and protection of holy ground."

"Certes," James replied. "We canna trust Leslie. He
could escort Margaret to Stobo with a hundred men."

"If he would take part in what was done to Wallace,
he willna let a pair of church doors stop him from getting
you," Quentin said. "He will want the Border Hawk's
head for this."

"But if he wants Isobel, he must agree to an uncompli-
cated and peaceful exchange. And he does want Isobel.
Be sure of that," he added quietly, glancing at her. The
words seemed to stick in his throat.

Isobel said nothing. She turned her head to look out
the window. James felt a deep tug in the region of his
heart as he watched her. He sighed and pulled at his
earlobe, feeling reluctant and torn.

He tried to convince himself that she was infatuated
with him, that she wrongly idealized him as some champion. The best course, he thought, was to send her away
from him quickly.

But what he felt for her was far deeper than infatua-
tion. Those feelings burned within him, stifled and un-
spoken, flaring into passion whenever he was near her.

He could hardly bear to send her back to Leslie, but
his original plans had been formed long before he knew

her. Isobel had altered the scheme at every step—in an unwitting, frustrating, and wholly charming manner. He had to stoke his determination to see this through. He had no other way of rescuing Margaret.

And besides, he reminded himself sourly, Isobel had been promised in marriage long ago. She deserved a home, and should be with a man who could truly safeguard her—even an English sympathizer whom James loathed. Surely not some forest brigand.

"You will be safe at Wildshaw, Isobel," he said to her impassive profile, uncertain if he meant to convince her, or himself, that she should go.

She shrugged one shoulder and did not look at him.

"You will be reunited with your father," he added, "if Ralph has kept his word to you."

"Aye," she said, and went on staring at the moonlit sky.

"The lass is tired," Quentin murmured, from his seat beside James. "Isobel, Jamie asked me to find a blanket for your bed. I put one there before supper and hung a curtain. And Alice sent along your satchel of clothing."

"And I brought up some fine French wine out of storage," Patrick said, "if you would care for a dram or two."

She rose from her seat. "Thank you," she said quietly. "I willna have wine, but I do need some rest. Good night."

She drifted through the shadowed room like a wraith, pushed aside the cloak that served as a curtain, and disappeared into the darkness beyond the narrow threshold of the adjoining room.

James watched her go, and felt his heart sink a little with each step she took. Now that the process of bartering with Leslie had begun, he felt more dishonorable, more traitorous than ever. She had given him her trust, and he was sending her away.

Patrick poured wine from a jug into the clay cups that had already been emptied that evening. He handed one cup to James, another to Quentin, and noisily swallowed the contents of the last one himself.

James downed his wine more swiftly than he meant

to do, and leaned over to refill the cup himself. "If you leave at dawn, you will be at Stobo by midmorn."

"Aye," Quentin said, eyeing him soberly. "And what will you do? Take the lass to Alice's house?"

James shook his head. "I dinna want to risk anyone taking her before this is done. Alice has Eustace and Henry there to guard her. I'll keep Isobel here at the Craig."

"Ah," Quentin said. The sage note in his voice made James frown at him. "While you have the chance, you may as well try to solve whatever 'tis between you and the lass."

"There is naught between us," James growled, and sipped from his cup, tasting the sharp sting of the red wine as it went down. "And you make a bold statement." He shot Quentin a grim look.

"Jamie, do you think we are fools?" Quentin asked. "I dinna think you can give her up to Leslie."

"I can," he snapped.

"Will she go?" Patrick asked.

"Aye." He stood. "I'll see to the hawk."

"The hawk is asleep, on that front perch in the mews, with his head tucked to his wing," Patrick said. "I looked in on him as I came up with the wine."

"Leave him be," Quentin said. "He's jessed, and tired. He'll sleep, and be safe."

James nodded. He rubbed a hand over his jaw, shoved his fingers through his hair, feeling unsettled, as if there was something he should do, and could not think what it was. "I'll have to work with him some more. His wing willna heal unless he stops bating and fussing. He has to learn to sit quietly."

"He will, though he's spoiled," Quentin said. "I have never seen any man with as much patience for a hawk as you have. But you look as if you havena slept properly for a week."

"I havena," James said. "You know what message to deliver to Father Hugh."

"We know," Quentin said. "And 'twill be done. Jamie, 'tis a dangerous scheme. Father Hugh knows Leslie quite well, I gather. We can trust the priest only with caution, I think."

"I agree," James said. "We'll let him deliver the message, but we canna tell him any more about our business. And I want you to get Geordie out of his hands before this exchange takes place. Father Hugh willna let harm come to Isobel, but we shouldna trust Geordie to a friend of Leslie's for long."

"The lad will be able to travel by the time we go back to Stobo," Patrick said.

"Good. I need one more favor of you both," James said. "I want you to travel to Dunfermline Abbey to see Brother John Blair. Find out what more he has learned about Wallace's betrayers, and what other news he might have. If Geordie needs further rest, you can leave him with John. I dinna want to risk harm to the lad by bringing him back here, unless he's strong enough to wield a bow and a sword again."

Quentin nodded. "Do you have a message for Blair?"

James turned to look out through the small window at the white and misted moon. The melancholy sight seemed to embody what he felt inside his own heart.

"Tell him that I have the prophetess," he said. "Tell him that she is willing to serve as my . . . payment for my cousin."

"I think," Quentin said slowly, "that you will pay more dearly for that cousin than you ever imagined."

James drew in a sharp breath. "Is that a prediction?"

Quentin stared at him through the shadows. "Aye," he said gruffly, and took a deep swallow of wine.

Chapter 20

James sat on the uppermost edge of the broch wall, watching Isobel, who stood far out on the grassy plateau of the crag. The wind, always steady and strong there, lifted her braid and blew her clothing against her long, slim body. The simple lines of her dark green gown, which she had taken from the satchel Quentin and Patrick had brought to her, lent her an elfin, beautiful appearance. When she lifted her head proudly, the sun, already past its high point, shone on the crown of her head and set a smooth gloss to her hair.

He recalled the heavy silk of that skein in his hands when he had braided her hair that morning. Scarcely a word had passed between them then, or later, when they had shared a breakfast of porridge and water.

He had not known quite what to say in the face of her silent mood. Even when he led her in a long tour of the crag, carrying the hawk as they explored the broch, the tunnels, and the caves, they had discussed only the features of the promontory—its rock, its tower, its water, its weather—and little about the man who had lived there for years.

She had not asked him more about his life as an outlaw on the Craig. He missed her curious, eager questions, her astute observations. He found that he wanted, very much, to talk with her. But he also saw the wisdom in silence.

Even more, he saw the merit in caution. He had touched her only when offering his hand to step up or down, although the rush of desire that went through him at such simple contact made him draw in his breath. He had not allowed himself to stand too close to her, or to look too deeply into her luminous eyes.

She would be leaving soon. He did not see much wisdom in strengthening the link that had already forged between them.

She had kept her distance, as well, he had noticed, lowering her thick-lashed eyelids, speaking softly, sharing wan, cool smiles. She had retreated into a reserve, where, he suspected, she was angry, resentful, and perhaps disappointed in him.

He knew that she dreaded the exchange that was to take place in a few days. He did, too. But he knew full well that it must go forward for many reasons. He wanted Margaret safe—and he wanted Isobel safe as well.

The tiercel chirred on his gloved fist, feet planted firmly, eyes sharp, his movements calm. James glanced at him. Gawain's mood was improved, for he had bated only once or twice so far that day, when startled or hungry. Perhaps a night's rest had helped the bird; perhaps he had finally begun to accept his new master's fist. Whatever it was, James was grateful, and more confident that the tiercel could be manned.

He sang the *kyrie* once again, as he had done often that day, humming it as he stroked the bird's breast feathers. Gawain looked out over the crag, over the sky and the forest. A flock of larks flew past, and the bird scarcely moved.

James was pleased by that sign of progress. He thought the time might be near when he could train the bird to jump to the fist from a leash, and then fly on a creance, a line long enough to allow the bird to fly a distance from the fist and back again. Before he could release the bird to freedom, he had to be certain Gawain could fly well.

But first, he wanted to treat the bird's sprained wing again, warming the fresh loaf of bread that Alice had sent through Quentin and Patrick. And Gawain's bent tail feathers needed straightening if he was to be allowed to fly. For both of those procedures, he would need Isobel's help.

He returned his gaze to her as she stood on the promontory. He would call her if she did not come back to the broch soon, for he wanted to tend to Gawain while the bird was quiet.

But as he looked down at Isobel, he only wanted to walk along the crag with her, to talk and laugh with her—to hold and touch her. That last urge filled his blood with fire. He sat, and watched her lonely, wind-blown figure, and did not move.

He knew that he had begun to treasure her. God help him, he might even have begun to love her. He could not define the tumultuous feelings that rocked inside of him—he was afraid to name them. He had never anticipated this turn of events when he had set out to find the prophetess of Aberlady.

Only one certain fact existed. No matter his own feelings, soon he would have to let her go.

Isobel felt the push of the wind and the warmth of the sun, and stretched her arms out for a moment, despite the ache of her injury. The sun's heat felt good on the stiff muscles.

She looked up at the mountain that soared beside the crag, and then gazed out over the dense green forest. So high up that she could watch veils of mist float over the trees, she felt truly free and unfettered for the first time in her life.

Until lately, she had not realized how closely her father had protected her at Aberlady. Since her mother's death, she had stayed inside its walls, going out only to attend holy day masses at Stobo, to ride occasionally with her father over the hills, and to go to market once or twice a year with her nurse. She had never questioned her life.

She had been confined and closely supervised, without true friends, and with few servants and kin. At Aberlady, she read poets and patriarchs, embroidered fine work, and practiced the skills needed to run a castle household. And she prophesied whenever her father had deemed it time for her to do so.

When her father had been taken in battle, the weeks of the siege that followed had begun a new education for her, one that James Lindsay had continued. She had

discovered not only untapped strengths, but a deep taste
for freedom. Ironically, she understood the extent of her
sheltering only once she had been captured.

Now James expected her to return to a protected life,
with an unwanted husband as a guardian instead of a
father. But she no longer could accept being an obedient
prophetess, letting her abilities be used by men who regarded her as a weak female to be directed—and even
more, as a political advantage.

Her visions were precious to her. She endured blindness each time for the privilege, and she did not want
the integrity of the visions compromised. Her gift of
prophecy needed to flow from the will of God, and never
again through the will of another.

If the siege had not occurred, and if James Lindsay
had not taken her away from Aberlady, she might never
have realized her own independence. She would be at
Aberlady still, the pawn of Father Hugh and Ralph Leslie, in her father's absence.

She sighed. She had to know that her father was safe.
The last vision she had seen—and which she was astonished to recall so easily—had been an image of her father in a dungeon. She did not doubt its truth, but did
not know if it represented past, present, future, or some
symbolic meaning.

The only way she could find out what had happened
to her father in reality was to go to Sir Ralph. She
hugged herself as she thought, and looked down. The
landscape spread out for miles, wide and crystal clear in
the sunlight, as if she saw it from the vantage point of
a bird. The beauty and the scope of the view was stunning, as marvelous as any vision.

She did not want to leave this, ever. Nor did she want
to leave the man who had brought her here. But she
knew that she must go, for her father, and for James,
who wanted his beloved cousin back again—more than
he wanted to keep Isobel with him.

She glanced over her shoulder at the broch. James sat
on a high edge of the wall, the goshawk on his gloved
fist. The outlaw was a solitary figure in brown, the sun
glinting gold over his head, the wind lifting his hair. He
looked like a legend come to life, a figure of wild, un-

tamed power and beauty. And yet inside, he was securely manacled to the past.

Isobel adored him, but he did not see it. He had shown her kindness and caring, had given her respect, had even erased the blindness from her with an exquisite kiss. The wonder of that had stayed with her. She knew that she could love him utterly, if he would only let her. If he had wounds, she wanted to balm them; if he had secrets, she wanted to keep them as her own.

High up on the broch wall, as she watched, James stood and lifted his hand to her. He waved slowly, and beckoned.

Her heart leaped. She lifted her skirt in one hand and walked toward the broch, hungry to be near him. She would even welcome his cool silences, if that was all he offered her.

She wanted far more. With this man, she knew now that she would never lose her freedom. With him, she could find safekeeping as well as happiness. But the forest outlaw did not intend to include a prophetess in his life.

She would have to accept confinement once again. For now, though, she meant to cherish the little taste of freedom that remained.

"Hold the jesses securely, now," James told Isobel. "Wrap them around your fingers."

She twined the leather jesses around her smallest two fingers, lost in the thick glove that swathed her hand, and looked up to see James's nod of approval.

Gawain settled his feet squarely on her fist and blinked at them both, turning his head and cocking his wild bronze eyes. Isobel shifted her hand as she tucked the end of the thong away. The tiercel lifted his gray and cream wings and squawked, fluttering rapidly in a partial, upright bate.

Isobel ducked, startled, as a wing tip batted her cheek, a blow harder than she would have thought. James reached out a hand to assist her, then withdrew it when the bird calmed.

"I have him," Isobel assured him, straightening her posture.

He looked at her doubtfully, and nodded. "Very well. I'll warm the bread and we can treat the wing." He turned away to rummage in the sack of food that Quentin and Patrick had left with them the previous night.

He had led Isobel to a small cell on the lowest level of the broch's mural chambers. The square space, whose broken walls were partly open to the sky, creating a wide windowlike area, had a stacked stone hearth that served, James explained, as a kitchen for the outlaws. She knew that Patrick and Quentin had cooked supper here for all of them last night.

Part of the chamber was cozy with heat, and a refreshing breeze came through the gap in the wall. The fire that James had started that morning still burned low, with a tangy odor.

James stepped to the hearth and set an empty iron kettle on a hook over the glowing peat bricks. He placed the bread, wrapped in cloth, inside for warming. After a few moments he took it out, sliced it partly in half, and handed the hot, fragrant loaf to Isobel.

"Can you hold it on his wing?" he asked. "I want to fetch water to use for straightening his tail feathers."

"If you fill another kettle, I can make us something to eat," she said. "Alice sent some food—I know we still have oats, onions, and some cooked chicken from her stores."

He nodded and left the chamber carrying two kettles. Isobel sat on a large stone slab that served as both a bench and a low table, and craned her neck to watch him stride across the grassy courtyard toward the well, where he filled the kettles with water drawn from a bucket on a rope.

She turned her attention to the goshawk, applying the warmed bread over the joint of his wing and shoulder as she and James had done before. When the bird grew restive on her fist, jerking his neck and lifting his wings, she wondered why James had not hooded him to calm him before leaving her alone with the task.

She frowned and admonished herself for even thinking of blindfolding the bird. Drawing a breath, she began to sing the *kyrie eleison* in a low tone, repeating it over and over.

Gawain had learned to respond to the pattern of sound. He grew motionless and watched her boldly. She remembered that hawks did not like to be stared at—although they could stare all they pleased—and glanced away, still singing.

She looked up to see James in the doorway, leaning against the stone frame, listening. She stopped, blushing, and he came into the room, setting the kettles down by the hearth.

" 'Twas lovely," he said. "Dinna stop. It calms the bird."

She could feel the heat in her cheeks as she began to sing again. James set one kettle of water over the fire, and turned to pull on the hawking glove that he had set aside.

"Here, let me take him," he said. "You did say you would make us some supper." He smiled.

Her heart gave a curious lurch to see that smile. She nodded and stood as James stepped toward her. She lifted the bread and held out her fist.

Gawain, perhaps startled by the movement of the bread, shrieked and clenched one foot tightly on her first finger.

Isobel gasped, a raw intake of breath, at the fierce pain. She tightened her fist in response to the excruciating hold on her gloved finger. She panicked, reaching out with her right hand to pry the clamping talons loose.

James hit her bare hand away. "Open your hand," he ordered. "Isobel, open your hand and cast him off!" He reached out and slid the jesses off her smallest fingers, then shoved at her arm.

Through a haze of pain and fear, she understood what he wanted. She tossed her arm and opened her fingers to release the bird. Gawain spread his wings and fluttered upward, kakking, and was brought up short by James's hold on his jesses.

"Come here, you gos," James said, and hummed the *kyrie*. The bird flapped down to his fist and settled there, fixing them both with a baleful eye. "Naughty lad," James muttered, and sat on the stone bench. "Isobel, let me see."

She sat beside him and drew off her glove, wincing.

Her finger was reddened and swollen, and as she turned it to show him, she bit her lower lip against the ache.

James took her hand in his, his touch infinitely gentle. "Can you move it?" She wiggled the finger and nodded. "Good," he said. "A hawk can break a bone like kindling wood, even through a glove, if he gets a tight enough hold. Even a strong man canna break the grip of a talon easily. The only way to loose the hold is to cast them off and let them think they are free." He studied her bruised finger. "You were lucky, lass."

"Why did he do it?" she asked. "I thought he was tamed."

"He will never tame," he said, keeping her hand in his. "He's wild, and manning will never change that. 'Tis why hawks must be handled with patience and respect. I know you showed him that," he added quickly. "But goshawks are high-tempered creatures. There is always a little danger in keeping a short-winged hawk, even the best of hawks."

She nodded and looked at Gawain. "Naughty lad," she said sternly. James chuckled. Still he did not let go of her hand, and she leaned a little toward him as his fingers cradled hers.

"He will always be a bit of a rogue, this gos," he said, and stood, stepping near the hearth. He fetched a bowl and a ladle from a shelf, scooped water from the second kettle on the floor, and brought the bowl to her. "Soak your hand here—the water is still cold from the well."

She dipped her fingers into the cool water with a sigh of relief. While she sat, James moved around the kitchen with the hawk, fetching Alice's sack of food and settling the spare kettle of water over the fire. He dumped in some oats, a whole onion, and the entire cooked chicken.

"I was going to cook our supper," Isobel said.

"Well, you canna do it just now, and I am starved," James said. "I have been making my own meals for years, lass. If you dinna mind simple foods, we'll eat soon."

"Simple, aye," she said, and laughed. " 'Tisna even cut up."

"With a hawk on my fist, I think I did well." He took

a long stick from the shelf and stirred the pot slopping some of the mixture over the side. Then he went toward a pile of rounded stones in a corner of the room, and carried several, two or three at a time in his free hand, over to the hearth.

"What are you doing?" she asked curiously, still soaking her fingers as she watched.

"When the stones are hot, I'll take them down to the spring. I promised you a warm bath. After enduring yet another injury with great courage, I think you should at least enjoy a bath." He glanced at her and smiled.

The feeling of warmth that flooded through her had nothing to do with hearth fires. "Thank you," she murmured.

He nodded and peered into the other kettle. "Now, can you help me? This water is boiling."

She set aside the bowl. "What are you going to do?"

"Cook a naughty gos," he said, and grinned when her mouth dropped open in surprise. "Nay, lassie. I'll show you. We need to straighten his crooked tail feathers."

He ladled boiling water into a deep wooden bowl, taken from a stack of two or three on a shelf with a few cups, and carried the bowl to the slab on which she sat. Isobel shifted over when James sat down. He placed the bowl of hot water between them.

He moved his gloved fist, with the recalcitrant hawk, close to his chest and smoothed his hand over Gawain's back. His long fingers, large-knuckled and strong, eased over the bird's plumage, and he uttered a few low, quiet phrases.

"Look at his tail," James said. "The deck feathers, those in the middle, are twisted. A quick dip in boiling water will straighten them out."

"That sounds risky, with him," Isobel said skeptically.

"Aye, 'tis," he said. "But we can do it together. I'll move him toward the water, and you grasp his tail and dip it."

Isobel grimaced. James grinned, fleetingly, as if he acknowledged the risk and enjoyed it. She wiggled her bruised, aching finger and nodded, holding out her hands. Her right arm, while stiff, was improved, and she could use that hand if she moved the arm carefully.

James lowered the hawk on his fist and murmured quietly, soothing his hand over the goshawk's back, coaxing him to spread his tail in a wide fan.

"Six bars out," he said. "See the gray bars across his tail feathers? That tells us his age. He'll have seven bars showing when he's full grown. Aye, you gos, you're still a young lad, and act like one, too."

"He acts like a bairnie who doesna get his way," Isobel grumbled as James lowered the hawk toward the water, spreading his hand firmly over the back and wings. Isobel grasped the soft feathers of the tail.

Shrieks, footing, a wildly flapping wing, and the dipping was soon over. James pulled his arm up, murmuring to the bird, and reached into the pouch at his waist. He withdrew a piece of raw meat and fed it to him; Isobel saw that it was a segment of the rabbit that Patrick and Quentin had brought for the bird.

"What a fine tail you have now," James murmured. "And soon you'll be soaring out there, where you belong. *Ky-ri-e e-lei-son*," he intoned, repeating the melodic phrase while the bird devoured the bit of food clenched in his talons. "*Ky-ri-e e-lei-son*." He sang it again, and then again, spinning a pattern of calming sound.

Isobel leaned her back against the stone wall behind her and listened, cradling her injured finger and closing her eyes. James's voice combined mellow serenity with rich power. She breathed in the sound, let it soothe over her and through her, its peace easing her doubts, her fears, her sadness.

Then she lifted her chin, drew a breath, and began to sing with him. Her voice, fainter than his, without his truth of tone, gained power in the blended harmony and rose into the air with assurance.

After a while, his voice hovered on a long, vanishing note. Isobel ended her own song, listening as the glorious thrum of his voice vibrated through her body.

"Isobel," James said softly into the silence. "I think my porridge is burning."

Chapter 21

Isobel tested the water gingerly with her bare foot. The water in the shallow end of the underground pool was indeed warm. After they had eaten their meal—the porridge and chicken had been overcooked but hearty—James had carried the hot stones to the pool and stacked them in the water for her.

She stripped out of her gown and chemise and set them beside her boots. The late afternoon sun sent amber beams into the cave, creating a warm rainbow sparkle in the trickling water.

She eased herself into the water and sat, sighing with delight. Above, on the crag's summit, she could hear James whistle to the hawk. He had told her that he intended to work with the tiercel, coaxing him to jump a short distance, on a leash, from a perch to his fist. While he set off for the task, she had eagerly gone to the cave, a square of linen tucked in her belt ready to be used as toweling.

She shimmied deeper into the pool and leaned back against the rim. The natural stone bowl had been rubbed smooth in some places by flowing water, and she stretched out and sank nearly to her chin once she found a comfortable niche.

Water lapped in a gentle cadence against stone and trickled musically down the ridges and furrows in the rock wall. She relaxed as tension flowed out of her. The warm water eased her aching arm. A current of colder water, carried from the deeper far end of the pool, swirled among the warmth.

She thought, dreamily, that she could stay here forever. Water had always given her a sense of tranquility.

As a child, she had loved going with her mother, along with a few children of Aberlady's tenants, to swim in a small lochan outside the castle.

She leaned back her head, wetting her hair, sluicing it through with one hand. Closing her eyes, she felt the drifting water surround her.

Blended with the myriad sounds of the water, she heard a low melody as James sang to the hawk somewhere overhead, out on the crag. Isobel smiled softly as she listened.

Splashing the water gently over herself, she smiled again as she thought how much the Craig resembled a paradise. She thought that she could easily spend her life in this solitary, beautiful place without regret—so long as James was with her. Then she sighed sadly.

She listened to the faint, true notes of his plainsong, blended in a melody with the water. The warmth, the lapping water, and the harmonic murmurs of the spring relaxed her deeply. The edges of her awareness dissolved into the harmony, and she saw delicate lights dance behind her eyelids.

Within moments, she sat upright in the water and grasped the edge of the stone. But she could not dispel the shimmering images that had already begun.

A man sat in the darkest corner of a dank chamber, his back leaned against the wall, his ankles manacled. His large frame was so thin that he appeared skeletal, and his long gray hair had lost its silvery tone under layers of grime. When he looked up, his striking blue eyes—so like her own—were hollow with a loss of hope. Then the shadows closed around her father's image.

She saw several horsemen in the forest, riding along a track in pairs, with Sir Ralph Leslie in the lead. He was strong and bull-like in build, his smile complacent, his posture commanding as he rode his dappled horse. He turned to look at the woman who rode beside him, her glossy black hair braided beneath a gauzy veil, her gown an embroidered and costly blue silk.

"Wife," he said, and smiled. The woman did not look at him.

Isobel knew that his bride was herself. She gasped,

gripping the stone rim of the pool, and opened her eyes, but all she saw was darkness, a broad field for the swirling images.

She saw the pilgrim again, as she had before, cloaked and hooded, walking past a church in the rain. This time he pushed back his hood as he walked toward the hawthorn tree. This time he knelt by the green mound under the tree and clasped his hands in prayer, while the goshawk fluttered past him into the tree.

Isobel saw herself approach him, her gown whispering over the damp grass. He looked up and smiled. When she reached out to him, he vanished into the mist and the rain.

Then she saw an array of battle scenes, men who struggled with each other on a field, wielding sword and ax, lance and mace, their blows heavy and hard, their armor bloodied and shimmering in the light of a misty dawn, and in a shaded wood, and beside a wide, calm stream. The sounds and sights of the battles faded, replaced by a lion overlooking Scottish hills.

She drew breath, and gripped the edge of the pool, and saw one last, vivid scene of a skirmish in the forest between men on horses and men on foot. James was among them, surrounded by riders. He swept out with his sword as they closed in on him. Blood darkened his face as he fell.

"James!" Isobel screamed. *"Jamie!"* She lunged out of the pool, splashing and puddling water on stone. Darkness enveloped her, and she sobbed and trembled, less alarmed by her blindness than by a sudden fear for James, wounded and defeated in her vision. She prayed mutely that she had not seen his death.

She fell to her hands and knees on slick stone and groped for her clothing. Finding them at last, she rummaged for the linen square, swiping it hastily over herself in an effort to dry her chilled, dripping skin. Her shaking hands were clumsy and uncertain, but she found her chemise and yanked it over her head, twisting her arm painfully as she pulled on the garment.

The murmur of the spring and the streams seemed much louder once she was sightless. The echo was so steady that it masked the sound of the spring itself, making it hard for her to orient herself. She stood, holding her gown, and turned hesitantly in what she thought was the direction of the ladder, the quickest way to the top. She knew that a doorway led out to the tunnel, but she feared getting lost in a maze of branches and caves.

"James!" she called out. "Jamie!" The strained echo of her voice seemed lost amid the rush of the water, which sounded like muffled thunder to her ears.

She took a few halting steps forward, and her foot stumbled in a puddle on the floor. She caught her balance, gasped, and turned again. Her hand extended in front of her, she found a wall.

She fumbled her fingers over its damp, knobby surface, following it as she took several careful steps. The surging rush of the spring grew louder, confusing her. Another step, and another—then she stepped out into nothingness and fell into the pool.

The shock of the cold water brought her upright, gasping and choking, in water over her head. She sank down and spun under the water, arms flailing. Then she came up, her chemise twisting around her, and sank again. She used the strength of her legs to bound back up to the surface, as her limbs remembered, from childhood practice, how to stay afloat.

Half swimming, half sinking, coughing and gasping and near panic, she pushed forward through bone-cold water, uncertain where the edge of the pool was in the enveloping darkness.

James tore off his boots and tunic as he called out her name, but Isobel had gone under the surface for a second time. He plunged feetfirst into the deep end of the pool and sliced through the water toward her. Isobel thrashed, sputtering, her hair spreading like a black cape. He swam toward her with swift, long strokes and grabbed her around the chest, pulling her against him as he headed, legs pumping, for the rim of the pool.

He lifted her over the ledge and heaved himself out of the water, breathing hard. She leaned over and moaned, her breath as ragged and labored as his. The frightened, wild look in her eyes alarmed him.

"Isobel," he rasped. He swept back the sopping curtain of hair that had fallen over her face. "Isobel, you are fine. I'm here." He tipped her head up and wiped water from her cheek.

"Jamie," she said, reaching out. The movement was awkward. She hit her arm into his shoulder, then she fumbled down to grasp his forearm. James stared at her, frowning. Isobel sat nearly nude before him, and did not seem to know it. She stared upward, her eyes glass-blue.

Beneath the wet, diaphanous cream silk of her chemise, her breasts quivered round and full; the fabric clung to her hips and pooled over her bare thighs. Desire streamed heavily through him, but his heart plummeted.

He lifted a hand and waved it slowly before her face. She neither moved nor blinked.

"Oh, God, Isobel," he whispered.

With a curdled sob, she fell toward him. He slid his arms around her and gathered her close. She muffled her tears against his bare chest. She was shivering and dripping wet, as he was.

"Soft, you," he said, and held her securely with one arm, while he stretched forward to snatch his dry tunic. He wrapped it around her shaking body. "Be calm, lass."

"I had a vision . . . s-several of them," she stammered, shivering violently. Late golden light poured downward, but the sunbeams no longer took the dank chill from the air.

"Tell me about it up in the broch, where we can both get warm and dry," he said. He stood, helping her to her feet, and snugged his tunic securely around her. Then he stepped away to gather his boots and hers, and dragged her dripping green gown out of the water, wringing it out.

Wrapping an arm tightly around her, he led her carefully through the door of the cave and guided her along the tunnel to the long flight of stacked steps beneath the broch.

In his sleeping chamber inside the broch walls, he gave Isobel a blanket from his bed, a length of plaid wool that was both thick and warm. While she removed her wet chemise, he turned carefully away and added wood to the low fire. Then he stripped out of his own wet breeches and snatched up his wide pilgrim's cloak against the distinct chill, exaggerated by damp skin and hair.

"Come sit by the fire," he said, turning to guide her. She settled on the floor beside the hearth with her back leaned against the wall and her knees drawn up beneath the blanket.

James could hear her teeth chattering. He sat beside her and pulled her within the circle of his arm.

"Wh-where is the hawk?" she asked, shivering.

"I put him in his mews," he said. "I thought he had worked hard enough for the day."

"D-did he come to your fist on the leash?" she asked.

"You are cold." He rubbed his hand up and down her back to help warm her. "He came like a dream, Isobel, flying the length of the leash, a few feet—though it took countless attempts to get him to do that," he added, chagrined. "But he did it. So I let him eat and put him on a perch. He'll sleep the night."

"You willna stay awake with him?" she asked.

"I will let him sleep tonight, and carry him through the day on the morrow. If he is a good lad, I will try him on a creance, a longer line that will allow him to fly the length of a field. I think he is ready for that. His wing seems stronger."

"He's finally taming," she said.

"As much as he can." He glanced down at her. "Tell me what happened, Isobel. Are you warmer now?"

"S-some," she said, her teeth still chattering. "I dinna know what began the visions," she said. "The pool was lovely—so comfortable, and I was relaxing, and listening to the water flowing, and to you singing, and then the visions just came. When I got out of the pool, I was blind, and . . . I panicked."

"What did you see? Can you remember?"

She paused, then shook her head slightly. "I know that I saw my father again, and you . . . you were in great danger, Jamie. I do recall that." She ducked her head toward her updrawn knees, huddled in the blanket. "My father was in a dungeon. I must find him, Jamie."

"Ralph Leslie will help you with that," he said in a grim tone.

"Aye," she whispered, her head tucked. After a moment, she drew a breath. "I saw you in an ambush, I think. I do know that you were in great danger." She made a little sound of frustration. "There were so many other images, of battles, and you and I in a garden. I couldna make sense of them."

He watched her, an idea forming in his mind. "Isobel," he said slowly. "You said that your father and the priest would ask questions of you, and you would describe what you saw to them."

"Aye, during a vision. But the vision has passed."

"Bring it back," he said quietly. "Tell me what you see. Let me help you remember it."

She tipped her head, thinking, and nodded. Then she leaned back her head and closed her sightless eyes, breathing deeply. For several minutes, all he heard was the crackle of the fire and the slow sound of her breath. Then he saw her eyelids flutter.

"I see a pilgrim, on the steps of a church in the rain," she said, and described the church. "He walks toward a hawthorn tree. The pilgrim is the laird of the wind, and the tree guards a secret. . . ." She went on in a soft voice.

James felt struck to his soul as he listened. He had heard something similar in the prediction that Father Hugh had circulated throughout the Scottish borderlands; but to hear it in full, from the seeress herself, stunned him.

She described Dunfermline Abbey in detail, even to the hawthorn that grew in the side yard, yet he knew she had never been there. He had walked past that tree not so long ago, cloaked as a pilgrim. He frowned; the only secret the tree protected was the grave of his friend's beloved mother.

Isobel tipped her head and continued. "I see a battlefield beside a wide, calm stream. . . ." The words went on, fast and low, and he listened carefully. Isobel created vivid images in his mind, as if he were blind and she the sighted one.

"A lion stands in protection over the hills of Scotland," he repeated softly. "Who is the lion, Isobel?"

She tilted her head, thinking. "Robert Bruce, earl of Carrick. By spring, he will take the crown of Scotland for himself, but it will be many years before his leadership triumphs over the English. Even then, his independence willna last forever. Over five hundred years will pass before Scotland and England can live in true peace, when roads are made of steel, and wagons speed over them without horses."

He stared at her, dumbstruck.

"The laird of the wind will be taken," she said.

James sat forward. "Taken by whom?"

"The hawk of the tower canna be trusted," she said.

"When will the laird be taken?" he asked softly.

She shook her head as if in protest. "Soon . . . soon," she said. She stilled as if she saw something new. "A folded parchment drops from the hand, tightly bound, that holds it. The laird of the wind holds the secret of the lion, and protects it with his life. I see another parchment"—she frowned—"but the ink on the page disappears."

A chill traversed along his arms. No one knew about the folded parchment that Wallace had dropped the night he was taken, which James had later returned to pick up.

Isobel sat quietly for several moments, then drew a breath and opened her eyes, tilting her head as if to listen for his voice. The hearth created warm lights in her sightless eyes.

"I am here, Isobel," he said quietly. She reached out her hand, and he caught it in his. "My God," he said. "You are a visionary, with a rare gift. No wonder your father protected you so closely, and the priest wrote down your every word. Do you recall what you said just now?"

She shook her head. "Just something about you, and about battles and Scotland." She shivered and drew the blanket higher.

He gathered her close to him for warmth and related to her what she had told him. He did not allow his quiet, calm voice to reveal his astonishment at her prophetic ability.

"Jamie, you may be in great danger if you proceed

with this exchange," she said. "The laird of the wind will be taken—"

He shook his head. "Danger always exists," he murmured. "Those of us who fight as rebels must accept that, so the threat of danger doesna bother me. And your vision didna reveal when something might happen. I could be in skirmish a week, a month, or years from now." He paused, glancing down at her. "And you might have seen a symbol regarding me. There are other ways to take down a man, my lass."

She tipped her head, looking perplexed. "How so?"

"He might never meet danger at all, and yet lose his heart." He watched her evenly, and the silence lengthened between them.

" 'Twasna a symbol," she whispered. "The danger is real."

"Mayhap 'tis," he murmured, watching her. "Isobel," he said after a moment. "That parchment you mentioned . . . I have it."

Her eyes widened, but remained blank. "What do you mean?"

"The night that Wallace was taken, he dropped a small object that he had hidden in his hand—and his hands were bound together, as you said. Later I went back and picked it up. 'Twas a folded parchment, just as you described." He paused. "You couldna have known that."

She sat up, her interest caught. "You still have it?"

"Aye. 'Tis a letter from Bishop Lamberton of Saint Andrews to William Wallace, which mentions a pact made between the bishop and Robert Bruce to support each other against the English. The bishop invited Wallace, with Bruce's sanction, to join in the secret bond. 'Tis well known that the Scottish Church has made a stand against the Southron force—but the letter reveals that Bruce of Carrick is part of that rebellion, too, and was willing to support Wallace."

"Dear God!" Isobel looked stunned. "If the English had such clear proof of Bruce's intentions, 'twould be the end of his hopes—and his life. The future of Scotland would be lost."

He nodded. "I have kept it, for fear that if I sent it

on to Bruce, or back to Bishop Lamberton, it might be intercepted," he said. "I had already decided to guard the lion's secret, just as the prophetess said."

She tilted her head, a crease forming between her delicate black brows. "I think you keep many secrets."

"I trust few," he said. "And few trust a traitor."

"I have faith in you, yet you dinna trust me."

He watched her face in the amber light and heavy shadows. What poured through him then was a blend of awe and respect—and, he realized, love. But a heavy current of sadness flowed, too. He would have to give her up.

"I do trust you," he whispered.

She laid her hand flat upon his chest, her palm bare against his skin. He wondered if she could feel the wild beat of his heart beneath her fingers. "Then tell me why you call yourself a traitor, when all I see in you is honor." She tilted her head as if she waited to hear his answer.

James sighed and rubbed his brow, thinking. For too long he had kept the dark memories to himself. His gut swirled with dread. No one knew the full tale, yet he wanted to tell her. The urge stemmed from far more than simple trust.

He sighed again. "The English took me prisoner last spring, and held me in Carlisle."

"Aye, you were released in the summer," she said.

"I was held with other Scots nobles, but when some of us were taken north in the summer, I escaped from the escort. Margaret didna get away with me. That was when Ralph Leslie took her to Wildshaw."

"And so you must get her back," she said. "I understand. But that doesna make you a traitor."

"While I was held in Carlisle, King Edward sent orders that some of us were to sign a parchment," he said. "We were to be executed if we didna obey. One day, four of us signed it, with false intentions. Not one meant to keep the pledge. Some of us were released later, and I was given into Leslie's custody. He was ordered to let me go—they hoped that I would fulfill the promise I had signed—but he thought to keep me a bit longer." He shrugged. "I didna agree, so I left his patrol once we were in the forest."

"What was the parchment you signed?" she asked quietly.

He hesitated, dreading the next words he must speak. "An agreement to hunt down Wallace and deliver him to the English."

She paused. "I willna believe you promised that."

"Believe it," he said brusquely.

"Others signed it, too, but you said none kept the pledge."

He drew a long breath and looked into the fire. "I kept it," he said, his voice hushed. "I led them to Will."

"Jamie, nay!" she breathed out.

"When I escaped, I came here and learned where Wallace was, far north of here. I set out, disguised as a pilgrim. I was followed. Leslie must have sent a man after me. If I had known that," he said emphatically, "I would have taken a different route or worn a different disguise. But I led them to Will unaware, stupidly. The next day, I discovered that soldiers were gathering at the house where I had met with him. I went there as fast as I could." He shook his head. "But I was too late."

Isobel leaned toward him. Her fingers found his face, traced along his jaw, her thumb brushing his lips, her fingertips cool and slim on his cheek. "You didna betray him."

"I did." He closed his eyes in anguish. Isobel's fingers were butterfly soft on his face. "I brought the bastards to him. If I hadna come there, he would be alive now."

"Jamie," she murmured, her voice earnest. "We both tried to warn him, help him. You didna betray him. 'Twas meant to be."

He sat silently, frowning, his lips pressed together. He had believed for so long that he had betrayed his friend, through folly, through carelessness, through selfishness—he did not know how he had done it, but it had happened. He wanted to cast away his pain and his anger, but he could not.

"Jamie—you said that I mentioned another parchment, on which the ink had vanished. That must be the one you signed."

"I dinna understand. We signed it in black ink."

"The vanishing words are a symbol," she said. "The pledge wasna real. The guilt doesna exist. You had no role in Wallace's betrayal."

He listened to her dulcet voice, felt the whisper of her touch, and felt the hard casing around his heart crack. He tried to answer, but his throat was tight.

"They would have taken him somehow. 'Twas meant to be. No one could have changed it," she said softly.

"There is one thing more," he said, in a voice so hushed that it rasped in the still air.

She looked toward him, waiting. He realized that her patience was a blessing. He trusted her. So much. He sighed out, heavily. "When they rode away with Wallace . . . I tried, with my last arrow, to take his life."

He heard the intake of her breath. "You knew what he was going to face," she said. "You knew his death would be inevitable, and cruel."

He nodded, unable to speak, his throat thickening.

Her hand found his. "That was a very great act of love," she whispered.

He had not felt the sting of tears since he was a child. He blinked them away, glad she could not see them.

Isobel leaned her brow against his cheek, the silk of her hair heaven-spun. "Jamie, you never could have betrayed Wallace. Those of us who love you know that. We have faith in you. When will you see that?"

He sucked in a breath. *Those of us who love you . . . we have faith in you.* The words were simple, beautiful, stirring.

He dipped his head, his cheek sliding along hers, and pulled her close, holding her, rocking her gently in his embrace. A few moments later, a few breaths later, he could command his voice.

"You saw all of this months ago," he murmured. "If only I had known you then. Ah, Isobel," he breathed out. "If you had prophesied this to me, we might have changed the outcome."

"We canna change what is fated by God. And I would prophesy for you," she insisted, her voice a warm drift against his cheek. "I would do anything for you."

His heart bounded. He held her close, sliding his fingers deep into her damp hair, feeling the warmth and the weight and the truth of her in his arms. Hardly able to think through what he did, or said, he slid his mouth along her cheek.

"Would you?" he murmured against her skin.

"Aye." Her arm tightened around his neck. "But an outlaw wouldna want the trouble of a prophetess."

"If he would trouble himself with a silly hawk," he murmured, dragging his mouth toward hers, "a wee prophetess might seem like a blessing."

He raked his fingers through the mass of her hair, tilted her head back, and took her mouth with a swiftness and a thirst that scarcely expressed his craving. His mouth moved over hers, and he drank some of her sweetness into his soul.

Chapter 22

Her heart thundered within her. She sighed beneath the pliant caress of his lips and surrendered gladly to the strength of the kiss. As he leaned, she tilted back, the flow of motion between them a silent play of giving and surrendering.

For an instant, tiny spinning lights glowed in the darkness inside her eyes, an exquisite medley of color. The light grew, whirling in her inner vision until it filled her sight with golden brilliance.

Firelight.

She gazed past his shoulder at hot golden flames. She gasped, and pulled away to look up at him, resting her hand on his bristled cheek, blinking to clear her sight, to be certain that it was indeed there. She looked into his thick-lashed indigo eyes.

His silent question was eloquent on his face. His fingers swept the curve of her cheek. She smiled, laughing softly. "Aye," she whispered. "I can see you now. Whatever magic your kiss possesses, 'tis wondrous stuff."

"The magic isna mine," he said, dipping toward her. She welcomed him, shaping her mouth to his.

"Nor is it mine," she whispered against his lips.

"Ah, then," he murmured as he took her down to the floor in a nest of warm blankets. "We must have created it between us."

"Aye," she breathed. "We did."

He stretched out beside her. The blanket slipped away when she shifted toward him; the hearth fire warmed her bared leg and her naked shoulder.

He gathered her into his arms and leaned down to kiss her softly, drawing his lips away so slowly that she

moved toward him for more. He smoothed her hair as
he gazed at her.

"No one else could kiss the blindness from me," she
said, watching him. "I am certain of that."

"I think I might kill any man who tries it," he murmured. The fierceness in his quiet voice sent a thrill
through her. "What of Sir—"

"Hush, you." She touched her fingertip to his lips.
"No man shall ever kiss me as you do, or touch me as
I let you touch me," she whispered. "I swear it."

He closed his eyes. "Isobel, if you swear such to me,
I will hold you to it."

"Hold me to it, then." She looked intently at him.
"And swear such to me yourself."

"I swear it, none but you," he said, on a breath, and
took her mouth again. She sighed as he delved between
her lips, gasping as the sweet, moist tip of his tongue
touched hers. She lay serene in his arms, and yet felt
her body whirl and spin.

The quick, fervent promise between them swept
through her, bringing a profound sense that here, with
him, she had found love and perfect refuge. She wanted
to give herself to him utterly, heart and body, without
regret. She wanted, fiercely, to stay with him, though she
knew that might never be possible.

Unwilling to close her eyes and see only darkness
again, she pulled back to look at him. Her gaze took in
the thick waving pattern of his hair, reflecting the gold
of the fire, and scanned his broad, smoothly muscled
shoulders and the width of his neck, where a pulse
thumped.

But sight could never give her enough of him. Blindness had taught her the value and the power of touch.
She traced her fingertips over his jaw—squared below
his ear, firmly curved at the chin, his beard textured like
sand. He closed his eyes as she touched his eyelids, the
lashes soft and thick.

The slope of his nose was straight and long, his breath
a warm caress, his mouth beneath it full, firm, and moist.
He took her fingertip into his mouth and sucked at it,
and she caught her breath at the sweet shock of the
sensation.

She slid her palm along his neck and down his sculpted, smooth chest, resting her fingers over his heart. He pulled her closer, his hand pressed to her lower back. Though the blanket and his cloak were bunched between them, she felt the hard heat of his body, and felt an answering quiver deep within herself, startling and exciting.

His hands stilled on her back, warm pools of touch. "Do you want this to happen?" he murmured, his voice low at her ear.

"Aye," she whispered fervently. "Aye. I have no doubts."

He pulled her into his warm embrace, the blanket cushioned between them. She hid her face against his shoulder. The danger she had foreseen, and the betrothal that awaited her, were certainties. A desperate foreboding urged her to seek comfort in his arms now. This might be the only time she would ever have with him.

She lifted her head and kissed the corner of his mouth, kissed his lower lip, cherished him with her mouth, her hands, the offer of her body. She opened her mouth beneath his and sighed, and pushed away all thought, all logic, immersing herself in what she felt, with touch and heart her only guides.

His fingers glided along her throat, sliding lower. Her heart pounded, an urgent drum, as he skimmed his hand over the rounded contours of her bared breasts. The warmth of his palm was so alluring that she arched into the cup of his touch.

As he swept the tip of his tongue into her mouth, his hand molded her breast. Her heart surged, her breath quickened. Soon she felt his other hand push through the mass of her hair, twining it, tugging her head back so that his lips could trace freely down her throat. All the while, his fingers swirled over her breast, and a radiating tingle spread throughout her body.

She smoothed her hand along the solid width of his chest, his skin warm over hard muscle, and found his flat, soft nipple, touching it lightly, curiously, feeling it tighten as hers had done for him. She heard the quick intake of his breath, and his hand skimmed over her abdomen. His fingers slid lower, cupping her gently, until she shifted toward him with a little moan.

He pushed the blanket away and drew her closer at last, his body warm and solid along the length of hers, his hands hot as they soothed over her back, the fall of her hair, her hips. He dipped his head and found her breast, bathing her nipple with his moist lips. The deep, keen pleasure coaxed another moan from her. His resting fingers, enticing her with their stillness, dipped gently into the hidden recess of her body.

His touch eased over her in exquisite caresses until she lifted toward him, feeling liquid fire pour through her limbs. The shimmering, beautiful cascade left her yearning, as if she hovered on the tantalizing verge of perfection. She moved deeper into his arms, fervent to seek out what her body promised and what her heart now craved.

Her hands slid over his abdomen, following the warm path of hair that led downward. The rigid, hot length of him filled her hands. He groaned low, shifted, and pulled her on top of him, settling her so that her legs hugged his hips and his body fit intimately to hers.

She leaned into his embrace, feeling his heart pound against hers as she fitted her mouth to his in a lingering kiss. The quickening cadence of his breath matched hers as he guided her hips with gentle, fervent fingers. She slipped over him like glove to hand, her small cry stifled against the column of his throat.

When she straightened, arching her back over him, he took her hands in his, palm to palm. That simple touch was as tender, somehow, as the sweet, hot merging of their bodies, as if what he pledged with his body was sealed with his hands.

An irresistible force flowed through her, a compelling stream of joy that brought in its wake a realization. The home she craved, the refuge she needed, existed in the love that had been created between them. Wherever he was, she belonged. The finest castle, the deepest forest, offered only a shallow sanctuary compared to what she had found with him.

Leaning toward him, she sighed out. He drew in a breath and swept her into his waiting arms, while her hair fanned out to cover them like dark, outspread wings.

The cold that accompanied dawn cut through the window and stirred him awake. James shivered and pulled the blankets closer, snuggling Isobel inside the circle of his arms, her nude body warm and soft against his. Her snores made him smile, and he tilted her limp head to quiet her breathing.

They lay together in his bed, in a nest of blankets and furs. He wished that he had thought to thicken his straw mattress and construct a curtain around the open, ancient stone bed to keep drafts out. He was used to his hard bed, sleeping quick and deep whenever he lay here.

But last night, the stark comforts of his chamber had supported joyful, sensuous loving. From the floor, as the embers faded in the hearth and the cool breezes increased, they had sought the shelter of the bedcovers. Neither was tired, and both readily explored each other and shared of themselves, deeply and completely. His blood and body surged at the memory, and he pressed his lips to her brow as she slept.

He sighed out and tucked her head against his chest, combing his fingers through the soft strands of her hair, a slow, cherishing gesture. This day, or the next, his friends would return with word from the priest. Soon, too soon, Isobel would walk into the church in Stobo and disappear from his life.

He wondered if he could endure the sacrifice that he had set for himself. He wondered if he could stand back and let her go.

She mewled in his arms in her sleep, and curled against him. He kissed her brow and the curve of her ear, and stroked the graceful swell of her hip with his hand. He trailed his fingers up her arm, over the delicate bones of her shoulder, along the full slope of her breast.

She stirred against him and lifted her face to his. As he bent to kiss her mouth, she circled her arm around his neck and pulled him to her, returning his kiss with fervor. She uttered a soft moan and ran her fingers through his hair, pulled him to her again. Words were not necessary. He understood what she felt.

He felt the same desperate sense that time slipped from them too quickly. He feared that he would lose her forever. But for now, he would fill her with joy, with his love, and take what she offered to him. Within days, the obligations that they each had would destroy what they had found together.

He swept his arms around her and dipped his head to kiss her, whispering her name. He wanted to tell her so much. Now, though he would stay silent and let his hands and body speak with gentle eloquence.

"But the creance is such a long line," Isobel said, standing beside James as he wound a long length of twine over his arm. "He has only hopped to your fist from an arm's length away. The creance line is a hundred feet long, you said."

"The length isna the problem, lass," he answered as he walked with her across a flat, grassy part of the crag summit. Gawain sat his fist and chirred as they went, while Isobel took long steps to keep up with James. "The problem is getting the bird to come willingly and quickly back to the fist. Once he does that, he will do it from a foot away, from a hundred feet away—or from a half a league away, without a line. The distance is naught to the hawks. Trust is all."

She nodded her understanding, and stood where he indicated. "Watch, now, and we will see what he does," he said. He checked the knots that attached the creance line to the leather jesses, and then shoved the other end of the line, tied to a wooden peg, into the grass.

He murmured to the bird for a few moments. Then he walked the length of the field, the creance unfurling behind him, and set the bird on a rocky ledge. He walked back to stand beside Isobel, and called to the bird.

Gawain sat, and busied himself preening his feathers. James called again, singing the notes of the *kyrie*, tugging on the line. The goshawk fluttered up, and then down, perching on the ground. James sighed out and walked over to pick up the bird, murmuring to him. He carried him back to stand with Isobel, looping the creance as he came.

Then he thrust out his arm and cast the bird off his fist.

Suddenly Gawain took to the air with a broad sweep of his wings, flying out and upward, the creance spooling out behind him. His gray and cream wings rowed, then glided, then rowed the air again, carrying him the length of the grassy field.

Isobel gasped at the sight, and James laughed out loud beside her. The hawk was beautiful and graceful, yet he possessed a keen, dreadful power, a master of the air, an archangel in his own realm. The sun glinted silver on his back as he sped onward.

He gained height. The creance waved and soared with him, then began to tighten. The goshawk drew up and glided over to perch on a high rocky outcrop along the mountain slope.

Isobel stared after the hawk. "Will he come back?"

"We shall see," James murmured, and raised his hand. The deep, clear notes of the *kyrie* rang out over the crag.

Isobel caught her breath and waited. Gawain cocked his head and turned. James sang the melody again, holding up his arm.

As if he had thought enough about it, Gawain took to the air with a dancer's grace, sailing back toward them, his wings cutting the air and spreading wide as he floated on a current.

Isobel saw how fast the bird approached and stepped back apprehensively. James stood rock still and waited, his arm out, while the hawk raked steadily toward him.

At the last instant, just as Isobel clapped her hand to her mouth to muffle a cry of warning, afraid the hawk would hit into James with his powerful talons, the bird tipped and slowed and settled to the fist with a nonchalant flutter.

James offered him a bit of meat. Then he grinned and looked over at Isobel. "Now that," he said, "is a goshawk."

She smiled and came toward him, lifting her skirts and half running the few steps. "That was beautiful," she said. "Sir Gawain, what a bonny lad you are!"

"Bonny indeed," James said, glancing at her. "Now

we'll see if he'll do it again—and again, and again. It may prove a long afternoon, lass."

"Ah well," she said, sighing. "What else have we to do?"

"What else, indeed?" He lifted a brow and gave her a twinkling look. She glanced at him and suppressed a smile, feeling heat sear her cheeks. A small rush of joy streamed through her at the thought of being in his arms again.

"Will the hawk come to me, do you think?" she asked.

"He may. We will find out, if you wish."

"I would like to try." She watched as James reeled in the line, murmured to Gawain, and cast him off the fist again.

The afternoon spun out, filled with disappointment as well as delight. Isobel stood beside James and watched the hawk, and together with him, soothed and cajoled Gawain. The goshawk flew or did not fly, bated or perched, ate or did not eat, according to his whim. But as the shadows on the crag grew longer, he complied more and misbehaved less.

And regardless of the state of his mood, Isobel noticed that the bird always seemed to respond in some way, subtle or great, to the low, serene notes of the *kyrie*.

As sundown neared, and pink-edged clouds spread across the sky, Isobel looked out over the forest. She sighed, aware of a curious sense, a blend of safety and power, high up in their eyrie. James looped the creance and tucked it in his belt, then turned to walk toward her, Gawain calm on his gloved fist.

" 'Tis wonderful here," she said as he stood beside her. "So protected, so far above the rest of the world."

"Is that what you like best? The protection of this place?"

She shrugged. "I like the isolation, and the feeling that no one can threaten us up here—that no one can come up here unless they know the secret way."

"Aye. This sanctuary provides protection—and a kind of freedom," he said.

"I spent my life inside a castle, seeing little of the outside world," she said. "I thought I was protected, but now I know 'twas false. I was kept as if in a prison, my life lived by others' rules. Here, I feel truly safe, and truly free." She reached out her hand, and he took it. "I want to stay here forever, with you," she said impulsively.

He stood silently, her hand tucked in his. She waited, heart thumping with hope, for him to express the same feeling.

"You have a great gift, Isobel," he finally said. "Your words should be heard by many. But you need the finest protection as well because of that. There are some who would use you, if they could, to tell them what the future holds."

"My own father . . . and the king of England among them," she said somewhat bitterly.

"Aye," he said. Then he sighed. "Isobel, I willna condemn your father entirely for keeping you as he did. He wanted to protect you from those who wouldna understand what you can do, and he wanted to ensure your ability to prophesy. The marriage he arranged for you is meant to continue that."

She watched him, tightening her fingers in his. "What are you saying?" she whispered, disbelieving.

He looked out over the forest. "That I canna give you what you need or what you want."

"How do you know what I want?" she asked, a little defiant.

"I know that safekeeping is important to you," he said. "I know that a home is important to you, too. You should live in a lovely place, a walled castle, with a garden, and . . . and roses for you to tend." He paused, his grip on her hand tightening. "A home where you can raise children, and know peace and plenty, and share your prophecies with those who will benefit by them."

"Love is important to me," she said. "Freedom is important to me. *You* are important to me," she added fiercely.

"Your gift is important," he said. "Rare and significant. If you shut yourself away with a man who must hide from the world, your prophecies willna be heard." He sighed. "A homeless outlaw canna safeguard a valuable prophetess. But a man who commands a stout castle and a garrison, and has the might of England on his side, can do that well."

"I thought you regretted sending me back to Ralph Leslie," she said, hardly able to keep the tremor from her voice. She curled her fist anxiously within his hand.

"I do regret it," he said quietly. "And I want you to go."

She scowled. "You want Margaret."

"Och," he murmured. "You know the truth of that." He did not look at her, though she stared intently at his profile. "Isobel, if you stayed with me, we would be hunted by Leslie, and by the troops King Edward would send out after us both. There would never be peace, or plenty, or a home for you."

"This is a home," she said. "If I go to Ralph, I will— I must become his wife, and . . . I canna bear that." She gripped his fingers, turned to him. "And King Edward will make me say prophecies for the English."

"Say them well," he said. "You will have all you want."

"All I want!" Fear and anger flared within her. "All I want is you!"

"All I want," he said sternly, "is for you to be safe. I have thought long about this. Your gift is remarkable and should be shared. You deserve accolades and luxury. I canna bring that to you. This is the only way." He watched the sky darken to lavender. The hawk kakked, shifted, stirred his wings.

Her heart slammed, her breath quickened. "There is one difficulty with sending me in barter for your Margaret."

"And what is that?"

"I willna go."

He lifted a brow, glanced at her. "You will."

She scowled. "When we go to Stobo, you can keep Margaret in the church when Ralph sends her in, and I will go out and tell Ralph Leslie I willna go with him."

"That," he said, "would start a bloodbath."

"Dinna make me go," she pleaded.

He breathed out a low, anguished sound and reached out, pulling her close, sliding his arm around her neck.

She wrapped her arms around his waist and held him, breathing out a little sob of relief, glad to be in his arms.

"I have to let you go," he said. "You must see that. You are the prophetess of Aberlady, too high in worth for an outlaw to keep for himself. And what about your father?"

"I dinna want to be owned by some man who will control my prophecies like sacks of wool to be taken to market," she said. "And there must be some other way to find my father. Father Hugh can help us, or your friend at Dunfermline Abbey." She bit her lip and squeezed her eyes shut. "We can find him, I know it."

"Nay," he murmured against her hair. "He is at Wildshaw."

"We hope. Jamie," she said, as a new thought came into her mind. "I will go with Ralph as you arranged, so that you can have Margaret back. If Ralph has my father safe, I will leave Wildshaw with my father. Then I will come back here to you."

He paused, hugging her close. "You canna do that."

"I can come back," she said. "Let me come back."

"Nay," he whispered. She looked up at him. The wind ruffled his hair, and his eyes were deep blue in the saturated sunset light. "Remember our bargain, when we first came up to the Craig. You said you would stay a few days, if I promised to let you go."

"I dinna want to be let go. I will come back here to you."

"Isobel," he said somberly. "Nay."

"I will," she insisted.

He sighed heavily and looked out over the forest in the deepening light. She stared up at him, her eyes pooling with sudden tears. "I understand," she whispered. "You want your freedom, and think you willna have it with me."

He closed his eyes briefly. "I want you," he said. "But I canna keep you. You will go with Ralph, and forget me in time."

A pain began in the center of her being. "Dinna say that. We need to be together."

"We have different paths, you and I," he said.

"We have the same path! We have the same needs—peace. Sanctuary. Love," she added in a whisper.

"If our lives had been different, Isobel," he said, "aye. If I had been simply the laird of Wildshaw, and you had been simply the Maiden of Aberlady . . . but 'tisna that way."

"Jamie," she said, burying her face in his tunic. "Jamie, dinna do this." She squeezed her eyes against tears.

"Soft, you," he said gently. He stood still and held her. "Isobel, my lass," he said after a while. "Look down there."

She glanced down, narrowing her eyes. "I see only trees. Your eyes are sharp as that hawk's. What do you see?"

"Quentin and Patrick. They are back faster than I thought."

She clung to him and watched. A long while passed before she saw the tiny figures of the two men running toward the crag. She dreaded their arrival, dreaded their message, and what the next few days would bring.

"Jamie," she said. "I am afraid."

He stroked her hair, a slow caress, and lifted his arm from her shoulders. "You will be fine."

She watched the two men for a few moments more, the wind whipping freely at her gown and her hair. Then she turned.

James walked away into the gathering shadows, the hawk on his fist.

Chapter 23

"Father Hugh insists on meeting privately with Isobel, in return for delivering our message to Ralph Leslie," Quentin said. "He wouldna take our reassurance of her safety. He wants to see her for himself. Otherwise, he says we canna use his church for our purposes."

James frowned and glanced at Isobel as he considered the news. Along with Quentin and Patrick, they had gathered in the kitchen area of the broch, and had just finished a meal prepared by Isobel of barley and onions, along with fresh bread and cheese sent by Alice.

"Father Hugh has always been protective of me," Isobel said. She poured more of the French wine into cups for each of them. "And I would like to speak to him," she added quietly. She did not look at James as she spoke, but her lowered eyes and the blush on her cheeks told him that she was aware of his gaze.

"Can we trust him?" he asked Quentin and Patrick.

Patrick nodded. "Aye, if we go with her."

"He wants to meet alone," Isobel said. "Where is he now?"

"He rode to Wildshaw to deliver the message," Quentin answered. "We traveled back from Stobo with the priest and Geordie, who insisted he was well enough to come back here. From Alice's house, Father Hugh rode to Wildshaw. The priest says he will ride over from Wildshaw to meet with Isobel in early morn. We suggested the old oak not far from Alice's house."

"A good choice," James remarked. "We can defend her more easily there if he arrives with a patrol of soldiers."

"He swore to come alone," Patrick said. "He's a priest

and a friend to the lass, and so he will be trustworthy in this."

"I dinna like it," James said. "Quentin?"

"I dinna like it much myself," the Highlander answered. "Too much could go wrong."

"I must go, or Margaret willna go free," Isobel said. "And I think 'tis time I left the Craig." She wiped crumbs off the stone table with her hand as she spoke, as if she was reluctant to look at them. "And I want to see Alice and Sir Eustace and the rest. I'll leave at dawn."

James watched her evenly as he swirled the wine in his cup. He wanted to reach out and grab her, hold her, ask her to stay. But he kept still through sheer mental effort.

If he had kept control over his emotions from the beginning, he told himself, he would not have complicated the matter by hurting the lass—and himself—deeply, in the bargain.

"I fear a trap," he said. "Leslie could snatch you."

She looked at him directly then. "You wanted me to go back to him," she pointed out. "I trust Father Hugh. I will go."

"We will escort you," he said. "You shouldna go alone."

She shook her head. "Dinna go with me. Please. You must stay away from the forest."

"We will escort you," he repeated. He knew that she thought about her prophecy, which had told her that some danger would befall him. But James did not fear that. He feared only for her.

Isobel opened her mouth as if to speak, then bit her lower lip and rushed out of the room. James rubbed his hand briefly over his eyes and sighed. He knew that she did not want to leave the Craig or proceed with the hostage exchange. And she was clearly still upset by his insistence that she leave him for her own protection.

"If we go with her to meet him, she will have a strong guard," Patrick said. "Naught can hurt the lass."

"That," Quentin said, sliding a frowning glance at James, "may have already happened."

"She doesna agree with our plans," James said.

"Is that what bothers her," Quentin drawled.

James scowled. "I assume you didna go to Dunfermline Abbey. You came back here more quickly than I expected."

"When we got to Stobo, two monks had arrived from the abbey with a letter for Father Hugh, who corresponds with the abbot," Quentin said. "I talked with one of the monks, who knows John Blair well. He said that John is making progress on his chronicle of Wallace's life."

James nodded. "Did the monk have news of the men who betrayed Wallace?"

"The lord of Menteith is the only man whose part is known for certain, and 'tis said he sent his servants and guards to do the task for him. There is little interest in searching out the identity of the others."

"I intend to seek out at least one of them," James said. "Leslie."

"Are you certain that Leslie is involved in the betrayal?" Patrick asked.

"I am," James said. Leslie knew about the parchment that James and the other captive rebel lords had signed, and James was sure that Leslie had sent someone in pursuit of him, the day he had escaped from Leslie's patrol and had gone to see Wallace.

"No official search will be made toward finding Wallace's betrayers. The Guardians of the Realm of Scotland have other matters to attend to, including their attempt to convince King Edward to appoint a Scottish bishop as co-guardian."

"What news of the earl of Carrick?" James asked, remembering Isobel's prediction that Bruce would gain the throne within several months.

"Robert Bruce renewed his pledge to King Edward last summer, but rumors persist that he secretly aids the Scots. Rebels never seem to be caught when Bruce goes out after them. Edward doesna trust the earl of Carrick as well as he used to. He's named an English commander to Kildrummy Castle, and told Bruce to be ready to answer to that man. Aye, the King suspects Bruce is secretly loyal to the Scots."

"The cause of Scotland may find a stout ally in Bruce

after all." James thought of the letter safely in his keeping.

Quentin began to speak, then hesitated, glancing at Patrick as if troubled. "There is something else that you should know, Jamie," he said. "The English have put Wallace's remains on display."

"I expected that," James said flatly. "Where?"

"His head is piked above the London Bridge, bedecked with flowers. And his limbs have been sent north to Newcastle-upon-Tyne, Berwick, Stirling, and Perth," Quentin answered. " 'Tis said that at Newcastle—" He stopped, looking at Patrick.

"The Southrons piked his right arm above the sewers in Newcastle as a final insult," Patrick said. "They say that his finger points north toward Scotland of its own accord."

James clenched a fist, fighting a wave of grief and anger. "He deserves peace in death," he growled. "He deserves honor."

"King Edward should be damned for scattering him about," Patrick said. "Will deserves a proper burial."

"Then see to it," James snapped bitterly, standing, hardly aware of what he said. Hurt and rage surged fresh and raw within him, clouding his judgment and his reason. Without waiting for a reply, he stalked outside.

After dark, he sat in the mews with Gawain on his gloved fist, murmuring to the hawk in the reddish light of the brazier. He had come inside after a long walk around the summit of the crag, as if the wind could blow away what tormented him. His anger had calmed, but his mood was grim and solitary.

He heard Quentin and Patrick coming down the gallery inside the broch walls, chortling over some joke, shuffling past the door of the mews to seek their pallets in other cells inside the ruin. He heard no sound from the direction of Isobel's small cell. She must have gone to her bed earlier, for he had not seen her after she left the kitchen.

Gawain sat quietly on the glove and stared wide-eyed at James, his eyes gleaming. He puffed his feathers and balanced on one leg, looking silly but contented.

James, on the other hand, was far from content. He shoved a hand roughly through his hair and blew out a long breath, startling the tiercel, which squawked and planted his upright foot.

The news of the further humiliation of Wallace's memory had deeply disquieted him. All evening, his thoughts had spun in a turmoil of rage and remorse; anger at the English for brutality and lack of respect; anger at Will for his sheer stubbornness and for his relentless pursuit of the English, despite King Edward's growing hatred for the rebel leader.

Most of all James was angry with himself. He felt partially responsible for every aspect of the tragedy. Isobel had helped to assuage some of his guilt, but he deeply regretted leading the Southrons to Will. He owed a debt to Wallace that he could never repay.

Another sorrow tore at him mercilessly, like the goshawk tore at bits of meat. He had delivered a keen blow to Isobel, and had wounded himself as well, by rejecting her so deliberately earlier that day. But he wanted her protected. He wanted her to have a home and a chance for peace in her life. As much as he despised Leslie, the knight could provide for Isobel what a forest outlaw could not. And he was sure Leslie would never hurt her, for the man valued her prophetic gift far too much.

But she would be lonely. So would he.

He sat upright, and stood abruptly, but could not escape the truth: he wanted her for himself. Setting the goshawk on a nearby perch, he drew off his glove and turned away.

His original plan had been the wisest, but he had not kept to it. He should have abducted the prophetess without a word of his intention. He should have kept her in silence, and traded her to Leslie in silence, and gone on his way. But he had not, and now he had lost his heart in the bargain.

He left the mews and went to his own chamber. When he approached his bed, the memories of loving Isobel there so tenderly, so recently, made him turn away.

Isobel was asleep in the adjoining room; he could hear a pattern of soft snores. Her head was tilted the wrong way again, he thought. She would not sleep peacefully like that—nor would he sleep, with any reminder that she was just a few steps away.

The curtain that separated their rooms was but a cloak, hung crookedly. He shoved it aside and went toward her bed.

He knelt and cupped her face with a gentle hand, shifting her head to ease her snores. Her cheek was warm and soft as a dove beneath his touch. And her face, tipped toward the glow of the moonlight, was beautiful enough to break his heart.

The yearning that rose in him in that moment stemmed from his awakening heart more than his body. His intense longing unsettled him; he was not accustomed to needing anyone.

The prophetess had said that the laird of the wind would be taken. That had already happened, he thought, during the siege at Aberlady. He had been taken by the gentle hand of a gifted lass, and he had just realized how utterly he had been defeated.

Unable to stop himself, he touched his lips to her mouth, pliant and achingly sweet beneath his. Afraid to wake her, afraid to stay with her, he stood quickly. Then he stepped through the shadows and shouldered aside the curtain.

His own bed was hard and cold when he lay down upon it, and did not warm before he fell asleep.

Pale dawn light streamed through the cold and darkness as Isobel and the others walked along an earthen path that led through the trees. Their journey from the crag into the forest had been silent and steady, with James in the lead, followed by Isobel, then Quentin and Patrick. No one spoke, and none of them paused or slowed as they came down from the crag, crossed the burn, and headed out over the hills toward the forest.

Isobel's step finally faltered as they neared their destination. She felt a sudden urge to run back to the safety and sanctuary of the high, dark crag that loomed behind them. But she went onward without protest, knowing that her meeting with Father Hugh was an essential link in the chain that would draw Margaret back to James.

The goshawk rode quietly on her gloved fist as she

walked behind James. In the broch, as they gathered to leave, James had mentioned that Gawain might slip back to a half-wild state if he spent a full day alone in the mews. When she had asked to carry the tiercel, James had reluctantly agreed.

The hawk's keen gaze darted all around. Isobel was glad that James had fed Gawain a full crop of food before they left, in order to encourage complacency in the high-tempered bird. She murmured softly to the tiercel, and he blinked at her. His round, piercing eyes seemed luminous in the dimness.

James turned to glance at her, his gaze as penetrating and wary as the hawk's. He turned away, his stride long as he followed the path. The hilt of his broadsword glimmered, its blade hidden in the scabbard strapped to his back. He gripped his bow, a full quiver looped to his belt, and wore a leather hauberk over his tunic. His head was swathed in a close-fitting chain-mail hood that reflected the pewtery light of dawn.

He was prepared for battle, as were Quentin and Patrick. Isobel could hear the creak of the leather and metal they wore as well. Grateful to have such a strong, loyal guard, she was frightened at the thought that they might have to fight on her behalf. She did not know what the future would bring for her.

She lamented that her gift only brought specific visions, never revealing what she wanted to know of her own life. But James had given little credence to her prediction that danger would befall him. She sighed, looking at his powerful back and the deadly gleam of his weapons. The stealth of their advance only added to her uneasiness.

After a while, a clearing showed through the trees ahead. James held out his arm, gesturing for the others to stop.

"I dinna see a priest," he said, after watching the clearing. "But the others wait for us."

Isobel craned her neck to look past him, and Quentin and Patrick stepped forward beside her. In the cold dawn light, several people stood like shadows outside Alice's house.

"Come ahead," James said.

"But Father Hugh said we must meet alone," she said, hurrying after him.

"Likely Alice decided that six men surrounding you and the priest is alone enough. And I agree with her," he added gruffly.

As Isobel entered the clearing, she saw Alice standing in the yard outside her little stone house with Eustace, Henry Wood, and Geordie Shaw gathered with her. Alice looked toward the group that entered the clearing, and rushed forward.

Isobel was soon enveloped in a hug so warm and deep that it brought unexpected tears to her eyes. Alice chattered to her softly, and then turned to wrap her arms around James.

In the midst of this, Gawain began an anxious bate, upset by so many people, faces, and voices. James helped her calm the bird while the others greeted each other and spoke quietly.

Isobel turned to see Eustace beside her. She gave a glad cry and grasped his hand, smiling up into his dark brown eyes, so comfortingly familiar. She had not seen him since the day of the skirmish in the forest, when her horse had run away with her.

"Eustace, you look well," she said, and kissed his leathery cheek. "I am so glad to see you."

"Isobel, lass," he said, smiling. "The life of a forest brigand has been good for you. I havena seen such roses in your cheeks, or such a bright sparkle in your eye, since you were a bonny wee bairn."

She felt herself blush, and looked over his shoulder to see James watching her. "When you saw me last, I was unwell," she said hastily. "But I am rested, and my arm is much improved. How have you fared of late?" He leaned down to tell her of his time at Stobo, then turned away to answer a question Henry Wood put to him. Isobel was pleased to see that the two men seemed to be fast friends.

Then she looked around to see Geordie Shaw step toward her, his cheeks bright in the dawn glow, his dark, curly hair tousled above the bandage wrapped around his brow.

"Geordie!" She smiled. "I was very concerned about you. 'Twas good to hear that you are recovered."

"Aye," he said, grinning. "When I learned we might fight Southrons for you and Margaret, they couldna keep me away."

"They should have," James grumbled, pausing in his low conversation with Alice. "Geordie, I want you to stay here with Henry and protect Alice." The boy made a face but did not protest. James looked at Isobel. "We should go," he said quietly. "The sun is nearly up."

She looked up at him. "I'll go alone."

His eyes were dark in the cool half-light, his face lean and hard within the steel mesh frame. "You willna."

"I need no protection from a priest I have known all my life. And I must see him alone if you want Margaret returned safely. You know that."

"Ah, well," he said. "That may be true. But you dinna know exactly where the meeting place is."

She hesitated. "Direct me to it, and I will find it."

"Dinna be foolish," he said, looking intently at her.

Alice approached them. "Let me keep that hawk while you both go to this meeting," she said.

"I think Isobel should bring the hawk with her," James said suddenly.

Isobel frowned. "Why?"

"If you willna keep a guard with you," he said, "at least take the hawk. If there is a threat, he will bate in a fury. That should give you some protection until we can reach you. We will be close by." He glanced at the other men.

"Aye, no one will want to get near that gos when he's fretting," Alice said. " 'Tis a good plan, lass, if you willna let Jamie be at your side. But he will never let you go alone, I think." She slid a look at James, who nodded gravely. "And I'm glad to see that," she announced.

"Naught will happen to me," Isobel insisted. "Father Hugh only wants to talk with me. I will be back soon."

James leaned close. "For a prophetess who can see danger for others," he murmured, "you can be thick as a stone about your own safety."

" 'Tis *your* welfare I care about, you great brigand,"

she said, low and fierce. Alice chuckled, a sound of pure delight, and turned away, pulling Henry and Geordie with her.

Isobel saw a flicker of amusement in James's deep blue eyes as he looked down at her. But his underlying expression of determination did not alter. His hand tightened around her elbow, a grip that accepted no argument.

He turned, and gestured to the others that the time had come to leave.

Chapter 24

An old oak tree rose at the center of a grove, its trunk massive, its wide, leafy canopy providing dim shade. Younger trees formed a circle around the oak. Beyond lay the forest, and in an opposite direction, an open moor. James headed toward the ancient oak while the others followed.

The roots of the gigantic trunk were nearly obscured by a sea of green ferns. James waded through the fragrant mass, ducking his head and shoulders beneath low-hanging branches. Partly hidden by a screen of leafy boughs, a deep, knotty crevice penetrated the tree trunk, creating a hollow space perfect for hiding, which he and his men had used before.

He grasped Isobel's hand and pulled her inside the narrow cavity, their bodies pressed close at hip and shoulder in the confined space. Quentin, Patrick, Henry, and Eustace swung up into the boughs and found seats along the wide, thick branches in order to keep watch.

Isobel looked up at the ancient, split oak, her eyes filled with awe. Slender beams of dawn light spilled through the leaves and touched off a diamond sparkle in her eyes. James watched her quietly, resting his hand on her shoulder. Then he looked past her into the grove, but did not as yet see the priest.

Gawain lifted his wings and squawked, stirring restlessly on Isobel's fist. She shushed the bird and murmured low to him, then lifted her arm to perch the bird on a knot of the tree just over their heads, while James tied the jesses to a branch.

He stood close to her in silence for a long while, their bodies warm in the small space, their breathing quiet.

Time seemed to suspend for him as he waited, his awareness of Isobel's body beside his almost painfully keen.

"Father Hugh should be here soon," she finally whispered.

"Aye," he said softly. "Someone will give the signal when he approaches." He looked down at her. "Let me go with you."

"Nay." She shook her head firmly. "Nay."

He sighed. "Then while you meet with him, we will hide in the tree, watching. Dinna leave the grove."

"Dinna leave the tree," she whispered. Her eyes, wide and limpid in the gloss of dawn, seemed to plead with him.

"If the priest should come with someone else—"

"I will be fine," she murmured. "Father Hugh willna let harm come to me. 'Tis you I worry about. You shouldna be seen."

He gazed at her. All else seemed to fade from his vision. He felt the insistent drum of his own heart and looked into her beautiful eyes. A wave of love, blended with desire, poured through him with stunning strength. He touched her cheek.

"Isobel," he whispered. She tilted her head up, her body snug against his, and her cheek brushed past his lips. He turned his head, seeking. A small shift of movement, and she flowed like a dream toward him until his mouth fitted over hers, swift and hard and hungry.

His hand found her cool, silken hair and he tugged gently to tilt her head, taking her mouth again in the silence, slipping his hand inside her cloak to find the graceful curve of her waist, drawing her even closer.

She gave a little soundless cry against his lips and circled an arm around his neck, kissing him with a fervor that made his heart pound. He leaned her back into the heart of the oak, drinking in her breath, her heart, her soul.

He was a fool to let her go anywhere, with anyone, he thought. He craved her, in his heart as well as his body; she was sustenance for his soul. He would not flourish without her.

But the memory of Elizabeth, whom he had not protected as he should have, would always haunt him. He could not let that happen again. Isobel had to leave the forest, leave him.

But for now, he held her in his arms. He framed her delicate, earnest, sweet face between the palms of his hands as if to savor it. He moved forward to kiss her again, letting his mouth linger over her lips, her cheeks, her eyelids, until his blood slammed through him, until his breath nearly stopped.

Until he knew, unquestionably, that he could not exist without her. And yet he must. His kiss gentled, grew poignant, lifted away.

"Jamie," she whispered against his cheek. Her fingers touched his jaw, trembling. "Jamie, I love you."

He closed his eyes and rested his cheek against her silken head. The echo of her hushed words sank into his soul.

He loved her, too. But if he uttered what he felt, he would never be able to follow the course he had set himself. He held her silently and kept his thoughts secret.

"The priest is in the meadow beyond the grove," Quentin hissed above them. "He's riding toward us. He is alone. Isobel, hurry, before he sees where you have been hiding!"

Isobel pulled away and looked up at James uncertainly. He nodded and reached up to untie the hawk's jesses. The bird stepped onto her offered glove.

When she glanced up at him, he saw the glint of tears in her eyes. She lowered her head and edged past him.

He touched her shoulder. "I will be here," he whispered.

"I know," she breathed. "I know." Then she stepped out of the hollow in the tree and vanished beyond the heavy branches.

He shifted his position to watch her walk away. Her body swayed gracefully and her cloak swept the ground behind her. Beyond the trees, the sun brightened over the heathery moor that stretched between the grove and another wide arm of the forest.

James watched while Isobel moved toward the sunlit edge of the grove and waited there. He realized then that she held the hawk's leather jesses as securely as she held the strings of his own heart. He felt the tug as an almost physical sensation.

He saw a man ride to the middle of the moor and dismount. The man walked toward the grove, dark-robed and short, his wide face pale beneath the shelter of his hood.

James saw Isobel greet the priest with clasped hands and a kiss on the cheek. They stood talking for a long while. The priest took her arm, urging her to walk beside him. Isobel seemed to hesitate, looking back toward the shadowed oak. Then the priest pulled gently at her arm, smiling. She nodded and walked out onto the moor with him, lean and willowlike beside his shorter, heavy build.

Inside the recess of the trees, James grasped his bow. A shiver went through the small hairs along his arms and neck. Isobel might trust the priest, but an inner sense told James to be cautious. He edged out of the hollow in the tree.

On Isobel's fist, Gawain bated, lifting his wings and squawking. Isobel stopped to calm him, and the priest put his arm around her, drawing her along with him.

James ducked to steal out from under the low-hanging oak boughs. He whistled to Quentin and the others, and heard them thump, one by one, to the ground behind him.

Before he could step out of the shelter of the tree, before he could cry out a warning, men on horseback surged out of the forest and crossed the heather-deep moor at a thundering pace.

James started running. Footsteps pounded behind him. He reached for an arrow and nocked it into his bow as he went.

Three of the men rode toward Isobel, and the rest cut across toward the grove. The priest stepped back as they came near. A soldier on a white horse leaned down and grabbed Isobel, swooping her onto the front of his saddle as he rode past, his horse's hoofbeats digging up heathery clods.

The hawk fluttered his wings wildly. As Isobel was yanked upward, she lost her grasp. The tiercel soared above the moor with swift wingbeats, slanted, and soon vanished into the trees.

James paused, staring, stunned. Both Isobel and the goshawk had been swept away from him in the space of one swift, awful moment.

He roared out and ran forward. As he went, he tried to steel himself against the agony that ripped through his heart. He allowed himself to think only about how many arrows he had, how long a bowshot he must take, how many men rode toward him. He saw the white horse carrying Isobel disappear into the dark rim of the forest, and he felt a surge of rage.

The other riders—ten or twelve in all—had nearly reached the perimeter of the grove. James stopped, knowing that he and his friends had a better chance against horsed soldiers within the shelter of the trees. Behind him, his friends arranged themselves, bows and weapons drawn. Henry Wood raised his longbow and released the shaft, which sailed between the trees and struck one of the soldiers in the chest.

James shot, too, scarcely looking where the broadhead landed before he nocked and pulled again. The horses came at him so fast that soon arrows were of little use. He drew his sword from the scabbard at his back and swung it brutally, teeth bared, legs planted apart, as the first rider came toward him.

Horses circled him, and he fought ferociously, his strength stoked by rage rather than fear. Isobel had trusted the priest, and she had been betrayed. She was gone. The hawk was gone. James could not think beyond his gut-deep need to cut past the men who confronted him and prevented him from going after what had been torn from him.

He had meant to send her away himself, but safely, always protected. This betrayal and capture had endangered Isobel. Fury burned like a yellow-red glaze in his vision. All that he saw took on a slow, terrible grace, as if he looked through the golden irises of a hawk.

In front, behind, beside, horses and soldiers surrounded him. He swung the two-handed sword savagely, driving a couple of the horses back, slicing at the thighs of the riders, his blade striking steel, bounding back, arcing down again.

He could not see his men. His vision was filled with

the heaving flanks and shoulders of horses, with faceless men in chain mail and bloodred surcoats, with glinting steel blades and cruel weapons swiping relentlessly toward him. He ducked and swung, turned, avoided a coming blow, spun, cut upward with the blade, turned again.

One of the soldiers cried out, clutching an arrow in his chest; another whirled away from clashing his blade with James to struggle with an unseen foe outside of the circle. James knew his men were there and fighting with him, though a heavy barrier of horseflesh trapped him.

He turned, seeing an opening as one of the horses shied back. But as James tried to slip past, the spiked steel ball of a mace was flung into the air and came down in a merciless arc.

He felt the shock of the glancing blow on his head and fell forward into darkness.

As he slammed into the hard earth, he thought he heard the cry of a faraway hawk.

Isobel looked frantically over her shoulder again, past the man who carried her across the front of his saddle. They rode at a steady pace through the forest, while she sat over his legs, trapped in the circle of his arms. Chain mail bit into her through her clothing. She had never seen the man before; his face was bearded and his dark eyes somber, and he seemed young. He scarcely spoke to her.

Far behind them, she saw Father Hugh, riding with two other guards along the forest path. She looked away swiftly, feeling ill with anger as she recalled how the priest had broken trust with her. He must have known that Leslie's patrol waited in the forest, ready to steal her away and go after the outlaws.

She had caught sight of James only once after she had been taken, when she had looked back wildly to see him running toward her through the trees, his bow drawn, his face fierce. Then a phalanx of horses had surrounded him, and the horse that carried her entered the forest, and the trees had obscured her view.

She knew that James had gone down. She had seen

the same sight in a vision, days ago. He had fallen inside a circle of horsemen, his face darkened with blood.

She gasped and covered her face with her hand. Her other hand still wore the hawking glove. Its weight reminded her that the hawk was gone, too. The awful realization of that double loss hit her with devastating force. She felt as if her breath might stop. Squeezing her eyes shut, she forced back tears as her captor rode on.

Kee-kee-kee-kee-eerr.

Startled, she looked up at the vast, swaying canopy of leaves overhead. A hawk swooped there, slanting his wings as he cut through the treetops. He glided like a sylph, the rising sun golden on the outspread fingers of his wings, touching his pale underside with light. His jesses trailed behind him like ribbons on the wind.

Excitement and hope stirred in her. She stared up at the goshawk and held up her gloved hand. "Gawain!" she called. "Sir Gawain, here to me!" She began to sing the *kyrie*. The guard holding her looked at her as if she had gone mad.

"Gawain?" he asked.

"Gawain is my hawk," she said. "He's just there."

He craned his head around. "The goshawk, there?"

"Aye. A valuable bird," she said. "I must have him back."

"Aye, gosses are naught but trouble to train, and that alone gives them worth. Yours, then, is it?" He shook his head. "He will not come back, now he's gone free. Before noon, he'll be as wild as the day he was born."

"He will come back," she insisted. She watched the goshawk swoop and soar, and then alight on the dry upper branches of a tall, dead tree. "He will. Stop here, and let me call to him." She looked at the guard. "Please, I beg you."

He looked doubtful and glanced over his shoulder at the priest and the other guards, who rode a fair distance behind them. "Well, any hawk named Gawain ought to be saved," he mused. He drew rein and circled the horse. "You must stay with me, though, and make no attempt to flee. I mean you no harm. Sir Ralph Leslie charged me with your safe arrival."

"My safe arrival," she repeated. "But what of the outlaws?"

He frowned. "We were told that they took you hostage, my lady. Our orders were to rescue you, and take prisoners for Leslie to deal with."

"I was no hostage!" She looked at him, her eyes wide. "Then he—they—might yet be alive? What happened back there?"

He shrugged. "I did not see. But I know that Sir Ralph demanded the leader be brought to him. Lady Isobel, look there. Your hawk is in that tree."

Isobel felt a surge of relief, both at the thought that James might be alive and at the sight of the goshawk. He was still perched on the high, dead branch, his head and wings silvery in the early light. She lifted her gloved fist and sang out to him. The tiercel seemed to look at her, then turned his head as if to ignore her.

"Gawain," she called. "Here, gos, sweet laddie, come to me!" She sang the haunting melody again.

The guard looked up with a doubtful expression. "A manned falcon would come to a call, but goshawks are stubborn birds, always wild, I think. But we'll try, if you must have your bird. Sir Ralph would not want to see a trained hawk lost."

Isobel nodded and continued to coax the bird and offer her hand as a perch. She reached into the pouch at her waist, remembering that she carried the hawk's food there. Withdrawing a piece of meat, she waved it and sang.

"Not like that, my lady," the guard said. "Use it as a lure. Have you got a creance in the hawking pouch?" She nodded, grateful for his help, and fumbled in the leather pocket, withdrawing a twine leash. The guard took it from her and tied the meat to it. "Now we need a few feathers to disguise it."

She dipped into the pouch again and brought out the feather that James sometimes used to stroke the bird. The guard took it, broke it in two, and thrust it into the meat like wings. She understood what he did, for she had seen James use a lure—a false bit of prey made of feathers and meat—to tempt Gawain. The bird had eagerly pounced on it while on the creance.

The guard tossed the line and its lure out and began to spin it over his head. "Call him, my lady," he said.

She did, singing the *kyrie*, pleading, cajoling, whistling.

Gawain lifted his wings and soared away, banking out of sight. Isobel lowered her head, devastated. She had failed to keep Jamie's hawk.

The guard gathered the reins and rode on. A while later, he stopped again. "There," he said. "The goshawk is up in that high elm now. He almost seems to be following you. Call to him." He lifted the lure and spun it in a high circle. Isobel sang out, holding out her hand, and sang again and again, until her voice grew hoarse with the call.

Finally she saw the goshawk. He cut through the trees, streaming toward her like a torrent of wind. She held the glove out and did not flinch, though her heart raced, though the guard ducked his head and exclaimed.

Gawain plucked the lure out of midair with his talons and dragged it with him to alight on her glove, as if he had done it a thousand times. Slanting a wild bronze glare at her, he dipped his head and began to tear at the meat. She grabbed his jesses with a trembling hand and wrapped the leather straps securely around her smallest fingers.

"God in heaven," the guard said slowly. "He came right to you. I did not truly think he would. 'Tis a valuable hawk indeed that does that. Come, Lady Isobel. Your betrothed wants you safe in his castle." He urged the horse onward.

"Bonny gos," Isobel said. She swallowed, her throat heavy with tears. "Bonny, bonny gos." She tightened her fist over the jesses as if she would never let go.

Chapter 25

A square tower and surrounding wall of gray stone emerged through the morning mist, set on the green crest of a hill above a river valley. As Isobel and the guard rode closer, she glanced over the man's broad shoulder. Father Hugh and the soldiers followed in the distance, now joined by a larger party of men.

Ahead, a narrow drawbridge spanned a rushing burn. The guard's horse pounded over the wooden planks, and the huge portcullis creaked just high enough for them to pass under the iron teeth.

Inside the bailey yard, Isobel looked around at a scene of early morning bustle as soldiers and servants hurried around the yard on various errands. Dozens of Southron soldiers in chain mail and russet surcoats walked past or stopped to mount saddled horses; lanky boys and barking dogs seemed to run in every direction; a servant guided a creaking, loaded cart, drawn by a small ox, across the yard. Smoke twined up from a slate-roofed, open-sided smithy, and from a smaller building, which Isobel guessed was a bakery from the tempting odors wafting toward her.

The teeming, chaotic yard was dominated by a massive tower keep of dull gray stone, which soared at the far end of the bailey. Sturdy wooden steps led up to the wide arched entrance on the second level. A man came rapidly down the steps, his chain mail glinting, his wine-red surcoat a rich burst of color in the gray mist.

Ralph Leslie lifted his hand in greeting as he came closer, his surcoat flapping about his steel-covered legs. He stopped beside her horse and fisted his hands on his hips, his expression stormy. He always reminded her, in both build and temperament, of a surly dark bull. That impression had not faded in the months since she had seen him.

"Lady Isobel," he said. "Thank God you are safe."

She shot him a grim look and did not reply. The guard who had brought her swung down, helped her to dismount, and stood beside her. A boy ran forward and led the horse away.

"My thanks, Sir Gawain," Ralph said brusquely.

Isobel turned to look at the soldier. "Gawain?" she asked.

The man's stern countenance warmed in a quick, appealing grin. "Your hawk and I share a name, my lady," he said, his dark eyes twinkling pleasantly. "And so of course I was happy to help you regain him. Good day, Lady Isobel. I hope you will be content at Wildshaw." He inclined his head and turned. Isobel watched him walk away, grateful to have at least one friend in this uncertain place. She turned back to Ralph.

He frowned and looked up at her; Isobel stood half a head taller, and had since the age of fifteen. But in contrast to her slenderness, Ralph Leslie was broad as an oak, his face square and high-cheeked, his chest wide, his fisted hands tough and sure at his waist. His brown eyes smoldered beneath heavy brows and a thick shock of iron-gray hair.

"Are you harmed?" he asked gruffly.

"Nay," she said. "Would it matter to you?"

He scowled and looked pointedly at the goshawk on her fist. "I see you have brought my goshawk all the way from Aberlady. A nice gesture of good will, Isobel. My thanks."

"Your hawk?" she asked, her mouth open. "*Your* hawk?"

He nodded. "Aye. I left that tiercel in the care of your father's falconer. He is a stubborn, hot-tempered bird, and I had no success in training him myself—though I am by nature the most patient of men," he added, smiling complacently. "How is it you got him to sit for you? I didna know you cared for hawks."

She still blinked at him in astonishment. "I—we—Sir Eustace set the hawks and falcons free from Aberlady's

mews but for the few we ate. We . . . we found this one
in the forest later. I didna know he was yours."

"You *ate* valuable trained birds?" He glowered.

"We were starving," she retorted. "Starving, and besieged by English troops! And no one came to our rescue who might have done so!" She looked pointedly
at him.

"By that you mean me," he said. "I did not hear of
the siege until too late. By the time I got there, the
castle was burned. Isobel, I would have come to you had
I known." He took her right hand between both of his.
"You know how I care for you."

"Where is my father?" she asked, pulling her hand
from his.

"Your father is here," he said slowly.

"Thank God. Where? Is he well?" She looked around
eagerly, hoping to see him coming toward her through
the crowded bailey.

"Isobel, he is . . . unwell," Ralph said.

She felt a wave of fear. "I must see him. Please. Now."

"Later," he said brusquely. "You and I must talk first.
There is much I want explained, and much I must ask
you. Your father is not ready for visitors yet."

"He will want to see me," she said. "I must go to
him, regardless of his condition."

"You must rest first," Ralph said. "And I believe your
father is not yet awake."

She frowned, puzzled that he would delay her meeting
with her father. She sighed. "Then I trust you have a
chamber prepared for me—since you went to the trouble
of having me escorted here," she added through her
teeth.

He turned and walked alongside her. "Of course," he
said. "I will have someone take you up there. Margaret!
Come here, girl!" He gestured.

Isobel looked around in surprise. A tall young woman
came toward them, her stride bold as a man's. Her russet
gown molded to her large-boned and lush figure, and
matched the thick crown of red hair that curled and
waved beneath a simple white veil. She did not smile,
but her round golden brown eyes, striking in her large,
plain face, seemed warm and intelligent.

"This is Lady Isobel Seton," he said. "Take her up to the chamber in the keep that I ordered readied earlier today."

"Lady Isobel," she said. "Welcome to Wildshaw. My name is Margaret Crawford."

"Margaret!" Isobel said, extending her hand. "I am so glad to see you at last."

The girl looked confused as she grasped Isobel's hand. "Let me take you inside, my lady. You must be tired after your journey."

"Journey!" Isobel turned to stare at Ralph. "I was taken by force. My faith in you and in Father Hugh was totally betrayed." Margaret, standing beside her, gasped.

"Isobel." Ralph looked evenly at her. "You needed a rescue, I gave you one. Go inside. You seem distressed, as well you should be by your ordeal these several weeks. We will discuss this later."

Isobel opened her mouth to reply, but a commotion at the gates attracted her attention. She turned, as did the others, to watch as the rest of the patrol, including Father Hugh, rode beneath the portcullis and into the bailey yard.

In their midst, a man was tied between two horses, his arms stretched wide, his long legs dragging in the dirt. A tangle of brown-gold hair hung over his bowed head and hid his face.

Isobel's heart lurched. "Jamie!" she cried out, and started forward. Ralph grabbed her wrist fiercely, holding her back, sending a shaft of pain through her right arm that she ignored. She looked at him. "Dear God, let him go!" she cried. "What will you do with him? He didna harm me, if that is what you think!"

"Do you care what happens to the brigand who took you?" he asked, his eyes narrowed. "Margaret, escort her to her chamber."

But Margaret was already running across the yard. She fell to her knees in the dirt and clasped her arms around James, supporting the sagging weight of his body. His head lolled, and Isobel saw that his face, so familiar, so beautiful to her, was half-covered in darkened blood.

She gasped and strained forward, but Ralph would not release her. On her other fist, Gawain launched into a fierce bate, beating his wings and squawking. She stretched out her arm to give him the necessary space for his fit.

"By hell, 'tis indeed my own damned hawk," Ralph muttered.

Isobel did not answer. Her gaze was fixed upon the injured man and the girl who held him tenderly.

"Guards!" Ralph called, looking around. "Get Margaret away from the prisoner and take him to the dungeon—if he yet lives."

"He lives," one of the soldiers answered. "Though scarcely."

Isobel swallowed back the sob of relief that rose in her throat. She could not let Ralph know how dearly she cared for the outlaw. She bit her lower lip anxiously as she lifted the calmed hawk back to her fist.

Pulled back by the guards, Margaret made an angry remark that caused them to let go of her and glance at one another. She whirled and stomped toward Ralph with a look of fury on her face, then towered over him as she gestured toward James. "You know that man is my cousin! Let him go, I beg you!"

"I cannot do that, Margaret," Ralph said calmly.

"Last summer, when you held him in custody, you were ordered by the king to let him go," she said. "You must do so now."

"Those orders were for a special situation, and none of this is a concern of yours," Ralph snapped. "He has committed crimes and offenses against the crown of England—and against me." He turned, pulling Isobel with him. The goshawk shrieked, and Isobel hushed him.

"If you put my cousin in your dungeon," Margaret said, striding along with them, "I will never go to your bed again."

Isobel gaped at Margaret, stunned.

"Margaret, hush," Ralph said. He stopped walking, and reached up to stroke his hand along her arm, while he gripped Isobel's arm in his other hand. "Easy, my lass. Easy, love." His voice, Isobel noticed, dropped and gentled. "Lady Isobel is my betrothed. I will explain all to you tonight."

"Betrothed!" Margaret said. "Betrothed! You willna see me tonight!"

Ralph leaned toward the girl. "Will I not?" he murmured. Margaret lowered her eyes and looked away. "Good lass. Now take the lady up to the tower chamber. Your eyes are the color of honey when you are angry," he said, low. "Golden as the eyes of a young hawk. Go on now, lass, and come to me later."

He let go of her and looked at Isobel. "You and I will talk, as well," he murmured. "Go on. I will send my falconer up to take that gos to the mews."

"The gos stays with me," Isobel said.

Ralph frowned. "I have a fine mews."

"He stays with me," she repeated. "Have a perch and fresh food brought up to the room."

He tipped his head in acceptance of her wishes. "That room already has a perch," he said. "Very well. Food will be sent for him. And for you." He turned and walked away.

Isobel stared after him. Then she looked up at Margaret, who was even taller than she was. "Margaret," she said gently. "I willna wed Ralph, no matter what he says."

Margaret's eyes brimmed with tears. "Come with me," she said stiffly, and stalked toward the tower doorway.

Isobel glanced back over her shoulder. A group of guards carried James, slung between them, across the bailey. She stood watching until they disappeared into a doorway in the base of a wall tower. Fighting against her own tears, she tightened her grasp on the goshawk's jesses and followed Margaret into the keep.

The chamber was on the uppermost floor, tucked into the corner of the great keep, a small room with a wooden planked floor, cold stone walls, and a single narrow window. Margaret ushered Isobel inside and stood by the door.

Isobel turned in the center of the room. The furnishings were simple: a bed, draped and curtained in red, a leather-topped X-shaped stool by the window, a wooden chest and a brazier, along with a tall wooden bird's perch in a corner. She set Gawain there and drew off her thick leather glove. Margaret murmured a farewell and began to pull the door shut behind her.

"Wait," Isobel said. "Please, wait. I know you must

be unhappy with me. You didna know about me. But I have heard much about you."

"Me? What would you know of me?" Margaret asked. She scowled. "I have heard of Isobel Seton, the prophetess of Aberlady. Many know that name. Sir Ralph has often said that he knows you well, and that you prophesy for him. But he never said he meant to wed you."

"My father arranged it long ago, but I dinna want it. I love another," she said in a soft voice.

Margaret shut the door and came forward into the room, her hands folded in front of her. "Does Ralph know you love someone else? Does he know the man?"

"You do," she said quietly. "Jamie Lindsay."

Margaret gasped softly. "Jamie! But how is it you know my cousin? He has never mentioned you, other than to talk of one or two of your predictions."

"I met him only recently." Isobel studied her thoughtfully. "Margaret, do you know how I came to be here today?"

"You have come to visit. Were you summoned by Sir Ralph?"

"In a way. Ralph ordered his men to abduct me from a private meeting with Father Hugh." Margaret looked confused, and Isobel hurried on. "I think you dinna know that Jamie contacted Sir Ralph with an offer of a barter—James was ready to trade me for you. But Ralph has deceived him. Deceived all of us."

Margaret looked shocked. "What are you talking about?"

"Sit down," Isobel said firmly. "We must talk." She went to the bed and sat on its edge, while Margaret sat on the stool.

As quickly and simply as she could, Isobel explained her first meeting with James in the besieged castle; she described the escape, the journey through the forest, and the tale of how the hawk was found and trained. She spoke of Alice and Quentin and the others, and mentioned briefly the days spent on the crag.

Margaret shook her head slowly. "I am beleaguered by this. Why would Jamie take you and propose a barter to Sir Ralph?"

"Jamie has been worried about your safety. He knew

that he couldna get you free by force of arms, so he took me—Sir Ralph's betrothed—and meant to use me as a ransom payment. But we . . . came to care for one another. And I wonder, now," Isobel mused, "if James was wrong about you, Margaret. Have you been held against your will after all?"

Margaret looked out the window, a high blush in her pale, freckled cheeks. "I am a prisoner here," she admitted. "But I bought peace for myself at the price Sir Ralph suggested to me."

Isobel sighed. "Oh, Margaret," she murmured softly.

Margaret nodded. "When Sir Ralph first brought me here, I was angry and frightened," she said. "Jamie had escaped during our journey here. He tried to take me with him then, but the guards kept me back. I screamed at Jamie to flee. I could tell by his face that he would come back for me. I knew I only had to wait." She sighed. "Sir Ralph gave me a choice between a cold, dark dungeon cell and the warm room off his own bed-chamber. I spat in his face and took the dungeon cell."

Isobel nodded, watching her silently.

"He never forced me," Margaret explained. "He was patient. He had me brought to him each evening. He would sit with me by the hearth in his chamber and speak to me about many things." She paused, looking out of the window, the daylight golden on her delicately colored skin and bright russet hair. "He stroked me gently, and told me that I was lovely, and wild, and . . . and that he wanted me. That he was sorry that he had to keep me confined. After a time, I came . . . willingly to him. No man had ever treated me like that. I am a plain lass. Men dinna find favor in me as they would in you, my lady."

" 'Tisna so," Isobel said. "I think you have an admirable spirit—and your bearing and coloring are high and strong. I know that Patrick Boyd is smitten by you," she added.

Margaret blushed deeply. "Patrick is a rough lad to appearances, but tender in his heart," she said. "But I didna think . . . nay. He thinks of me as a comrade. A brother, even more than a sister. They all do, for I followed them when my own brothers were with them, and afterward. I love them all, I think," she said, and sighed. "But none of them love me."

"Jamie and his men are all fond of you, and they do see you as a woman," Isobel said. "I can swear to the truth of that. And they are determined to rescue you from Wildshaw."

Margaret smiled a little. "They would rescue any one of their comrades, my lady. I have always liked the ways of men, their freedom, their strength. I like shooting a bow, and running free, and wearing breeches—though Ralph had this gown made for me." She fiddled with the fine wool. "I am not soft, but I am a woman. Ralph sees me that way, and he says he likes my rough ways. My wildness." She shrugged. "Mayhap I was unwise to let myself be charmed by him, but it was pleasant, in a way, to be treated like other women, to be kept close, protected. But I didna like it for long." She made a face. "I want to be let loose from here."

"I do hope that most women have reasonable freedoms, and the respect of the men in their lives, if they dinna have the same privileges," Isobel said. "I myself was guarded at Aberlady, by my father, and Father Hugh, and Ralph as well." She looked at Margaret. "I wasna truly free until I was taken hostage by Jamie. I know that sounds odd, but 'tis true. Until then, I didna know much about life, or about love. I envy the life you had with Jamie in the forest. I would be glad to live like that with him, but he . . . he willna hear of it."

"Ah, but I know Jamie. He doesna care if a woman leads a life of her own choosing—he was practically raised by Aunt Alice, after all." Isobel chuckled with her. "But if Jamie wants you protected, there is good reason for it."

Isobel nodded. "Aye," she said, and sighed. "He has good reason, I suppose. He wants me protected because of the prophecies. And because he thinks I want a home like this one."

"Do you?" Margaret asked.

Isobel shrugged as rising tears suddenly constricted her throat. "I just want to be with him," she blurted.

"Och, Isobel," Margaret said, her voice gentle. "Please forgive my misbehavior in the yard. Meeting you was a shock to me. I have a high temper." She watched Isobel and sighed dreamily. "I think that Jamie must love you as well as you love him."

Isobel smiled wanly, not so certain of that herself. "There is naught to forgive. And soon I will tell Ralph that I willna wed him." She paused. "Tell me . . . do you love Ralph Leslie?"

Margaret shook her head. "He has treated me well enough, but he holds me here against my will. He insists that he will never let me go, and he ensures that I canna leave the castle."

"How so?"

"He instructs the garrison to keep watch over me," Margaret replied. "And he binds my ankle to his bed at night, and at times during the day."

Isobel gasped. "He keeps you as if you were a beast?"

"As if I were a prisoner," she reminded her. "Which I am. After all, I was captured by Southrons while I ran with a band of Scottish rogues. And if you ever saw that dungeon cell, you would understand why I made the choice I did."

"Margaret," Isobel said. "I must get down to the dungeon. I must see Jamie. Can you help me?"

"I might be able to persuade Ralph to let me see my cousin. And I think I can convince the guards to let us both in to see Jamie."

Isobel nodded with relief. She looked toward the door. "Will Ralph come soon, do you think?" she asked. "I want to see my father. Ralph said that he is here, but unwell. Have you met Sir John Seton? He would be a guest of Sir Ralph's."

Margaret drew her slight brown brows together over her tawny eyes. "Sir John Seton is your father?" she asked. "Certes—Isobel Seton. I should have realized. . . ." She heaved a long sigh. "Isobel, we must get down to the dungeons for certain."

A chill crept over Isobel's skin. "Why?" she asked warily.

"Because your father is there," Margaret said. "Ralph brought him here months ago. Sir John Seton was among the prisoners released from Carlisle Castle with me and Jamie."

Chapter 26

A gray haze intruded into his pleasant dream of floating upon a dark sea scattered with flower petals. James opened an eye halfway and blinked at dim surroundings. Still groggy, he tried to recapture the dark peace of the dream. But it had been replaced by distinct sensations of cold, damp, and pain.

He realized that he reclined against a cold stone wall. Shifting a bit, he felt the burden of heavy iron cuffs around his wrists, attached to a long chain. The damp straw beneath him gave off a musty, unpleasant odor, and the chamber was dark and chilly.

The more he came to awareness, the more fiercely his head ached. He could scarcely see out of his left eye, which felt sore and swollen, and his mouth and jaw felt tender. A deep breath revealed that his right side had a bruised or cracked rib. Judging by his wounds, he had been dealt a number of blows.

He dimly recalled the ball of a mace coming toward him and the sound—like the deep toll of a heavy bell—when it struck the side of his head through his chain-mail hood. Blackness had followed that, and little else; his mind felt oddly blank.

With effort, he sat straighter, emitting a breathy groan. His head seemed to spin with dizziness as he looked over his surroundings: dark, slimed stone walls; a thin chink in the wall that admitted more chill than light; matted straw, tossed sparsely over the earthen floor; a low arched door of latticed wood and iron. Beyond the door, he saw a section of a dark wall, its rough stone faintly aglow with the light of a torch, ensconced out of sight. He heard no voices in the corridor.

He pulled forward slightly and felt the tug of the long chain behind him, which ran loosely through a ring embedded in the wall and linked to the manacles on his wrists. The movement of his arms was limited by its length. His feet were still booted—though his armor and weapons were gone—and his ankles were cuffed with broad bands of iron, joined by a chain just long enough to allow him to walk.

If he had the strength for that. Every muscle in his body hurt, but none of it compared to the slamming ache in his head. He leaned back, licked his dry lips, and looked around the cell.

Then he noticed the man in the shadowed corner, only a few feet from where he lay. Chained in a similar manner at wrists and ankles, and clothed in a torn tunic and breeches, the man looked ancient and skeletal. He had long, bony limbs, and his hollow face was surrounded by a wild tangle of gray hair. But his blue eyes burned with awareness, like jewels in his haggard face as he watched James.

"Name?" the man rasped out.

James blinked at him. *Name.* He was certain he had one. He slowly scanned the dungeon while he thought, looking at the scummed walls, his iron-linked feet shoved into dirty straw, his hands, grimy with dried blood, resting on his updrawn knees. *Name,* he prodded himself. *Ah.*

"James," he said. That was it. "James Lindsay."

"The Border Hawk?"

James thought about that. "Aye," he said slowly, sure now.

"Jesus God," the man murmured, shaking his head.

"Pleased to meet you." James felt almost drunken—woozy, relaxed, strangely ready to laugh at his poor jest.

"Nah," the man barked. "John Seton."

James frowned, seeking the mental niche where the familiar name belonged. He almost found it, but his head ached too much to follow the thought. "John Seton?"

"Laird of Aberlady," the man rasped.

He stared at the prisoner. Aberlady was as familiar as his own name, somehow, and yet sounded hollow and strange. He blinked to clear his thoughts, but only caused himself more pain.

"We were at Carlisle together, lad," John Seton said. "I recall seeing you there. You were held in another cell with the lass Margaret. We were all taken northward by Leslie's patrol, but you escaped. You didna know me then, but I heard who you were. Your name is well known."

James scowled so deeply that the wounds on his temple and his swollen eye throbbed. He made an effort to piece together what the man told him with what he was trying to recall.

Carlisle—Margaret—Seton of Aberlady . . . Isobel. *Isobel.*

He narrowed his eyes to focus on the prisoner. Those blue-gray eyes, set in a gaunt, handsome face, were nearly luminous. He had seen them before, in a gentle lass. Suddenly the whole meaning came together with stunning force.

"Jesu," he breathed.

"Nah, John," the older man grunted.

"Ish—Ishbel," James murmured, his swollen lip stumbling clumsily over her beautiful name. "You are her father."

John Seton lifted a brow. "What do you know of Isobel? Have you heard of the prophetess of Aberlady? Have you recent news of her?"

"Aye, news," James said. He sighed. "Aberlady was besieged and burned to the ground, sir. I was there."

John Seton lowered his head. "I had heard that rumor from the guards," he said. "So 'tis true."

"Aye, sir," he said quietly. "I torched it myself, to keep the English out."

Seton drew a long breath, and was silent for several moments. "And Isobel?" he growled.

"I took her out of there safely. She is here—at Wildshaw." He looked around the crude arch of the doorway, at gray stone walls, all familiar to him from years ago. *His home.* He was in the base of the northwest tower, where two dungeon cells were located. "Aye, here at Wildshaw," he muttered.

"Here?" John barked. "How do you know that?"

"Ralph Leslie has her," James answered. He leaned his head back against the wall and swallowed hard. "I tried to reach her," he mumbled. "But they took her faster than I could—"

"What are you talking about?" John Seton growled.

But the powerful ache in James's head swamped his reason, and the peaceful darkness returned. He welcomed it.

Cool, gentle hands stroked his face. Then a damp cloth sponged his brow, slicked over his eyelids and temple, stinging as it cleansed. He winced, his eyes still closed.

"Jamie." Her voice, a sound he loved, seemed part of the calm blackness in which he drifted—but for that annoying wet cloth. "Jamie, I'm here," she whispered.

"Ishbel," he said. His lower lip hurt fiercely when he spoke. The pain jarred him to greater awareness.

"Aye, 'tis Ishbel," she said, laughing a little, catching back a tiny sob. She kissed his mouth, and the light angelic touch banished pain for a moment. When the lip throbbed again, he opened his right eye—the other eye felt as big as a side of beef—and looked at her.

She knelt but a handspan from him. The light from the tiny window crevice, behind her, haloed her head with silver. Even in deep shadow, her eyes were utterly beautiful. "You're awake. Thank God," she whispered. He heard the tears in her voice.

"Ishbel." His mouth was dry. "I'm fine," he lied, and sat up stiffly, leaning his back against the wall. The iron chain between his feet scraped quietly over the stone floor.

She tipped a cup of water to his lips. The water spilled cool and fresh into his sour, swollen mouth, and he swallowed. "Oh, Jamie," she whispered. "I love you. . . ." Her words dissolved into a small sob.

"I know," he murmured. "Love you, Ishbel. I do." He mispronounced her name deliberately that time, like a caress, hoping to hear her laugh again. He was glad to utter the words to her at last. They brought a sense of peace like a prayer.

She gave him an exquisite, watery smile, and leaned

forward to place her cheek against his. She smelled like flowers and sunshine, a font of blessings in this dark hell. He raised a hand to circle her waist, the chain heavy on his wrist.

"Isobel, we must hurry," a woman said.

Isobel half turned and nodded. She touched her fingertips to his face, tracing like a butterfly over his lips, his jaw, his brow, smoothing over the tangle of his hair.

"Jamie, the goshawk—" she began.

"He's free," he said. He recalled that the bird had flown away. He did not want her to fret, although he was greatly concerned about the tiercel's welfare. "I know."

She shook her head. "I have him. Gawain is here with me."

He felt a strong surge of relief. "Good," he said softly. "Keep him safe." He reached up to touch her cheek, the chains jangling. She felt like heaven beneath his fingers. Her skin was damp with tears. "You stay safe, too," he whispered.

"Isobel," John Seton murmured from the other side of the room. James turned his head slowly.

"I need to speak with my father again," she murmured. "He is here, too—just as I saw in the vision. Do you remember?"

He frowned as he tried to recall, and nodded stiffly. "Aye," he whispered. Her presence, and his memories of time spent with her, were as rejuvenating to him as fresh air, sharpening his awareness further.

She smiled again, wan and loving, and got to her feet. The soft hem of her skirt brushed his hand as she turned. He caught at it with his fingers, and let go.

Someone else stood before him; he looked up at the long folds of a russet skirt. She knelt beside him, and he narrowed his one good eye. "Margaret," he said. "Dear God, Meg—"

His cousin smiled, her eyes teary, and leaned forward to kiss his brow. "Jamie. I am so glad you are awake. When they brought you into the yard, I feared you were dead." She took his hand. "I brought Isobel here to see you and her father both," she said. "We had to beg the guards to let us in secretly. We canna stay long, or Sir

Ralph will find out. We brought food for you." She indicated a sack beside him.

"You brought Isobel, and yourself. 'Tis enough."

Her mouth worked as if she held back tears. She drew
a breath. "Isobel told me about your plan to ransom me
free from here. I—thank you, Jamie. And she told me
about you—and her." She glanced at Isobel, who murmured quietly with John Seton. "I like her well," she
said. "If you wouldna have me, that is." Her eyes twinkled, but he saw her sadness, too.

James twitched his upper lip. "*You* wouldna have *me,*
lass," he drawled. "Though I would have begged." He
tried to smile, tried to recapture the teasing tone they
often used together.

"Och, you would never beg for anything, you brigand.
And you and I argue too much. That lass has a gentle
spirit. You need that far more than what I could offer
you."

"You have fire," he said. "Brave Meg."

She sighed and squeezed his hand. "Oh, Jamie, I am
so sorry. 'Tis because of me that this has happened."

He shook his head. "I should have attacked the gates
weeks ago," he mumbled. "Should have demanded your
release. Instead, I thought he would release you in exchange for . . . his betrothed."

"Jamie, you couldna attack this place. The garrison is
over two hundred strong. You didna have the troops.
Your plan was well formed and would have worked. But
Sir Ralph acted dishonorably." She leaned forward.
"And Isobel said she would never have gone to him, in
the end. She wants to be with you."

He sighed, closed his eyes briefly. "All my plans come
to naught where that lass is concerned," he said. "Meg,
I just want you and Isobel to be safe." His mouth was
dry again, and his lip hurt keenly, but he went on. "You
should be with your kin, and she should be . . . with
someone who can protect her and her gift."

"She should be with you," Margaret said crisply.

"Nay. She is a true prophetess—a visionary. I thought
Leslie would provide well for her and protect her regardless of my prejudices, and his own faults. But I was
wrong."

"Aye, you were wrong." She dipped the cloth in a wooden bucket and wiped his face. "Will you nae listen to your heart, you great loon? Who best to protect her—*and* her gift—but the man who loves her?"

James stared at her. "She wants a peaceful life. A refuge, a home. I canna ensure those for her."

"She might have wanted a safe sort of life once," Margaret said. "But she wants—and needs—you."

"I am an outlaw," he said hoarsely.

"You're a great bonny fool, too," Margaret said. She wet the cloth again and slapped it against his temple. James winced and caught at it with one hand, chains chinking.

"Ow," he said. "And how am I a fool? I want the best for her," he muttered, his temper sparked, as it often was, by his outspoken cousin.

"What gives you the right to choose what would be best for her? I know you were thinking of her, and of her gift. But let her declare for herself. And as for you—" She sat back on her heels, anger lending her eyes a tawny color. She drew a breath, swelling her bosom.

James slid a glance at Isobel. Both she and her father had turned to stare at Margaret.

"And as for you," Margaret went on, "you are gloomy with your own pain. Aye, 'tis a heavy burden, and I willna belittle it. But you are caught by that net of cares you carry over your shoulder. You canna reach out for happiness, even when it smacks you in the face!"

"Meg—" he said.

She gestured toward Isobel. "You send her to safety, and away from you, because you love her. But I think Isobel would risk all to stay with you. You could both be content, even now, on your high crag!" She folded her arms over her chest in a huff. "And now look at you! Canna even see! And nae wonder!"

James cleared his throat uncomfortably. He glanced again with one eye at Isobel. She watched them, eyes round, cheeks bright pink, a terrible stillness in her.

"We wouldna be content, Meg," he said gruffly. "There would still be the matter of you and Sir John, trapped here."

"Och," Margaret said. "I have been working on that."

"What do you mean?" James asked. She shrugged, and blushed.

"I have been doing what I can to gain my freedom," Margaret replied. "As for you—"

"Jamie did what he thought was best," Isobel said.

"Isobel, is this true? Do you love this outlaw?" John Seton asked. "I thought you seemed overfond of him moments ago, but this—"

"Aye, 'tis true," she said, looking at James.

"As Meg says, I have been a great bonny fool," James said, returning her gaze as well as he could with one opened eye.

"And you, Border Hawk," John Seton said. "If you love my daughter, would you ask her to live the life of a brigand? She has a gentle spirit, and a precious gift. Her life should center around what God wants of her. I always tried to see to it."

"I do love her," James said quietly. "But I would never expect her to live an uncertain life with me. I want her kept safe, just as you do."

Isobel stood slowly, still looking at James. She seemed distant, though she stood only a few feet from him.

"Isobel, I have made a grave mistake," John Seton said. "You canna marry Sir Ralph. He has proven himself to be treacherous. But I dinna think you should wed a brigand, either. Your gift is far too significant to waste like that."

James scowled at that remark, but said nothing, watching Isobel. She looked from him to her father, and clasped her hands in front of her, twining and untwining her fingers. James saw a wary look in her eye, almost caged. He sensed that her temper rose within her like a wave, but she kept ominously silent.

"Her gift is hers, to use as she would," James said softly. "And not as others direct her."

John Seton cast him a sudden glare, and turned to look at his daughter. "Isobel, you need a proper husband to care for you. One of the guards here tells me news I heard what is said of the Border Hawk—that he betrayed his friend, Sir William Wallace. I had great respect for Wallace."

"He didna betray Wallace," she said quietly. "He

tried to help him. He is an honorable man." Her defense of him stirred deep gratitude inside James as he watched her.

"Still, such a rogue isna the husband for the prophetess of Aberlady," John Seton said.

"Mayhap no one is," she said. "Mayhap you are both wrong."

James saw that she was angered and confused, torn between her father and him. He leaned forward, wanting to comfort her, inwardly cursing the chain that held him back. Margaret stood, hands folded, watching all of them, oddly silent.

"Tell us what you want most, Isobel," James said.

"Aye, what do you want?" her father barked.

She stared at each man in turn, and fisted her hands in determination at her sides. "I want both of you to be free," she said, low and fierce. "I would give whatever I have to see that done. I would give my own life to see it done!" Her chest heaved softly, and her eyes burned like blue flames.

James sat straight, awed by the beauty and ferocity he saw in her. "What then, for yourself?" he asked.

"I have long wanted protection," she said, stepping back. "And—like both of you—I thought I needed a safe place for my visions to come to me. But I have changed in the time since my father saw me last, and since I met James. Now I want something more than safekeeping. Now I know the visions will come to me, wherever I am."

"You have had visions recently?" her father asked.

She ignored him. "I want freedom, too," she said, flattening her palm on her upper chest. "I want to live where my heart will be most glad, whether 'tis in a castle or a cave. But I want to choose that for myself. And I want to decide when and for whom I will prophesy." She paused, and raised a trembling hand to cover her eyes suddenly. "Ah, but what does it matter, now? It may be too late for any of that."

"What a bonny speech, my dear lass," a voice said. "I am sure we can find a solution to suit you."

*　　*　　*

An icy chill plunged through Isobel, and she whirled around.

Ralph Leslie stood on the other side of the latticed door. He smiled at her, inserted a large iron key in the lock, and swung the door open. Two guards stood behind him.

"In fact," he said, stepping into the cell, "I have learned a great deal listening to your conversation in the few minutes since I came down here. Let us hope, Isobel"—he reached for her, but she moved away—"that it's not too late for you, at least." He reached out again.

"Get away from me," she said through her teeth.

He inclined his head politely. "I would not care to mistreat the prophetess. Bid your father farewell. And your lover," he added in a growl. He looked at James. "Did you touch her, when you kept her with you?" he snarled. Isobel drew in a quick, wary breath.

James stared at him, evenly, silently.

"Return to your chamber," Ralph told Isobel. "I have matters to discuss with these men. Go on. Margaret, take her out of here," he barked. Margaret stood beside John Seton and made no move to leave.

Isobel backed away from Ralph, glancing over her shoulder. James rose up slowly, sliding his back against the wall, gaining his feet through the strength of his legs and sheer will. His gaze was stony as he glared at Ralph Leslie, despite the swollen left eye and bruised jaw.

Her heart lurched when she saw him stand, his fists clenched beneath the iron bands, his legs solidly placed. He was weak, she knew, but she saw stubbornness and rage bring him to his feet as if his injuries were nothing. She stepped back again, watching Ralph, until she stood within inches of James.

"Isobel," Ralph said. "Get you to your chamber."

Her own anger surged. She fisted her shaking hands and echoed James's stance. "You played us false!" she cried. "You held Margaret dishonorably—you betrayed me with Father Hugh this morn—and you promised to search for my father, when you had him all the time. I trusted you. My father trusted you!"

"I found Sir John in Carlisle and brought him here."

"In chains?" Isobel demanded.

"You brought me here then, as well," Margaret said. She went over to John Seton and supported him as he slowly stood.

Ralph shrugged, glancing around at all of them. "I recently accepted the command of this stronghold from King Edward in return for my oath of fealty. What could I do but obey when I was ordered to imprison rebels here?" He narrowed his eyes and came toward James. "You escaped that day, but you willna manage that this time."

"Dinna be so certain," James growled.

Isobel stepped between them. "You could have given my father a gentlemanly confinement, regardless of your orders. He was always a friend to you. Have you no loyalty?"

"Does he? Do any of you place your loyalty where it belongs, in the king's peace? Seton has been an active rebel, behind my back," Ralph said. "I had the betrothal promise. I saw no reason to court the favor of an old rebel any longer."

"I didna tell you of my secret politics," John Seton said. "Only a few men knew, whose loyalty to Scotland has never wavered. But then, you didna tell me that you intended to declare for the English king again. You told me that you planned to choose for the Scots once and for all."

"Why would you trust such a man?" Isobel asked her father. "Why?"

"For you, lass," her father said quietly. "For you. With so much strife in Scotland, the best safety lies with English allegiance. I thought a Scottish knight with English ties would protect your interests—and your gift— better even than I could, for I couldna declare for England myself. I thought him a practical man. Father Hugh continually praised him."

"We were all deceived," Isobel said. "Father Hugh betrayed me this morn."

"I was deceived, not you," John Seton said. "You have never liked Ralph and the priest, but I gave them my trust because they both showed concern and admiration for you. Ralph told me," he added in a low growl, "that he loved you, Isobel, and that he would lay down

his own life before he would let harm come to you. And
so I gave your hand to him."

"I told you what you wanted to hear," Ralph said.
"And I do care for Isobel. So much so that I accepted
the English offer of command at Wildshaw. A Scottish-
born knight with so much English influence is an ideal
husband for the prophetess. You wanted her wed to a
man of might. Now I have that, more so than before."

"I want her wed to a man with a sense of honor!"
Seton shouted, stepping forward. Margaret, nearly as tall
as Seton, kept her arm around his waist when he sub-
sided against the wall.

"Honor is not always practical, nor powerful," Ralph
said. "Even the most honorable of men can fall into
treachery. Ask James Lindsay."

"You know naught of honor," Isobel said.

"Nor does Lindsay, it seems." Ralph turned to look
at Isobel. "I have a letter in my possession, bearing his
signature. A pledge to turn Wallace over to the English.
And he led us there nicely." He looked at James then.
"Just as I thought you would if I let you go. I allowed
you to escape that day, Border Hawk."

"You think you did," James snarled.

Ralph leaned toward him. "I was there that night, Lindsay, when you were hiding in the forest, shooting at Wallace's guards." He clapped a hand on his own arm. "I
caught one of your arrows myself. And so I made certain
that word went round about your deed that night. 'Twas
simple to begin a rumor that you betrayed Wallace." He
tipped his head toward Isobel. "Her prophecy had already suggested it. I merely made sure my tale fit with
her prediction."

James stared at him silently, his nostrils flaring, his
eyes like steel shards. Then he flattened his back against
the wall, sank his weight into the wrist cuffs, and lifted
his booted, manacled feet, slamming them into Ralph's
gut.

Flung backward by the force of the blow, Ralph lay
gasping on the floor of the cell. He rolled to his side,
groaning, as the two guards rushed in from the corridor.
One of them helped Ralph stand. The other stepped
toward James, his hand on his sword hilt.

Isobel cried out and threw her arm across James's chest, staring wildly at the guard. The man halted. Sir Gawain looked at her, his eyes narrowed, his face somber. Then he stepped back slowly, removing his hand from his sword.

"What stops you?" Ralph gasped out. "Toss the woman aside."

"I willna touch a woman in anger," Gawain said. He turned and looked at Ralph. "Nor will I punish a man for doing what I would like to do myself." He spun on his heel and walked out.

"Damned chivalrous bastard," Ralph muttered. "Isobel, get out of the way." He stumbled to his feet, breath wheezing, face pale, and drew a dagger from a sheath at his belt.

"Isobel, move," James murmured.

She grasped him more tightly, her hands trembling on his arms. "If you harm him," she said as Ralph stepped closer, "I swear to you that I will never say another prophecy again."

Ralph turned his gaze on her. The cold resolve that flickered there made her fearful. "We shall see about that," he growled. He grabbed her arm in a fierce hold, wrenching her toward him, stepping back. Pain seared through her shoulder, and she cried out.

"Bring the other woman to my chamber!" he yelled to the remaining guard as he dragged Isobel out of the dungeon.

Chapter 27

Ralph opened the door and pushed Isobel ahead of him into the tower bedchamber. She walked away from him, going to the far corner of the small room to stand beside the goshawk's perch. Gawain kakked loudly and clenched his talons.

"He is hungry," she said, sliding a glance toward Ralph. "And he has been alone here too long. He slips back into wildness quickly." She remembered that James had once remarked that if she had no other protection the goshawk would do. She picked up her glove, shoved her hand inside, and nudged her fist toward Gawain.

The tiercel stepped onto the glove, his bronze eyes glinting at Ralph, who stood by the doorway. Isobel cast a sideways glance at the man, and went to the wooden chest, where she had left the hawking pouch. She took out a strip of raw meat, wrapped by James before they left the crag, and laid it on the glove. The hawk clutched it with a foot, dipped his head down, and tore at it with his beak.

Ralph stepped toward her. "You have become quite a falconer since I saw you last," he said. "But I found this bird to be far too wild and truculent. He will never learn to hunt. His temper is too hot. I would have let him go, but your father said he would take over the care of him."

"Jamie was sure that his first owner ruined him," she said, sliding him a glare. "Now he comes to Jamie like the wind." She spoke quietly, but relished the words.

Ralph came nearer. "And you? Do you obey Lindsay's commands, too?"

She half turned away. "Dinna stare so. Gawain doesna

like it. In fact," she said as the tiercel raised his head to glare at Ralph, just as she did, "I think he doesna like you. Mayhap you should leave." Gawain worked the last of the food down his throat and stretched his beak open. Isobel murmured to him and stroked a finger down his breast.

Ralph stayed, folding his arms as he watched the bird. His taut mood hung in the air, making her uneasy. The bird sensed it, too, for he pulled in his feathers tightly and swiveled his head, his eyes gleaming amber beneath slanted white brows. She watched him for signs of bating, and murmured softly.

"Did Lindsay teach you how to handle that gos?" Ralph asked.

"Aye," she said, stroking the bird.

"Just what else did he teach you?" he murmured smoothly. His flat stare disconcerted her.

Isobel made a few small, airy noises to the bird while she tried to compose her answer. "He taught me about freedom," she said carefully.

"Freedom!" he scoffed. "You learned that from an outlaw, hiding on a damned crag? He held you hostage, and called it noble, I suppose. And you believed his vows of liberty for himself, and for Scotland." He shook his head. "I often feared that you had poor experience of people, Isobel—of men. This is certain proof."

"I understood what Jamie spoke about. After all, freedom," she continued stubbornly, "was what you, and my father, and Father Hugh saw fit to take from me."

"We took naught from you," he said. "We agreed among us that you needed guidance and safeguarding."

"I know differently now," she said.

"I see. Tell me what else this outlaw taught you." He came toward her, standing so close that she felt tension roll off of him like heat from a fire. He touched her head, slid his hand down the gloss of her hair. "Were you a keen pupil for his wisdom?" he murmured.

"Leave me," she said quietly, firmly, turning her head.

His hand fell, hot and heavy, upon her shoulder. "Did he touch you?" he asked. His fingers flexed for an instant, strong as a hawk's talons. She held back a wince, remaining calm and stony under his gaze and his hand. She did not reply.

He trailed his fingers down her back, touched her waist. "Did he touch you like this? Or this . . ." His hand slid up her arm, and his broad thumb grazed over the swell of her breast.

She stepped away, her heart pounding anxiously. The bird lifted his wings, kakked, stretched his beak. "Be gone, Ralph," she said. He came with her, turning as she turned. She could not get away from him within the small confines of the room.

"You've grown wild in spirit since you left Aberlady," he murmured. "You were gentle, once. Biddable. You need some reclaiming now that you've . . . tasted freedom." He touched her hair again, sifting it back. She jerked her head away.

"Dinna touch me," she said.

Ralph grabbed a fistful of her hair, painfully, and pulled her head down toward his face. She uttered a small cry. The tiercel raised his wings nervously, clenching his feet on her fist. "If that outlaw touched you as a man touches a woman," Ralph said between his teeth, "I will kill him slowly, until he screams for mercy and begs forgiveness for cuckolding me."

Gawain shrieked, and launched upward from the fist with a heavy flapping of wings, tightening the jesses as he pulled up. Isobel raised her arm and resisted the bird's strength. Ralph let go of her, and she stilled utterly, until the hawk slowed the frantic beating. Her heart slammed at a furious rate.

"What a troublesome hawk," Ralph commented bitterly.

"He wouldna be so troublesome if you werena here," she said, keeping her voice quiet. "And as for forgiveness, 'tis you should beg it of James Lindsay." She assisted the hawk back to her fist. "You betrayed him, and all of us—and Scotland, too." She wanted to shout and rave at him, but the hawk's nervous presence demanded that she sound calm and patient, no matter the content of her words.

"I did what needed to be done. Wallace was a firebrand. Many wanted him stopped, Scots as well as English. I am not alone in helping him toward his execution, my lady. And I will continue to do my best to see that his comrades are brought to justice. Peace will come to Scotland," he said. "The king of England's peace."

"Peace will come to Scotland," she agreed. "But under a Scottish king. King Edward will never rule Scotland." She glanced up and saw Ralph's face change as if he had been struck.

"You have seen this," he hissed. "When?"

Isobel walked away and sat on the wooden chest by the window. She did not answer as she whispered to the goshawk.

"By God, you prophesied for him!" Ralph crossed the room after her and sat on the chest beside her. "What did you tell him? What does he know?"

"What secrets does he know that you dinna know?" she asked. "I have forgotten what I saw. That should hardly surprise you."

He grabbed her arm, his fingers pressing deep. "Tell me."

"I canna." She tried to pull her arm away. "Why does it matter to you? What is it you want of me?"

"I must know what you predict," he said. "I must have a record of every prophecy you say—you, my wife."

"You canna own me, or my gift," she said.

He rubbed a hand over his brow, frowning to himself. "I will send for the priest. He will sit with you, and you will prophesy again. You will tell me what you told Lindsay."

"Why does is matter? 'Tis my gift to use as I please."

"Nay!" he said, looking at her. " 'Tis mine, if you are my betrothed, and my wife. And I have promised it to King Edward."

She stared at him, horrified. "What are you saying?"

"I have promised the king that I will bring him the prophetess," he said. "And he in turn has promised me a great reward. A very great reward." He licked his lips.

A chill traversed her spine. "You would turn me over to him? As if I were a—a bag of gold, or a silver bowl, or a bit of land?" Her voice rose indignantly. The hawk stirred restlessly, and she scratched the tops of his feet, heedless of the wicked talons, while she watched Ralph.

"Two weeks from now I am to appear before King Edward and introduce you to him as my wife. You are to prophesy for him, and if he is pleased, he will be generous to us both. You must predict a golden future."

"You are mad," she said. "I canna do that."

"He summoned me recently, Isobel. We must go."

"He sent his lieutenants to besiege Aberlady in order to get to me," she said. "Surely he received word that I had escaped. Or word that I had died in the fire." She glared at him, recalling what he had told Alice about her supposed death.

"Father Hugh told me that you were alive—he learned it when he cared for the wounded outlaw lad. And so I sent word to the king that I had you. I told him you were my wife."

"Presumptuous," she said.

He waved his hand in a dismissing gesture. "I intended to have you back from the outlaw as soon as possible. A betrothal is as good as a marriage, and besides, Father Hugh can wed us quickly. The king sent word immediately with the date of our audience with him in Carlisle. He expects you. And he expects a full account of your prophecies."

"I willna prophesy for the English king," she said.

"He will not be thwarted," Ralph said. "Nor will I. You will do this. I have no choice, therefore you have no choice."

"I will never prophesy for him," she said, standing. Ralph stood, too. Her greater height did not give her confidence, nor did it lessen the fear that rose when she looked in his dark brown eyes.

He took her arm again in a grip that made her teeth set on edge. "You will see the future for Edward of England."

"If I told him what I know of the future," she said slowly, "you would not receive a very great reward."

He tightened his lips until they were white. "Then you must tell me what you see of the future, before you tell the king. You will do that now." He pushed her toward the bird's perch. "Set that hawk away and we will begin."

"Nay." She shook her head, slowly, firmly, locking her gaze to his, though her knees trembled with fear.

"You always did what your father told you," Ralph said. "I expect the same from you. Your new taste for liberty will gain you no benefit with me." He laid a hand to his dagger. "If you like freedom so much, I can cut those jesses and let the cursed bird go free," he said. "If you do not want to see that, then set the tiercel away from you."

She realized she had no choice, for she could not bear to see the goshawk lost or harmed. She pressed her lips together in angry silence, and turned to put the bird on the perch. Ralph shot out a hand and grabbed her arm.

His silence was heavy and dangerous as he pulled her toward him with an inexorable strength. He slid a hand around to press her lower back until her body met his, her breasts flattened against his broad chest, their clothing thick and warm between their bodies. His eyes were dark, greedy, frightening pools.

"The priest has warned me that taking physical pleasure of you could compromise your prophetic gift." His breath blew hot in her face. "But if you have given yourself to the outlaw, and yet prophesied for him, then we know you kept the gift. For that, I suppose," he murmured, nuzzling his lips along her cheek, "I must thank him, before I kill him."

She jerked her face away and pushed against his chest. "Stop," she said. "I didna say that I gave myself to him."

"You did not need to say it," he said. "I saw it in your face. In his face. I might find it in me to forgive you for that someday, if you promise to give yourself to me alone, and give me full guardianship of your power. No man can possess you as completely as a husband." He gave her a taut smile.

"I will promise naught to you," she gasped. His mouth was hot and slow on her cheek, her neck. She shivered violently and pushed at him, but his grip was too strong to break. On the perch beside her, Gawain fluttered and kakked, and walked back and forth restlessly.

"What if I prophesied for him before I gave myself to

him?" she asked, gasping again as he snugged her hips to his. "Then we wouldna truly know if the gift remains, would we?"

Ralph stilled suddenly, as if all the heat fled from him at once, turning him to ice. His grasp on her arm was iron-hard.

"Tell me," he growled. "Tell me what you did. And tell me exactly what you told him." His fingers flexed on her arm, opening and tightening, wickedly strong. She cried out and struggled against him.

The tiercel shrieked loudly, spread his wings, and leaped up from the perch. He landed on Ralph's hand, only inches from the perch. Gawain beat his wings furiously and shrieked, and his muscular yellow feet clenched convulsively, talons digging deep.

Ralph roared and let go of Isobel, stumbling back, batting wildly at the bird. Isobel ran toward them, watching in horror.

"Cast him off!" she said, and tried to get in close to grab the jesses. "He will let go if you cast him off!"

Ralph flung his arm outward, again and again, in a frenzy. The goshawk finally released him and beat his wings to rise toward the ceiling.

Isobel leaped upward and caught the ends of the jesses, pulling the bird down to her with all of her might, holding out her gloved hand as she did so. Gawain settled to the fist with a flutter and perched quietly. He blinked a bright eye at her, and then at Ralph, and bent his head to calmly preen his feathers.

Ralph sucked in air as if in severe pain and examined his hand, spewing vicious oaths. Isobel murmured to the bird, stroked him, and watched Ralph without moving toward him.

"He broke my finger," Ralph said, holding up a bloodied, swollen first finger. "I cannot move it. Cursed bird!" He winced and curled his other hand over his injured finger.

"Hawks are dangerous to keep," Isobel said. "You should have remembered that. You should have been more wary. He didna like you so close to him. Or so close to me," she added, stroking Gawain's shoulder. She was not sure why the goshawk had leaped onto

Ralph's hand, but she was immensely grateful for the intervention.

"What is the trouble here?" a voice asked from the doorway. "I heard the screams from the stairs."

Isobel whirled to see Father Hugh standing in a shadow by the door. He stepped into the room.

"That foul bird broke my finger," Ralph muttered, holding his wound up to show the priest.

Father Hugh came forward to peer and shook his grayed, partially shaved head. "Hawks never seem to favor you, Ralph," he said. He glanced at the tiercel on Isobel's fist. "Is that the same gos that you left at Aberlady?"

"Aye," Ralph muttered. "And he's not long for this world. You should have eaten him when you had the chance, Isobel," he growled, and stepped toward her. She gave a little shriek and retreated.

"Enough!" Father Hugh snapped. " 'Tis just a bird. Have some sense. Wrap the finger and stop complaining. I came to tell you that I just spoke with Margaret. She's waiting in your chamber for you. She's complacent," he added.

Ralph shot him a dark look. "Margaret," he said, "is incapable of complacency. I want a proper wife—this one."

"Have patience." Father Hugh turned to look up at Isobel. He, too, was considerably shorter than she was, his build sturdy and tough, his jowled face still handsome. "Sit down, lass, and talk with me." He took her arm and led her to the bed, seating her on its edge, sinking down beside her. He folded his ink-stained hands inside his sleeves, resting them on his broad belly.

"Isobel," Father Hugh said, "this morn in the forest—"

"You betrayed my trust," she snapped. If she had listened to Jamie, she thought, none of this would have happened.

"I agreed to let a patrol follow me because I was greatly concerned about your welfare. We had to rescue you from the outlaws. There was no need to meet as the outlaw wanted."

"What about Margaret?" she asked. She glanced at

Ralph, who sat on the leather stool, nursing his wound, which he had wrapped in a cloth he found in the wooden chest.

"She is content enough here. 'Tis unfortunate that Lindsay believed she was being held against her will. She has been . . . a willing companion for Ralph these several weeks."

"Surely you know better than that," she said.

He shrugged. "I am concerned with your well-being, not hers. Your honor was unjustly threatened. We saved you. Where is your gratitude?"

"You stood back and allowed me to be taken prisoner."

"Dinna be harsh," Father Hugh said. "Ralph loves you and wants you for his wife. And he wants you to become prophetess to a king. Has he told you the news?" He took Isobel's hand.

She withdrew it, reaching over to stroke the bird's breast. "Aye, he told me. And I willna do it."

She saw Ralph exchange a quick look with the priest. For a moment, the two men looked like brothers, she thought; twins in shape, coloring, and especially in their dark determination to control her even more closely than they had before. She would not let this happen. She could not. Those days were ended.

She thought of James in the dungeon, and felt as if her heart twisted inside. She would do whatever she could to free him, and the others, from the schemes these men had planned.

"Isobel," Father Hugh said, "for years I have carefully recorded and interpreted your visions. Over the last two years, I realized that they were too significant to keep to ourselves. I began announcing them from my pulpit— this you knew about." She nodded, listening. "And I sent copies of the predictions to the Guardians of the Realm, and to other Scottish nobles."

"But why?" she said, genuinely puzzled.

"I believe they are truly extraordinary, the work of God. You could speak for kings, Isobel, and so you will. I have been preparing a volume of what I have recorded and notated so far. I mean to send it to the pope himself.

A few months ago, I sent a collection of your words, bound in fine leather, to King Edward."

She stared at him, incredulous. "You did this without my knowing? Those are my words, Father. I endured blindness and—and the rigors of your safekeeping to say them."

"We didna need to consult you, lass," he said, not unkindly. "You would have asked us not to do it, in seemly modesty."

"Then *you* were the one who brought King Edward's attention to me," she said. "And Aberlady was besieged because of it!"

"I didna know the king would react that way. But your father favored keeping your words private, sharing the prophecies with a select few," the priest said. "Sir Ralph and I decided to go to King Edward. We thought it best." He beamed at her. "And now the king of England wants you for his own prophetess. We couldna be more fortunate in our patron."

"Patron!" She stood. "You intend to gain money for my prophecies?"

Ralph stood and took her arm. "I will be honored and proud to see my wife so favored."

"To see yourself so favored," she said bitterly.

"The prophecies are what matter," Father Hugh said. "They are remarkable for one of such youth, with meanings we can only guess at now. I will ask the king to finance my study of them."

"I will never take part in such a plan!"

"You need us, Isobel," Ralph said. "You understand so little of the power you possess. You are like ink for a pen, clay for a hand. Someone must control your potential." He looked at the priest. "Father, she prophesied for the outlaw, and refuses to tell me what she said. I asked her to summon the visions for me here—but she refused that, too. We must be certain that she tells us all she has seen. I have a way to convince her to begin, I think."

"Aye, then," Father Hugh said. "Sit, lass."

She backed away, edging toward the door.

"Come here, and give me that damned hawk," Ralph

said. He paused to rummage through her hawking pouch, pulled out the small leather hood, and strode toward her.

"He'll foot you," she warned as he came nearer.

"Let him try," he said, grabbing her arm to pull her to him. She thought about flinging the hawk in his face and running, but he managed to hood the hawk in one swift, forceful movement.

Gawain squawked and struggled for a moment, and stilled on her fist. Ralph pulled Isobel toward him, his gaze locked to hers. She resisted but lacked the strength to counter his power. He pulled out a dark piece of cloth, which he had tucked in his belt, whipped it over her head, and tied it firmly behind her.

Darkness descended over her suddenly and completely. She gasped and pulled at the blindfold, but Ralph grabbed her free hand and held it behind her as he shoved her, step by unwilling step, across the room.

"I found the cloth in the chest," he said. "And I thought, what if blindness was forced upon you? You just might prophesy more readily. What do you think, Father?"

"An intriguing idea, my son," the priest said. "Dinna hurt the lass, now. She is valuable to us. Sit her there easily, aye. Here, Isobel, let us set the hawk on this perch."

She felt the glove and the goshawk taken from her, and heard Gawain chitter, but knew he would be calm with the hood on his head. Ralph took her hands—she knew it was him, for his fingers were roughened, the strong, direct touch of a man who worked with weapons and gear and horses—and tied them behind her.

"Why do you do this to me?" she asked. "Father Hugh, why do you join in treacheries with Sir Ralph? I trusted you. My father thought you a worthy priest."

"John Seton has always looked after the welfare of his only child," he said. "And so I have cared for the welfare of mine."

"Your—child?" She tilted her head, frowning. Then the meaning of his words stunned her. "Ralph is your—son?"

"Aye. My son," the priest said. "I watched him fight in his childhood, wanting to be equal to other lads, though he was the bastard of a priest and of a Scottish heiress who died at his birth," he said. "I found a noble household to foster him, and I instilled him with pride and ambition. 'Twas all I could give him to protect himself in this temporal world. Now, Isobel," he said quietly, "the darkness is upon you. That should produce prophecies in you."

"Nay," she cried, turning her head, trying to shake off the blindfold, and shake off the fear. "I willna do this for you."

Ralph's hand, heavy on her shoulder. "You will, lass," he said. "Our talk of freedom and wildness, and that accursed gos over there, has shown me the perfect way to tame you."

"Tame me?" she asked, her heart pounding.

He bent close. She could smell his breath, feel its heat. "I will keep you awake for as many days and nights as it takes," he said. "Without food, without sleep, listening only to me." He caressed her shoulder as if she were a bird, and he spoke in a hushed, patient whisper. But she heard a cold element in his voice, like ice entering her veins.

"When you are ready to obey me"—his hand trailed over her shoulder, grazed over the top of her breast, lifted away—"as your husband and your master, then we will have prophecies of you great enough to please a king."

"Nay," she whispered, bowing her head.

His hand rested on her hair, stroking, and he laughed.

Chapter 28

James faced the stone wall and reached up to grip the chains. With the strength of his arms and shoulders, he raised his body until his feet cleared the floor, then lowered himself and pulled up again. He repeated it until his muscles ached for release, until the sweat rolled off of his brow and dampened his back and chest.

"You'll exhaust yourself," John Seton observed.

"What else have I got to do?" James muttered. He wrapped his hands around the chains, placed the soles of his feet against the wall, and extended his legs. He folded inward and shoved out again. "I have lost strength over the past few days from the head wound and from the fine feasts they serve us here."

John Seton grunted. "I worked my body, too, in the beginning. Now I just want to survive. A small bowl of porridge each morn, and a little watered ale through the day, doesna make much brawn or will in a man."

"Well," James drawled, looking up at the ceiling. "There's always the supper hour."

The wooden planks that formed the flat ceiling were the same boards that formed part of the floor in the chamber overhead. The upper room was used by garrison soldiers as a dining hall. Whenever the men gathered for supper, talking and stomping across the floor, small scraps of food would trickle down between the planks and fall to the dungeon floor. John had showed James how to harvest the best bits quickly, crawling on hands and knees, before the mice scurried in and took the rest.

"Aye," John said, looking up. " 'Tis usually bread crumbs or cooked barley, but I have a fierce taste for some meat."

"They might kick some chicken bones through the door cracks for you," James remarked. He lowered his feet and turned to sit, wiping sweat from his brow, licking his hand to conserve the salty moisture his body lost.

John Seton watched him. "Your eye looks better. The swelling is less and the bruises are fading. Can you see?"

James looked around, squinting. " 'Tis improved."

"Do you see an old fool?"

James looked at him, frowning. "Nay," he said slowly.

"Aye, you do. I was wrong about you, lad."

"I wouldna expect you to favor the outlaw who wooed your daughter and lost her," James murmured.

"Ah, you havena lost her," Seton said. He half smiled and shook his head. "She loves you well. I saw it in her eyes. But I have lost her. I took her words to heart," he said, rubbing his gnarled fingers over his brow. "And I have been thinking. Isobel is right. I treated her unfairly these last few years. Now she has rebelled against me. I always thought she was a timid, gentle lass, but she's changed."

"Timid? Nay," James said, pinching back a smile. "But she is gentle and ever will be—though like a breeze, or a stream of water. There is great endurance beneath that soft nature."

"Aye. She is stronger than I thought."

James nodded. "She is. But I willna lose my own strength. I intend to get out of here, and get to her, somehow."

Seton smiled, rueful and wise. "I was wrong about you, and I ask your pardon. You have been here for—four days? Five? I dinna see a traitor. I see a rebel, and a man I admire. I see honor and determination in you, and great love for my daughter." He looked at him soberly. "Do you have a plan for escape?"

"I have thought over the possibilities," James said in a hushed tone. "If Margaret comes back, she might be able to get a key. Failing that, Ralph Leslie may return, and I will be waiting. He came near me once, but I didna hit him hard enough. Let him come near me again," he said, drawing out the chain between his hands, a cold slither of steel. "If I threaten to break his neck, he will have to order us free, with weapons put in our hands. That, at least, would give us a chance."

"There are two hundred soldiers in this place," Seton said.

"And one guard who seems to favor us. There may be more. With but a few soldiers on our side, we can win our freedom." He saw Seton's doubtful expression and sighed. "What other hope do we have, John?" he asked grimly. The man nodded.

James turned and placed his feet against the wall. He sat up, went down, curled up, went down. He felt his muscles tighten and stretch, and felt power surge through him.

He would be ready, he thought. The time would soon come when he would use the strength he garnered now.

She wanted a bath. Isobel turned and walked the length of the room again, counting the steps, reaching the bed on the eleventh step, turning to walk back to the bird's perch. She shifted her arms, her hands tied behind her back, and twitched her loosened hair over her shoulder with a toss of her head.

She wanted a hot bath, clean hair, a fresh gown, a good meal. Most of all, she wanted the reassuring warmth of Jamie's arms around her. If he were here, his love would wrap around her like a cloak, and she would sleep soundly at last.

Tears prickled her eyes behind the blindfold. That would not do; she had discovered how much dried tears itched. She sucked in a breath and dispelled them. Ten steps, eleven.

Her toe touched the base of the perch. Gawain chirred, and she stood beside him and sang the *kyrie* softly, its haunting strain calming both her and the bird.

Turning, she walked through darkness. The sound of larks, and the newborn coolness in the air wafting through the window, told her that morning had come. Soon Ralph would return.

Her knees were wobbly with exhaustion, but she stayed on her feet. If Ralph came in—as he had done before without warning—and found her sleeping, he would pull her up, not roughly, but wholly unforgiving.

is determination to treat her like a hawk to be broken
as deeply frightening.

Because of his constant attention, she had not slept
or more than an hour or two since he had tied and
lindfolded her. She had scarcely eaten, and all she had
en was the gritty darkness of the blindfold.

And all she had heard, when Ralph was there, was his
oice, softened, cajoling, convincing her to listen to him,
let him take care of her, to give in to his wishes and
s wisdom for her. His hands, soothing over her, and
s voice at her ear were a travesty of James's genuine
atience and kindness, both with the hawk and with her.

On his father's practical advice, Ralph had allowed
largaret to come to her briefly, a few times each day,
bathe her face and hands and assist her with her
odily needs. The girl had been instructed not to speak;
alph had stood outside the door, listening, to make
rtain. Isobel had felt his malevolence seep through the
ick oaken door.

But she had found real joy in Margaret's whispers and
acing hugs. The girl's sniffling tears only saddened her
d brought tears of exhaustion and frustration to her
asked eyes.

Now, though, an hour or two of sleep had strangely
eared her head. She paced through the ever-present
irkness, trying to ignore the sharp hunger in her belly
d the equally keen fear that invaded her thoughts.

If she prophesied, she could have anything, she told
erself. If she gave in to Ralph, he would allow her any
quest within reason. He had told her that repeatedly,
a whispery voice, while his hands traveled the con-
urs of her body. He had not ventured beyond sweep-
g, slow caresses, though he promised her more when
e became his wife.

That was not something she wanted to think about.

The latch of the door rattled, and she heard the door
ening. She jerked around, stepping away when she
ard his heavy foot on the floor.

"Isobel." Dear God, how she hated that voice, which
e had once found pleasant. "Come and eat. I know
u are hungry."

She shook her head silently and backed away until sh‹
reached the bird's perch. Ralph crossed the room.

"You are far more stubborn than I ever would ha‹
thought." His hand touched her head. She tilted aw‹
with a little sound of protest. "And I have no time ‹
wait upon your whim any longer. You must give up th‹
wildness you favor. In a day or two, we will journey ‹
see the king."

She said nothing, her head lowered, all of her sens‹
alert. She heard the goshawk stir nervously on the perc‹

"Today," Ralph said, "we might let that hawk go."

Isobel swallowed heavily and remained silent. Sh‹
sensed Ralph reach out to the bird—a creak of leathe‹
the chirr of the hooded bird, blinded and trapped as sh‹
was. Subtle sounds told her that Gawain tore at som‹
meat, so she knew Ralph fed him.

"After I let the hawk go, I think I will go down ‹
the dungeon and set your lover free. Free to go to Go‹
that is."

She licked her dry lips to speak. "You—you will k‹
him?" she whispered. Her heart pumped so hard th‹
she felt faint.

"I will," he said. "And your father. Unless you ‹
what I ask of you. My patience has gone dry, Isobel
He paused. "I do not jest. I do not bargain. The ki‹
awaits us, and expects worth for his coin. He will n‹
bargain with me in this matter. He will not grant t‹
tolerance that I have given you."

She drew a breath and brushed past him, counting h‹
steps as she crossed the room, giving herself time ‹
think. She did not doubt that Ralph would kill Jam‹
She could not bear the thought. And her father, to‹
would die. Ralph had loyalty only to himself. Even M‹
garet, who had won Ralph's favor, would likely fall v‹
tim to her lover's evil nature. And the hawk would ‹
set free as a last blow. Isobel would lose everyone s‹
loved if she clung to her stubbornness now.

But she could endure survival and safety for the‹
Her own fate hardly mattered to her when compared ‹
the immeasurable value of those other lives. If sh‹
acquiesced, Ralph would be generous with her. Sh‹

would not be harmed; she would have all that she needed—all but love and freedom.

Without those, without Jamie, she might wither away. But if he died, she would surely cease to flourish. Her choice was obvious. The alternative was unthinkable.

She would give up her own chance for joy and peace in exchange for the good of those she loved. But she must speak now, while she had the strength of resolve, or lose the courage.

She turned. A black, empty feeling crept through her, a heavy shadow that sucked up hope and erased brightness from her future. But the knowledge that Jamie, her father, and Margaret would live sparked at the center of the darkness, like a candle flame in an abyss.

"What do you want of me?" she asked in a hollow tone. She knew well what he wanted. The question became a statement of surrender. She felt detached, increasingly numb in spirit.

"Prophecies," Ralph said simply. "And your hand in marriage, this day. I want my wife to be the king's prophetess."

She held her blindfolded head high. "I ask a marriage boon." He was silent, but she knew he watched her. She felt stripped naked, threatened, by a stare she could not even see.

"I want them released," she said. "My father, James, and Margaret. If you promise to let them walk out of here unharmed, I will agree to what you want."

She heard his step on the floor. "Reasonable enough," he said, surprising her. "I will let them go after we are wed."

She turned away, facing the window, feeling its soft air upon her face, her hands. "Leave the goshawk with me. He is mine. You willna release him."

"Aye," he said gruffly. "I will tell my father to prepare for the wedding." He paused. "Isobel. I hope to make you proud of the husband you have chosen. You will be greatly admired in the English court."

She kept her back to him. "I love another man. But I will wed you in barter for his life, and the lives of my father and Margaret. I must have your solemn oath of honor on the bargain."

He was silent, standing by the door.

"Swear it," she said. "On what you most value."

"I swear they will go free," he said. "On the pain of my love for you." He opened the door and left.

Isobel's hair gleamed like a skein spun from midnight as Margaret combed it out before the brazier's glowing heat. The girl had assisted Isobel through a bath, and had wept freely, while Isobel sat cool and silent. Isobel watched the goshawk, fed and unhooded, as he sat his perch, and knew she was as trapped as he was.

Freed of her blindfold and wrist bonds, Isobel took no satisfaction in the release, or in the longed-for bath or the hot meal that followed. Ralph had given her a gown and surcoat of deep blue Flemish samite, trimmed in silver embroidery and tiny glass beads. The gown and surcoat, along with a silk chemise and a veil of fine, translucent gauze, were exquisitely rendered, finer than anything Isobel had ever seen. Ralph told her that he had purchased the cloth and had the garments made in Edinburgh months ago, in anticipation of their wedding.

She would not have cared had the clothing been rags. She stood passively while Margaret dressed her. Through the silence, Isobel sensed Margaret's pain and disappointment keenly.

"I am sorry," Isobel whispered. "Truly sorry. I know you love Sir Ralph."

"I have lost my affection for him," the girl hissed. "But I weep for you, Isobel," she added in a hushed tone. "And I dinna know what I will tell Jamie, if Ralph truly lets us go."

"Tell him," Isobel whispered, "that I wish him peace in his life." She looked away, feeling a stony numbness collect inside of her. "Only that. There is naught else to say."

Margaret nodded as she combed out the length of Isobel's hair. She arranged the veil over it, draping its tail under Isobel's chin and bringing it up, then crowning her head with a circlet of rolled silk.

A knock on the door preceded Ralph and the priest. Ralph had changed into a tunic and surcoat of fine black wool trimmed in fur in honor of his wedding. He stared at Isobel and bowed his head slowly. Margaret stood, but Isobel remained on the stool beside the brazier.

"Is it time for the ceremony already?" Margaret asked.

"Soon," Father Hugh said. "Margaret, go tell the guards to fetch our guests and bring them to the chapel."

"Guests!" Isobel burst out.

"Surely you want your father and . . . the outlaw to witness your wedding," Ralph said.

Isobel stared flatly at him. "Nay."

"Nevertheless," Father Hugh said. "Margaret, go. Now." The girl gave Isobel an uncertain look and hurried from the room.

Father Hugh sat on the wooden chest and took out a rolled parchment, an ink pot, and a quill. "We want you to summon a vision for us, Isobel. We must know what you told the outlaw."

"Of course, you will keep your promise to prophesy for your husband," Ralph murmured. " 'Tis a mark of good will if you do that for us now." He produced a bowl of water. "Gaze here."

Isobel bowed her head. She did not look at the water or at the men. She drew in a breath, and heard, in her mind, the calm, mellifluous tones of Jamie's voice, singing the *kyrie eleison*. She heard the sounds of water trickling down a stone wall. Then she saw the glistening rills flow into a pool, inside a paradise she would never again enter.

Peace streamed through her, gentle and serene. She realized that here, at least, in her mind and in her memories, she would find the refuge of the love she needed so desperately. And the visions, no matter what came afterward, brought her a true sense of joy, as if heavenly voices soothed her and told her secrets.

She tipped her head and watched new images form. Men in shining, bloodied armor, wielding broadswords and axes; a tall, white-haired, aged king on his deathbed; a Scottish nobleman running through heather and bog, newly become a rebel, a renegade, and a king; and the single lion, the banner of Scotland, raised in victory over a field by a flowing burn.

She began to speak.

Chapter 29

James reached out his hand, chain links jangling, and assisted John Seton in the arduous task of climbing the steep stairs in ankle cuffs and chains. At the top, they walked into the yard, surrounded by guards.

James blinked in the fading daylight. Blue shadows gathered along the high enclosing castle walls, and the massive gray stone keep was silhouetted against the red sun as it sank in the west.

James looked around warily. One of the soldiers who had escorted them out of their cell had tersely announced that they were to be taken to the yard, but had not explained why.

A crowd of soldiers gathered at one side of the keep, in front of the chapel that jutted out into the bailey. The guards escorted James and John toward the crowd. Three lancet windows along the side of the small building reflected the glowing sun. James gazed at the design, remembering that his father had built the chapel for his mother, a lifetime ago.

On the steps, beneath the deep pointed arch of the entrance, James saw Isobel, Ralph, and another man, a priest, whom he recognized from Isobel's ill-fated meeting in the forest. As he walked closer, craning his neck to see above the heads of the soldiers gathered before the chapel entrance, he realized why they had been brought here.

"My God," John said. "She's being wed, here and now, on the steps of the church." He moved as the guards urged them forward.

James stepped ahead slowly, chains dragging on him,

foot and hand. But the profound weight of his sinking heart was a thousandfold heavier.

The ceremony had already begun. As he edged closer, he heard the priest's voice speaking the Latin of the ritual. He heard Ralph's reply, strong and sure. And he heard Isobel's uncertain answer.

She looked like a saint or a queen, framed within the graceful curve of the entrance arch. Gowned in sumptuous blue, with silvery glints striking off her sleeves and hem like diamonds, she stood willowy and elegant beside Ralph's husky, vigorous form. The shimmering folds of the veil lent her face a fragile, ethereal loveliness. She was more beautiful than he had ever imagined.

James stared, enthralled, stunned, struck deep to his soul.

Isobel held out her hand, and Ralph slipped a ring on her finger. He moved toward her, and she turned her face slightly so that he kissed her cheek. Ralph raised his head, looked out over the crowd of soldiers, and found James and John standing among them. He smiled, bitter and triumphant, and turned away.

Isobel did not look at them at all. Ralph took her arm and spoke to her, looking up at her as if in adoration.

"Bastard," John growled. "I am her father, and denied a place at her wedding. He wouldna invite me to watch closer than this for a reason. He knew I would raise an objection."

James spun away, squeezing his eyes shut, hardly able to think as a tide of rage and anguish plunged through him. He felt as if he had taken a killing blow, as he had when Elizabeth had burned to death at Wildshaw years ago, dying in this very yard; as he had when Wallace had been taken. He had survived those invisible, grievous wounds.

He did not think he could survive, this time.

He stood like a stone, his back to the chapel, hearing the cheers of congratulations among the English guards. Besides him, John Seton watched his daughter.

"Jamie," Seton said in a low voice. James heard the odd note in it and turned, ever alert to danger. "Look at her."

He scowled. "I canna."

"Look," John insisted. "You must."

James reluctantly lifted his gaze, narrowed it on her face, so beautiful, so heartbreaking. Then he noticed the odd tilt of her head, the blue ice glaze of her eyes.

"Jesu," he breathed. "She is blind."

"Aye," John growled. "She's prophesied only recently, I would think. Jesus God. The bastard has taken her in wedlock when she was most defenseless and least able to act for herself."

James felt his rage rise to a nearly uncontrollable level. He fisted his hands, felt his belly muscles tighten. He looked instinctively for a weapon, and had none. He, too, was defenseless and unable to act.

" 'Tis done," John Seton said. "They are going inside the church now. The doors are closing. Father Hugh will say a mass to solemnize the occasion. And we will be taken back to our cell, having witnessed the match."

But the guards who surrounded them guided them toward the gate rather than the dungeon. James heard his name being called and looked around, puzzled.

Margaret ran toward him, skirts flying around her strongly muscled legs. She reached his side and grabbed his forearm above the manacle. "We are being released," she said breathlessly. "They are sending us out of here!"

James frowned at her. "What do you mean? What has happened?" Around him, the escort urged them hastily past the great iron-studded wooden doors of the entrance, which had been pulled back. They walked beneath the vaulted tunnel of the foregate, which sloped downhill. James looked at Margaret in astonishment as they reached the other end of the vault, where the portcullis gate lifted slowly, pulleys squealing. Outside, the drawbridge had already been lowered.

"What is going on here?" he asked Margaret. They were escorted across the drawbridge, the booted feet of the guards stomping in strong, unmatched rhythms. The air was fresh and keen, but the shock of the marriage ceremony had drained all the joy from his release. His feet thudded over the grass at the other end of the drawbridge, and his cautious gaze already scanned the valley, the hills, the forest in the distance.

Beside him, he saw John Seton blinking up at the trees, the sky, the green expanse of the valley below the castle with a look of wonder on his face.

The guards stopped around them. One man came forward with a large iron key and bent to unlock John Seton's leg and wrist manacles, while other guards lifted away the chains. They turned to do the same for James, while he held his arms out patiently and watched the faces of the guards.

Not one, he noticed, would look him in the eye. One by one, they turned away and crossed back over the drawbridge. John Seton, on Margaret's arm, stepped ahead, the wind blowing through his gray locks as he looked around.

A single guard remained to unlock James's ankle cuffs and lift the weight of that chain. The man stepped back and looked at James. He saw that it was the same soldier who, a few days earlier, had refused to harm Isobel or him in the dungeon.

"My thanks," James said quietly.

The man nodded. He handed James a folded, sealed parchment. "This is Sir Ralph's note of safe passage, allowing you to leave Wildshaw land and return to the forest."

James looked dubiously at the parchment he held. "Why?"

"A wedding promise, as I understand it. The bride required your freedom—all three—as a condition to the marriage."

James closed his eyes briefly, feeling yet another blow, this one poignant and tender, but no less painful. He nodded. "I see," he said. He turned to walk after Margaret and John.

"Beware, Lindsay," the knight said. James turned, frowning. "Soldiers are hiding in the woods, ready to ambush and murder all three of you. A wedding gift from the groom, I think."

James watched him intently. "Why does a Southron knight warn me of this?"

The man shrugged. "Your lady is lovely. I would not like to see her distressed by the news of your death."

"She isna my lady," James said harshly.

"Ah, but she is. I saw it in her eyes the first day she came here," the man murmured. "I see it in yours now."

James glanced away, glanced back. "Tell me the whole of why you take this risk. You have the chary look of a knight, a soldier, not one to fall for a bonny, sweet face. Even hers."

The man huffed a short laugh, and shifted the chains in his arms. "I have heard of your bravery and cunning for years."

James shrugged. "Old triumphs. Few trust me now."

"Many men do, though you do not even suspect their support," the knight said, looking at him evenly. "I was there the night Wallace was taken. I was part of Sir Ralph's guard. And so I saw what Leslie and the others—Menteith and his men—did. And I saw what you did. That was uncommon bravery, sir. It became clear to me then which men were honorable that night."

James watched him with the sudden, odd sense that he had discovered a loyal friend. "Go on," he said cautiously.

The man glanced away, over the hills. "I felt fouled that night for what we did. Men trust and respect you more than you know, Border Hawk. They are English soldiers, garrisoned here at Wildshaw. But the story of that night is well known here. We know the truth." He turned to look at James, his eyes a deep, rich brown. "Many of us regret what happened that night, and afterward, to Wallace—and to you. Not all Southrons admire betrayal and injustice, you know."

James stared at him in astonishment. "What is your name?"

"Sir Gawain of Avenel, in Northumberland."

James smiled a little, and nodded. "Gawain," he said, half to himself. "Certes, she would have known the name would have significance someday. I am pleased to know you, Sir Gawain," he said. "And you have my thanks. You have saved our lives this day. Should you ever find yourself dissatisfied with your king and his cause in Scotland, you are welcome among the men of the Ettrick Forest."

Sir Gawain nodded. "I will remember that. There is one last thing you might want to know," he said. "On the morrow, Sir Ralph intends to escort his bride to an audience with King Edward at Carlisle. They will have to pass through the forest. I thought you might want to bid your lady adieu."

James nodded, frowning. "I might," he said slowly.

Gawain pulled the dagger out of his belt and tossed it into the grass at James's feet. "You will have need of a weapon in those woods beyond."

"I am sincerely in your debt," James said. He pulled out the knife and stuck it in his belt. Then he nodded to Gawain and turned to walk down the grassy slope that led away from the drawbridge.

His step had lightened considerably with the chains removed. But he still carried a leaden weight in the region of his heart. And he could not bear to look behind him.

"That hawk is getting fat," James said. He stretched out on the floor beside Alice's blazing hearth, leaned his head on his hand, and looked up at Ragnell. The hawk perched on the back of Alice's chair, her silver foot glittering in the firelight, and glared at him with a royal, reddish eye.

"She's fat because I am overfeeding her," Alice said. "I dinna want her to fly away. And you, my lad, are drunk."

"Nah," James said as he took another sip of dark Rhenish wine from a leather flask. "But I might be soon."

Alice sighed audibly and frowned at him. James cocked an eyebrow at her and took another deep swallow. He watched his aunt turn her frown upon all of them, one by one: his own men, along with Eustace, John Seton, and Margaret, who curled on the floor by her aunt's chair. The small main room was crowded, dim, warm, and uncomfortably silent.

"And what's to be done with him?" Alice asked.

"Leave him be," Patrick muttered. "He's heartbroke."

"If he wants to dive into his cups, let him," Henry Wood said. "'Tis what I would do, though 'tis unlike him."

"After all he went through this day," John Seton said.

"we canna blame him. He fought like a demon in the forest when those soldiers attacked us. If you lads hadna come along to finish them off, we would all be dead, not a quarter mile from Wildshaw's gates. All that, and witnessing that accursed wedding, too. Let him down that wine, and I'll drink with him."

Eustace and Geordie muttered agreement, watching James. He ignored them all and sipped from the leather flask again. He disliked the stuff, and had not intended to get drunk. But the more they discussed it around him the better the idea seemed.

"Heartbroken he may be," Margaret said. "But he can do something about it." She scowled at him.

"I havena decided," James drawled, "what I will do about it." The painful mixture of anger, confusion, and hurt that had roiled in him all evening had not faded with the wine. He wanted to believe that Isobel loved him, only him. But he could not help but wonder about her choice.

"Isobel doesna want a forest outlaw, it seems," he said, and sipped at the wine. "Naught makes that so clear as a wedding."

" 'Tisna clear to me," Margaret said. "Dinna be a sodding fool. Go get her, and find out for yourself."

"Margaret, lass," John Seton said kindly. "He doesn need the sharp side of your tongue, now. Have a care."

"But Gawain of Avenel told him about Ralph's rout through the forest for a reason," Margaret said. "H gave Jamie the chance to win her back. Jamie, you cann ignore that."

"She chose luxury and the protection of a garrison— in my own castle—over life with a brigand. And wh could blame her?"

" 'Twas against her will," Margaret said. "Ralp forced her into the marriage by threatening your life and the life of John Seton. And mine, too, I think."

"You said she wished me peace in my life and wer about donning her wedding finery. Which I could neve have afforded for her," he muttered. "She made th practical choice."

"I saw her with him, Jamie. She hates and fears hin

He will use her prophecies for his own gain. Steal her away!"

"The English king will favor her," he said. "She will be honored. She willna be harmed."

"She willna be *happy*," Margaret snapped. "Do you love her?"

He gazed into the fire. "Aye," he growled. "But I willna take another man's wife. Even a rogue has morals."

"Make her a widow," Quentin said quietly.

James slid the Highlander a long look. Quentin folded his arms, stretched out his legs where he sat on the bench, and regarded him calmly.

"Make her a widow," he said again. "I will help you."

"And I," Henry said.

Eustace leaned forward. "I know Ralph Leslie well," he said. "And my loyalty has ever been to John Seton of Aberlady and his daughter. But, James Lindsay, you have my full respect." He gazed steadily at James. "So I will help you take the lady."

James frowned, glancing around the room. They all looked at him in turn, nodding, murmuring agreement.

"I will be at your back," Patrick said. "You know that."

"And I," Geordie said, sitting up where he lounged on Alice's bed. "I've a good hand with a sword."

"Now that I have a fine meal in my belly," John Seton said, "I believe I could run with you lads."

James listened silently, looking at each one, frowning.

"You know my hand is steady with a bow," Margaret said. Her gaze was like dark amber in the firelight, her face strong and proud. "And I have a grudge with Ralph Leslie myself."

"As do we all, on Margaret's behalf," Patrick growled.

"If you have a doubt as to why the lady married him," Alice said, "then stop her escort and ask her yourself."

James scanned each face in turn, his throat tightening. Their firm loyalty stirred him to the roots of his soul. The trust and support of these few willing, loving friends were riches enough for a lifetime.

But there was one whose shining, gentle faith in him was as elemental to his soul as water was to his body.

As long as she was missing from his life, as long as she
was threatened, or lived somewhere without happiness,
he would feel it. He would know it, and he would never
begin to find the peace that he so long had craved.

"Aye, then," he said grimly. "We have a task ahead."

Isobel walked across the small chamber carefully, still
blinded, counting the steps to find her way through the
darkness. She reached out, groping past the bird's perch,
and took the leather glove from the wall peg where she
had left it. Then she stroked the bird, found his jesses,
and untied them, leaving him free on the perch.

During the ordeal of a wedding supper with Ralph,
Father Hugh, and a few English knights, she had considered the matter of what to do with the hawk. Aside from
kind words from Sir Gawain, she had heard little from
the other men. Her thoughts had strayed continually to
Jamie, who had his freedom, and to his hawk, who did
not.

Now that she knew what it was to be trapped, jessed
and hooded, she could not keep Gawain against his will.
If the goshawk stayed with her, he must choose to do
so. She did not expect intelligent loyalty from a hawk.
But she had to know.

She stood by the window, raised her empty gloved
hand, and gave him the choice. With lifted chin, she
chanted the melody of the *kyrie*. After a moment, she
sang again. Then she stood quietly, and let the wind call
him, too.

She heard the goshawk rouse his feathers and chirr.
Then came the rustle of lifted wings, and the soft
whooshing rhythm as he flew across the room toward
the window.

He landed on her glove with a sure settling of wings,
the grip of his talons strong.

Isobel blinked back tears and whispered praises to the
bird as she carried him back to the perch. She slipped
the jesses on his feet with quick, certain fingers, even
in darkness.

"My advice to you, my son," Father Hugh said, "is
to wait."

"Wait!" Ralph protested.

Isobel listened from her seat upon the edge of the bed. She folded her hands in her lap, sat silently, and felt immense gratitude toward the priest.

"Wait," Father Hugh said. "The blindness doesna last long. A day or two, mayhap only a few hours, and she will be sighted again, and willing."

Never willing, Isobel thought to herself.

"She isn't even a virgin," Ralph whined. Isobel knew that he was surely drunk, judging by the amount of wine and ale he had consumed at supper.

"We canna change that," Father Hugh said. "Although if I were you, I would have sought revenge rather than release the knave who did that to her. But remember this, Ralph. Her prophetic gift is fragile in nature. As long as she is blind, I believe that she is still in the state of grace brought on by the holy word of God that comes through her."

"Damn," Ralph muttered.

Isobel sat straight and demure, and kept her eyes wide open, hoping to appear saturated in grace. The idea occurred to her that she could keep Ralph away from her as long as she remained blind—or claimed that she was.

Then she sighed. Both men knew the blindness would go away in a day or so. Her reprieve, even if she managed to extend the time, would end.

She heard Ralph cross the room, and sensed him standing in front of her. "One kiss," he said. "She is my bride."

"One chaste kiss to celebrate the marriage," Father Hugh agreed. "But we canna offend the integrity of her prophetic gift. You willna touch her until the blindness passes."

"By then we'll be in Carlisle, visiting the king," Ralph said.

"A fine place for a nuptial celebration."

Ralph grunted without enthusiasm. Isobel felt his fingers slide along her chin, felt him tip her head up as he bent forward. His lips touched hers, pressed, opened lightly. She closed her eyes instinctively, and kept her mouth tight and flat beneath his. He renewed the kiss, slanting his mouth over hers. Although the kiss did not stir her, she found it wine-flavored and gentle, if full of need. She offered neither protest nor response.

He lifted his mouth from hers. "Good night, wife." She heard his booted step as he left the room, heard the door close behind both men. Her eyes flew open.

For once, she was deeply glad that the blindness lingered.

Chapter 30

A fine web of mist hung between the trees as the group made their way along the forest path. Leather trappings, chain mail, and the stomp and snort of the horses created layers of sound as they traveled through the cool, silent morning. Isobel rode at the center of a group of fifteen men, flanked by Ralph and Sir Gawain. Father Hugh rode in front with several soldiers, and another six were armed and mounted behind.

She glanced at the hawk perched on her fist, and then at the misty green forest with silent wonder and gratitude. As always in the hours after the blindness departed, she savored whatever she saw. A night's sleep had restored her vision completely, but she had been unable to hide the fact from Ralph and Father Hugh. She could only try to ignore Ralph's eagerness, and her own dread, as they readied for the journey to Carlisle and set out.

Ralph was wary about riding through this part of the forest, she knew; he had ordered a full patrol. As they rode, he seemed anxious, his eyes scanning, his hand on the hilt of his sword.

"Did the guards I sent out yesterday before the wedding return yet?" he asked Sir Gawain as they rode.

"Nay, sir," the knight replied. He kept his eyes ahead.

Isobel stared at him and then at Ralph. "You sent an ambush to meet James and my father and Margaret?" she asked, horrified.

Ralph slid a glance at her. "No need to concern ourself."

"Since the guards did not return, my lady," Sir Gawain said, "we should worry more about them than about the outlaws." His firm tone helped to reassure her that James was unharmed.

As they rode along, a cloaked figure suddenly stepped onto the path ahead of them, holding a large hawk on a gloved hand. The hawk had a silver foot, and the figure was statuesque and bosomy. The soldiers at the front of the group halted.

Alice! Isobel thought, and craned to see.

"Sir Ralph," Alice called. "I beg a word with you."

"Do not stop here," Ralph said. "She is—*ah!*"

He ducked as Ragnell came flying toward them, cutting through the double column of men. Soldiers leaned sideways in alarm as the huge red-tailed hawk swooped past and slanted sideways to disappear between the trees. Alice slipped away, too.

Frightened out of his wits by the female bird, the tiercel fell into a ferocious upside-down bate, squawking and flapping. Isobel held out her arm to accommodate him, while Ralph snarled and looked around, his hand at his sword.

A slight rumble of sound gave the only warning. An enormous log burst out of the treetops, suspended sideways on long ropes, and swung down toward the front group of guards and the priest. The men had no chance to jump aside as the log crashed into them, sweeping them off their horses like chessmen off a board. Among the mist-veiled trees, a few men scattered like deer.

"After them!" Ralph screamed as he tried to control his startled horse amid the chaos. Isobel struggled to hold both her horse and the frantic hawk, who still dangled from her arm by his jesses.

The soldiers of the rear guard galloped off in pursuit, leaving Ralph, Sir Gawain, one guard, and Isobel still mounted. Father Hugh and several others lay moaning or unconscious on the ground, while their horses stomped and circled on the path ahead.

Isobel saw three men and a woman walk out of the forest and come toward them. She gasped, and Ralph swore, grabbing the hilt of his sword. Isobel barely remembered to shift the calmed goshawk back to her fist as she watched them come forward, her heart beating in anticipation and sudden, wondrous joy.

James strode between the trees, a bow in his hand, a sword at his back. Beside him, Quentin and Patrick carried bows, and Margaret followed, wearing a tunic and trews, a loaded bow in her hands. She stopped a short distance away and raised the bow. Patrick and Quentin trained their arrows on the men still lying on the ground, while James advanced toward Isobel and Ralph.

"What are you waiting for?" Ralph yelled at the soldier mounted behind Sir Gawain. "Use your crossbow, man!"

The guard looked at Gawain, then shook his head in refusal. "I will not shoot at a women."

"God's bones!" Ralph snapped. "Gawain! Take care of them!"

Sir Gawain shoved back his chain-mail hood, his thick dark hair whipping in the breeze. "I find that I cannot do that, sir," he said, and circled his horse to ride toward the outlaws. The guard followed. Ralph gaped, then snarled curses after them.

James came closer, his stride long and sure. Quentin, Patrick, and Margaret came behind him, their arrows aimed at Ralph. Isobel then saw her father standing at the edge of the path, and watched as Sir Gawain and the other soldier halted their horses near him.

Ralph grabbed the hilt of his sword. Instantly three arrows pointed directly at him, and he lowered his hand without a word.

"What do you want?" he demanded. "Do you mean to rob us?"

"We might," James said. "You do carry a treasure—the famed prophetess of Aberlady." He stopped on the path, gripping his upright bow. Isobel read wariness in every line of his body and saw a fierce, cool glint in his dark blue eyes. She felt a desperate urge to leap from her horse and run to him, but the restrained power she saw in him made her uncertain. She wondered if he was furious with her for marrying Ralph.

"If you attempt to take her, you commit an offense against King Edward," Ralph growled. "And against myself. She is my wife—as you know."

"I wish to speak with Lady Isobel," James said bluntly. Isobel gazed at him, eyes widened, heart quickening.

"She does not speak to robbers." Ralph slid his gaze around, as if looking for the return of his guards, or for the recovery of the men still on their backs on the ground. "Step aside." He urged his horse forward. "Come, Isobel."

Patrick released his arrow. The bolt slammed into the ground, and Ralph pulled his horse back quickly. "The man said he wishes to speak with Lady Isobel," Patrick snarled.

He nocked another arrow. Behind him, the others stood guard over the fallen soldiers, some of whom began to stir.

James stepped toward Isobel and looked at her, his gaze keen and penetrating. His stance was easy, but his hands wrapped around the upright bow were white-knuckled. She held the hawk on her fist and gazed down at him, maintaining only an outward calm.

"Lady Isobel, tell me this," he said formally. "Will you choose safe passage through the forest this morn"—his quiet, mellow voice seemed to resonate in the core of her being—"or will you follow a different path . . . with an outlaw?"

She caught her breath, her heart bounding wildly. "Jamie—"

"Let us pass," Ralph interrupted. "The king awaits her as his honored guest. If you think to harm the prophetess, you will be hunted down by the king's own men. Isobel, all of them will die if you leave me," he added in a growl. "I will see to it."

She hesitated, biting at her lower lip, glancing at Ralph. His dark, malicious glare underscored his promise.

"I have had Edward's men after me before, and I have been threatened by you before," James said in dismissal. "Isobel, let me hear from your own lips which path you choose to follow."

Yearning welled inside of her. "Jamie," she murmured. "I—I made a choice yesterday. You are free now because of it." *And I am trapped,* she thought. She closed her eyes in anguish.

"She has answered you," Ralph said. He took the reins of her horse and pulled her ahead with him. "Clear the way. You promised safe passage if she made her choice. Even a forest rogue has to keep such a promise."

James snatched her bridle. "Not necessarily," he growled. "Isobel—do you travel willingly to see the English king?"

"Nay," she said. " 'Tis much against my will."

"Ah," James drawled, "then you must be in need of a rescue."

"I am!" she said breathlessly, grasping at the hope he offered.

He yanked out his dagger and sliced through the taut rein that Ralph held. Then he shoved her horse aside and squared his stance in the path as Ralph came toward him.

Isobel circled her horse, murmuring distractedly to the agitated hawk on her fist, and halted by the edge of the path. John Seton, on foot, and Sir Gawain on horseback, flanked her protectively.

Ralph grabbed the hilt of his sword and tried to draw it free. In one swift, powerful motion, James angled his bow like a staff and hit Ralph in the chest, unseating him. The man fell, slamming down on the ground with a loud grunt.

Isobel had never before seen such fury on James's face. He strode toward Ralph, who lay on his back, awkwardly attempting to pull his long, heavy sword from its scabbard. When the blade came loose, James flicked it deftly with his bow and sent it spinning. Ralph rolled to scramble away, and James bent down to haul him to his feet by a handful of wine-colored surcoat.

"Dinna go anywhere just yet," he said, "I have a few questions for you." He shoved him backward until Ralph stumbled against a tree. James jammed the long side of his bow under the shorter man's chin, pinning him high against the trunk, almost pulling him off his feet. Ralph grasped at the bow with both hands. "Did you touch her?" James asked, towering over him.

"She is my wife," Ralph said. " 'Tis not your concern."

"Did—you—touch—her?" James enunciated in a deep growl.

Ralph blinked rapidly and did not answer. James tightened the press of the bow on his throat.

Isobel murmured to her father, and he turned to help
her dismount from the horse. With the hawk on her fist,
she lifted the hem of her blue silk gown and crossed the
path. Quentin and Patrick followed, aiming half-drawn
arrows at Ralph.

"James," she said. "Stop. He didna touch me."

"Is it true?" James asked Ralph, who nodded, his
face red.

"Isobel, get back," James snapped, without looking at
her. "Now tell me this," he said to Ralph. "Why did
you betray William Wallace? Were you part of a
conspiracy?"

"Menteith brought the others into a scheme of his
making," Ralph gasped. "I did not learn their names.
Wallace stepped beyond his place," he went on. "His
rebellion interfered with Scottish nobles who sought
peace with England. 'Twas—'twas decided that he
should be—prevented from acting further. We wanted
peace with England."

James made a sound of loathing. "You wanted land
and wealth even more. So you helped destroy the greatest voice for freedom in this land! And then you went
after me, starting the rumor that I was a traitor and
helping to hunt me down. All that, I think," he growled,
pressing the bow close, "to ensure your claim to
Wildshaw."

Isobel gasped and placed her hand over her mouth,
astonished. On her other fist, the hawk beat his wings
and squawked.

"Aye." Ralph narrowed his eyes. "And now the
woman you want is mine, and lady of Wildshaw. That
pleases me well," he rasped out, nearly choking, though
his eyes glittered.

James stared at him, his breath heaving. Isobel sensed
the tension in him rise to a frightening level. James
stepped back suddenly, pulled the bow away, and landed
a violent blow to Ralph's belly that dropped the man to
his knees with a retching groan.

James turned away, his face dark with anger. "Quentin," he growled, "make her a widow if you want. I
willna sully my hands with thet foul bastard any
further."

Ralph uttered a roar and leaped after James, dragging on his legs, pulling both of them to the ground. Isobel saw the flash of a dagger as it plunged toward James's back.

She screamed, and the hawk bated furiously, pulling upward with such strength that he threw her off balance. She fell in a tangle of blue silk, her gloved hand opening when she hit it against the ground.

The goshawk tore away from her fist with a flurry of wings. He veered and rose into the air, shrieking. Isobel stumbled to her feet and looked up at the vanishing hawk, then down, gasping with fright and panic, as James and Ralph wrestled with the dagger. The others gathered to watch, while Quentin, Patrick, and Margaret stood with their bows ready. But she knew none of them would shoot for fear of striking James unintentionally.

Ralph held the blade at James's throat, but James had a deadly grip on his wrist. They twisted and turned again, until James reared back and slammed his head viciously against Ralph's brow. Ralph fell back, the knife tumbling from his hand.

James lay panting, then rose to his knees. He stood and turned away slowly, wiping his face. Isobel stepped toward him, then screamed as Ralph rolled, snatched the dagger, and threw it blade first at James's back.

James whirled to avoid the blade, just as Ralph sank with a horrible cry, an arrow sunk in his chest. James dropped to his knees and bent over him.

After a moment, he looked up. "He is dead," he said flatly.

Isobel covered her face for a moment, overwhelmed, feeling suddenly ill in the aftermath of panic. She drew a shaking breath, and then looked up to see the others gather around the body. Her father walked toward them, leading Father Hugh, who looked gray and stricken. A few guards stepped forward hesitantly, and Sir Gawain turned to speak with them.

James stood and strode toward Isobel. She rushed the few steps toward him, wrapping her arms around him. The warm bliss of his embrace surrounded her, and his lips touched her hair.

"Oh, God, are you hurt?" she gasped.

"Nay," he said. She sank against him and sobbed out as deep relief and anguish both washed through her. "Soft, you," James murmured, holding her. "Soft, now."

"The hawk—" she said.

"I know, " he whispered, cradling her head. "I know."

"James," she said after a moment. "Who shot Ralph?"

James was silent. She felt him lift his head and watch the circle of people. She looked up with him.

Margaret dropped to her knees beside Ralph's body, her bow still clutched in her hand, the nocked arrow gone. She covered her face with one hand and bent as if she sobbed.

Patrick knelt beside her and pulled her into his arms. He held her tenderly, his big, rough fingers gentling over her hair.

"Dear God," Isobel said.

"Meg saved my life," James said. "I owe her much."

"We both owe her much," Isobel said, touching a trembling hand to his sweaty, beard-rasped cheek.

Then, overhead, she heard a cry. Looking up, she saw a streak of gray and cream. "Gawain!" she breathed out. "Look!"

The goshawk sailed overhead like an angel, the underside of his wings pale, his legs golden. He canted sideways and sliced between some birches, calling as he went.

"We'll have to get him back," James said. "He's jessed and could tangle in a tree." Isobel nodded and stepped away from his arms. Her glove was still on her hand, and she tugged it on more firmly as she took off after the hawk. The bird cut between the trees, vanishing into the forest. Isobel ran after him, holding her skirts high on her legs as she sprinted. James came behind her, running left to take a different angle into the forest.

The hawk sailed through the treetops, darting in and out, looking like a shining prince when the sunlight, burning off the mist, caught the tips of his wings.

Isobel watched him row the air, then glide, row and then glide, rising high and skimming low, effortless and masterful. She called out after him, holding out her arm. He dipped and wheeled in a circle, and she followed.

She heard James among the trees, calling and whistling as he ran. She saw him, dashing between the trees with loping strides, his hair winging out behind him. By then she had lost the bird, and stood still, breath heaving, to watch and wait.

Then she lifted her head and began to sing the *kyrie*. Her voice rose and fell with the natural rhythms of the chant. Moments later, hearing *kee-kee-kee-keer,* she ran toward it.

"Ky-ri-e e-le-i-son." To the left, the melody rose again as James took up the chant. Sung in his mellow voice, the plainsong rose and dipped, flowing like a tranquil current, easy as a hawk in flight. His voice created a serene veil of sound that drew Isobel toward him.

As she ran, she glanced up to see the goshawk wheeling, gliding, landing in a high treetop. She skimmed over the forest floor, skirts billowing, hair flying, and felt an exquisite sense of freedom that matched his glorious flight.

James waited. She slowed, her footfalls gentling on the ground as she went to him. He pointed, and she looked up. The goshawk sat on the pinnacle of a tall tree, the early sun striking silver off his wings and head.

James drew breath and began to chant again. The beautiful melody rose in a gentle arc, undulated and floated out. Isobel felt entranced as she listened. The hawk fluttered, dipped his head, and began to preen himself.

"Mayhap he willna come down, this time," she said. "He may have decided that he wants to be free."

James looked up. "I canna blame the lad for that," he said, "but he's still jessed. If he wants to go free, we'll have to get him back long enough to remove the bands. Hold up your fist, Isobel."

She held up her arm and waited. The goshawk stared down at them and lifted his head to the sun. Isobel began the *kyrie,* but the bird ignored her pointedly, turning away on his branch.

Then James took her free hand in his and began to sing with her. Their voices, deep and delicate together, wove and twined around each other, forming a perfect harmony. The chant swelled and grew, and filled the forest with tranquility.

The hawk raised his wings and streamed downward, angling toward them. He called as he came, as if joining in their song, and fluttered onto the outstretched glove. Isobel laughed softly, tears springing to her eyes as she looked up at James.

"He came back," she said. She smiled at him through the shining pearls of her tears. "He saw us as one master."

James wrapped the jesses securely around her fingers, then reached into the leather pouch at her waist to fetch a bit of food for the bird. While the goshawk bit at his reward, James looked down at her.

"He saw two masters, I think," he said, leaning close, "with one heart between them."

He lowered his head to give her a lingering kiss. He wrapped his arms around her and drew her close to nestle her against his body, while the hawk perched on her fist and blinked at them, chirring softly. James slanted his mouth deeply over hers. After a while, he drew back to look at her, sifting back a lock of her hair.

"Keep a good hold of that hawk for now," he said.

"Oh, I will," she answered, smiling.

He chuckled. "I meant that the wind is gentle today. Never let a hawk go on a soft downwind. 'Tis a sure way to lose a valuable bird."

"You never told me that before," she said.

"Ah, well," he said, drawing her close under his arm to walk with her. "There is much left to teach you, my lass."

She smiled. "I think I've learned a great deal about hawks already."

"Aye, you have," he murmured. "We both have. But there's more, my love. Much more."

Epilogue

James stripped out of his breeches and dove into the water, cleaving the still surface with a muffled splash. The chill hit him like a shock, and he rose, gasping for air, and dipped again, gliding through the water, warming his muscles as he went, his powerful strokes creating wavelets of foam.

He swirled at the far end, kicked out and turned back, sensing the warmer water at that end, heated by the pile of hot stones that he had left in the shallow end. He surged upward in the center of the pool and stood chest high, sluicing back his hair and opening his eyes.

Isobel stood at the side of the pool, watching him. The firelight from a single torch flooded an amber glow over her tall, slender figure, clad in a simple silk chemise. She smiled.

"They have all gone to their beds," she said. "Quentin, Patrick, Margaret, Gawain—and Gawain the gos, too. We talked so long after you left us that I thought you wouldna wait for me."

He swirled the water with his hand and smiled. "I would wait for you forever, lass," he murmured, lying back in the water, floating a little, watching her. "Come in."

She tipped her head and smiled. "I was hoping that we wouldna have visitors to our high crag so soon after our marriage, husband," she murmured.

"We've been wed a month," he said, smiling. "And I have matters to attend to in the forest and at Dunfermline. Quentin and Patrick, and Gawain of Avenel—who is proving a fine ally—brought some interesting reports to me."

"I know." She looked down and trailed a toe in the water. "I wanted to hear the news everyone had, too. Margaret said that Alice and Eustace are getting on quite well. They walk in the woods and giggle like bairns. Margaret thinks it wonderful. Even Ragnell likes Eustace."

He grinned. "Now that is a good sign. Alice has been lonesome a long while. What of your father?"

"He and Henry and Geordie have gone to Aberlady to look over the damage. My father wants to rebuild soon, but he wants to consult with the Guardians of the Realm on whether he should. If they ask him to wait for fear of another English attack, then he means to join your band of rogues."

"He is welcome with us. Years may pass before John or I can hold our own castles. Wildshaw is still held by the English."

" 'Twill be yours soon enough. Quentin said local men are talking quietly of joining the Border Hawk again. You may have enough men one day to take Wildshaw back."

"I intend to," he said. "And I mean to discuss that matter with Robert Bruce myself." He splashed a wavelet toward her. "Come in the water, lass."

She tilted her head, clearly still intent on delivering news to him. "Quentin said Father Hugh left to go on a pilgrimage to Dunfermline, and then to Saint Andrews," she said.

"I know. Quentin told me of it. Father Hugh may even continue to Canterbury and then on to Saint James at Compostela. He feels a deep need to cleanse his soul of the pride that he thinks caused his son's ambition, and resulted in his death."

Isobel nodded. She dropped down to sit on the edge of the pool, drawing up her chemise and swirling her legs in the water. " 'Tis warm at this end," she said. " 'Tis cold where you are."

He surged forward and stopped a few feet from her, dipping down to submerge his chest and shoulders in the water. "Come in and find out what 'tis like," he said.

She shook her head. "Margaret feels the burden of killing Ralph," she said, frowning as she watched the rippling surface of the pool. "I said what I could to comfort her."

"She did what had to be done," James said. "But she must find her own peace with the matter."

"Patrick asked her to wed with him, did you know that?"

"That doesna surprise me."

"She refused," she said. "Though she loves Patrick, she likes her freedom, too. She needs time to think."

"Aye, well," he said, "some of us take our time to decide who to wed. And some of us know from the first moment." She cast him a glance, and he smiled, coaxing one from her.

"Did you know from the first moment?" she asked.

"I knew my heart had been breached like a castle wall, that first evening," he said softly. "But it took me a little while to accept defeat."

"Ah, naught could ever defeat you, brigand." She tipped her head to look at him. "I heard Quentin and Patrick tell you that they saw your friend John Blair in Dunfermline, and that he has urgent news for you," she said. "Will you leave soon?"

"Aye," he answered somberly. "I want to show him the letter from the bishop concerning Wallace and Bruce. I want John to deliver the letter to Bruce himself, with a note that includes the words of the prophetess of Aberlady—a hopeful message for him, I think, for she predicted he would be king of Scotland soon, and eventually save Scotland from English domination."

"Did she?" She smiled. "I would like you to tell Bruce about that. Quentin said you have another matter in Dunfermline too."

He sighed. The summons from John Blair involved brief mention of a clandestine task. The news made it imperative that he go to the abbey quickly. "There is something I must do."

She watched him. "Jamie," she said softly. "Have you not yet found peace, after all that has happened?"

He pushed the water toward her until it rippled about her slender legs. "Come in and find out," he said, easing.

She shook her head. "You come out. I am cold."

"Let me warm you." He surged forward and stood, reaching out to take her waist, pulling her into the water with a deep splash. She gasped, her chemise floating around her like a cloud in the water. He grasped it and pulled it off in one easy motion, while she lifted her arms to assist him.

She draped her hands around his neck and curved her body into his. Her breasts felt divinely soft and heavy against his chest, and her body fitted to his like glove to hand.

"I didna want to come in," she said. "The reflections in the water and the sound of the spring could bring on a vision."

"You dinna want another vision?" he asked, dipping his head toward her, brushing his mouth across her cheek.

"Not just now," she answered.

"And if you had one," he said, "would I not kiss the darkness from you?"

"Aye," she breathed, turning, seeking his mouth.

He enfolded her in his arms and covered her lips with his in a deep kiss that stirred his body and soothed his soul. She wrapped her arms around his back and drew him down into the water with her to their chins, the warm currents swirling about them.

"Jamie," she whispered against his cheek. "I want you to find peace now that this is over."

He framed her face in his hands, her wet hair streaming down to pool like midnight around them. Her eyes were wide and beautiful, opalescent as moonlight. He kissed each eyelid, kissed her brow, and drew back to look at her.

"Part of me may never find true peace, lass," he whispered. "One deed weighs on my heart still. I may never find the forgiveness I seek. But I am thankful, each day for the serenity you have brought into my life."

"I know that something remains unresolved in your heart," she said. "I know that. But here in this paradise with each other, we will always have sanctuary."

"Aye, love," he said, bending to kiss her, to surround himself with her, soul and body. His hands drifted down to her waist, pulling her closer. "Peace is here, with you.

Requiem

The hawthorn tree stood in a gentle slant of dawn rain, its leaves turned upward to catch the moisture. A man in a pilgrim's cloak walked past the abbey church. He pulled up his hood against the soft rain and crossed the small yard on the north side of the church. The tranquil sounds of plainsong floated out from within the abbey, where the monks sang to welcome the somber, rainy hour of prime.

A few people clustered in the arched shadows of the north door of the abbey church, watching him. He knew them well, friends all, and he treasured their faith and support.

But this task he had to do alone.

A simple wooden box sat on the grassy mound beneath the hawthorn tree. James knelt on the ground beside the box, the grass dampening his knees through the folds of the old brown cloak. He bowed his head and folded his hands in prayer.

The box was neither large nor small, its sad contents the earthly remnants of what had been a brilliant and courageous man. Rain beat a quiet rhythm on the wood. James reached out a hand to brush the drops away.

Over the last weeks, Quentin and Patrick had traveled to four towns in Scotland and northern England in search of the mournful reminders of the unjust death of a great leader. They had gathered his bones into the box and brought it to Dunfermline Abbey, where kings, saints, and leaders of Scotland had been laid to rest for centuries.

James quietly murmured the prayers he had chosen to honor his friend, and then stood. A cavity in the

ground had been opened earlier. He removed the cloth
that covered it, and lifted the box, setting it deep into
the earth.

He spaded the soil, shovelful by shovelful, over the
box. When that was done, he patted the sods back into
place, carefully fitting them so that the secret grave
would never be noticed.

He had refused the help of his friends, though they
stood and watched from a distance, murmuring their
own prayers in reverence for the dead. He was grateful
that they understood that he needed to do this alone.

The prophetess had once spoken of the laird of the
wind, who had a penance of the heart. He fulfilled that
penance now. Every prayer he said, every shovelful of
earth he lifted, was done as an act of humility and an
act of love—and as a request for forgiveness.

He owed William Wallace that much, and far more.
The rest of his debt might take a lifetime and into eter-
nity to repay, but at lease he had begun. Now, perhaps
he could find the peace that had eluded him for so long.
Now, perhaps, he could begin to forgive himself.

When he had finished, he stood in the rain, folding
his hands in prayer. "*Requiem aeternum dona eis, Dom-
ine,*" he murmured. "*Requiescat in pace,* my friend." He
turned away.

She waited for him. Her eyes were beautiful in the
rainy half-light, filled with a love that was offered without question, in full faith. Her gentle spirit gave him a
sense of redemption that freed him to love in turn.

The hawk on her gloved fist chirred and fluttered his
wings, flying the short distance to the hawthorn tree
where he settled to wait out the rain.

Isobel smiled and came toward James, gliding over the
damp grass like a sylph, like an angel. He watched her
in silence.

Then he held out his hand.

Author's Note

At Dunfermline Abbey, a hawthorn tree grows in a small graveyard on the north side of the church. Long-standing tradition says that William Wallace's mother is secretly buried under the tree. But a lesser-known tradition claims that Wallace himself may be buried beside his mother.

According to local legend, the Benedictine monk John Blair, along with a friend, collected Wallace's remains from the four towns where they had been piked on display. They placed them in a secret grave near the abbey, possibly beneath the same thorn tree where Wallace's mother lies.

John Blair, who was Wallace's confessor and a rebel fighter himself, retired to Dunfermline Abbey after Wallace's death to write a chronicle of his friend's life. The Latin manuscript was apparently sent to Pope Boniface, but has been lost to history. Supposedly, the fifteenth-century poet Blind Harry used Blair's chronicle in writing his own well-known life of Wallace.

Whether or not the legend of the grave is true, I could not resist exploring its fictional potential. I am grateful to Mr. Bert MacEwen, of Abbot House in Dunfermline, for telling me about the legend. At the time, we stood looking at the hawthorn tree, which was in spring bloom. The hawking techniques described in this novel are, for the most part, taken from early treatises on hawking, such as *The Boke of St. Albans* and *A Jewell for Gentrie*. I was fortunate to be able to observe two falconers and their birds, a tiercel goshawk and a red-tailed hawk, and to speak with several falconers regarding modern and medieval techniques. The high-strung temperament of the goshawk in this book is, as far as I understand it, certainly within the realm of possibility.

Prophets and prophetesses were by no means unheard of in medieval Scotland, and respect was accorded them by commoner and king alike; the witch hunts of medieval Europe, for the most part, occurred outside of Scotland until the late sixteenth century. The best known Scottish medieval prophet is Thomas of Ercildoune, or Thomas the Rhymer, who predicted events that have actually transpired up to the twentieth century. Historical evidence indicates that Thomas of Ercildoune may have acted as a spy under Robert the Bruce.

As for who actually betrayed Wallace, the historical record, as so often happens, does not reveal the full truth. Recent popular opinion implies that Robert Bruce, earl of Carrick, who became king of Scotland after Wallace's death, may have had a hand in it. The evidence, however, indicates that Bruce, if anything, secretly supported Wallace.

Scholars of Scottish history, including G.W.S. Barrow, the best authority on Robert Bruce and the wars of independence, suggest candidates for the deed who are far more likely, if less well-known, including Lord Menteith, a Scots noble.

James Lindsay and Isobel Seton were created—as I hope is true of all my characters—within the stream of historical truth, shaped and defined by what did happen as well as by what could have happened, long ago. I hope you enjoyed their story regardless of myth, fact, or supposition.

I love to hear from readers. Please visit my website at http://members.aol.com/KingSL/, and e-mail me from there, or send a self-addressed, stamped envelope to P.O. Box 356, Damascus, MD 20872 for a reply.

And be sure to look for *The Heather Moon*, my next Scottish tale, to be released in the spring of 1999 from Topaz Books.